I0586502

ABOUT THE AUTHOR

Peter Knyte was born and grew up in North Staffordshire, England, where more by chance than design he first stumbled across the works of J.R.R. Tolkien, Arthur Ransome of Swallows & Amazons fame, David's Gemmell and Eddings through their Legend and Belgariad series, and met Jonathan Livingstone Seagull through the eponymously named title by Richard Bach.

North Staffordshire and the Staffordshire Moorlands are also where Peter developed his love of walking and the countryside.

After leaving Staffordshire, Peter moved to Middlesbrough, Birmingham, London and Leeds during which time he grew to love Neil Gaiman's Sandman comics, Asimov's Foundation series, and Rider Haggards tales of She Who Must be Obeyed and King Solomon's Mines.

Peter still lives in Leeds, West Yorkshire, where he continues to enjoy walking and the countryside, as well as gardening, motorcycling, rock climbing, snowboarding and cooking.

The Ashes of Time is his sixth novel and the third and final part in his Flames of Time Trilogy.

For more information please visit:
www.knytewrytng.com

OTHER TITLES BY PETER KNYTE

The Embers of Time
The Ashes of Time

Through Glass Darkly
By a Blue and Crimson Light

The Ghosts of Winter

Forthcoming titles
A Shadow on the Sky (Glass Darkly series)

Short Stories
Death and the Creator

THE FLAMES OF TIME

PETER KNYTE

COPYRIGHT

Copyright © 2015 Peter Knyte.
Second edition 2019
Peter Knyte asserts the right to be identified as the author of this work.
All rights reserved.
First paperback edition printed 2015 in the United States and United Kingdom
A catalogue record for this book is available from the British Library.

Paperback ISBN: 978-0-9930874-0-0
eBook ISBN: 978-0-9930874-1-7

No part of this book shall be reproduced or transmitted in any form or by any means, electronic or mechanical, including photocopying, recording, or by any information retrieval system without written permission of the publisher.

Published by Clandestine Books Limited

For more copies of this book, please contact:
info@clandestine-books.co.uk
For general enquiries or to report errors in this book please email: info@clandestine-books.co.uk

Interior designed and set by Clandestine Books
www.clandestine-books.co.uk

Cover art by Piere d'Arterie

The Flames of Time

Clandestine Books Limited
Peter Knyte

DEDICATION

For Richard Bach, J.R.R Tolkien, Robert Heinlein, Isaac
Asimov, Henry Rider-Haggard, Doris Lessing, Kenneth
Grahame, Robert Pirsig, and countless others for changing
the way I think.

ACKNOWLEDGMENTS

With thanks to everyone who has patiently listened to me ramble on about my writing, and then somehow still managed to find words of encouragement and enthusiasm.

Also special thanks to Jon and Tasha Williamson, Lisa Bath, Philip Hall, Shirley M Addy for providing the invaluable feedback and proofreading of this title, which has enabled me to improve it in countless ways.

I hope I can return the favour sometime.

DISCLAIMER

This book is entirely a work of fiction, and while it plays fast and loose the names of historic figures, places and events, no part of this book should be viewed or understood to be factual, or attempting to be factual in any way. This story is set on other worlds of imagination, which at best may bear a superficial similarity to our own, and in all probability, will be wholly different and bear no resemblance to any actual people, personalities, locations, circumstances or events whatsoever.

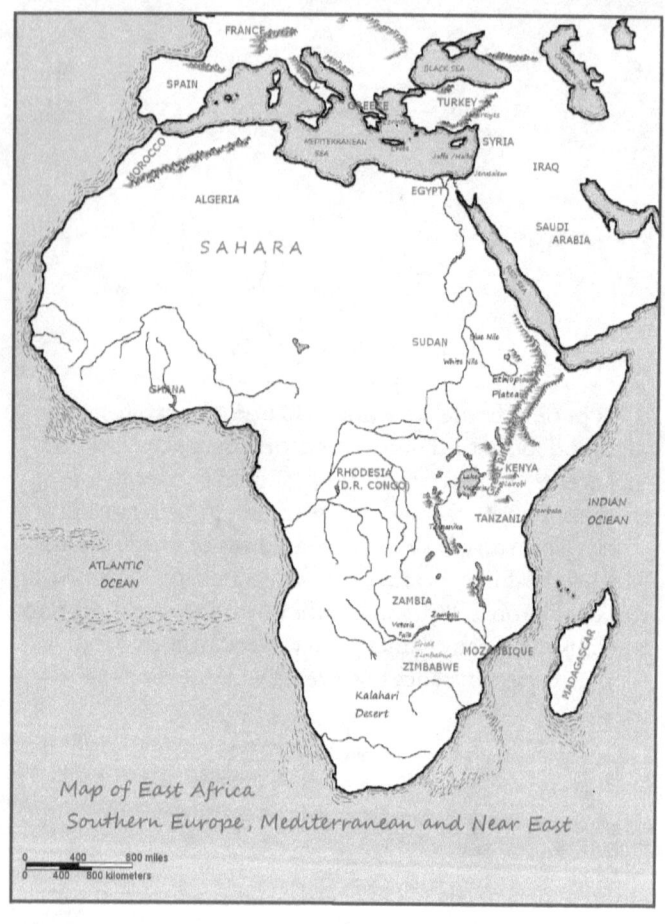

Map 1 – East Africa, Southern Europe, Mediterranean and Near East.

Map 2 – Eastern Mediterranean, Egypt, Red Sea and Turkey.

Map 3 – Greece, Crete and Mediterranean islands.

PREFACE

I HAVE KNOWN THE MAN for over sixty years, and I have known his plans for almost all that time. Yet have I waited, yet have I hoped that he was lost or changed or intent upon some other purpose, and yet has some part of me known he was not.

During all that time, he has been, and still is, my friend. Perhaps it is because of this that I have nurtured the hopes and prayers that his insights and ideas were delusions, an eccentric blemish on an otherwise flawless character.

But now I finally know that those hopes were in fact my own delusion, my own eccentric blemish, for he has left my home not one hour ago looking barely ten years older than when I first met him in 1934.

I almost dared think he had become an old man, like myself, as he arrived, stepping slowly out of the car. The falling snow and his careful steps across my icy driveway deceiving me further, as he made his way through the wintry conditions toward my open door.

But as he stepped into the light, plumes of hot breath appearing from that generous smile, I could no longer mistake the steady gaze, the powerful posture and the impossibly young face that I had last seen sixty years previously.

I realised in that moment the extent of my self-deception. That his ideas and the force of will required to manifest them were never just eccentricities, but very real, very terrible intentions. Goals that he had no doubt been working steadily toward achieving, not only for his own personal benefit, but also for what he perceived to be the benefit of humanity as a whole. The first incredible step toward which, was the attainment of his own physical immortality.

I could imagine it all as clear as day. The same uncompromising nature which had brought him this far, would unhesitatingly plunge the world into chaos, an abyss that we would have to claw our own way out of.

In the process humanity would be irrevocably changed, and in his mind, enhanced, improved, without thought to the suffering and anguish that must surely be endured along the way.

Knowing all this, I still shook the hand that he extended, still led him to my fireside and offered him my hospitality. Still listened to his compliments upon my home and my person.

Knowing all this, I still assured him I was with him, as he told me that the time was now at hand for action, and that within a few short years he would initiate his plans.

Why I didn't speak out against him, try once again to dissuade or divert him from his course, I cannot say.

That I must oppose him I have no doubt. Though it takes more will and more life than I have left, I must stop him.

I must expose his plans to the world, and in so doing expose them to the full light of day, in order to unleash the horror, shock and refusal that must surely follow.

But to expose his plans I must expose the man, my friend. I must cause him to be known, to be hunted and finally to be destroyed.

I may already be too late.

May the world forgive me for waiting so long.
Suffolk 2001

AFRICA

HIS NAME IS ROBERT MARLOW and we first met while I was travelling through Africa in 1934.

I was twenty-two years old in body, but I fancy, a little older in spirit, and although I'm told I was always a serious, or 'adult' child, my maturity had become all the more pronounced with the death of my father eighteen months earlier.

My father was the only family I'd ever really known, my mother dying while I was still very young, and the Great War removing the only other faint traces of a family tree.

So, I grew up with him on the outskirts of a remote village in Shropshire, a day-pupil at the local boarding school, forever leaving my friends and travelling through the evening twilight back to the empty family home and my often distant, reclusive and resented parent.

I felt like I'd barely escaped for my university studies when he unexpectedly died. For while I'd known his health was failing, we weren't close enough for him to tell me just how ill he really was.

Suddenly I was alone, with no idea what I should do with my life, and enough money not to have to think about it for a while.

The house I'd spent my whole life hating seemed even bigger and emptier without my father, but I rattled around inside it for a few months, just going through the motions, until one day I stopped.

It was as though I had no idea where I was. The house, so familiar to me, simply made no sense anymore. I knew what everything was, but didn't understand what it was doing there or what it was for, and then gradually, I came to realise it was my own self that I didn't understand. It was me that had no purpose or use.

In a trance I moved through all the rooms of the house in the hope of finding something that might remind me of what I was supposed to do, but there was nothing. Eventually I wound up in my father's old room.

He had moved out of the master bedroom when my mother died, and now his things lay where he'd left them, in his attic room. It's one small window looking out over the side garden and the undulating Shropshire plain.

In front of that window on the desk lay his journal with pen and ink close to hand, along with an electric table lamp for use in the evenings.

Feeling even more lost and out of place in this room which I'd entered so rarely in the past, it took me a moment to realise these things would never be used again, my father would ever pick up this pen and write another entry in this journal, or need the light of the lamp to illuminate the desk.

Unless… I sat down in the fading afternoon light and switched on the lamp, and then almost involuntarily, I saw my hands open the journal before me, and I began to read.

At first, it felt like a violation of his privacy, and I almost closed the journal and walked away. But as my eyes scanned the handwritten pages before me, I realised that at least in part this record was intended for me. The things he would have said to me, if he'd ever been able to shake off the loss of his wife.

The entries for the last few months were a little patchy and introspective, as his health and will declined. But I continued to read, one entry at a time in reverse order, and as I did so, the sense of violation was replaced by a feeling that I not only could read these entries, but that I should read them.

Perhaps sensing his end was near, the last few weeks contained a flurry of entries, several of them referring to earlier journals, and his desire to re-read them with a view to organising and annotating them before it was too late.

I'd had no idea there were other journals, though as I thought about it, I'd always known my father had kept one. Nor did it take me long to find them, all carefully bound and labelled on one shelf in the corner of our small library. It seemed natural now, after having read the most recent journal to read those that preceded it. So, I settled into one of the library armchairs next to the shelf of journals, selected the first and earliest journal and began.

They went back to before I was born, before my father was even married, when he had apparently become a missionary in Africa.

He'd travelled around a bit, but had eventually settled in Kenya, in a small mission ninety miles or so outside Nyrobi (Nairobi).

The penmanship in his African journals was markedly different, more eccentric and alive, clearly lacking the care and precision of his later years. There was humour too and passion, aspects to my father's character I'd hardly experienced. And then there was Africa, the heat and dryness, the sights and scenes of his everyday life there could not have been a greater contrast to the pleasant and safely undulating life of Shropshire.

As though to illustrate the point further, just as I was reading an entry in my father's journal about his first experience of the torrential African rains, I heard a soft patter of rain outside the library windows. I could see nothing of the outside through the perfect black reflection in the French windows, but in a moment I had the key in my hand and they were open. The rain was coming down in the large idle drops that only ever seem to fall in the Summer, splashing across my face and hands in a half-hearted erratic fashion so different to the horrendous downpour described by my father. Somehow the sheer contrast made me come to a decision. I would go to Africa, perhaps I would retrace my father's steps. I didn't know, but it would be a start.

The arrangements were deceptively simple, my housekeeper and a solicitor could take care of any day to day considerations whilst I was away. My father's journal contained a fairly complete, if dated list of travel requirements. I was even able to book passage from Portsmouth, just as he had done over thirty years earlier.

The ship now stopped in a dozen more locations, but it somehow managed to ply the route in the same four and a half weeks each way, four times a year. It was a brief fantasy, but for a moment I thought there might even be some of the same crew still working the route.

In what seemed moments the scent of north Africa was in the air and the bay of Gibraltar lay before me. The journey around the coast to Mombasa was like a dream.

At some point I must have partially awakened from my confusion for I decided to start keeping my own journal, a naive, unfocused rambling for the first few entries, becoming gradually more direct and informative as I became accustomed to ordering my thoughts before attempting to put them down on paper.

By the time I arrived in Mombasa the writing had become a regular habit, and I remember sitting on the balcony of my hotel pen in hand, watching as the ship that had brought me there pulled out into the Indian Ocean and turned southward back the way it had come.

From Mombasa the journey to Nairobi across the Taru desert was spectacular and fearful in its barrenness, with every inch of the train line bought in human suffering. But I did arrive, and over the next eighteen months, time seems almost to have stood still. So entranced was I with the new sights and sensations, the Athi Plain and lowlands, the highlands and Great Rift Valley; a more appropriately named sight I hope never to see; and of course, the elusive and ever distant Mount Kenya.

At the end of those eighteen months I was beginning to feel some guilt at my prolonged absence from

England, especially with the murmurings of unrest in Europe, but my thirst for Africa was barely whetted. As such it was with a divided mind that I set out again inland from the capital toward Mwanza and the southern edge of Lake Victoria, through the eastern rift and hopefully along the way past some Maasai villages my father had visited as a missionary.

It was after I had only been travelling for a week, putting up at a hunting lodge for the evening I was told at reception that I was not the only Englishman resident. A large party of gentlemen had been there for a few days, including several English.

This seemed like a promising change, for despite running into quite a few Europeans in Africa, most seemed somehow settled, especially amongst the missionary communities. The size of this group, immediately made it sound more lively, thinking this I instantly resolved to linger for a short time should they prove amiable.

With that I took myself off to my room to get refreshed before they turned up.

So it was that they found me. I was sat on the lodge's western veranda with a tall glass of something cooling, watching the hot sun sink into a distant bank of cloud. They arrived at a good, but not hasty pace, the dying sun illuminating them in a thousand shades of flame. Fragments of conversation spilling into the growing twilight as they drew closer.

Leaving the horses with the hotel staff, they moved toward the front of the lodge, odd individuals waiting and then forming into companionable groups before entering the building and leaving my sight.

I sat for a few moments wondering how long I should wait before going in to introduce myself, only half aware of the last quarter of sun, and the growing din of a thousand night-time insect voices being raised in joy.

'It almost sounds like the night rejoicing in its

dominion over the day,' someone said from the doorway behind me.

I hadn't heard his approach, but somehow the unexpected voice hadn't startled me, and I was able to offer my affirmation before I stood and beheld the man for the first time.

He stood in the doorway to the veranda, his travelling clothes still dusty from the ride, a tall glass of iced water in one hand. He was just slightly above average height with deep auburn hair made almost black by the dying light and a deeply tanned complexion that suggested he'd spend years beneath the African sun.

'It doesn't matter how many times I see it, it always fascinates me, whether over land or sea, forest, mountain or moor, it never seems to set the same way twice. Yet somehow here in Africa where the horizon stretches so far…'

With these words his gaze had drifted back to the west and the last fraction of crimson disk as it slid into the quenching bank of distant cloud.

As though released from a trance he turned back to me with an apology, and offered me his name and his hand. 'Robert Marlow, at your service.'

Moving inside from the now dark evening he explained that the reception had told him of my arrival, and that I was travelling with just a guide and a couple of servants. As such he'd come straight over to make sure I didn't go in to dine before he'd had the opportunity of inviting me to join him and his friends for the evening.

As we moved through the reception it was immediately apparent that the group were well accustomed to their own mutual habits, as everyone who I'd seen ride in had now moved through into the bar area for a drink before changing. Anticipating this, Marlow led me straight to them, stopping only briefly in the doorway to introduce me to his companions.

'My friends! We have with us another visitor from

England, Mr George Whitaker. Who has kindly agreed to join us for dinner this evening, so please make him feel at home.'

'It is a wonder there are any Englishmen left in England, there are so many of you in Kenya alone!' piped up one obviously Gallic member of the group.

'This is Jean Louis de Gris, our resident artist and philosopher,' replied Marlow, '… and possibly one of the worst shots in the whole of Africa!'

'Ah, do not listen, M'sieur Whitaker, it is Mr Marlow himself, who has to wait until the quarry is almost upon him before he shoots.'

There was much good-natured laughter at this, and then as conversations came to a natural close, two or three individuals would disappear briefly, to return a few minutes later changed and refreshed for dinner.

And so it was, being already changed, that I at least briefly got to meet everyone as the group gradually dwindled and then swelled again ready for dinner.

Dinner itself was a very good-natured affair. Polite yet informal, during which the conversation split and fragmented a hundred times, only to be re-united with the advent of a popular topic. I was politely quizzed about my background and tastes, and in my turn I questioned and observed the members that made up this sociable and welcoming group.

I discovered that they had mostly been on tour together for the past three years, and had gradually come together through chance encounter, but had stayed together through mutual interest. They had wandered around Africa, at times only a few hours away from myself, in search of life and sport and spectacle. Occasionally individuals would leave for a while to re-join later.

Their company reminding me greatly of my time at Cambridge, or what it would have been like in such surroundings, before my father's waning health had obliged me to abandon my studies.

The only permanent members of the group seemed to be Jean, a slightly older Frenchman with distinctly military bearing, Marlow an Englishman just a few years older than myself, with the deep tan of someone who'd grown up somewhere much sunnier than England. A slightly older and gentle giant of an American called Harrison Sutherland, who was both tall and broad with an unquenchable appetite for cakes and sweet treats of every type, and an Italian about my own age called Luke Cassanelli, who had the blonde-hair, blue eyes and slender physique of a movie screen actor.

The four of them had apparently met through a mutual friend in London, before travelling out to Africa with Marlow, who had then been in the early stages of planning a trip.

Jean and Harry were clearly the older and most settled members of the group, with each regularly poking good natured fun at the other.

The Frenchman had a little more grey in his hair and beard, but he clearly took great care in his appearance, trimming his beard Napoleonic goatee style which made me think he must have held the role of quite a senior officer in the army.

In contrast both Marlow and Harry couldn't be less military in their aspect. Harry, while taller and broader, had the unmistakably round-shouldered build of the habitual academic, while Marlow moved and stood more like a natural athlete.

As the evening wore on we relaxed again in the bar with brandy and cigars. Marlow began to question me upon my immediate plans, and hearing that I was intending to travel inland to see the southern end of Lake Victoria and the spectacular Bismarck rocks, he suggested I delay my visit for a few days and join them on their hunt for a man-eating lion.

Apparently, the creature had recently killed a young man from a nearby village, thus becoming a monster that would almost certainly attack people again. Many tribesmen and locals had already gone to hunt the beast, but after a week without success, they were now beginning to give up the search to return to their farms and villages, presuming the animal to have moved off.

'We know it must be a rogue,' said Marlow, casually. 'As male lions never go out to hunt unless they're no longer in a pride. We also know from a couple of eyewitnesses that it's far from being a grizzled old beast, typical of the usual rogue. So it has probably been ousted from its pride for some temporary infirmity, from which it unusually seems to have recovered.'

'Yes, but what makes you think this beast is still in the area,' I asked.

'Well, it's nothing definite, more a general feeling for the type of animal. If it were just an old male, past its prime and evicted from its pride by a young buck, then I think we'd have seen it move by now. These creatures soon lose their strength outside the pride, they get harassed by animals that would normally give them a wide berth and are forced to move on from their resting place or their kills before they're ready.

'This lion is different, if it is still in its prime, then it can probably hang on to both its kills and its resting places. And once a big male lion has had a belly full of meat, it can lie back and rest for over a week before it really needs to eat again. As you probably know it's the females that usually do all the work, so unless it's already adapted it'll rest until it gets really hungry.'

I had known this already, and on reflection could see Marlow's point, but how would one go about hunting such an animal? Spotting a pride on the savannah was one thing, but a solitary animal, that was another thing altogether.

'We also know a rogue lion similar to this one was reported a few weeks ago, moving up from the south,' continued Marlow. 'Where it's thought responsible for the deaths of several domestic cattle.

'Now, if this is the same animal, then these reports indicate it's in no hurry to move on from a good hunting ground. In one case it stayed in the same area for nearly two months before the local farmers managed to make their livestock too difficult to get at. So, if it's here, there's a good chance it'll stick around until something forces it to move.'

I had to concede the possibility of what he was saying, and as such agreed to stay around for a while in order to help out with the hunt.

I didn't have to wait long. After retiring for the evening, it seemed as though my eyes had closed for no more than a moment when I was woken by Jean hammering on the door and telling me to get dressed quickly, the lion had been spotted.

Apparently during that very evening, the beast had stirred, killing a calf and its mother, and seriously wounding the farmer who'd stumbled across the creature after it had fed.

I dressed immediately and reached the waiting Jean at a run. As we mounted the horses in the early morning light, he told me that the others had been gone for only a few minutes, but that they'd set off at a furious pace.

As we followed, he also told me several members of the group had continued to talk after I'd retired, and that Marlow had admitted his growing dissatisfaction with hunting, or more specifically the long-range rifle hunting.

Jean openly voiced his concern, informing me that Marlow had on more than one occasion allowed his prey to get dangerously close in order to enhance the thrill.

'It can only be a matter of time,' he said. 'Before such risks end in disaster.'

Coming across a farmer we discovered that in our haste we'd gone slightly off course, and to our dismay, added half an hour to Marlow's lead. By riding far less carefully than the terrain demanded we managed to reduce this by a little, but by the time we arrived at the scene we knew we were probably already too late.

Directed by a couple of servants left behind by the group, we arrived over the crest of a low hill, slightly to the side of where the main group must have discovered and then driven the lion.

Looking around, we saw Marlow some three hundred meters ahead standing over the body of a large lion. As we approached, we could see he'd removed his jacket and holster and left them a short distance away with his rifle, choosing to face the beast instead with a sword!

The right sleeve of his shirt was ripped off at the elbow, with the torn fragment hanging from his wrist by the cuff. The pale fabric slowly being turned black as it was soaked by the blood flowing from a deep gash in his forearm.

As we came alongside, I could see the blade from his swordstick had entered deep into the animal's throat and probably become lodged in the spine, severing the carotid artery and quite possibly the spinal cord in one blow, killing the beast instantly.

There was a low cloud of dust around the pair, but as it settled, I could also see a pool of dark blood spreading out from the animal and around Marlow's feet.

I could barely believe what I was seeing, as Marlow, apparently calm, stepped forward to pull his blade free, followed a moment later by that dark pool of African life, halting it spread as the beast's heart pumped its last, and then being absorbed into the parched earth.

Removing the blade seemed to break the spell for the group as well, and as Marlow turned back toward us, Nunn, a stocky American who had joined the group only a few months earlier, unleashed such a torrent of oaths and curses at the foolishness of the stunt, that for a moment I thought he was going to punch Marlow.

He didn't, but his sentiment was clearly echoed by several of the others, some who spoke out, others whose expressions spoke volumes.

Jean who was beside me remained silent, just looking at his friend with an expression I can only describe as one akin to sorrow. Eventually someone remembered Marlow's arm and managed to bandage it and get the bleeding to stop, but it did nothing to quell the barrage of disapproval and criticism.

Somehow, we managed to make our way back to the lodge, amongst the grumbling and griping which didn't stop for a moment. It was still only late morning, but already the day was promising to be stifling, so whilst the others were distracted, I took the opportunity to slip away and visit one of the villages my father had briefly stopped in.

It was a largely fruitless exercise, like several of the other villages I'd visited, but I'd almost succeeded in putting the morning's events out of my head, until I came within sight of the lodge again. When, I swear I could detect the change in atmosphere from quarter of a mile away.

Dinner that evening was absolutely wretched, with long bouts of silence followed by half-hearted attempts at conversation. I passed on dessert altogether, and would have done the same with the main course too if I felt I could have done so without appearing to be rude.

Somehow it all reminded me of how long I'd been away from home, and the nagging idea that often came with it, that life was a serious matter and I was just avoiding my responsibilities by playing at being an adventurer in Africa.

CATHEDRAL OF STARS

THE NEXT FEW DAYS were a sombre affair, with much of the camaraderie I'd witnessed on the first evening being replaced by short tempers and stand offishness. The only topic of conversation was of course, Marlow and the lion, and anyone trying to avoid it was sought out and questioned before being preached at.

Marlow himself was no exception, and several times I was aware of him being taken aside for a 'serious talk' by different members of the group. At one point there was even talk of calling a priest for him.

Then they began to drift away. One's and two's at first. Nunn, the American, just disappeared. Packed his things and left before anyone else even woke up, no message or even so much as a note. Another two, which I hadn't spoken to much, including a young Yorkshireman, left the same day. Both stayed to say goodbye, and then left with long faces and many apologies.

After another two days over half the group had gone and we were down to seven of us. Marlow, Jean, Harry and Luke, as well as Peter McAndrews from Edinburgh and another Italian Silvio Jesuino from Florence.

I can't explain why I stayed, especially with my other commitments nagging at the back of my mind.

Perhaps not having seen the actual act made it less real, or more alarmingly, perhaps of all the people there I could almost understand why Marlow had done it, and what it must have felt like to face such a beast without a rifle.

As soon as the last of those leaving had gone, a semblance of the old atmosphere returned, and at dinner that evening, four days after the hunt, the conversation was once again light and entertaining. It was obvious there was much being left unsaid, and eventually the darker aspects of our thoughts began to be voiced.

Harry, almost apologetically, started us off.

'You know, I don't think I could ever go back to my old life. I've got friends and family that I'd sorely like to see again, and for a while I know I could enjoy their company, as well as the woods and the fishing, especially in the fall.

'You folks would just love New England in the fall, there's more shades of red and gold than a person can count, and every house you visit smells of apples and berries. I dare say there may even be a few ladies who wouldn't mind listening to a tall tale or two of far off lands.

'But, I know after a couple of months the routine would begin to get to me. I'd start thinking about Africa or India, and then about what I was going to do with my life. Not that I know what that is yet, just that I've got to keep on looking. If it takes me the rest of my life, that's the one thing I do know!'.

There was a lull for a moment or two, with a few murmurs of agreement, and then Marlow took up the theme.

'My friends,' he began, resignation written in every line of his face. 'I think we all knew this time was coming. As I've said to some of you before, the hunt for me has lost its appeal. You've all seen the… foolhardy attempts I've made to try and recapture some of the meaning or challenge, but I understand now how that isn't possible, and no amount of risk taking or gambling with my life is ever going to bring it back.

'Having said that, I've got to keep looking for something. I realise it may sound foolish, and perhaps even naïve in its sentiment. But I honestly feel that we've just been practising, or playing at life, and the time has come to live it in a fuller sense. Like Harry, I don't know what that is yet, I just know it's time to figure it out.'

As I listened to these new-found friends of mine discussing this issue, and trying to understand one another better, I thought I was perhaps a little ahead of them in reaching these conclusions.

I'd left England with the half-formed idea of retracing my father's footsteps across Africa, but I'd known even then that what I was seeking wasn't a greater insight into my father, but a greater insight into myself.

Jean who'd been silent up until now, leant forward to refill his glass, but in such a typically expansive and Gallic manner, that I couldn't help but smile in anticipation of what he was about to say.

'Well, I am not sure I can quite believe what I am hearing! My friends who I thought all so cheerful and content in their sojourn around Africa, I discover are all miserable, and bored of their privileged lives. You will all be telling me next that you have seen the light of true socialism and wish nothing more than to spend your time toiling on the land and eating raw vegetables!'

'And to think, some people suggest sarcasm is a lower form of whit,' interjected Peter with a wry grin from the other side of the table.

'It is either that,' continued Jean, unperturbed. 'Or, you are all about to tell me you wish to find the true meaning of life. And, that you are prepared to spend the rest of your lives traversing far-flung, exotic and no doubt highly attractive areas of this planet in order to do so. Such sacrifice mes amies! Such sacrifice.'

'You perhaps have a better idea, Jean?' asked Marlow with just a hint of pique in his voice.

'Ah, Robert! You have found me out, I do not. But that is not the same as thinking your idea either possible or in any way credible. It is simply not sensible for a person to discover these things, they are… too big. The best we can aspire to do is decide what we shall do, from the list of things that we can do. The rest we must leave to history or the next life.'

'We will all meet our maker soon enough, I think.' suggested Silvio, amiably. 'Maybe such a question can wait until then?'

'Gentlemen!' replied Marlow holding up his hands in mock surrender, 'I realise this is a difficult question, but to not ask it merely because of its size, or the trouble we think we may face in trying to find an answer, that can only be an excuse, surely?'

'Robert, it is not just a question of…' began Jean, only to stop abruptly and turn his head to listen.

It was very faint at first, but as we all sat and listened

the sound of distant drums began to grow stronger, fading in and out of the night-time air. As one we moved to the door and out onto the western veranda. It was dark out now, a sliver of moon and the clear arc of stars the only illumination across the entire Serengeti. Several of the lodge staff and guides were already outside, listening intently to the sound.

'The talking drums,' muttered someone behind me as the sound once more faded out. I noticed Mkize the Kikuyu guide I'd hired in Nairobi standing nearby. Not knowing how long I was going to be staying I'd asked him to stick around for a few days on the off chance I wanted to continue my journey. I quietly called to him and asked him if he could tell me what the drums were saying. He hesitated, obviously struggling to interpret, but after waiting for a moment while he listened, he eventually managed to translate.

'An elder comes,' he began, '...a chief of many villages. He brings the... dream to the Singing Stones.'

We stood listening for a while longer, unsure if these ethereal sounds would convey anything more, and then as those more knowledgeable than ourselves disappeared back to what they were doing, we also moved back inside.

Whatever they meant, the subject offered a very tempting distraction, and whether consciously or not, when we returned to the dining room where we'd been sat, everybody was pre-occupied with the drums and what this strangely cryptic message and form of communication could mean.

Several of us had heard the drums before at local events, where they were played to tell a tale during some festivity or ceremony, often whilst other members of the village enacted the story in dance. But these instruments were generally about the size of a tambourine in surface area, and were played with two curved drumsticks. The sound from such could reach for quite some distance, well beyond the average Maasai kraal, perhaps up to quarter of a mile before becoming inaudible amongst the sounds of the day or night.

But the drums we just heard, sounded much further away, none of us had encountered the like before, though all were curious to find out more.

After throwing the subject around for a while and realising we were all as ignorant as the next, we decided to ask the lodge manager if he could find someone to tell us more and possibly conduct us to the place referred to in the message, the Singing Stones, for whatever was about to take place.

The following morning shortly after breakfast, the manager returned with a local Maasai guide, who through an interpreter, informed us that it was not an elder or chieftain who was coming but rather a 'Laibon' or shaman.

He also informed us that the Singing Stones mentioned were a Maasai sacred site only a few days travel across the Serengeti. The exact nature of the ritual we couldn't decipher even with the interpreter.

As an afterthought, I asked the Maasai guide about the drums and why I hadn't heard them used over such distances before. He looked thoughtful for a while, admitting it was indeed strange, such ceremonies only took place every six or ten years, but even so, the big drums which had been used last night were only normally used for war, or other very important things. Anyway, we would find out more as we got closer.

That we would be setting off to see this ritual was a forgone conclusion, the temptation provided by a change of scene was just too great. The Maasai guide that we'd quizzed about the drums agreed to show us the way, and within no time we were off into the Serengeti.

Getting out into open ground again was exactly what we all needed after being cooped up around the lodge for the past four days. Jean arranged for a couple of local guides to come along with us to help out with the making and breaking of camp, so I asked Mkize to travel with us also, as I still wasn't sure how much longer I was going to stay with the group, and he was just about able to translate what the Maasai was saying when he did rarely try to communicate with us.

After a couple of days, we'd been progressing well, when we came across a Maasai enkang or 'Kraal' which Nbutu our guide disappeared towards as soon as it came into view. We continued on our way for a short while, passing within several hundred feet of the village as we did so.

Just inside the broad thorn fence which surrounded the place, we could clearly see Nbutu talking to two of the village men. There were several Maasai women also visible and numerous children playing in and around those peculiarly small straw-topped huts that the Maasai seem to have to bend double to get into or out of.

We pulled up our horses in the shade of some trees at the top of a nearby rise to await Nbutu. He returned nearly an hour later with the two head-men from the village. He conversed with these for a moment and then addressed us via Mkize.

'I have spoken with the Laibon of this village about the drums that were sent out across the sky. They say they have been waiting for us and that the drums were sent to bring us to the Singing Stones.'

Well, that caught us all off guard, the implications of what was being said taking several moments to register, after which everyone started asking questions at the same time.

Nbutu and the two elders stood before us in that politely aloof manner so characteristic of this tall people, waiting for us to order our questions in a way they could understand.

Eventually Mkize just stopped trying to hear what each person was saying and simply turned his gaze toward me. At this the group fell silent allowing me to ask the questions on their behalf.

'Mkize, could you ask them what they mean. How could they even know about us let alone be waiting for us.'

With the smallest of nods, he turned and relayed my question as best he could, and then listened as one of the elders responded.

'They say the spirits of the mountain have told them,' came back Mkize's reply, 'They have seen you kill the lion with your hands and take the first step on your journey.'

Realising that Mkize had told us the first part of the message, the same elder addressed him again. The upshot of which was that we should ask no further questions, all would become clear at the Singing Stones, where the spirits would talk to us themselves.

With the smallest of nods to Nbutu, which he returned, the two elders then returned to their village.

As I turned back to the others, everybody seemed to be struggling to absorb what had been said, let alone understand how it could be possible. We all knew the Maasai to be painfully honest and truthful in their dealings, so it was senseless to imagine they might be making the story up. But it was Jean who, regaining his composure, or at least his wit, before the rest of us, broke the silence, and brought us all back to earth.

'Well, it seems we will be saved the arduous task of deciding what it is we are to do with our lives,' he said rather sarcastically. 'As the "Spirits of Africa" seem to already have something in mind.'

As we remounted our horses to head off after Nbutu, who had simply started walking, I could hear all my thoughts played out in snippets of conversation from my friends.

'How could they have known we would come?' 'It had been our decision to seek out the source of the drums, nobody had volunteered or suggested we go.' Let alone what journey it was they referred to and what they could possibly have meant by the spirits talking to us themselves.

It took another two days to get to the Singing Stones, the first unfortunately seeing us almost oblivious to the wonder of our surroundings, as we struggled increasingly with the terrain and severity of our climb. But as we gained altitude it also got a little cooler, and the ground which was parched down on the valley floor, now started to show signs of moisture and life.

The further we went the steeper and more rugged the ground became, until eventually Nbutu indicated it was time for us to walk, leaving our horses and camp equipment behind with the local men Jean had brought with us.

It's amazing how much more you see and feel when you're on foot. As we walked, I think we all became more aware of the land through which we travelled. Not just because of the increased danger, but also because we were closer to the ground and perhaps had to make more of an effort to look around and understand where we were.

On several occasions I was stopped in my tracks by one or another of my friends as they paused momentarily for some water or to get their breadth, only to become transfixed by the ever-changing vistas and panoramas of the land around us.

It seemed that with every step the views became more spectacular. To either side of us stretched the ragged line of the Eastern Rift and the flanking highlands, complimented in the foreground by the undulating plains, bush and grassland that we'd just passed through, all interspersed with the rocky kopje outcroppings and watering holes or dried-up tracks of parched riverbeds.

Climbing further up we eventually started to work our way through an endless maze of gorges and shallow valleys. First one, then another, gradually increasing in size and depth, until we were snaking our way upward almost entirely blinkered by narrow canyon walls, only sporadically escaping into the open air and the views beyond.

It was tough going at times, climbing dried up

waterfalls, or finding our way through long stretches of craggy rocks and boulders, but the ground finally started to level off, and we began to see signs that we might be approaching our destination.

First one of us then another would spot something, an unnatural pile of stones, or an exposed rock face daubed in paint, or etched with a symbol. The more we saw the closer it felt we must be getting, until suddenly as we got to a wider part of the canyon which held the remains of a recent camp fire, Nbutu instructed us to halt.

The light was beginning to fade by now, and I couldn't help but think we might be better off just pushing on. But apparently it was the dusk that Nbutu was waiting for, and when we asked him about moving on, he told us simply that we were near, and that the final steps could only be walked once the sun had set.

It seemed an odd phrase for the tall Maasai to use, but I was happy to have a few moments rest and drink some water from my canteen, so decided not to quiz him further.

In any event we didn't have long to wait for sundown, and while we'd only known him for a few days, I found I trusted this taciturn guide of ours not to leave us high and dry with no prospect of shelter or refuge for the night.

A few minutes later as the last remnants of the day disappeared, Nbutu now content for us to proceed raised his spear and, pointing up the side of the gorge where we'd been waiting, and instructed us to climb.

I didn't quite understand why it was now our turn to go first, but it appeared my doubts weren't shared, as first Marlow and then the others one by one started to scramble up the loose earth and stone that formed the canyon side. It was only a minute's work to make our way up there, but as I came to the top I was nearly sent reeling back down again by the sight that I saw before me.

Hidden entirely from our view below, the ground levelled out to form an open grassy area scattered with smaller rocks, boulders and stunted trees. But while the ground fell away to our right, revealing the twilight landscape of the rift and surrounding countryside, to our left, the exposed rock grew out of the earth, higher and higher as it circled that side of the grassy area until it formed a giant overhanging wall of rock in front of us. Immense in its scale, it towered over us at an impossible angle, jutting up into the night sky like a savage tooth.

Adding to this amazing view, and highlighting the jagged fang of rock even more against the night sky was a brightly burning fire, which flickered and leapt beneath the overhang, casting its uneven light across the rocky wall and out into the night.

Eventually, having just stood and stared for who knew how long, we somehow started to make our way over to the fire. But as spectacular as the scene was from further away, it became all the more so as we drew closer and started to discern pictures and patterns painted across the surface of the overhang. First one thing then another, subtle shapes, and pictures of animals or hunting scenes drawn around and with the shape of the rock, to lend a depth and texture to the various depictions, and giving them a strange life upon the 'canvas' of the rock.

More than once I nearly tripped as the flickering light made the images seem to jump and move, until I was no longer watching where I was walking.

'It could almost be a map of this country,' remarked one of my friends. 'With the places and animals that are found there.'

It was breath taking in its scale and craftsmanship, but as we walked across the open ground toward the overhang I finally managed to bring my attention back to the group of figures around the fire and our purpose in coming here.

We walked over and stopped a few meters in front of the fire, the magnificently painted rock face soaring above our heads. There were a dozen men on the other side of the fire right next to the base of the rock face, faces turned to the fire, waiting without talking. And another three a little closer to us, obviously elders or chieftains of some type, who turned as we drew closer, and then moved a short distance forward to meet us.

None of them were talking, and I could clearly hear the crackle and burn of the fire once we stopped and stood before them.

Like all Maasai elders, there was little of ornament or decoration about these three, to signify wealth or status, they simply were who they were with no pretension, and no need for badges or titles.

They clearly weren't surprised to see us, and after Nbutu, with much deference, introduced us, they got straight down to business.

The first one to speak to us gave his name as Nelion, was stood in the middle of the three and slightly to the front.

He was a little shorter than the others and facially quite different, but it was the scar across his shoulder and upper arm that really singled him out.

Like many Maasai he wore a hide cape draped over one shoulder and loosely around the body, thus showing the entire shoulder and arm. It was obviously an old wound that ran across his body like a personal representation of the Great Rift, weathered and rounded, but in places still as angry and jagged as the day it was made.

'It has been many years since anyone has walked upon the path that now lies beneath your feet,' he began, waiting for Mkize to relay his words. 'Longer still since the spirits of this place have welcomed any of your kind to their home, so long have your people been lost, walking with closed eyes... But you have come to this place now and so my brothers and I welcome you.'

I wasn't quite sure what we were supposed to make of this, let alone how we should respond, and I could see some of my new friends looking at one another questioningly, until Jean, who it seemed had a little more experience of such things, responded.

'On behalf of my friends I thank you for your welcome.' he said, with perfect diplomacy, 'Your words are wise, for there is much we do not understand, and more still that we do not know. What is this path or journey of which you speak, and how have we taken the first step upon it?'

It was the turn of Lenana the elder on Nelion's right to speak this time, stepping forward he raised his spear to point straight at Marlow's bandaged forearm.

'We have seen you slay the lion,' he said simply, with a look of some sympathy on his face. 'And we have seen you do this with your own hand and by your own will.'

'We have also seen in your heart that you do this not as the hunter,' continued Batian, the third elder, who had so far not spoken. 'Or as the hunted. But because you must.'

'You are not the first amongst your people who have come to know you are lost,' Nelion continued, after a short pause. 'Nor are you the first to seek what you have lost in the land and the water and the animals of the earth, only to discover it in none of these things.

'But still you will continue your search,' he went on, looking upon each of us in turn now. 'Though the path may destroy you, and separate you forever from the rest of your kind, still you must continue.'

I was both confused and intrigued by what these men were saying. Their words seemed to echo around my mind, just beyond the grasp of my understanding. At the same time their knowledge of Marlow's confrontation with the lion troubled me, and their talk of how we were seeking something lost, that was also a little too reminiscent of the conversation we were having just before we heard those distant drums, not to be unsettling.

And then the soft heartbeat of the drums began again. So slow and quiet to begin with, then quicker and louder, twisting into a suggestion of rhythm, before calming and quietening back to a whisper.

They were close this time, with none of the fading

we'd heard before. Their soft murmur conjuring to my mind the fond remembrance of a hazy childhood summer and, judging by the wistful expressions that flickered across their faces, the same pulse brought similar thoughts to my friends.

'It is time,' said Nelion, quietly. 'The spirits have come and the dreaming begins.'

At these words, several of the men who had been stood at the back, came forward with various bowls and containers, which they held whilst Nelion and the other shaman combined and mixed their contents into a broad serving bowl.

There was no way of knowing what these substances might be, but as the shaman worked, and their deeply lined features were thrown into even deeper relief by the flickering firelight. I could see the swirling liquid they created begin to steam and bubble, before finally clearing and turning a translucent white that shone in the darkness.

I couldn't help but be mesmerised by the process, and when the drums began to swell and grow again, I felt their influence upon my mind like the soft tendrils of steam or smoke that rose from the shaman's potion. The darkness had surrounded us now, and even as I looked around at my friends and the scene beneath that painted rock face, I felt as though I were somehow becoming intoxicated. My caution and cares falling away, as the drums and the firelight became all that I knew.

I viewed the scene now as though from a distance. Saw Nelion and the other shaman first put the bowl to their own lips and drink of its contents, before holding it out to us.

Even now, lulled by the impatient drums, I still felt a sharp pang of fear as the bowl was offered, a momentary realisation of the situation we were in, and the risks we were taking, and then the drums had me again, and I saw Marlow step forward and take the bowl, hesitating for only a moment, before raising it to his lips and drinking deep of the contents.

He turned and offered it to Harry, who drank without hesitation, before passing it to me. I saw myself take the bowl, and raise it to my lips, all the while without understanding why I was doing it, and then I drank before passing the bowl on to Jean.

The drums were everywhere now, racing up into the sky before whirling and diving back down to the fire, and the figures across the wall leapt and danced with the flickering firelight to their joyous rhythm.

In that moment I was lost, and yet… and yet… had lost the will to care.

THE CHASE

I WAS THIRSTY, the air was dry and my heart was thundering in my chest with the effort of keeping my legs moving. The gazelle was wounded and couldn't run for long, but it was fast as the wind, and we needed to get to it where it dropped before it was claimed by one of the big cats, vulture or hyena.

I was in the wall, spear in hand, bare-foot across its craggy surface, jumping and racing to catch the animal before me.

I'd lost track of the others and the fire and soon I didn't even remember the wall, the hunt and the chase was all there was. I was no longer sure which way the animal had gone and was just plunging on, lungs burning, legs straining in the hope of coming across it. And then my father was with me, running alongside, as he was when he was young, life, enthusiasm and energy radiating from him.

We ran to the very tip of that rock face, hot and dry, and then plunged headlong into the cold pool of stars, where we swam and floated, splashed and dived amongst a thousand points of light.

Eventually, when we could swim no more, we climbed back onto the land and just laughed and talked. Walking and resting, first in Africa, then somehow back in Shropshire and then in other places where I'd never been, with other people I'd never met. The world just seemed to open up before us, the past, present and future like so many pages in a book.

But like all dreams it had to come to an end, and on awaking I could feel much of the precious memory begin to slip away from me, evaporating like the morning mist beneath the heat of day.

I was on my back beneath that colossal rock face, the morning light illuminating its smoke-darkened surface in a warm golden light that made all the painted figures seem more restful, content to just lie across the surface and cease their efforts to jump free.

Mkize was already up and talking with some of the Maasai as they prepared food over the now much lower remnants of last night's bonfire.

I felt refreshed and rested both mentally and physically. And had been placed on my own sleeping matt, with a bowl of cool fresh water on the ground beside me.

Sitting up to drink the water provided, I looked around, I could see the same had been done for all my friends.

Marlow was already up and was just a few meters off from the group, sat watching the sunrise, so I got up and walked over to join him.

As I sat down beside him, I noticed he'd unwrapped the bandage from his forearm and was unconsciously tracing the lines of the twin gashes with his forefinger. He smiled up at me as I sat down.

'We think of these people as being so primitive in comparison to ourselves,' he observed, as his gaze returned to the sunrise. 'But sometimes, I wonder whether we haven't got it the wrong way around.'

'Yes,' I responded, knowing what he meant. 'It was an extraordinary experience, and honestly, I'm not sure what to make of it yet, but I feel very grateful to have been able to take part.'

'Can it really have been just a dream, George?' He asked, taking his eyes off the horizon to look at me.

I had to demur at such a straight forward question, 'What else could it be?' I responded. 'I'm not sure I'm ready to start believing that I've just spent the evening talking to spirits!'

'Perhaps, but I do think Nelion was right,' replied Marlow glancing over at me. 'Our world, with all its science and culture is lost. We've advanced so far in some ways, but at the expense of so much else.'

Jean and Harry were the next to come around, closely followed by the others. The evening had obviously put us all in thoughtful mood, but Jean, Silvio and Luke seemed not to have taken to the experience in the same way as the rest of us. Though their low spirits may have seemed worse in contrast to Harry who was positively giddy with his recollection of events.

'Astounding! Everything seems so clear, so obvious. I don't know how I can't have seen things this way before!' Was all he seemed able to say, amid his incessant questioning of what everyone else had seen and experienced.

Of the three Shaman there was no sign and Nbutu would say only that they had gone. As such with apparently nothing more to hear or be told, we began to make our scant preparations to return.

We did have to wait for a couple of hours for both Jean and Harry who were determined to loiter. Jean so he could do a 'quick' sketch of the rock face and its multitude of figures and symbols, much to the confusion of the Maasai. Harry so he could try and find a way up to the top of the cliff and the source of the drums.

Needless to say, they both took far longer than they'd planned and it was mid-morning by the time we eventually set off.

Heading back down though was much easier going than it had been on the way up. Obviously, it was now a slight decline most of the way, but we also seemed to run into fewer delays. So much so that even with our late start we still managed to get back to our horses and temporary camp by the end of the day.

After a full day of walking we were all tired and ready for a good rest, but as we sat and lay around the fire after our evening meal, the conversation turned toward the previous evening, and the dreams we had each experienced.

Harry was obviously going to be the one who started us off, he was just desperate to find out what everyone else had experienced.

'I know I've gone on about this perhaps a bit too much, but last night changed the way I see things and I'd really like to know if it was the same for any of you.'

'You keep saying that, Harry,' Peter said, as kindly as he could. 'But you don't actually tell us what you saw.'

'Well I'd say it was more a case of what I lived than what I saw, for the time I spent talking to those... spirits seemed as real as talking to you now. But if hearing about my night will help loosen your tongues, then so it is.'

'I remember taking the bowl from Rob, not that I realised I'd decided to drink until it happened, so I guess the moment must have just overcome me. Anyway, I watched it go to you George, and then Jean, and then I remember looking back at those three elders to see what they were doing. But as I looked over toward them, I noticed over their shoulders, back on the rock face, there was a symbol I hadn't seen before, a strangely geometric circle of marks.

'It was low down so I figured one of the Maasai must have been stood in front of it or some such, but I was sure I'd seen it somewhere before.

'Well I just couldn't place where I'd seen that

symbol, so I kept looking at it, trying to figure it out, then I noticed this symbol was carved into the rock, maybe even chiselled, not painted like all the others. Finding this strange I turned to mention it, but of course you were all no longer there, in your place was my old archaeology professor, Dr Zimmerman.

'Now I had, or have a great deal of respect for my old professor, and had stayed in fairly regular contact up until his death a few years ago. So, once I got over the idea of seeing him again, we just took up where we'd left off and it seemed like the most natural thing in the world. We talked about the symbol and where else it had been seen, with our memories conjuring us to the places we discussed.

'I think I was aware that I was dreaming or under the effects of Nelion's potion, but only distantly. Even so, that distant awareness was enough for me to be conscious of the fact that my old professor was steering our conversation, ever so subtly, along the lines that Nelion had mentioned.

'The symbol and slight variations on it, seemed to always represent flux and stability, and had been found at the core of so many early faiths and mythologies, often relating to world origins, or the nature of reality as shaped and agreed by the gods.

'After a while I thought I could guess where he was leading me, until eventually he came right out and told me.'

'Our world, Harry,' he began, indulgently. 'Or rather your world now, has never been good at considering some philosophical questions. Often, we prefer to leave the consideration of deeper matters to more spiritual minds. But there are questions, which we should have considered, decisions or agreements that may no longer serve your interests, that could even become limits. It may even be time for the world you know to leave its Gods behind and be shaped again in our own image.'

'When put so bluntly, I must confess I found it all a bit overwhelming, and admitted the same to my old friend.

He was sympathetic, and assured me that I was under no obligation to go any further, there were others. Including you Rob, who he showed me brief glimpses of, who may be more comfortable taking such steps.'

As Harry recounted this last section of his dream, I perceived a pronounced discomfort in the faces of the two Italians. Neither of them said anything, but I saw them glance at each other, and I watched Silvio as he both uncharacteristically and unconsciously touched the cross and chain around his neck.

Marlow was also noticeably quiet, a deep frown of concentration on his face as he stared intently into the fire.

For the first time, I think Harry started to pick up on some of the tension around him, and he became a little more hesitant as he continued.

'I had to think about my Professor's offer for a while, but as some of you will know, I've never been one to accept things quietly. So, I began to ask questions, what agreements had been made, and how did they limit us. I didn't get the answers I wanted of course, perhaps I didn't push hard enough, or ask in the right way, but after a while I got the message that reviewing such things was not in the nature of the process.'

'Instead, others appeared, who I didn't know, and our conversation turned to the nature of life, death and faith, including my lack of purpose. But I don't think my heart was really in it, and eventually they drifted away. I just wasn't sure what I was supposed to do, so I chose to return to the rock face and the carved symbol. Professor Zimmerman accompanied me back, offering what encouragement he could, before he too walked back into the night.'

There was a pause for a while, with just the sound of the crackling fire. Nobody questioned the nature of Harry's experience, but eventually Jean piped up with a question that I think several of us had been thinking of.

'You mention seeing Robert in your dream, but

what was it you saw him doing?'

'Well I know this will sound kind of strange, but I saw you walking and talking with that lion, Rob, the one you killed. I could see its mane still soaked with blood, so I know it was the same one.'

'That's alright Harry,' Marlow responded, wearily. 'What you saw was right.'

He seemed almost resigned as he began to speak, as though he knew beforehand that we wouldn't comprehend what he was saying, but that there was never going to be a better time.

'I too remember taking the bowl from Nelion as you all saw, and drinking deep of its strange contents. Anyway, it didn't take long for the drug to start having its effect, and soon I felt myself becoming entranced by the fire and the shadows dancing around us.

'I don't know at what point I lost track of everyone else, but after a while the lion that I killed, appeared from the darkness on the other side of the fire and came toward me. I don't know how, but I knew it was there as my guide, so when it turned, I followed. Away from the fire and into the drum-filled night beyond.

'We walked for a time before coming to another fire. It was in a broad, open place with just stars above, and a host of figures gathered around. As we approached, my guide abruptly bunched up his back legs as though to sit or jump, but instead lifted his front feet off the ground and... stood up to reveal a man in a lion skin cloak. Now upright, he turned with a completely natural motion and welcomed me to the group.

'They were stood in a circle a comfortable distance from the leaping flames, all talking either with those next to them or across the circle, a confused and raucous babble. As I looked around, I saw that many of them were also wearing the skins of animals, whilst some were clad in leaves or grass and a few shimmering individuals seemed to be garbed in running water, mist or cloud.'

'My guide had waited for a moment whilst I took in the spectacle of the group, before he addressed me in his deep rumbling voice.'

'You are welcome in this place, O' son of man. We are the spirits of this world, those responsible for the shape of its plains and rivers, its oceans and shorelines, the high places and the deep, all that you see and touch has been shaped by us.'

'His golden-eyed gaze ranged over those around the fire as he spoke these words before returning to rest upon me.'

'I'm not quite sure how it happened. I talked at first of my attempt to find meaning through the hunt, a challenge that would test me to my limits, in order that I might grow and expand those limits. This seemed to cause much debate amongst the group, conversations and questions flying in all directions.

'Why did I need this challenge, where would it stop and what did I hope to become by forcing myself through such trials. I tried to ask questions in return, only to have them evaded or ignored.

'Though I couldn't see what fuel it was burning, the fire seemed as though it was getting brighter and bigger and hotter. I felt dizzy with the heat and the frenzy of conversation, and then it all suddenly became clear and cool.'

'You represent the forms of all that has been shaped in this world, all that can be known and touched, but man is becoming something that you did not shape, and the world in which we live is also becoming something that you did not shape.

'As I uttered the words, the one question that I must ask became clear in my mind… Which of you shaped our minds, our thoughts, the aspect of us that represents our real natures?'

'It was as though a thunderclap had suddenly deafened me to the group around. The moment froze as they stopped and simply looked upon me. And then the fire seemed to respond, its light and heat increased, several of those stood around raised their hands to shield their faces, and then took a step back from the heat. It was scorching, I could hardly breathe the burning air, let alone look at the brilliance at its centre.'

'And then, I don't know why. I stepped forward, the pain overwhelming, toward that inferno of light and heat, until I touched it, the flaming essence of reality. For the briefest moments I saw and understood everything, before I was overcome.'

'The rest you know, I woke up early this morning on my sleeping mat, with my memories of the dream fading with each passing second.'

BEGINNINGS

THE FOLLOWING MORNING, as we began our journey back to the lodge it was with a mixture of emotions. After Marlow's account of the previous night Silvio had become increasingly agitated, until finally after many a false start, he gave us his account.

In his dream, he'd encountered his grandfather, who he'd adored from childhood, but who, after a long and painful illness had finally taken his own life, and was therefore damned.

This subdued even Harry's enthusiasm to hear about our dreams, for even though the encounter had no overtly malevolent elements, it clearly distressed the Italian more than he wanted to admit.

Added to this we were awoken early the next morning my Mkize who was concerned that the rains were coming. The chance of which while we were so far away from the lodge was enough to focus our minds on something other than the dreams.

By the time there was enough light to see, we were well on our way, but the rain clouds could already be seen over the distant horizon, and all of us who'd been caught in the rains before knew that meant we were in for a soaking. It was just a question of how far we'd get before it started.

The Savannah and brush are strange places just before a storm, the animals and even the plants seem to know that an abundance of water will soon be available, and with it the end, albeit temporarily, to harsh adversity and the struggle for life.

Suddenly the dust and dryness will be transformed into a verdant playground and every living thing seems to have a spring in its step and foolishness at heart.

Whether because of this or not, I don't know, but with the clouds racing across the heavens toward us we were making a desperate attempt to quicken our speed, only to have seemingly every impediment possible stand in our way, from a group of buck elephant that were intent on pushing trees down along our path, to a swarm of hornets that likewise seemed intent on going exactly where we wanted to go.

On the first day we travelled late into the night and set off again early the next morning whilst it was still very much dark. Even resting our horses as we travelled by walking alongside them for part of the day rather than stopping, but we'd still travelled no more than half the distance to the lodge before the first big, fat drops of water started to land around us.

Within minutes the rain was an opaque sheet on every side, and we were reduced to blindly following the grey shape of the person in front, nose to tail, trusting our guides to somehow find their way through the downpour.

After an hour in the saddle, making no noticeable headway, I began to lose track of where we were and what we were doing. Even the rain became less a downpour and more a series of tiny rivers and streams flowing over my cloth-plastered skin.

By early afternoon we were surely the most wretched individuals in Kenya. But just as it seemed there was no end in sight, the rains stopped and we were released.

It often happens like this right at the start, for although the rains can go on for a week or even two in exceptional years, they frequently include a prelude as though to warn unwary travellers of what's to come.

Needless to say, we didn't need to be told twice, and within moments had picked up our pace. It was difficult going now with the earth sticking in thick wet lumps to the horse's feet, but we pushed on and miraculously managed to get within sight of the lodge before those heavy raindrops once again started to fall.

I've rarely been so happy to see a place in my life, as I was that evening, entering the lodge with Marlow, Harry and the others, tired and worn from the journey, straight into the welcoming arms of a stiff drink and some hot food.

We'd arrived slightly late for dinner, but the lodge manager, somehow anticipating our return that evening, had not only prepared an abundance of hot water for bathing, but had also arranged a simple yet hearty meal.

We were all washed and changed in double-quick time, the luxury of being dry and the hot filling food ameliorating our frayed nerves and tired frames.

Thoughts of the drums and Nelion's dreams put aside, if not forgotten, for a short time.

Despite our tiredness though, there was still work to be done resurrecting our equipment from the day's watery onslaught.

The lodge-staff were a wonder here, and did a sterling job with everything. But the rifles and much of the personal or delicate equipment merited our own attention. As such, following on almost straight after the meal, we retired as a group to the bar with a drink and a rifle or other piece of equipment, rags, brushes, tools and oil for an industrious and good-natured end to the day.

I awoke the following morning to the same sound of distant thunder and drumming rain that I'd fallen asleep to the previous night.

The comfortable bed and fresh bedding had worked wonders on my mood and general feeling of well-being, and I stretched out of bed in the most slovenly fashion before glancing out of the window at a grey and very waterlogged Africa.

A leisurely wash and shave later and I was ready to stroll downstairs for some breakfast and a day of housebound idleness.

Amazingly, I was the first one to rise, so decided to wait until one of the others came down before going in to breakfast. I didn't have long to wait before Jean meandered down to join me, followed intermittently by the others.

Following breakfast, I went to sit beneath the sturdy shelter of the western veranda to watch the rain as it continued to fall. At times it seemed to lighten, almost as though it might stop again, only to come down heavier than before a few minutes later.

From time to time as the downpour eased off, a figure or two could be seen darting from one building to another on some errand. But on the whole, everyone was quite comfortably confined to the lodge and stables.

A new batch of newspapers had been delivered while we were away, so the morning slipped by in easy distraction as we each reacquainted ourselves with the goings-on of our respective homelands.

In the afternoon, following a light lunch, the group began to fragment along the lines of our individual interests. And after a few minutes casting around for something to do, I was just beginning to think I'd have to entertain myself by editing my journal, when Harry came over and suggested a little sabre fencing in one of the stable barns near to the lodge.

As we made our way, stopping off to pick up the

gear, we also picked up Jean and Marlow, who were just in the act of resetting their chessboard.

'It is no good,' said Jean, in mock irritation. 'He is not even trying to beat me. Perhaps you will concentrate more with a sword back in your hand, my friend.'

A few minutes later, this time with us being the ones darting through the rain, we were installed in a clear corner of one of the big barns. Harry and I started and then following Harry's undeniable victory, Marlow took a turn against him. Theirs was a much closer match, but again Harry prevailed, albeit by a narrow margin.

'Rob, while it's enjoyable to beat you for once, it would be considerably more gratifying if you'd at least pretend to be paying attention.' Harry said, with a tone of gentle irritation in his voice.

'I'm sorry, Harry, and to you too Jean for the chess,' Marlow apologised. 'You're both right, I haven't been giving you my full attention.

'There is in fact something preying on my mind from our meeting with Nelion at the Singing Stones.'

'I thought you might be holding out on us,' chipped in Harry, with unrestrained zeal. 'What else did you see, Rob?'

Hanging his sword and mask on one of the tack hooks along the wall, Marlow turned back toward us with a troubled look on his face.

'I've been trying to make sense of it myself, though in some ways it is clear enough. The account I gave you of my dream was honest, but it's what I saw when I touched that blinding flame at the centre of the gathering that I didn't explain as fully as I might.

'The pain, as I've said, was like nothing I've ever felt, but as I plunged my hand into the blaze, there was more beside the pain that was washing over me.

'At first it seemed like it was just a flickering image or two, but then I began to see groups of images. Moments of time that began to slow down to a speed I could comprehend.

'I can hardly describe the sensation. You see, whatever I thought about suddenly appeared in greater detail, places I knew, times and events I recognised. It was still blurred and confused at the edges, but slowly I began to exercise a deliberate influence over the things I saw.

'It was amazing,' he continued, sitting down on the end of an upturned water trough. 'I remember thinking this kind of knowledge could be both wonderful and terrible. But as I thought it, I started to lose control of the visions that appeared to me, and had to struggle to understand what I was seeing. Dark futures of things that humanity may or will experience, the growth and decay of our societies, and those great societies that have come before us, all flashed before my eyes.

'It seemed so hopeless, but just as I could feel myself beginning to fall away from the flame, the conversation we had back at the lodge, about our lack of purpose, came back to me. And, as the thought entered my mind, it was as though the flame understood what I sought.

The images were still coming too fast to begin with. It seemed like the entire history of humanity passing before my eyes in moments. But eventually it slowed and I recognised that this sentient fire was showing me birth, death and survival throughout the ages. Yet there was nothing more, for just as we began to develop, to show potential, we began to decay, both as individuals and as societies. We simply didn't exist long enough to reach beyond the petty achievements of our short lives.'

'Robert, I am not sure I like where you are going with this... vision of yours.' Jean added in a concerned voice. But Marlow hardly seemed to hear him as he continued.

'What could we achieve if only we had more life, while I touched that flame everything was a question, and every question was answered. In response, I saw wonders you would not believe, slow at first, but my control was fading, and the images started to slip though my fingers again, back to a blinding, burning light. Still I hadn't seen enough, and I couldn't let go until I'd asked one final question.

'In my mind's eye I stepped further forward into the flame, the pain overwhelming and revitalising my mind, raw energy coursing through every fibre of my being, and I grasped the bright centre of that inferno with both hands before shouting my question into its heart.

'Where can humanity find more life?

'The response was as dispassionate as the rest. I saw everything, but couldn't control it, there was just too much. I grabbed fragments as they passed and tried to force them into my memory, but couldn't stem the flow for long enough.

'I don't know at what point I passed out,' finished Marlow. 'But I know my memory contains only a fragment of what it should. The part that remains though, it speaks to me of something I barely dare contemplate... Immortality!'

For a moment Marlow was like stone, motionless after his tale, he was sat on the end of the water trough, looking distractedly at the ground lying between us.

It was Harry who spoke, finally breaking the silence. 'Surely an impossible dream, Rob, do you remember nothing more?'

'I can recall pieces, Harry, fragments of a whole so large I simply couldn't grasp it.

'But I know the answer is out there, humanity has held immortality in its hands before, but has lost it or buried it or forgotten it. There may even be those amongst us who still know the secret and walk this earth untouched by the ages.

'What I do know is that this secret can be found, and brought forth once more into the light.'

As he said these last words, he seemed to regain some of his focus, and standing up, he looked straight at us.

'And, I think I know where to start looking.'

It was Harry's turn to sit down, though I suspect we'd all have accepted a seat right then if there'd been anything else around.

'I've been trying to decide,' he continued, as we all struggled to gather our wits, 'Whether or not it would be fair to tell you all this. And I'm still not entirely decided as far as the rest of the group are concerned, but I think it would have been unfair of me not to tell some of you the truth before I go.'

'Go? What do you mean before you go?' Jean demanded. 'Robert, we are your friends, you cannot be thinking of just disappearing in the night without first telling us of your plans or asking us if we would accompany you.'

We talked for another two hours in that barn. At times it felt like I must have been dreaming, but eventually we all walked out together, dashing back to the lodge through the mud and rain.

Marlow had agreed he would share this additional information with the group before deciding what to do next.

After we returned to the lodge, he took himself off to his room to prepare. Luke had spotted us returning and it took just one look at us for him to know that something had transpired.

Jean was at the fore and as we'd agreed in the barn, he prepared the way by telling Luke and then the others that we had been discussing Nelion's dreams again and that Marlow now had something he'd like to share with us.

It was almost an hour before Marlow re-appeared, bringing with him several large rolled up maps and assorted other paperwork.

We'd taken over a small dining room, which had yet to be set for the evening, and whilst there was a certain anticipation in the air, everyone was cordial and mostly happy to have the distraction, though Silvio was still notably quiet.

Marlow began by apologising for not telling them

the whole story at the start, and then recounted what he had told us in the barn.

For this second telling he'd obviously considered how to explain things better, and now it was a more forceful, structured account, leading straight to the conclusion that he intended to search for the places and things he'd seen.

That it was shocking we all knew and accepted. That it would not be accepted well by Silvio and Luke was something that none of us had really considered.

'This is wrong,' insisted Luke.' It is against the law of God to seek such things. I do not understand what poison we drank to give us such dreams, but it is the work of the devil my friend and it will drive you to your destruction.'

'For the sake of our friendship, let us just wait for the end of the rains, then go to find some of the fresh new game. The savannah will be rich with life soon, the bush in flower and full leaf. Let us go and enjoy it and forget this primitive nonsense.'

Harry immediately objected to this. That it was unusual and unorthodox could not be doubted, but primitive and devilish he simply didn't agree with.

That the atmosphere remained cordial for almost the entire duration of our talks was a testament to the friendship that existed between the group. But after an hour of constant back and forth discussion, of maps and illustrations, and even of Luke bringing down his bible it all fell apart.

Silvio, who'd been quiet for most of the conversation, stood up, and after expressing his regret at our decision, and stating in very simple terms that he felt what we were proposing was not only wrong, but dangerous and against everything he believed in, he walked out.

After that I don't think any of us expected to find the common ground we so desperately sought, and eventually Luke also took his leave of us.

'I would like to be able to wish you well on your

venture,' he finally said, slowly standing up from the table around which we'd been sat. 'But I cannot. I do believe you are stepping onto a truly dangerous path my friends, so I will pray for you no matter which way you choose to travel. May God go with you.'

With that Luke also turned and left.

The rain was still heavy so there was no way in which Luke and Silvio could leave the lodge for at least another couple of days. But as soon as they were able, I knew they would depart.

Without anything needing to be voiced, the matter was completely dropped whilst Luke and Silvio were trapped in the lodge with us. They in their turn made no mention or comment upon our plans, and for a brief few days all was superficially as it had been. We talked and dined together, played cards and distracted ourselves with the other limited games and entertainments available to us.

At one point, possibly the closest any of us came to the subject of our plans, I came across Jean on one of the verandas, desperately trying to recapture the scene beneath the cliff face, from his memory. His original sketch having been entirely destroyed in the complete soaking we'd got on the journey back.

Eventually though, the rains did subside, and Silvio and Luke took their leave. We were all there to see them off, and although we enquired politely about their immediate plans, there was still very definitely no further mention of ours.

As they rode away from the lodge, leaving the five of us behind, I couldn't help but wonder what could be going through the minds of my companions.

From being a large and gregarious group that had travelled around Africa for over two years together, they had in the space of a few short weeks fractured and split to leave just four of their original number, plus myself.

I couldn't be sure, but as I looked at them after Silvio and Luke had ridden out of sight, I thought I could see the same thoughts present in their expressions.

THE PATH

IT WAS ANOTHER TEN DAYS before we were ready to leave the lodge and start our long trip down country toward our destination in Rhodesia. It was going to mean travelling through some unfamiliar territory into what had once been known only as "the interior".

But it felt good to be busy, and to be heading far beyond the territory any of us had explored before. The practicalities of such a journey demanded some additional preparations, and aside from waiting for the last of the rains to finish, we also needed some guides and servants.

Provisions and currency had to be sent for and then transported to the lodge, along with more ammunition and all the maps we could obtain of the territories we'd be travelling through.

By the time we were finally ready to set off, the anticipation was unbearable. But go, we did and it wasn't long before we were surrounded by the now verdant and rich Serengeti. The dark red soil was still soft under foot after the rain, and every tree and bush in full leaf or flower, much to the enjoyment of the insects and birds

We were initially heading inland, leaving the Great Rift behind us and toward the eastern edge of Lake Victoria. From there we were planning to find a boat to its more southerly shore and then south again, over the surrounding highlands, and hopefully down one of the rivers feeding into Lake Tanganyika, that longest of all African lakes.

If we could make it that far and then find another good boat to take us down its great serpentine length we'd be half-way to Rhodesia.

We were making good time through the bush and savannah, and after a couple of days had crossed the invisible boundary into Tanzania.

With the travelling and activity the group morale seemed to improve, and it wasn't long before we were once more sociably chatting over an evening meal and being victimised by Jean's unforgiving French sarcasm.

'Perhaps I should start writing my memoirs?' he'd spontaneously commented one night whilst we were sat around the camp fire over a 'digestif' pipe or two.

'Like George here, with the journal in which he is always writing. A record of my thoughts and sensations, as well as perhaps a note or two upon my previous achievements and… conquests.' he said, smiling as Harry exploded with an involuntary cough and puff of sparks from his pipe.

'Conquests, Jean? Are you sure the world is ready for such revelations?' Harry responded, tamping down his pipe and attempting to re-light it with a thorny spill from the fire.

'Oh, I did not say I would necessarily publish such gentle… histories, but I think perhaps I should start to record them,' retorted Jean with a very self-satisfied glint in his eye.

'Ah, more of an aide memoir,' responded Harry again, struggling to restrain his smile. 'To help you remember the details in years to come perhaps.'

'I have an excellent memory, thank you, Harrison,' Responded Jean, with an air of mock offence at the barely restrained laughter from Peter, Marlowe and myself. 'I was thinking more as a general record, for what I might use it in years to come, who can say. But if I were to wait until I had the purpose before I start to keep the record, then I should never begin.'

We talked some more about journals, their pro's and con's and I explained about my father's writing being the inspiration for my own, and my trip to Africa.

As for the purpose, I had to confess myself just as much at a loss as Jean. As the fire burned and we emptied and refilled our pipes it became Harry's turn to become more serious.

'You know, as I think of it now, despite my earlier comments, Jean, I do begin to wonder whether you should consider keeping some kind of record of this journey.

'Like the rest of you, and please forgive me for putting it so bluntly, Rob, I have no idea whether we've embarked upon a journey of fools, or something entirely more serious.

'We cannot know one way or the other at the moment, but if it should prove to be the latter, then a record of this… gentle history, may well become of interest and even importance.'

'There's nothing to forgive, Harry,' responded Marlow, with a gentle smile. 'Whilst the lucidity of my dreams was enough to convince me that I had to investigate them, it's only right all of you should retain your scepticism.

'Especially, as it's far from certain that I will be able to take us straight to our destination, though I have been attempting to commit as much as possible from my dreams to paper in order to ensure nothing that might be useful is forgotten. Even so, there will still be times when an educated guess is all I can offer.'

We'd talked our way to that calm time of night, when sleep was almost upon us and contemplation comes easily. So, after throwing the conversation around for a little while longer, the talk gradually went down to nothing before we each turned in for the night.

Another couple of uneventful days travel saw us at the shores of Lake Victoria, and aboard a medium-sized barge that plied a route up and down the eastern shore of the lake between Mwanza and Kampala. We'd been fortunate to catch it heading south, and even more fortunate to find it with enough space for both us and our horses.

I hadn't appreciated the sheer scale of the lake until

we were upon it, a warm south-westerly breeze pushing us away from the water's edge as we travelled.

The expanse of water was enormous, though apparently shallow by comparison with the other great African Lakes, and strangely warm as a consequence, it seemed less a lake than an inland sea.

At over two hundred miles wide and three hundred long, we were still skirting the edge comparatively speaking, even if at times the eastern shore was just a hazy blur on the horizon. Of the western or northern shores we never saw sign, even with the small telescope that Jean carried.

But as impressive as it was during the day, at night after the last trace of sunset had faded from the west and only the starlit sky remained to be reflected in the water, it must surely have been one of the most beautiful places on the earth.

The boat seeming to sail through the heavens themselves. Not that its motions were appreciated by the hippopotami, who we could hear baying and calling throughout the night from the shore. As for the crew, they were oblivious to the Lake's charms. For them, to be sailing upon and beneath that field of stars served them only to navigate in the darkness.

We arrived at Mwanza on the south-eastern edge of the lake in the early morning on the third day, a small but bustling port right on the edge of the lake and framed in the distance by the smoky outline of the surrounding highlands.

It was fairly rudimentary by comparison with Nairobi, but had a big enough population to merit a number of larger and obviously European-style buildings. Not that we got to see much of them.

Within an hour of touching land we'd found another barge going in our direction, ferrying a middle-aged Dutch couple who were heading the same way as ourselves, on their way to a missionary outpost located in the highlands at the head of the river that fed Lake Tanganyika.

It was too much of an opportunity to miss, so

foregoing a stay in Mwanza we simply moved our things from one boat to the other and then set off once again.

After stowing our things, we made our introductions to Dr and Mrs Reiss. They were an affable and polite couple, who were moving from one mission to another as part of their calling, and were obviously as accustomed to Africa and its ways as we were ourselves.

They'd assumed, probably from our rifles and other accoutrements, that we were in Africa for the game, and we did nothing to dissuade them of this at first.

But as our first day together wore on, and we continued to talk, I became aware that we were all avoiding their questions. I didn't think they'd noticed, but it occurred to me then, just what difficulty we might have later on trying to explain the real nature of our journey. And it wasn't long before I began to see the same realisation on the faces of my companions.

It was Marlow who eventually set the Reiss's straight, with a half-truth about going to explore the enigmatic stone ruins known as Great Zimbabwe. This seemed to satisfy their curiosity for a while. But something, possibly our hesitation in telling them we weren't just travelling for the sport, must have caused them to become suspicious and for the rest of the day as we plied our way across the lake, they continued to politely quiz and question us about our trip.

Eventually we made landfall again, and with good African soil beneath our feet, we turned away from the water and toward the misty highlands in the south.

The Doctor and his wife were a pleasant enough couple at first. But as we made our way, their missionary calling gradually started to get the better of them and it wasn't long before Mrs Reiss was attempting to give instructional talks to the servants. Including Mkize, who succumbed so automatically as to make me realise he was long familiar with such… good intentions, and knew very well how to best deal with them. In stark contrast, poor Jean made the unfortunate mistake of 'declining to wear his faith on his arm' and consequently seemed to be trapped in one long debate after another with the good doctor and his wife.

It was going to take about six days to get to the Reiss's new mission, and whilst there was no hint of a trail, the going was steady and good, so we were able to escape from the Reiss's and the main group occasionally, in order to go hunting, often rejoining them late in the day and hence avoiding much of the evenings sermonizing to the servants.

After four days though, they'd obviously started to get curious about our journey again, and upon returning early from one of our hunting trips, with some plump ground roosting birds and a small warthog, Harry as near as caught them going through his things.

The following day, as we crested the highlands and started to make our way downhill, Dr Reiss and his wife, openly started questioning our motives for going to Rhodesia and Great Zimbabwe. They'd obviously heard about the troubles being experienced there and the lawless mining town culture that prevailed.

Either that or Harry's things had not been the only luggage they'd searched, and they'd found something else, possibly even my journal.

Harry managed to deflect them for a short while by showing off his knowledge of archaeology, whilst Peter spoke enthusiastically of the hunting and game available along the Luangwa and Zambezi. But eventually they couldn't even be distracted by questions about their new mission or more theological debate with Jean, and we were forced into just repeating the same thing over and over.

By the time we arrived at the Reiss's new mission and the river that would hopefully take us to Lake Tanganyika, we were all too happy to be getting away from them.

There was a small river boat that plied the route every two months, but we'd missed it by a couple of weeks so were forced to sell our horses and hire several native canoes instead, which meant spending another night with the Reiss's whilst everything was organised, and then taking our leave of them first thing the following morning, after yet another sermon for the servants.

It was a four-day journey to reach Tanganyika, which was good going bearing in mind we had to go ashore each night to camp. But in reality, it meant four days of cramped conditions and no shelter from the sun and humidity of the open river.

All of this put us rather out of sorts by the time we reached the lake. Not helped, it has to be said, by the Reiss's, who it turned out had written a letter, outlining their concerns to the police official in the small lakeside port where we'd finally left the canoes. To add insult to injury, the letter was of course covertly conveyed by one of the fishermen we'd employed to take us down the river.

Fortunately, the official in question was not only a Frenchman, but also a Gascon like Jean, and though they'd obviously never met before, within half an hour they were like brothers.

The following day saw us aboard another barge the Liemba, with the police official's best wishes and a bottle of Armagnac exchanged for some of our coffee and a few cigars from Jean's personal stock.

From Tanganyika we next made our way south, back into the more southerly reaches of the Great Rift and over the border to Zambia. From here we travelled just to the west of Lake Malawi to join the recently flooded Luangwa River.

The riverboat had been due for nearly a week when we arrived. But it was another three days before it finally came steaming around the bend in the river to the irrepressible joy of the local children and adults, who all turned up at the small wooden dock to see what it had brought.

We were all getting a bit tired of the constant sitting

around or waiting for boats by this point, and more than once I wondered whether we might not have been better just travelling back to Mombasa and getting a boat down the coast before travelling inland to our destination. But we'd decided we'd see more of Africa this way, and that we were certainly doing.

The river boat turned out to be an old paddle steamer, which had definitely seen better days. But it was sound and remarkably, quite reliable normally, on this occasion being delayed only by the detritus freed by the rains and now floating in great free-form pontoons down the river.

We made good time down the Luangwa, and got a first-rate view of the Muchinga Escarpment as it rose majestically to our right, framed to the fore by a constantly changing landscape of verdant bush, forest and grassland. There seemed to be an equally impressive array of African wildlife coming down to the water to drink or bathe, all with a wary eye to the boat as we passed by.

Despite the size of the boat, the narrowness of the river and the debris that still littered its surface meant we weren't often able to travel much after dark. But occasionally, where the river had broadened out and slowed down a little, we were able to travel through the twilight and see some of the big cats and other night-time predators as they too prepared for the evening.

Being on the boat also gave us more thinking time, in contrast to our time with the Reiss's and in the canoes, which had required our focus to be more firmly on the day-to-day practicalities.

Now, aboard the Liemba, with comfortable cabins to sleep in and abundance of deck to walk around, a dining room and bar, we were once again able to work out our plans for Rhodesia.

'I think the temple lies no more than a day's walk from the ruins of Great Zimbabwe,' began Marlow, as we tried to make the best plans we could with the sketchy maps at our disposal. 'I'm not clear on the relationship, if any, between the two, but I do know the temple is much older, and lies beneath the ground as part of a cavern complex.

'I also know that to some extent the entrance to the temple has been deliberately blocked.'

'And in this place, there lies some artefact which holds the secret of eternal youth?' quizzed Jean, with more than a hint of doubt in his voice.

'No, I don't think so, Jean,' responded Marlow. 'Here, I hope to find a map.

'As I mentioned before, when I was first trying to describe my vision, I simply couldn't keep hold of all that I was seeing. But, as I lost control, and the images began to race past me in a blur, there was one thing I could take hold of.

'Through the perhaps thousands of years of events that I saw while I was looking into the fire, I caught glimpses of others, both men and women, who had done the same. Some came more than once, and as I saw them, they surely saw me. But there was one man, whose unchanged face I saw again and again.

'Over what must have been an eternity of time he returned to stand in the centre of that fire as calm and collected as though he were reading the fire like you or I might read a newspaper.

Finally, the last time I looked at him, I was sure he looked straight back and saw me, for a moment later the vision in the fire changed to show me his home, and then flashes of numerous others that had come to visit him, followed finally by some kind of map showing locations related to each of those that had visited.'

'Of the details I can tell you little else,' continued Marlow, anticipating our questions. 'But what I can say is this. If the man I saw at the centre of that inferno was real, then he not only held the secret of everlasting life, but I think he was trying to mark a route by which others could also find it.'

Perhaps it was just my imagination, but as Marlow was outlining these additional details, I was sure I saw in the faces of my friends, and possibly even Marlow himself, the doubt and foolishness of pursuing such a fantastic goal diminish slightly.

The other details that Marlow could give were sketchy at best. The face of the figure he'd seen was of no clear racial type or descent, but seemed wild without being unkempt or manic.

As for the location of this individual's home, Marlow described seeing a particular view of a valley, and another of Great Zimbabwe, but as we sat on the sun-bleached deck of the riverboat with some cooling drinks, we struggled to patch together anything specific enough to try and find on a map.

By the time we left the riverboat on the lower Zambezi, we'd travelled through some spectacular country that I would sorely have liked to stop and explore.

From mist shrouded grasslands and verdant forests to starkly bare cliffs and mountain-sides the landscape changed almost by the hour. But as we entered Rhodesia we came across an entirely different landscape that in contrast, I'd have been more than happy to pass through with far greater speed.

This was the rough country of mines and miners, who were ravaging the countryside in search of ever less plentiful precious metals and the promise of wealth.

The centre of this chaos was Salisbury, as big if not bigger than Nairobi, and bustling with a life and energy tainted by the danger and menace that always walked hand-in-hand with greed.

REMAINS

WE KNEW WE'D HAVE TO BE CAREFUL making our arrangements once we got to Rhodesia, so as not to attract unwanted attention of either the official or unofficial kind. So we'd decided to spread out the purchases we needed to make, especially of explosives, and excavation equipment between Salisbury and Fort Victoria, our next stop along the way.

It could've been a dicey situation, with any kind of mistake immediately making us appear more suspicious, but Peter was our salvation.

He'd studied and worked as an engineer for a few years, so was familiar enough with the things we might need to school us in our purchases. He knew exactly when to haggle, what to substitute and how to make it look like it was something he'd done a hundred times before. A single day in Salisbury and we were off again with all haste, out once more into the wild.

It was the same at Fort Victoria, look as business-like as possible, get in, find a guide and some more supplies, and get back out into the country before anyone had time to grow suspicious.

With a local guide we were able to make our way to the ruins in just a couple of days. The area had long ago been explored and abandoned by the miners and mine owners, so there were just a handful of officials to get around and then we were on our own.

I think I'd been expecting ruins on the kind of scale you find in England or France. Either a roofless old building, built on a grand scale, that could almost be confused for something that was still being built, or an anonymous grassy bank surrounded by a few scattered rocks.

Nothing prepared me for the miles of overgrown ruins and suspiciously angular rock formations that we now found ourselves wandering amongst.

It wasn't too obvious at first, you could almost mistake them for little stony outcrops, almost but not quite natural, just peeking out through the clumps of brush and acacia or tall grass.

But as our guide led us on, those stony outcroppings became more numerous, and then started to be interspersed with larger pieces of shaped stonework that formed architectural features, until it was impossible to imagine how anyone could mistake the massed remains of an ancient city all about us.

From the moment we entered the area I decided to keep an eye on Marlow to see how he'd react as we got closer to our destination. At first, as we began to explore and to get a feel for the sheer scale of the place, he seemed as curious as the rest of us, pointing out the more telling bits of ruin.

As we progressed further though, the curiosity in his expression seemed to be replaced by uncertainty and then confusion. Until, as we crested the lip of the valley that lay to the fore of the Great Zimbabwe fortress, its silhouette clearly visible on the distant horizon, something seemed to change within him.

The sight of the valley momentarily struck us all. Its entire length seemed lined with caves or the remnants of stone structures.

The scale alone was breath-taking, but to see it in ruins, without another soul in sight, had an even more shocking impact.

I just wanted to stare and wonder at it all, but with an effort I forced my attention back to Marlow.

As soon as the valley and fortress had come into

view, he visibly stiffened, and then started looking from right to left, and back again, as though searching for something.

As I stood there surrounded by those ghostly ruins, the hot sun beating down on us as probably the only visitors the place had seen in decades, I knew he'd recognised something.

Despite never having been there before, he'd looked around and obviously seen features he knew.

After stopping to point out the fortress and caves from our viewpoint on the valley lip, our guide took his pay and his leave, and we were left alone.

Harry had been musing and enthusing happily to himself when Marlow interrupted him.

'The place we're looking for is several miles from here around the curve of the valley and beyond. With luck we should get there before nightfall.'

'You have memories of this place from your dream, Robert,' quizzed Jean, with a strained neutrality to his voice.

'Yes, Jean,' responded Marlow, simply. 'Though the ruins of this place are but a shadow of the image I have in my mind, there's enough for me to recognise it.'

As we travelled down into the valley beneath the fortress, I couldn't help but wonder what images from the past might be filling Marlow's mind.

Did he see the ghostly outlines of mighty buildings where now only a few broken walls stood? Or was he jostling and walking amongst the city's former residents as they went about their long-lost daily routines? He seemed quiet as we walked, his face and actions unreadable.

Unlike the rest of the city, the old fortress, as it was thought to be, was still an imposing structure at the top of the valley wall above us, and I knew I wasn't the only one who would have liked to go and look around it. But it didn't seem to figure in Marlow's vision or dream-memory, so we continued on past, along the floor of the valley and away from the densely packed rocky remains of the city, back into open bush.

An hour or so later, as we rounded the bend in the valley which Marlow had mentioned, the ground levelled off and then started to rise slightly, until a few miles distant the valley seemed to bend again.

On that next bend, directly ahead of us, we could see a strange geological feature. It looked like the valley floor suddenly rose to form a shelf or high step.

Turning half toward us, Marlow raised his arm to indicate that this giant 'shelf' was our destination.

The walk wasn't difficult, and threading our way through the still leafy trees and grasses would have been pleasant, but for the constant incline and lack of breeze, which combined with increased humidity, made the walk just a little bit too warm for comfort.

Even so, we made it to the shelf before nightfall. And, after pulling a quick thorn fence together around our camp, we just had time for a brief scout around.

The climb up to the shelf had been too steep for the horses while they were laden down with our equipment, but by reducing the weight they were carrying we managed to get them up there, then either carrying the equipment up ourselves, or using the horses to pull it up on a rope.

The shelf itself was rockier under foot than the main valley floor, and while there were enough trees to provide us with some shade, they were less densely packed together and seemed older, more contorted somehow.

There was still plenty of brush growing beneath the trees to hide potentially dangerous animals, though it was probably only lion or hyena that would have been able to make their way up here.

At the back and side of the shelf the valley walls were almost sheer, and around a hundred feet in height, but on the side with the spring and ruins that Marlow had told us about, the ground sloped at a moderate angle for fifty feet or so, before once again becoming sheer.

In all fairness I could see why this site might have been chosen for a temple or chieftains dwelling. It was nicely sheltered and easily defendable, both attractive qualities to primitive societies.

But more than that, its prominent position at the head of the valley made the shelf both very visible from the valley floor, and the whole valley floor very visible from the shelf. All of which must have added to the place's status.

The sun always seems to set quickly in Africa, but as I finished my quick reconnaissance of the shelf, and took a moment to watch the evening shadow as it raced across the valley bottom, I couldn't help but wonder whether the animals of this place were aware of what was happening as that great shadow swept toward them each night. Did they move instinctually toward the far edge of the valley to escape it's reach for just a few minutes more, or did they just accept the inevitable approach of night, and instead step gently into its cool embrace?

The additional height of the shelf, gave us a few more minutes of gloom before the night proper descended, and making my way back to the camp, before it got too dark, I found most of the others already returned and in restful mood.

Their thoughts and conversation mirrored mine on the location. Marlow and Jean, who'd also been looking around, had arrived back a minute or two before me and, navigating our way through the thorny barrier that had been gathered around our camp, we all settled down around one of the fires for the evening.

It was an uneventful night. Shortly after the meal I'd found myself nodding off, and whether because of the day's walking or comparative quiet of our camp, I slept without stirring for the entire night.

In contrast, it seemed Marlow had a restless night and, waking early, had borrowed Mkize and one of the servants to take a look at the site we'd found just after we arrived.

By the time I finally stirred both Harry and Peter had also headed over, and I was left with Jean. He had woken before me, but was determined to finish his breakfast and coffee before joining in the excitement.

The ruins we'd found on our arrival were only a short distance from our camp, so once properly awake I walked over with Jean.

When we got there, it was obvious the others had already been hard at work to uncover some of the more interesting bits of stonework. Even from a distance as we approached, it was clear we were looking at the remains of a significant structure.

It was obviously old judging by the stones that had been uncovered, which while clearly carved and shaped also showed signs of significant weathering.

There were still identifiable bits of column, and wall, all piled together forming an enormous, and for us, surely impenetrable barrier.

As we approached, it seemed Marlow and the others had come to the same conclusion, but unperturbed were in the act of discussing how to get around it.

'What about the explosives?' Marlow was in the middle of asking, as we joined them. 'If we could get far enough into the pile, could we blow some of these larger stones outward.'

'No, no,' responded Peter, shaking his head. 'We don't have anywhere near enough dynamite for that kind of thing. We've got enough to break up some of the rocks, perhaps clear a few small obstructions, not to perform a major demolition.'

'And bear in mind, Rob,' chipped in Harry. 'While we're trying to get through, we don't know how far back this rock fall might go, or how fragile the cave or structure beyond might be.

'Which leaves us with going around as the better option,' continued Harry, in a thoroughly business-like manner.

'And that means excavating the sides… and you two are just in time,' he said, indicating Jean and myself.

It wasn't long before my restful night was just a distant memory, as we each took turns at the backbreaking work of digging down and around the large lumps of stone that stood in our path.

Fortunately, the rainy season had happened in Rhodesia as well, and the earth was still moist enough to keep the dust to a minimum.

Within a couple of hours, we'd found the edges of all the big pieces of shaped stone and had started to penetrate down through the surrounding earth and rubble to expose the gaps.

It was exhausting work, and once the sun was directly overhead we had to stop for fear of getting sunstroke. But by the end of the day, and with considerable effort from Mkize and the small number of other men we'd brought with us from Kenya, we'd managed to expose the extent of several larger rocks and find a head-sized gap into a large space between one enormous boulder and the surrounding bedrock.

We couldn't be sure how far down the hole went, but as the gloom increased, and the ambient light outside reduced, we threw a couple of torches down into the hole, to see if we could make anything out of the interior.

There was definitely a good drop inside, but as soon as the torches hit bottom they seemed to be extinguished in a pool of water, presumably the build up from the small stream which trickled out from amongst the rocks and soil that blocked the entrance.

It was too late to do anything more so we decided to call it a night and talk through our options back at the camp.

One completely unexpected luxury we were able to avail ourselves of was the water coming out of the rocks, which turned out to be a warm spring, though without any trace of the salts and minerals normally associated with a volcanic or thermal spring.

While the day's work had tired us all out, the progress we'd made and the challenge of finding a way through the pile of rocks, was enough to keep us talking late into the night.

It was clear to us all we hadn't really come prepared for the scale of the work before us. Yes, we had some tools, and some explosives, but we just hadn't anticipated the large stonework that faced us.

This left us with two options.

We could either go back to Fort Victoria, re-equip, and risk the authorities getting curious about us. Or, we could stick it out and risk losing several days before finding out whether we'd be able to get in.

In the end we decided to spend another few days trying our luck before making the decision. That way we'd at least have a better idea of what kind of help we might need if we did end up going back to the Fort.

To say that we all slept well that night would probably be an understatement. But the following morning, despite our aching limbs, we were all up early and heading over to the site together for another day's labour.

We'd decided to focus on one side of the rocks, excavate as far as we could and then if we didn't have any luck, start work on the other side.

In the light of day, and with a fresh perspective, I think we were all quite pleased to see how much we'd already managed to get done.

Just as importantly, we were eager to see if the fresh dawn light would allow us to see any further into the gaps and crevices we'd unearthed.

We'd already figured out there was a large space behind some of these rocks, but we hadn't been able to tell whether it was the cave proper, or just a large cavity amongst the debris.

Unfortunately, the morning light turned out to be

coming from just the wrong angle to penetrate any of the gaps, so there was nothing else for it but to start work and try again later.

With no better options, we resumed work in the place we'd made the best progress the day before.

We'd managed to get far enough back into the debris on this side to discover the leading edge of a great rock that obviously formed a substantial part of our obstruction, possibly even the same rock that framed the top edge of the rock fall.

There was clear evidence this titanic lump had been shaped and worked by human hands, but strangely only on one side, with just unadorned rock on the other.

'My, friends,' said Jean rather suddenly, after we'd all been digging away for a couple of hours and the heat was beginning to get uncomfortable. 'I believe I see how these pieces of stone may have once fitted together.

'Surely, what we now uncover, this stone, shaped and carved as it is on just its lower side, this was a roof of some variety, perhaps supported by the remnants of the pillars we have found, to form a sheltered entrance into the cave beyond?'

'What, and you think this great slab may have just swung straight down obscuring the entrance?' I asked, slightly irritably, not quite understanding the significance or value in such speculation.

'Exactly, George,' Jean responded, ignoring my ill temper. 'Which suggests, does it not? That by focusing our excavation upon the edge of this megalith, and digging down to its base, we may discover the side or mouth of the cave which it once sheltered, as well as possibly the floor leading into that cave.'

It was as good an idea as any, and as such after a brief discussion yielded no better plans, we decided to focus our efforts in the manner suggested by Jean, digging straight down the edge of that great stone.

It was tough going, and we nearly came unstuck by

two large rocks that it was only just within our power to move. But after another few hours work the progress was clear and several feet of the megalith's edge was now visible, as it butted up against what was hopefully the bedrock forming the cave mouth. There were small gaps here and there down the exposed edge, which seemed to reveal the same cavity we'd glimpsed from above. But we were still unable to see for sure where it might lead.

It was Harry's turn next in the hole working with Mkize in the last shift before we'd be forced to take shelter from the mid-day sun. The two of them taking it in turns with the shovels and passing the loosened earth and stone back up to myself and Jean at the top, while Marlow and the others took a break nearby.

'There seems to be a slightly wider opening down here,' shouted up Harry, between shovels of earth. 'But there's another damn rock blocking the way.'

I could see what he was talking about over his shoulder, just as the gap between the bedrock and the roof slab seemed to be broadening out, the top of another stone had been exposed. Harry was kneeling down now and had managed to get his arm into the hole up to the shoulder.

'I can feel the join between the three rocks. It definitely gets broader, maybe even big enough to get through.'

This was enough to spur us on, and within a few minutes Harry had scraped away nearly a foot of earth, exposing more of the gap and the new rock that seemed to be blocking it. There was still no telling how big it was, or how far down it went. But it was clear that whilst it filled the gap between the other two much larger stones, it wasn't a perfect fit by any means, and Harry was able to push as much earth through the gaps between the three bits of rock, as he was able to shovel out.

The sun was getting high in the sky again, and we would all soon have to take a break to get away from the heat, but this looked like it could be a breakthrough, so I stood and shouted the others to come up and take a look as well.

I could hear Harry mumbling something under his breath as he knelt down to stick his arm through the gap again. Not that I could hear the words, but I could tell something about it was aggravating him, until eventually he just stood up and started stamping on the exposed top of the smaller rock and insisting it should move.

It seemed like a futile gesture, and I couldn't help but smile as I saw him kicking at what could've been another huge boulder, but then the thing moved, just six inches at first, and then another couple, and then suddenly the entire rock fell away.

The dislodged rock was obviously bigger than Harry had expected it to be, because as soon as it disappeared into the cave, a lot of the earth and smaller stones he'd been standing on went with it, closely followed by Harry with a yelp of surprise.

STEPPING STONES

MKIZE WAS SCRAMBLING OUT, helped by Peter, but there was no sight or sound of Harry from the hole, as I called out his name.

The others had obviously seen that something was up, and had raced up to join me. I briefly explained what had happened. The earth around the hole we'd dug, and the gap that had now opened up into the cave, forming a steep sloping funnel.

We sent Peter and the severely shaken Mkize to retrieve a rope and some torches from the camp, while the rest of us waited and continued to call after Harry.

'I'm going to try and get down to the mouth of the

hole, and see if I can see anything more from there,' said Marlow.

It was a good fifteen feet down, surrounded by loose and crumbling earth, and with very little at the mouth to hold on to or stop yourself from sliding straight down into the darkness below. But by using one of the shovels as a makeshift rope, we managed to lower him most of the way, and he was just able to slide the last few feet and brace himself across the opening to see down into the hole.

'Harry! Harry! Are you all right?' Marlow was shouting into the opening. 'I think I can just make him out. Yes, he's waving.'

A moment later and Peter had arrived with the ropes and torches and we were inside and had found our friend sitting at the bottom of a bank of earth, just above the pool of water that had extinguished our torches.

He'd obviously been winded, and he was holding his head as though that was hurting.

It made for a worrying minute or two not knowing how badly he was hurt, but after Jean offered him his dampened handkerchief and some fresh water he recovered enough to explain.

Apparently, in a graceful attempt to stop himself from sliding into the hole, he'd grabbed at his shovel, the handle of which had unfortunately swung round and hit him squarely between the eyes, dazing him quite badly.

Much relieved that it was only his ego which was seriously hurt, we helped him to his feet and started to look around the cave.

It was a good fifty feet tall in places and at least half that again wide.

As we lit more torches and were able to see further into the darkness, we began to realise just how much rock and earth was blocking the entrance. We could've spent weeks trying to dig our way in, even with the proper equipment, and still not managed it. The rock fall blocking the entrance was colossal.

Realising how lucky we'd been, we turned back to the cave, which was fairly clear of debris, but at the same time was quite plain.

The floor seemed to have a slight incline, down which a small stream of water flowed in a purpose-built channel, before swelling to form a sizeable pool behind the natural damn of the rock fall.

On closer inspection, it was clear both the ceiling of the chamber and the walls had been worked, to give them a smooth and regular finish, whilst the floor seemed to have not only been smoothed, but also laid with expertly carved paving, seamlessly incorporated into the bedrock of the walls.

Checking that Harry was fit to walk, we moved up the incline toward an elegantly carved tunnel, that was broadly rectangular but with slightly bowed sides, which we could see at the back.

'This is amazing workmanship, for an ancient structure,' commented Harry, still holding Jean's damp handkerchief to his brow. 'I don't know of another pre-mediaeval structure outside of Egypt that displays such geometric regularity.'

The stream was partially paved-over in the tunnel, creating an almost stepping stone like effect, with glimpses of water between each step. But as the tunnel broadened out into a second cave, the channel once more became exposed, leading initially to a curious nine-sided pool in the middle of the room, lined in plain white stone. This pool was in turn fed by an identical channel on its opposite side, coming into the room through another tunnel.

We must've been the first people to see these chambers in who knew how many hundreds or even thousands of years, yet the place seemed pristine.

This second room was slightly larger than the first, but seemed to show similar signs of human craftsmanship on the floor and ceiling. But as we moved further into the room and spread out around the central pool, our torches illuminated the walls, which were not only shaped and smoothed, but also carved into exquisite reliefs of figures, scenes and even writing.

More striking still were the colours and ornamentation of these relief's, rich ochres, reds and yellows intermixed with the brightest cobalt blue, black, and in places even gold leaf, as well as what may have been either precious stones or coloured glass.

'That cannot be,' said Harry walking over to the nearest wall, his aching head and handkerchief forgotten. 'This is… cuneiform lettering, in southern Africa.

'It can't be, it just isn't possible.'

'Perhaps it was some remote colony or settlement, of which the archaeological world has yet to learn,' suggested Jean, helpfully as he toyed with what appeared to be a metal bracket or sconce of which there were several fitted around the walls.

'No, no, you don't understand, Jean. This isn't just slightly out of place, this is wholly out of place,' responded Harry, never removing his eyes from the walls of the cave, 'To find… Egyptian remains in such a place would rock the foundation of our understanding. Norse or even Dynastic Chinese, would all be outrageous, but all would somehow be more expected than this.

'This… not that I'm an expert, but… and the detail, such carving. It cannot be.'

I could see Harry was completely overwhelmed, his gaze and out-stretched hands throwing fantastic shadows in the flickering torchlight as they moved back and forth across the wall as though not knowing where to start.

We'd all been so distracted by the discovery of the wall-writing, and Harry's response that I'd forgotten to keep track of how Marlow was reacting. I turned now to see if I could discern anything in his expression or manner which might give some insight into his thoughts, but he was no longer there.

'Where's Rob?' I found myself asking before I

realised.

This returned everyone to the present, even Harry turned away from the carvings to look around.

'I'm sure he was standing right beside me,' said Peter.

Jean dashed back through into the first cave to see if he was still in there, but returned a moment later without finding him.

Realising he must have gone on, we tore ourselves away, and followed the stream into the next passage.

Though identical in construction, this tunnel seemed much longer than the first, and with more of the metal brackets along its length, before it eventually opened out into a third chamber.

This was also highly ornamented, the walls carved again into exquisite relief, and another central pool. But now with three tunnels leading off, further into the earth, each guarded as it were by a pair of intricately carved black obelisks the height of a man and covered from tip to base in more cuneiform.

He could have gone down any of these tunnels, but there was only one which carried the stream, and almost without hesitation we crossed the room and followed its stepping stone path, calling out Marlow's name as we went.

Again, this tunnel seemed long, but as we neared its end, we could at last see the glow of Marlow's torch.

As the tunnel opened out, we stepped into a much larger cavern of warm shimmering light reflected from the surface of a large, clear and apparently completely natural pool, which sat in the middle of the cave.

This cave was quite different to the earlier chambers we'd seen, and aside from the floor, which was still made up of that seamless paving, the dome and walls appeared to be simple unworked rock.

With relief I saw that Marlow was stood on the far side of the pool by a large stone altar-block, which seemed to be the focal point of a ring of more black obelisks surrounding the pool.

He'd jammed his torch into one of the metal brackets on the wall to free his hands up, and now as though oblivious to our search, simply gestured for us to join him.

As we made our way around the pool and the obelisks, the reflected light from the water gave the entire cavern an almost naturally lit air. Jean stopped and managed to wedge his torch into another of the metal brackets, to free his hands, after which the rest of us did the same at various other points around the cave.

'It's here, in this altar,' continued Marlow, walking around the large carved piece of stone. 'I'm sure of it. As soon as I set foot in this room, I recognised it from my vision. And the map, I'm sure it lies in here somewhere.'

'Can we not break into it?' enquired Peter. 'Perhaps bring down one of the picks from outside.'

'That may damage the map in some way,' responded Marlow. 'While I know it's in here, I have no idea what it could be made of or how fragile it may be. It could even comprise part of the fabric of the altar itself for all I know.'

'I agree,' said Harry, taking control of the situation. 'We need to find out how to open it, as it was intended to be opened. I suggest we start by washing it down. This is an ornate object and secret joins could easily be hidden amongst the multitude of detail, which might just be shown up by a little water.'

'Might there not be some clue in the writings or carvings upon the walls in the other chambers?' asked Jean.

'Yes, that's a good point,' conceded Harry. 'Perhaps you and George could take a look while we start with the altar.'

It suddenly struck me, as I was retracing my steps with Jean, back through the earlier chambers, that this was all getting very real. We were moving beyond the possibility that this could be a simple co-incidence, or lucky find, and rapidly toward the confirmation of Marlow's vision as a very tangible and objectively verified reality.

We'd gone back to the original ante-chamber which Harry had literally fallen into, and stopping briefly to let Mkize and the others know we were going to be some time, we started to search each room methodically.

As we were finishing in the second chamber having found no sign of altars or maps amongst the various carvings, I turned to Jean to voice my misgivings.

'I also share your growing confusion in this matter, George,' he responded, with a degree of resignation in his voice. 'Robert is amongst my closest of friends, but I tell you openly and without hesitation, that I considered this vision and our journey to be no more than a fanciful dream, invented by an unconscious mind whilst under the influence of a powerful narcotic.

'But I look upon this ancient structure,' he added, reaching out and touching one of the exquisitely carved relief figures. 'And the boulders and earth which blocked its entrance, and I cannot explain how this could enter into a man's dreams through the medium of a drug.

'Nor, as a modern man, can I accept there is a mystical influence at work here, but as a philosopher and lover of wisdom, I can no longer deny the possibility that this is exactly what is going on.'

'But surely you cannot think that block of stone could hold the secret of eternal life, or even a map that would lead us to it?' I asked, almost desperate.

'No, George, I do not,' Jean replied, with a small shake of his head. 'Or at least I hope not.

'To me the idea of such a thing is both terrible and wonderful at the same time. A ridiculous fantasy for children or perhaps a myth for simpler times.

'For such a thing to be a reality, in our modern age, would change our world too much.'

We continued to search through the rest of the chambers, including the ones we'd not previously visited. They turned out to be quite extensive, with some suggesting they may have been used for accommodation as well as ceremonial purposes. But there was nothing anywhere to indicate how to open the altar.

We returned to find that Harry, Peter and Marlow had had similar luck with the altar itself.

'The only possibility I can think of is that some part of this can be lifted off by brute force,' suggested Harry, defeated.

With no better ideas, we gathered round and agreed to focus our efforts on the uppermost rim just a few inches below the top of the altar, where the pattern of the carvings provided some grip.

We took the strain and all tried to lift. There was nothing at first, but a second later the top moved just a fraction before seeming to get jammed.

A small gap had appeared at one end of the altar a few inches further down from where we'd been lifting, and Peter just managed to get a pencil into the gap before we had to let go, and the top slid back down.

As we recovered our breath, we had a look at the gap that had been exposed. If the pencil hadn't been there then we still might never have found it, so well was the join crafted.

It hadn't been hidden by the detail at all, but right in the middle of one of the plain areas of stone running right around the altar.

We decided to focus our efforts on the opposite end of the altar top, in the hope of lifting it and then jamming something into the gap, hopefully if we could gradually raise each end, we'd eventually be able to remove the lid altogether.

It was still heavy going, and required the sacrifice of both Jean's pen knife and Harry's petrol lighter, but we managed to raise the lid high enough to be able to twist it round across the top of the altar and expose the space within.

It seemed the lid had been a solid piece of stone, which had been fitted snugly onto the base via the thick rim.

Once this was out of the way it revealed a small interior cavity and a box wrapped in some ragged cloth.

Peter and Marlow very gingerly removed this object laying it on the floor next to the altar. After a moment's hesitation Marlow knelt down and carefully removed the cloth, which itself seemed to carry the faintest of colours and markings.

Within was a simple hardwood box dark with age, about eighteen inches long by about six inches square. The lid seemed to be carved into a relief similar to some of those we'd seen on the walls of the other chambers.

It was sealed with some form of gum or resin, but after carefully breaking this seal with Jean's now crushed pen-knife, Marlow slowly lifted the top of the box to expose the contents. Inside was a large scroll, perhaps sixteen inches long, rolled around two delicately carved ebony rods. I wasn't sure, but I thought I caught the scent of sandalwood as the box was opened.

'It seems fairly robust,' said Marlow, carefully removing the scroll, standing and then slowly unrolling it on top of the cross-wise lid of the altar.

Miraculously the parchment of the scroll was still flexible enough to be unrolled without cracking. And as it was unrolled the contents were revealed, but it wasn't a map. The scroll just contained more writing.

'I thought it was supposed to be a map,' commented Peter, echoing the confusion of the rest of us.

'It was', responded Marlow, a thoroughly confused expression upon his face. 'I was sure this was it. Even the scroll and box seem familiar to me now.'

'Do not despair my friends,' interjected Harry. 'You may in fact be looking at a map without realising.

'I know it seems strange, but to the peoples of the ancient world the idea of cartography as we know it today was almost unknown. More useful to them was a description of the landmarks, distances and directions. Often passed by oral tradition, but occasionally, carved, or as we may have here, penned.'

'But how can we find out what this says if none of us read this language, and there is no map to guide us.'

'This is certainly beyond my level of skill,' answered Harry. 'We would need to get this translated by a scholar far more familiar with the language than myself. Cairo is possibly the closest, but I have a friend who works within the Armenian library of Jerusalem, who may not only be able to help us with the translation, but who could also be relied upon to be discrete.'

The air inside the cavern was beginning to get a little smoky from the torches, so we decided to retire back to the surface to discuss the matter further.

The afternoon sun and heat was in stark contrast to the cool and shade of the underground temple, and following our return to the surface, we decided to withdraw back to our main camp in order to more comfortably discuss what we'd discovered and weigh our options.

Jean started us off.

'This is an interesting situation, my friends, one which I hope you will forgive me for saying, Robert, I did not think we were likely to find ourselves in, and which I am not sure I yet fully comprehend.'

Everyone seemed in agreement, and even Marlow managed a wry smile before Jean continued.

'We have followed your vision, Robert, given to you it would seem by that strange potion brewed beneath the Singing Stones, and that has led us unerringly here, to this temple, which, if I understand Harrison correctly is a significant archaeological find.

'Not only that, but we have now also discovered this scroll, which again, if I understand correctly, may lead us to yet more remarkable things.

'Now, I know I cannot be the only one who finds this... Incredible.'

'No, Jean, you're not the only one,' responded Marlow in a sympathetic tone, but with an increasing passion in his voice. 'This is a remarkable thing for anyone to accept, including myself. There have been times on this journey when I have thought this to be all pure madness, and by choosing to pursue it we have become mad men.

But this temple with its ruined doorway, that tranquil pool and the scroll we've now retrieved. These things are not just our imaginings, they are real and whether they fit in with the way we see the world, or belong to something we can't yet explain, we should take them seriously, without hesitation or doubt.

'The only question for me,' continued Marlow with a tone of determination I hadn't heard in his voice before. 'Is where I go next.'

'I'm with you Rob,' responded Harry without delay, 'I don't yet know where this ride is taking us, I don't even know whether I'll like where we end up, and I certainly don't know how these things can have come about. But I know this place is real, and that for me confirms there's at least an element of value in what we're doing.'

'But are we sure we really wish to achieve this goal?' retorted Jean. 'If this should by some miracle lead to the means of attaining unending life! My friends such a thing could change and damage our society in ways barely imaginable.

'To suddenly increase a lifetime beyond measure, it could have psychological repercussions upon even the strongest mind. Perhaps undermine a person's faith, damage their relationships with loved ones and friends.

'How, for example, could a marriage survive if just one member chose to become young again? How would you or I feel at the sight of our parents or even grandparents made younger than ourselves?'

'They're all good points, Jean,' responded Peter, with an unexpected enthusiasm. 'But take a look at it from another angle. Surely a longer life would fit right in with those exalted socialist ideals of yours? With just a few more years might not a person overcome even the most humble birth, to acquire the education and opportunities of their more fortunate peers. What would it take... another fifty years, perhaps a hundred? Before your long-awaited peaceful revolution delivered itself.'

'Perhaps so,' conceded Jean, thoughtfully. 'And yet, with immortality a man could become many things, not all of them so good.'

It was dusk by the time we finally finished debating the pro's and con's of our situation, and what we should do next.

Harry was eager to share the temple discoveries we'd made with the world's academic community, but also begrudgingly accepted that to reveal such a find might well jeopardise our chances of pursuing the thing further. As such, after much disagreement and compromise we all eventually agreed to document the site as best we could, before concealing it pending our own further investigations.

To ensure the details of our discovery weren't lost through some accident, we would also lodge copies of our notes with Harry's university in America and with Jean's lawyer in Paris. These documents would be sealed, to prevent anyone reading them, and would include directions to the site as well as an illustration of how we had gained access.

We would then journey to Jerusalem to discover what the scroll and wall writings said.

Despite the disagreement, it was still an amicable decision once made, and then it became just a question of breaking the work down into its necessary actions for the following few days.

Documenting our findings was going to be the single biggest task, and for that we were going to rely heavily upon Harry to identify the areas where we should focus.

Jean would then attempt to capture as much detail as possible of the relief carvings and inscriptions in a number of sketches and rubbings.

Peter and myself would simultaneously attempt to

survey and map the layout of the temple, its dimensions and the alignment of the corridors and chambers we'd discovered within it, as well as to describe as best we could its construction materials and the location of the different elements being documented in more detail.

The idea being that we'd be able to figure out where each sketch or rubbing was located within the complex, even after we'd left the site.

Marlow had decided to focus entirely upon the final chamber. He was convinced he'd missed something or not understood his vision correctly, as such he was going to attempt to document the layout and detail of the cavern, its obelisks and perhaps most importantly the altar.

We'd also asked Mkize and the other men to work on a couple of makeshift ladders for the entrance and a cover that we could place over the hole before filling the earth back in, once we were ready to leave.

It was interesting work once we got into it, and there were several details within the chambers we only really began to pick up on once we started to examine them in a more systematic way.

In fact, it was only the gradual build-up of smoke from our torches that made us take a break now and again, until the air had cleared.

But even with our dedication the level of detail was always going to be too great for us to be able to capture anywhere near all of it.

Perhaps if we'd had better lights to enable us to take better photographs it would've been different. But without them, having to record everything by hand became at times a frustrating and overwhelming experience, especially for Harry.

Over the course of the next week though we eventually managed to capture enough detail for him to give his reluctant approval to leaving the site, though he still made us leave a message inside indicating when and by whom the temple had been rediscovered, just in case.

REVELATIONS

BLOCKING THE HOLE UP and then back-filling it along with the rest of our excavations, was an oddly frustrating experience, which just seemed to jar with something inside me.

I understood why we had decided to keep the discovery a secret, but on some level, even with the veracity of Marlow's vision literally staring me in the face, I still found the idea of trying to follow it further foolish.

At the same time, foolish or not, I was still eager to find out more about this place, with its elaborately carved walls and enigmatic writing.

As soon as we were sure the site was once more secure, we started our journey back to Fort Victoria, from where we intended to travel to the coast and then hopefully by ship northward to Mogadishu, Mombasa, the Red Sea, Suez and finally Jerusalem.

The journey back was relatively straightforward. We stopped briefly to look around the mighty ruins and speculate once more about the people who once lived there. But with no sudden revelations or vivid descriptions from Marlow they seemed a pale imitation of antiquity beside the perfectly preserved temple we'd just left behind.

It had been several weeks now since the rains, and the flush of greenery and growth that had followed, was just beginning to fade. In areas with less tree cover, dust began to accompany us as we walked, and I found myself thinking thoughts that until recently would've been unthinkable for me… that it might be good to leave Africa for a short while, not to go back home, but to explore somewhere new.

Another couple of days and we were back at the Fort, once more intending on a quick change around, to get in, make the arrangements we needed to make and get out again, but on our arrival, Marlow discovered a telegram from Luke waiting for us.

There was no real detail, simply the statement that he'd had a change of heart and would like to re-join us.

The telegram was just over a week old and had obviously missed us by a few days. In any event he was heading back to Nairobi and was expecting to be there in another weeks' time, which meant he was probably travelling through the Red Sea as we spoke and we might just be able to get a message to him before he headed inland from Mombasa.

The surprise and pleasure at getting this good news was apparent on everyone's face, and whilst it hadn't even been two months since he'd left with Silvio, all that had happened somehow made it seem longer, and we were all eager to see him again.

After sending a return telegram to try and catch Luke, we enquired about the timetables for ships heading up the coast to the Red Sea. We knew there was likely to be something heading our way sooner or later. But, as chance would have it, the same passenger liner I'd originally caught to bring me to Africa was due to call at Maputo in the next week on its quarterly trip from Portsmouth to Suez.

It didn't leave us much time to travel to the coast, but more by luck than planning we managed to get passage down the Limpopo, and ten days later we were steaming into port at Mombasa on the Portsmouth to Suez ship.

Luke was waiting there for us on the quayside ready to come aboard, along with the various cases and trappings we'd left at the lodge.

There was a momentary awkwardness when we all stood facing him again, which was soon brushed aside by the ever-enthusiastic Harry, who seemed perennially oblivious to such things, and in no-time we were exchanging tales of our respective travels, much to Luke's wonder and amazement, and as soon as our respective belongings were aboard we retired to one of the deserted lounges with our pipes and cigars to catch up properly.

Mombasa was also the point at which Mkize was leaving us, and it was with genuine regret that I prepared to say goodbye to him and thank him for his help.

I think, if I'd had a better idea of where we were going and when we'd be returning, I might've been able to convince him to travel with us a little further. But he was understandably reluctant to leave his homeland again so soon after returning, so I walked with him down the gangplank, before shaking his hand and saying goodbye.

Back in the lounge with the others, and Luke was describing how him and Silvio had made good time after they'd left us.

Despite the rain and sodden earth, they'd managed to get back to Nairobi and then by train to Mombasa without incident.

Silvio had apparently continued to be troubled by the visions of his grandfather, and as they travelled and discussed their plans, he'd eventually decided to return to Italy to see his family and visit the grave.

Luke had accompanied him back to Italy with the intention of visiting his own family in Rome, before perhaps heading off for a little skiing and to visit friends just the other side of the Swiss boarder in Austria.

'It is always good to be back in Rome,' continued Luke, looking relaxed. 'Even over the winter, the city is still a welcoming and warm place to its returning sons, and at times it can seem as though every doorway, shop or coffee house contains a welcome and a smile.

'As it happens, while I was away our old priest, Father Francisco, had retired and had been replaced by Father Andrea. He was a young man from a family I knew, and had travelled a little in his youth. Before I realised it, I was talking to him about Africa and the friends I had left behind. I even spoke of the visions we'd received and the journey upon which you had all started and how I felt I could not accompany you in pursuit of such things.

'I don't know why exactly, but while talking to Father Andrea I began to think differently about some of my decisions, and sensing this he asked me to visit him again at his home later in the week to discuss the matter further.

'I won't bore you with the details of our discussion on my next and subsequent visits. What I will say, is in the following weeks he helped me to realise such a goal as yours is not in itself intrinsically wrong.

Rather, it is how we choose to pursue such a goal that is of greater consequence, and the principle that we should not neglect our daily lives lest we forget our devotions or responsibilities.'

'Well said,' responded Jean. 'Your Father Andrea is something of a philosopher perhaps?'

'Perhaps so, Jean,' Luke conceded, thoughtfully. 'But the guidance he gave me does not mean I am yet fully supportive of your choices or your goals.

'All I know for the moment is that the value I place upon our friendship is enough to enable me to travel with you a little further.

'That and the fact,' continued Luke, with an infectious smile. 'That I now have several irrefutable moral arguments with which to confound even you, Jean.'

There was much laughter at Luke's comradely challenge, and the friendly raillery that ensued reminded me greatly of the first night when I'd encountered this group those few, short, exceptional months ago.

As Luke was finishing his story, we were informed the ship was about to get underway once more, to start our northward journey.

It was Marlow's turn to look thoughtful now, and excusing himself, he informed us that he'd very much like to watch our departure from Mombasa. Jean also excused himself to accompany him, leaving the rest of us to continue our conversation with Luke.

'You know, I think he loves this country,' commented Peter, once Marlow and Jean had left to go up on deck.

'I've journeyed with him in a dozen countries, including England, but there's something about him when he's here in Africa...'

'It is a strange land and no mistake,' responded Harry. 'Some think it is the cradle of humanity, the place from which we all came, and yet by comparison with almost every other area of the planet, we know next to nothing about this continent and its history.'

We talked for a little while longer before we were interrupted again by a steward informing Luke that his cabin was ready, and with that, we each took the opportunity to go our separate ways until dinner.

The comparative luxury of the ship and a real bed was something I found very easy to get accustomed to. And, several days later as we pulled into Suez after making our way through the Red Sea, I found myself almost reluctant to disembark, even momentarily toying with the idea of staying aboard and returning to Portsmouth.

We'd arrived in Suez in the early morning, a light mist floating on the surface of the great canal giving the thoroughly false impression that the day might be cool and refreshing.

But after finding a berth on one of the cleaner cargos ships it didn't take long before we were disillusioned of that impression.

It may have only taken a couple of days to reach the other end of the canal, but it was two days of living in a steel sweatbox.

In places the desert came right up to the waterfront, bringing its scorching heat with it. In other areas as the canal broadened out into one of the lakes along the way, the dry heat of the desert was replaced by an even more suffocating humidity that left us all feeling lethargic and wanting only to sleep. By the time we disembarked in Port Said on the shores of the Mediterranean the shade and cool of the town seemed like paradise by comparison.

From Port Said it was a well-established and easy sea route to the ancient port of Jaffa and from there a relatively short dusty car journey to the old city of Jerusalem.

Harry had apparently travelled quite extensively around the Holy Land and took the greatest of pleasure in pointing out some of the biblical landmarks and features that were located along our route.

His commentary made the journey pass all the quicker, and before we knew it, we were slowing down in order to navigate the busy streets of modern-day Jerusalem.

A blur of new sights and sounds later and Harry informed us we were entering the Old City, through the great Jaffa Gate after which it seemed only a heartbeat before we were pulling up outside our hotel, which was located just on the edge of the Christian quarter.

Harry had telegraphed his friend, Dr Chukjadarian of the Armenian Library, from Maputo, to let him know we were coming, and had then managed to call once we disembarked at Jaffa.

As always with Harry though, it was impossible to bypass his enthusiasm for long enough to build up any kind of picture of his friend, but we didn't have long to wait before meeting him.

The hotel was a big old building, with the main entrance through a shady and cool courtyard at its centre. The car had dropped us off outside the hotel's heavy street doors, that opened onto a small piece of verdant paradise, complete with lemon trees and glittering fountain, beside which in a comfortable wicker chair sat a flamboyant figure that could only be Harry's friend.

'Chuk!' bellowed Harry as soon as he laid eyes on the figure.

'Harrison!' exclaimed the impeccably dressed stranger, immediately jumping to his feet and striding across the courtyard to grasp Harry's hand. 'Finally, you have returned, my friend, it has been far too long.'

'I could never visit frequently enough for my liking,' replied Harry. 'How have you been?'

Harry had talked at length, but told us very little about 'Chuk' as we'd travelled here, and I was beginning to see why.

He was a slender man of average height, and at first glance appeared to be somewhere in his late thirties, but as he came over to meet us, it became clear he was probably closer to Harry's age, if not a little older.

It also became clear that the crimson cravat and matching breast-pocket handkerchief weren't the only flamboyant aspects to a character that seemed almost able to eclipse even Harry's for enthusiasm and eagerness.

Exuberant hello's out of the way, Harry eventually remembered his manners and turned back toward us to perform the introductions.

'My friends, I am very pleased to be able to introduce you to one of my best and oldest friends. George, Rob, Jean, Luke, Peter this is Adroushan Chukjadarian, or as he's known to his many friends, Androus.'

'Or of course, Chuk if you prefer,' interjected Androus, smiling generously. 'As some of my much older, if not wiser friends still call me.'

That got an almost apologetic look from the still grinning Harry, before he continued on.

'Chuk, these are the intrepid adventurers I told you about in my wire.'

'Splendid, Harrison, splendid,' responded Androus expansively. 'And for my part I am also most pleased to meet all of you, and not a little intrigued as to this strange text with which you would like my assistance in the translation.

But where are my manners, you have no sooner arrived in Jerusalem than I have hijacked you and kept you standing outside your hotel, when you must all be eager to clear the dust from your throats and freshen up.'

With that Androus all but ushered us into the hotel proper. The rooms were spacious, airy and light, and whilst none of us had views of the more famous Temple Mount, the small deep-set windows we did have, afforded very pleasant rooftop views across parts of the Old City, and to the Citadel Tower and one corner of Omar Ibn el Kattab Square.

As I took a few minutes to settle into my room in the hotel and look out over the antique rooftops, I suddenly felt a little… displaced by the extent of the change in our surroundings. To go from the solitude and comparative austerity of Africa to the bustle and hubbub of Jerusalem, with all the sounds, sights and smells of a vibrant and busy city, just seemed too great.

I was still feeling that displacement when I became aware of a knock at the door. One of the hotel staff with some tea and dates. Thanking him, I absently poured myself a glass of the tea as he left the room, and was instantly assailed by the aroma of mint.

It was almost shocking in its intensity, but at the same time seemed so in keeping with the place.

Having not tried it before I sipped it at first, and then drank the rest of the pot thirstily, revelling in the heady aromatics and mild sweetness of the drink as it refreshed and invigorated me.

It was exactly what I'd needed to bring me back to myself. As I finished the tea, I once again looked out of my small window across those antique rooftops, but now it was with a curiosity and eagerness to explore, that I just hadn't felt before.

I found Androus, and the others downstairs waiting for me in one of the lounges. They'd already unrolled the scroll across one of the tables, and Androus was hungrily devouring it as I approached.

'This is very interesting,' he was saying, looking up

briefly to acknowledge me as I arrived, 'It seems to be written in an early Babylonian style... quite remarkable!

'I didn't realise your familiarity with the script was anywhere near so advanced, Harrison, let alone to use it to write so well in Babylonian. I really must applaud you.'

'I didn't write this, Chuk,' responded Harry in a very careful tone, 'This scroll is at least several hundred years old.'

'Harrison, why do you try and tell me this? You know as well as I there are no Babylonian scrolls. Clay tablets, stone inscriptions, even precious metals stamped with a word or two. But scrolls, no. This is an elaborate joke at best, a poor hoax at worst. But this is not a real Babylonian scroll.'

'Now, I didn't say it was a real Babylonian scroll,' continued Harry earnestly. 'But Chuk, if this is written in Babylonian, then it was done so several hundred years ago, at least. And I am very sure that if you look at this more closely, you'll be able to see that it is very real.'

'That cannot be, you know as well as I the Cuneiform languages were only recovered from obscurity eighty years ago. Prior to that they have been lost for over a thousand years, if not two thousand for Babylonian...

'Ah! You are thinking perhaps this is a blind copy? A clueless scribe copying from a tablet to this scroll without understanding the nature of that which he copies?'

'I would prefer not to speculate before you've had a proper chance to study it, Chuk,' Harry responded, carefully. 'All I can say at this moment is the place in which we found it is possibly even more remarkable than the scroll.'

'Then why will you not tell me more about this place? It sounds like the context it provides may help.'

'For now, Chuk. We've agreed that your objectivity in the translation is of far greater importance to us than the authentication.

'Allow us to impose upon you in this way, and I

promise we will explain everything once we have the translation.'

Androus was far from happy at being kept in the dark about the scroll's origins, but on the trip over we'd all agreed that until we knew him better, it would be best not to tell him anything about the temple or Marlow's vision. It would also, as Harry had said, guarantee Androushan's objectivity.

With obvious reservation Androus agreed to carry out the translation as best he was able over the next few days, although Harry had already saved him a good piece of work by copying the scroll into a much more manageable notebook he'd obtained on our journey here. With this in hand Androus took his leave and returned to the library to begin work.

It was a glorious day, and with no further progress possible for the rest of us, until we had a better idea about the contents of the scroll, we decided to take a break and enjoy the city around us.

I had to confess to Harry, that barring the obvious mentions in the bible my knowledge of Jerusalem was otherwise quite lamentable.

This like a red rag to a bull was enough to inspire Harry to a fever-pitch of enthusiasm, and before I knew it, we were off with Peter somehow sucked into the whirlwind of our passing.

Despite their rather churlish grins at our predicament, Luke, Harry and Marlow somehow managed to escape the enforced guided tour, and headed off separately, Marlow and Jean to the suq, Luke to wander around some of the old churches.

It was an exhausting avalanche of sights and sounds, but I'd be doing Harry a disservice if I didn't also confess to being both fascinated and exhilarated by his tour. The layers of history and culture revealed by him at every step as we walked, almost jogged, around the city.

Narrow alleyways festooned with a wild array of hanging clothes and fabrics, distracted our attention until Harry pointed out the massive arched buttresses that supported the great city wall which towered above the stalls.

Then the short street where the doorways of a dozen different historic styles could be seen, one next to the other.

Everywhere we went there were clues to the city's ancestry, the countless spires and domes that stretched upward, the walls and pillars which supported and the ancient roads walkways which separated.

All this of course before we approached the Temple or Majed Mount, and the last vestige of the second Temple, the elegant Dome on the Mount and the grand Al Aksa mosque.

It was nearly seven o'clock in the evening by the time Harry 'allowed' us to return to the hotel, where we found the others, apparently also only recently arrived, relaxing in the cool of the courtyard with more of the wondrously pungent mint tea.

It seemed we'd all made the most of our time and were now ready for a relaxing evening.

Marlow and Jean had popped into the Armenian library to see how Androus was doing and to invite him to offer us his initial opinions of the scroll over dinner at our hotel.

But to their slight surprise they'd been ushered away without sight or sound of our reluctant epigraphist, with only the message that he was busy and hadn't got the time to see them.

Not knowing what to make of this response they'd decided to leave him be and return to the hotel alone.

It seemed the hotel had only a handful of other guests, and following a delicious meal, the manager invited us to take our drinks up to the hotel roof to better enjoy the sunset and the evening air.

We'd heard the almost mournful strains of the call

to prayer as we were finishing our meal, and as we moved out now onto the paved and balustraded rooftop, the city seemed to have become more restful.

The horizon, had been almost exclusively painted from a limited palette of deep reds, purples and blues by the recently sunken sun, with just the odd wisp of cloud here and there coloured over with a watery lilac or yellow for contrast.

I was struck by how different the night was in Jerusalem. In Africa it would be filled with the sound of uncounted insects, so pervasive after a while as to seem like the sound of silence itself. Yet here in the middle of this ancient city surrounded by ten thousand souls there was a different, urban stillness.

Marlow had engaged the manager in conversation after he'd shown us to the roof. And watching them for a moment, I could see an almost identical blend of tranquillity and wonder in their faces as they looked out across the city at the thousand hazy blinking lights of the valley beyond.

I've no idea what time we finally made our way down from that rooftop and retired for the evening, but it seemed scarcely moments later that I was being roused from my slumbers by Jean knocking on my door.

'George, George, get up Quickly! Androus is here. He's found something in the scroll.'

It took me a second to collect my wits, but throwing on some clothes I followed Jean into the lounge we'd used on the previous day.

The staff were around and about, preparing the hotel for the demands of the day, and had considerately supplied us with a large pot of coffee, that I now helped myself to as I entered the lounge. Androus was there, eager for us all to arrive, while at the same time making a close examination of the original scroll and the box we'd found it in.

Beside him were Marlow, Harry and Jean and now myself, joined a few moments later by Peter and an obviously tired Luke.

At which point we all started to try and make sense of why Androus had disturbed us all so early.

Putting the scroll carefully back into its box on the table in front of him, and picking up his coffee, Androus seemed almost agitated as he started to talk to us.

Recounting how he'd left us yesterday with the copy of the scroll writings and made his way back to the library.

Confessing his doubts and misgivings about spending his time on what must be a hoax. Then when once settled back at the library how he'd become curious about the fake and who would have the skill and inclination to craft such a thing.

It hadn't taken long before he was completely absorbed.

'It seemed sketchy at first,' he continued. 'The language was indeed Babylonian, but it seemed poorly done. Cuneiform as a script is wonderfully phonetic, so with just a few words it becomes easy to identify which of the many languages the script is being used for. There are some words that are the same in Persian as they are in Chaldean and Babylonian, but there are others that change over time or which we only find in certain languages.

'In this way it is very like the modern English alphabet which can be used to write in French, German, Spanish or Italian.

'Now, the scroll begins in a standard enough format - I am Xiusutra conqueror of time, longest of breath, source of the waters and master of the deep etc. Odd phrases of which some seemed vaguely familiar or reminiscent of other texts, but some of the words were unusual, even archaic.

'I can't be sure, but time and again, these words seemed to me like they may be derived from the same common root as the Babylonian word. The rough meaning is clear enough though, but words were just a tiny bit off.

'It was interesting to be sure, for this to be a hoax would require some considerable expertise and time.

'But then I noticed a mistake. As I'd sketched out the opening oration or statement, I'd been a little hasty in my translation of the author's name, and now when I looked at it, I realised it was actually spelled as Ziusudra.'

Androus stopped for a moment then, as though ordering his thoughts.

'Now Ziusudra was known to the Greeks as Xisuthrus, whose story is recounted by Eusebius of Caesaria, via Alexander Polyhistor and the writing of Berossus high priest of Marduk in Babylon.'

Androus' bright crimson handkerchief had somehow found its way into his hand and as he paced back and forth before us, he applied this to his forehead as he made to refill his coffee cup.

'Am I right in remembering Xisuthrus was another name for the biblical figure of Noah?' asked Harry rather wide eyed.

'No, no, no, Harrison, there is an association, yes, but it is far more complex and quite the other way around.' responded Androus rather wearily and taking a breath before continuing.

'One of the oldest pieces of human writing that the modern world has yet discovered, is on a series of tablets found in southern Iraq just over two hundred years ago.

It tells the tale of the deluge or the flooding of the earth up to the heavens, and a man who built a boat to survive.

This is where the comparison with the far simplified biblical account ends. Because, as a reward for his efforts this figure Utnapishtim or Ziusudra is given the gift of 'breath eternal', he is then removed to a faraway place by the gods, this place is variably known as the origin or source of the rivers.

He is also, as Xisuthrus, described as being a king who ruled for over sixty-four thousand lunar months or five thousand years.

In the same tale he is also described as being visited

by the legendary Gilgamesh of Sumeria who also seeks the secret of life everlasting.'

'My dear, Androushan, this is all very well,' interjected Jean, calmly. 'But it hardly seems something that would require you to work through the night on, or to disturb us at such an early hour for.'

'You are quite right, Jean,' responded Androus with a weary smile and stretching his back slightly as he walked over to the window with his coffee. 'But do please indulge me as I have indulged you.

'The final point I wished to explain was that name of Ziusudra is a fairly recent addition to our understanding, and has been known to the modern world for less than twenty years, from a single fragmentary tablet of an even more ancient Sumerian origin.'

'If I am to come to the point then for disturbing you all so early, then I should perhaps begin by confessing that when I came here yesterday, I was fairly convinced that your scroll was some elaborate fake.

'But now, when I look at the evidence… For that scroll to not only be written in old Babylonian, but to feature words cleverly constructed to seem like archaic versions of that already most archaic language, and then for that same scroll to contain a name so recently added to our understanding. Well, gentlemen I think I can safely say that in the last twenty years there have only been a dozen people in the world capable of such a thing.

'None of whom, to the best of my knowledge, would have any desire or inclination to create such an elaborate fake.

'All of which leads me to the incredible conclusion, that as unexpected and impossible as it may seem, the scroll you have presented to me, may in fact be genuine.

'Now, I do not wish to labour this point, but you have to realise that if there is any chance, however remote, that this scroll contains the words of such an ancient figure. Well it could quite possibly be the single most important document to be found this millennium.'

To say that Androus' words took us all aback would be something of an understatement.

We looked at one another for several moments without a word as the implications of what he was saying sank in. Finally, Marlow broke the silence.

'Thank you for bearing with us Androus, I realise we've made your job that much more difficult by not disclosing the circumstances leading up to the discovery of the scroll, but I think when you've heard and seen what we're about to show you, you'll understand.'

INSIGHT

I T TOOK A WHILE TO PREPARE the sketches, maps and illustrations we'd made at the temple back in Africa, during which time, the hotel manager appeared again with the offer of breakfast and fresh coffee.

I didn't think Androus would be prepared to wait now we'd finally agreed to tell him the rest of our story, but he was clearly fatigued from his night's labours, and he leapt at the chance of a break and some food.

When we returned to the lounge, now filled with the bright morning sun, and thoughtfully provisioned with fresh fruit and more coffee, I think we were all a little more alert and less on edge than we'd been after being roused straight from our beds.

But as Harry began to tell Androus about our encounter with the shaman and the visions, it was still difficult to read the expression on the Armenian's face. Eventually though, after Jean showed him the picture he'd managed to reconstruct from memory and his sodden sketchpad, he started to ask questions and show a more pronounced interest in the information we were laying before him.

By the time Harry began describing our journey through the ruins of Great Zimbabwe and our entrance into the temple I honestly thought Androus was going to faint. And when we started to show him the sketches and illustrations of the temple layout with its carved reliefs and writings his entire frame displayed such an intensity of constrained energy, I thought he'd burst. Several times he moved as though to speak, only to close his mouth again and press his colourful handkerchief to his brow.

Eventually, after Harry had finished the story and Androus had spent several minutes just looking from one sketch to another, he suddenly stood up, stepped back from the table and walked over to the window.

None of us spoke as he stood there, everyone just waiting to see what he'd make of it.

'It is real!' were his hoarse first words when he eventually turned back to us. 'You have discovered what may be one of the most significant archaeological finds imaginable… The chronicles of Ziusudra, Noah, Xisuthrus, Utnapishtim, call him what you will.

There are figures from history on that scroll of whom we have never heard, along with the tales of how they sought him out and what they found when they did.

Not only that, but you have found this record in an ancient temple, which may itself rival the wonders of Petra, with walls covered in a whole library's worth of probably unknown knowledge from the ancient world. Incredible!

'It is evidently a dream,' he went on half smiling, as he walked back from the window to join us. 'Yes, an elaborate fantasy conjured by my unconscious mind after I have inadvertently fallen asleep at my desk in the library.'

'But then, if it were a dream you would not be asking me to keep this discovery a secret while you pursue who knows what further course?'

'That's why we came to you, Chuk,' responded

Harry apologetically. 'Because I knew we could rely on you to keep this to yourself, at least for the moment. And because we need to know what's on that scroll if we're to figure out where to go next.'

'Of course,' replied Androus, with a small wave of his handkerchief. 'You wish to retrace the steps taken by those who journeyed to the temple, in the hope that you may find their legacy.'

He hesitated for several agonising moments, a sad smile still upon his face, as he looked at each of us, before finally continuing.

'You know me too well, Harrison!' he said, looking more determined now. 'I can and will assist you. This information cannot be lost to mankind again.'

It seemed remarkable to me how quickly Androus could change in both his mood and overall perspective. It reminded me far too much of my own doubts and changing perspective.

'There is however something else I must tell you.' continued Androus becoming more focused, but also more hesitant. 'I have translated more of this scroll than I have yet told. I am still less than sure of the precise meaning, but from what I can make out this temple is not the only one to have been built by this Ziusudra.

'Following the passage I described to you. The author, Ziusudra goes on to inform the reader it is once more time for him to move on. Sealing and burying his second temple before consigning it to the vagaries time, after which he will 'renew his breath' at the first great temple in the east.

'He doesn't describe where this first temple is located, or whether he plans to build another after he has renewed his breath.

'What he does tell us though, is the date at which he is writing, in the form of two king lists. Lists that it was very easy for me to identify, lists that indicate this man was writing his scroll seven hundred years ago in a language that was lost to the rest of humanity in 1000bc.'

On hearing this, we all sat there paralysed.

Somehow dealing with a half-mythic figure from distant antiquity was easier to comprehend than someone placed within the very real time frame of a few hundred years.

I saw the consequences of what Androus had said, registering on the faces around me.

Intuitively, I turned my attention to Marlow to see how he'd react. Though my own shock still had the better of me for a moment. I looked at him sitting back in his chair across the table from me, and saw for a moment that same expression I'd so often seen on his face as he regarded a sunset. A calm so complete as to be almost unsettling, accompanied by a quiet, barely noticeable smile.

For the first time I think he noticed me watching him, and for a moment he looked straight at me, that strange stillness in his eyes, captivating and calming me. Until he looked away toward the others.

It took a moment for my wits to come back to me after his gaze moved on, but as they did, I found myself unexpectedly reminded of the lion Marlow had killed back in Africa.

Had that beast actually come close to killing him, I found myself wondering. Or had even the great golden eyes of that monster been becalmed by this man's gaze.

Shaking such nonsense from my head, I realised I was missing what was being said.

'That's good news, Androus,' replied Marlow, cheerfully. 'It means our quarry is not as far distant as we'd anticipated.'

I looked at my friends as he said this, and in particular to Harry, who had a better understanding of what was being said than any of us.

There was nothing obvious about the way in which he reacted, but as some of the others started to talk and speculate about this information, Harry looked almost winded by what he'd heard and for the longest time just stared at Marlow.

We were all tired, the early morning and excitement having taken its toll on us, especially Androus who despite his meal still looked hollow with fatigue.

So, after our various speculations and discussions had started to die down a bit, I suggested a break until the evening to give us all the opportunity to rest and more fully consider our situation.

There was a general agreement at this and after the briefest of goodbyes Androus took his leave, followed in quick succession by the rest of us.

I stayed behind to give Jean a hand in putting everything away. Despite being tired I didn't think I'd be able to get any more sleep just then, so once the scroll and associated sketches, rubbings etc were put away, I decided to go for a walk instead.

Before I'd come to Jerusalem, I think I'd had a very stereotypical image of what it would be like, all sand and rock with the odd faded bit of scrawny vegetation for some equally scrawny goats to nibble upon. As a consequence, the reality when we'd first arrived had been something of a shock.

One particularly pleasant surprise being the rich and verdant public gardens that exist in various parts of the city.

I'd come across one such garden at the far corner of the Armenian quarter during the whirlwind tour I'd had with Harry, and as I left the hotel, it was to that park that I made my way.

Being careful to avoid the route most likely to be taken by Androus, past the library, and the risk of getting drawn into further conversation and speculation.

It was still quite early, and the cool morning air helped to clear my head a little as I walked. I hardly remember reaching the gardens, let alone stopping to buy tea and dates along the way. But I managed to find a nice secluded seat in the shade of the great buttressed wall where

I could just sit and think.

I'm not quite sure how long I stayed there, watching the birds, insects and occasional other small animals as they made their way around that small corner of paradise. But as the sun climbed higher in the sky and the heat started to penetrate even into my shady corner, I decided it was time to move on in the hope of finding another cool spot.

I hadn't gone far and was just contemplating taking my tea glass back for a refill when I ran into Jean, sketchpad in hand, doubtless in search of some scenic vista to commit to paper.

There was a momentary uncertainty as we each tried to divine whether the other would like some company, and then realising that neither of us had any objection, we moved on together.

We eventually found a likely sketching site with a good view of the Citadel Tower, toward the northern end of the gardens in the shade of a giant bay tree. We'd nearly missed the spot and were just about to make ourselves comfortable on the grass, when Jean spotted one of the neighbourhood cats jumping through the surrounding bushes and onto a wall hidden by the foliage.

A minute's exploration revealed two low walls belonging to some anonymous ruin, open and visible to the park on the other side, but appearing to be nothing more than a clump of young trees and bushes from the direction in which we'd approached. Perhaps because it was such a splendid view of the park and distant Citadel tower, a new wooden seat had been positioned just inside the walls to better accommodate those wanting to sit in the shade and admire the view.

It was a relaxing spot, the dappled shade from the Bay made all the cooler by an occasional breeze channelled down the hill by the great wall to our left. Jean had his view and as we sat and talked, I observed him as he sketched. First laying out the proportions of the scene in pale hard pencil before beginning to fill in the detail with a softer, darker lead.

There was no real attempt by either of us to try and avoid the subject at hand, and after we'd both expressed our favourable opinions of Androus, we turned our attention back to the scroll and the unfolding mystery before us.

I confessed to Jean how I found the entire business just a bit too strange, without even allowing myself to think about the consequences if it were true.

'I know very well what you mean, George,' he responded, whilst continuing to sketch. 'I keep thinking of myself as entering into some childish adventure story, wishing the world to be a different, more exciting place than it is. A world where the cure for all mankind's ills could actually be sat in some ancient and dusty jar beneath a remote and exotic ruin.

'But then I scold myself. Am I not also a lover of wisdom, a philosopher, poet, and artist,' he said, gesturing almost deprecatingly at the sketchpad on his lap? 'As such, do I not strive to break with convention and consider the world objectively for myself?

'Yet I find myself thinking in such a… conventional, small way, about this journey, viewing it as a childish exploit, too incredible for a grown man who should know better.'

Jean had a point, and I had to acknowledge I'd been thinking about things in a very similar way.

We talked for a while longer, discussing all manner of things in and around the subject, including the wonders of antiquity that had somehow survived the centuries, only to be discovered again in our modern age.

From the obscure Neolithic structures and cave paintings dotted around Europe, to the great ziggurats of South America, or Stupas of India, not forgetting the abundance of poetry, sculpture and prose left behind by the Greeks, Romans and other cultures, and the amazing discoveries still pouring out of Egypt's Valley of the Kings.

Eventually, I think we rediscovered some

semblance of our enthusiasm and perhaps even 'childish' wonder for such things, but in doing so we'd talked the morning away.

Not that it wasn't a nice spot, but the shade from the Bay was moving round with the sun and as Jean was putting the finishing touches to his drawing, we started to think about retreating to a tea shop to see out the hottest part of the day.

My legs were just beginning to toast as the shade from the tree encroached upon our seat, and I was starting to get a little impatient with Jean's 'final touches'. When I noticed through the shrubbery surrounding us, someone bearing a striking resemblance to Luke.

He was strolling back and forth on the other side of the Bay tree, evidently waiting for someone to join him. Calling Jean's attention to him, he agreed it must be Luke, but whom could he be waiting for.

Whilst the intrigue was momentarily amusing, especially from our childishly covert vantage-point, we reluctantly gave in to the more elevated sides of our natures, and decided to go over and relieve Luke in his wait, before heading off on our way for tea.

Jean finished his sketch and was just putting his pencils and other equipment away, when I noticed the approach of a demurely dressed young woman who Luke turned and walked toward as soon as he saw her.

With elevated natures once more forgotten, and our sense of intrigue rekindled, we 'reluctantly' conceded that Luke may no longer require or desire the company we'd been about to offer, and that an altogether more circuitous route to the tea-house would be the more diplomatic choice.

Having said that, there was something about the way they approached one another that made me hesitate for a moment.

They seemed a fraction formal for a meeting of friends or even lovers, which Jean commented on also as we watched.

As they met the young lady immediately extended her hand upon which Luke respectfully placed a kiss. But having done this he then seemed to retreat a step, before they started to talk, or rather, before Luke seemed to talk while the young lady listened, only occasionally commenting or asking a question, to which Luke would again respond at length.

Strange though it seemed, there could be any number of reasonable explanations for it, so as the couple turned and began to walk, we decided to make a discreet exit and leave them to it.

We may not have been spies, but after making ourselves comfortable in one of the local tea-houses, neither of us could resist the temptation of wondering who the young lady might be.

'Surely, she must be an old acquaintance, a friend of the family perhaps, or even some visiting Italian dignitary with whom he has some link?' I scurrilously suggested to Jean's exaggerated disapproval. 'The latter would certainly explain the apparent formality of their meeting and Luke's very respectful kiss of the lady's hand.'

In any event, revitalised by our mint tea and with our better natures firmly subjugated for the day, we decided to head back to the hotel via one of the bigger suq markets.

A couple of hours later loaded down with knick-knacks from the market, including some new paper for my journal, stuffed dates and a tourist map of the region, we finally stepped into the comparative cool of the hotel courtyard.

The day had caught up with me by now, and the prospect of an afternoon nap was rapidly becoming my greatest priority.

But as we stepped through the street doors into the courtyard, I discovered both Harry and Peter had beaten me to it.

Though both looked perfectly comfortable in their slumbers, Harry had clearly nodded off while in mid-read, judging both by the book that lay carelessly at his feet, and the reading spectacles still clinging precariously to the end of his nose. While Peter on the other hand displayed an obvious forethought and preparation, and seemed all the more comfortable for his shady high-backed rattan chair, footstool and hat, which covered his eyes.

Stopping only to retrieve Harry's book from the ground and place it on the table beside him, I decided to forego the al fresco sleeping arrangements of my companions in favour of my room, which was now mercifully cool. Throwing my things down as I entered. I splashed a little water on my face and neck before lying down and falling straight asleep.

I could have quite happily slept through until the following morning, but after a couple of hours, feeling much refreshed and absolutely ravenous, I resisted the temptation to roll over for another forty winks and forced myself to get up.

After a quick wash, and putting the things away I'd so unceremoniously dropped a couple of hours earlier, I made my way down to the lounge to see if anyone else was up and around.

It seemed Androus had returned, and barring Jean, I found them all in the lounge that was fast becoming our second home.

Androus in particular seemed to have benefited from the rest and had lost that hollow look in favour of the gentle exuberance he'd displayed on our first meeting.

Nobody appeared in any great rush to get back to business, so we waited for Jean to join us in his own time, which he did about half an hour later, following which we settled down to once more discuss our situation.

It went pretty much as I was expecting at first. Harry with some support from Androus attempted to convey the magnitude of what we'd so far discovered, to be countered by Marlow and Peter with the prospect of what we could yet discover given just a little more time.

It was a very civilised discussion, and with the benefit of a bit more rest, especially for Androus, we were all more relaxed about the points being made.

But ultimately, as Harry very succinctly put it, 'It came down to what we were going to do next'.

Not telling the world about the 'discovery of the century' was one thing, but to just put things off indefinitely without any specific plan or direction was another.

The scroll was all we had for now, Marlow's dreams had led us to the temple, but there was nothing more coming from him.

Unexpectedly it was Androus who seemed to offer the solution to Harry's question.

'There is something I missed in my first reading of the scroll,' stated Androus, hesitantly. 'It may yet be nothing, my own misinterpretation of those unusual root-words.

'As I told you earlier on today,' he continued, slipping unconsciously into his sceptical academic mode. 'This scroll contains a narrative supposedly written by the fabled Utnapishtim or Ziusudra, a figure mentioned in the chronicle of Gilgamesh.

'Well, after resting this morning I had just a little time to further study the scroll before coming back over to join you.

'In that time, I examined the version of the Gilgamesh story contained on the scroll, hoping that my familiarity with it would make the task a little easier.

But I discovered that while the scroll version is similar in some ways it is quite distinctly different in several others, not the least of which being that Gilgamesh in the scroll version is successful in his quest and returns to his home immortal.'

'Unbelievable,' broke in Harry, almost unconsciously. 'Are you sure Chuk?'

'I am my friend, the details I will be able to improve upon with time, but the overall meaning is clear.

'However, that is not necessarily the most interesting diversion from the story. As you'll recall Harry, in the story of Gilgamesh we had before, he returns to his home unsuccessful, but wiser for his journey and accepting of his worldly lot, goes on to be a good king for the rest of his life and brings prosperity to his city.

Almost as an afterthought the chronicle describes how Gilgamesh inscribes the tale of his travels onto a block of stone which he then buries beneath the city gate and in so doing metaphorically re-founds the city upon his newly obtained wisdom.

'All very interesting, the stone has never been found, but it has also never been really looked for.

'Now, curiously that same stone is mentioned in the version of the story contained on the scroll, but it is described as being carved while Gilgamesh is at the African temple. Its surfaces covered not only with the tale of Gilgamesh but also a description of the path beyond to the great temple.

'Now the text is unclear, but the words used to describe the first great temple at the start of the scroll are very similar to those used in the description of the stone buried by Gilgamesh.

It's also described as lying "beyond", but as the scroll is supposedly written by Ziusudra while he is still at the African temple, it would be strange to describe his current location as beyond, you'd be much more likely to say, here or, in this place.

'Naturally, if my translation is correct then the implication is clear. The stone buried by Gilgamesh beneath the gate of his city, contains not only the story of his quest, but also directions to the first great temple of Ziusudra.'

'How much longer do you need to confirm your interpretation, Androus?' Marlow asked, eagerly.

'Another day perhaps two, to confirm my translation of this section,' responded Androus. 'Weeks if not months for the rest.'

I felt an energy fill the air as Androus spoke these words, with their suggestion of a way forward in our quest. I couldn't help but look around the room at the faces of my friends to see the anticipation growing behind their eyes also, even Jean couldn't hide is curiosity now.

'We know that the African temple was perhaps four thousand years old before it was abandoned,' commented Harry, looking earnestly at Androus. 'If the first temple was used for a similar period before the African temple, then it could date back to seven or even eight thousand years BC.'

'That would indeed be a remarkable discovery,' responded Androus. 'Let alone if it were to contain some form of written language.'

'We could perhaps do a little research on Uruk, Gilgamesh's home,' suggested Harry, with a large and increasingly infectious smile on his face. 'Perhaps figure out how to get there and what permissions we might need to do a little digging. You might even think of coming with us Chuk, and continuing your translation on route.'

AZURE

OUR JOURNEY AHEAD, into the heart of Iraq, turned out to be a bit more involved than I'd first imagined.

In essence I think I'd become accustomed to the way of doing things in Africa, and had forgotten the first fumbling steps I'd made, when I'd initially ventured forth from Nairobi, massively over equipped with things I didn't need, and surprisingly short of the things I did.

Having said that, travelling in Africa had proven to be more a logistical problem than anything else, and of course, I'd had my father's journal to give me an idea of routes, guides, weather and a thousand and one other things.

The Middle East was different, there were more subtle considerations to be taken into account, political sensitivities to consider and permissions and licenses to be gained, as well as up-to-date information to be sought. All of which took time, and demoralised or discouraged us almost as much as it delayed. But eventually, nearly a month later, we managed to get all our ducks in a row, and we were ready to go.

Androus' local knowledge facilitated the process immensely, but as we found our way through the last of the red tape, we were still struggling to get the information we wanted about our destination, the ruined city of Uruk or Erech as it was otherwise known.

Both Androus and Harry knew of at least two partial excavations that had been carried out, but it was proving more difficult than we'd anticipated to get accurate records describing the parts of the city uncovered.

This was information that would be critical to our own search once we got on site. So we had to get our hands on it quickly, before our various visas and permits ran out, and we'd have to go through the entire application process again.

The following few days saw a frenzy of activity as we scattered across Jerusalem like madmen, trying to find everything we needed. While at the same time crossing the t's and dotting the i's with both the new government in Iraq and the British military presence still in the region to confirm our passage and archaeological exploration rights.

Peter and Harry went off to sort out the equipment we might need again. It would be inconvenient securing this in Jerusalem and then transporting it all the way to Uruk, but not having to purchase it en-route would enable us to maintain a lower profile.

It was non-stop for a while, but somehow, three days later we were underway.

There was still a lot we'd have to sort out on route, but we were going to be stopping, albeit fleetingly, in several large cities and towns along the way and Androus had friends he was confident of being able to call upon.

I'd been looking forward to getting out and about again, back under the stars and into the wild. But within hours of setting off, stuck in the back of a car in all the heat and dust, I was wishing for nothing more than my cool comfortable room back at the hotel.

The further we went the less pleasant the journey became. The recent instability in the region had all but destroyed the local rail network, so we no sooner moved from car to train than we had to unload and transfer our things back to cars or trucks, and then back onto a train.

I don't know how he managed to concentrate with all the disturbances and inconveniences along the way, but somehow every time I saw him, Androus seemed to be writing in his notebook or consulting one of the increasingly dusty reference books he'd brought with him.

Despite the irritations of the journey I couldn't help but be entertained at the distractedly eccentric figure he cast, with his bright silk cravats, always perfect moustache and pile of great learned volumes surrounding him.

By the time we reached Baghdad, Androus had managed to confirm his interpretation of the Gilgamesh story on the scroll. The stone buried by Gilgamesh beneath the city gate, did indeed seem to have been carved while Gilgamesh was still at the African temple, which meant the directions it carried must refer to the first Great Temple.

Not only that, but there were more details of how Gilgamesh had obtained the secret of 'breath eternal' from Ziusudra and returned with it to his home. Where, according to the scroll, he would, 'Become the envy and the enemy of all mortal men'.

For this reason, Gilgamesh was also bestowed with a poison that would gradually, 'steal his breath and eventually seem to kill him, so that he may pass 'beyond' before taking up his new true life.'

Leaving Baghdad, we managed to secure half a day's ride with an American diplomatic convoy, but the comfort and space of their vehicles was short lived, after which we were dropped off to make our own way again.

Now, if Androus was a picture of eccentric abstractedness then Harry, when we were once more 'dropped off' was a picture of pure aggravation and irritation.

He was struggling with the mass of maps and illustrations of the ancient city in order to try and divine the most likely location of the city gate. But whereas Androus was able to muddle along with his limited library, Harry was wrestling with a dozen, oversized maps, pictures, books and notes. He even had a couple of recent photographs taken by the Air Force while flying over the area.

For the final leg of the journey we were once more on horseback and trekking through an almost perfectly flat landscape. In fact, the terrain was so uncompromisingly level, the ruins of the city came into view hours before we actually drew anywhere near them.

To begin with they could've been mistaken for a natural rocky outcropping on the horizon, but then as we got closer and closer, oddly geometric angles and shapes began to be visible, and then patterns and lines in what had previously looked like simple mounds of earth.

The entire place was made of mud-brick. Thousands, millions of them worn and sculpted by the wind and weather but still identifiable after thousands of years. As we drew closer to the outskirts of the great city wall, I could finally make sense of what I'd been seeing. The walls, even today were still massive structures, but over time they had worn and weathered, sand had built up in places, while elsewhere sections of wall had fallen away. But being made of brick it had fallen in regular pieces, probably the same sections in which the bricks had been laid all those years ago, leaving behind oddly regular holes and gaps.

There were numerous breaks in the wall, easily big enough for us to ride the horses through, but dusk was approaching and we'd been warned by one of Androus's contacts in Baghdad that the ruins were still to this day occasionally inhabited by groups of brigands. So, with this in mind we circumnavigated the walls for a while in search of a good place to make our camp.

It had been a humid and hot day and with the exception of Harry and Androus we were all glad of a chance to rest and enjoy the cool of the evening.

We decided to make our camp just beyond one of the larger openings in the city wall, on the north-west side of the city where the mighty ruins would shelter us from the prevailing winds. Winds which we'd been warned could whip up to a biting gale within minutes in this wide-open borderland between desert and marsh.

I'd been expecting the camp and the environment to be similar to those we'd made in Africa. But the more we saw of this country the less that seemed to be true, and now as we stopped the differences became stark.

When I first arrived in Africa, I remember thinking the place had an odour of decay about it, which over time I'd become accustomed to, and now apparently took for granted.

But here in the desert I realised what I'd thought of as decay in Africa was also the fertile odour of life, even in the dry season. An odour that Uruk just didn't have, for here the earth was almost sterile in its barrenness. Incapable of sustaining life, robbed as it was of every particle of moisture by sun and wind.

The others were busy setting up the camp and directing the half dozen European friendly Kurdish servants we'd been able to hire for the necessary chores.

An hour or so later and our small camp was complete, and we were settling down to see whether Harry had been able to figure out a plan of action for the following day.

The ground was still warm beneath our feet, as we gathered together around a low, flat topped mound of earth.

Harry had the best of his maps with him, and he now spread it across our impromptu table to show us where we were and what we knew about the city behind us.

It wasn't particularly good news, as the details just weren't there. Even with the multitude of references he'd been able to find, both in the scroll and elsewhere, the landscape around had simply changed too much.

All Harry could do was suggest where we concentrate our efforts on the north-west side of the city. There was little else to be done until the next day when we could get into the city and have a look around.

I was surprised at just how cold it was the following morning, and half expected to see a coating of dew on the baked earth when I got out of my tent, but if there had been any, it had been soaked up by the parched ground almost instantly.

We were up and about in no time, and the first order of the day was to get our bearings by making our way into the centre of the city, where most of the previous excavation work had taken place.

After Harry's rather sombre outline of the situation the night before, we were hoping the orientation of the civic buildings, which we knew had been partly excavated would give us a bearing upon a likely main gate.

Riding into the ruined city was an almost unreal experience. We were talking amongst ourselves when we set off, but on entering the city the conversation quickly subsided as we started to see what was left of the city.

At times it was exactly what I'd expected, baked clay walls mostly collapsed and ruined with little to indicate what kind of structure the remains had once formed.

But then a few meters further on they'd become almost whole. There were staircases and windows, upper floors and untold niches and shelves built neatly into the fabric of the structures. All they needed were a roof and a few odds and ends of furniture and the place would be habitable.

It gave the streets a ghostly air, as though the inhabitants were just hiding, and life would spring up again as soon as we passed the corner.

Finally, the streets started to broaden out and we reached the heart of the city with the faded remnants of its mighty civic buildings.

Previous excavations had been concentrated in this area and though the buildings were cleared of debris and dust giving them a peculiarly sharp quality, they were obviously less intact than the ordinary houses we'd passed along the way.

It was nevertheless a fascinating place, especially in the company of Harry and Androus who translated the anonymous piles surrounding us into a wonderful picture of life as it may once have been.

But as good as their understanding was, it quickly became clear there was no mighty avenue leading conveniently to the gate we wanted, and that the city had grown or evolved in a more haphazard way, without any kind of plan or structure.

This left us with no choice but to split up and examine each of the gateways individually for anything that might indicate it was the one we were after.

Anticipating that this might be necessary we'd each brought some basic hand tools to clear away the accumulated sand and debris. I was with Harry and Peter, while Marlow was with Androus, and Jean with Luke. We agreed to meet back at the centre at midday and then we were off, each group in a different direction.

Harry led the way for our group and we headed out on a slightly more northerly road than the one we'd used when entering the city, but it was much the same in its varied state of preservation, and I could easily see how the different roads could quickly become confusing.

While we were making our way, Harry explained the difficulty of the task ahead of us.

'Even when we've located the main city gate, it still won't necessarily be straight-forward to find the inscribed stone or stones mentioned on the scroll,' he began, earnestly. 'Its location is described as beneath the city gate, but that doesn't necessarily mean under the columns. It could just as easily mean under a portion of the road outside or inside the gate, or within the columns of the gate itself, and checking each of those options can mean a lot of excavation.'

Once we got to our first gateway, it turned out to be quite a bit smaller than some of the others, so we were able to quickly move on clockwise around the city walls to the next gate, which looked a little more promising.

Once we got to that gate, it didn't take me long to realise that I wasn't a natural archaeologist.

After half an hour of carefully scraping away the built-up soil and dust from one of the gate posts with a hand trowel, I was ready to move on convinced there could be nothing else of interest to us here, but Harry insisted we just keep at it.

It was hot again now, and as the sun climbed higher into the sky it became ever more difficult to keep in the shade. We were definitely working on one of the larger gateways, not that I could tell, but according to Harry the gate posts, whilst mostly brick, were topped and bottomed in sandstone, and that was likely to be only used for higher status structures.

We cleared the posts themselves and discovered stone footings that continued across the road to form a stone threshold.

This was buried beneath several inches of baked hard earth, but again, Harry and Peter just kept on working.

I was taking a break, stretching my spine and quietly praying that one of the other groups would discover something to save me from this backbreaking task, when

Harry suddenly lurched up and away from the patch of road that we'd all been clearing. Peter recoiled as well, reacting to Harry's sudden movement.

There didn't seem to be anything on the ground that could have caused such a response, but Harry had gone as white as a sheet, and was staring fixedly at the stones we'd been unearthing.

Peter fetched some water from one of the horses, perhaps thinking Harry was feeling the heat, but a moment later Harry seemed to come back to his senses enough to explain.

'The stones, can you see the pattern in the stones that we've uncovered?' he asked, still pale but apparently calming down.

I looked and there was some sort of vague circular pattern that looked like it might be repeated in a carving on one of the bigger central stones. A stone that I was fairly sure Harry had been excavating in the centre of the road.

I indicated to him I'd seen it, but for the life of me still couldn't understand his response.

We'd uncovered all manner of carvings, and patterns around the place, each of which we'd duly sketched or described for later examination.

This one, while perhaps a bit bigger, looked no different to any of them.

Regaining his composure, Harry spoke again very deliberately.

'This is the symbol I saw in my dream beneath the rock face in Africa, when we drank from the potion made by Nelion.

'The memory of it faded once I was awake, and I couldn't remember exactly what the symbol had been like. Well now I do, and that is it.'

It was our turn to be shocked.

I looked at Peter and then back at the symbol in the ground, but I just couldn't seem to get my mind around what Harry had just said.

Africa and the night at the Singing Stones seemed like a distant memory to me now, but I remembered Harry's enthusiastic account of his dream and his meeting with his old archaeology professor.

I tried to pull myself together, but Harry was talking again and I hadn't heard what he was saying. He looked at me quizzically for a moment and then repeated himself.

'I said, it would be quite some coincidence if the carved stone we're looking for happens to be buried beneath that symbol.'

We had a little more time before we were due to head back and meet up with the others, and we used it to quickly uncover the rest of the stones in the centre of the road, and the pattern that they made up.

The symbol itself was a relatively straight-forward circle, but with nine identical radial markings breaking up its circumference, almost like the markings on a clock face, or the key stones of an arch.

We didn't quite have time to expose the outer stones that mimicked the nine-points of the clock symbol on the central round stone, but it was clear the outer circle was exactly the same, even down to the alignment of the radials.

It almost seemed unnecessary to document what we'd found, as I couldn't imagine this wouldn't be the first place we'd come back to excavate.

Harry though was a stickler for detail, and after we'd uncovered as much of the threshold as we could, he then insisted we sketch not only the symbols, but also document the sizes, and make a quick positional sketch so the others could see exactly what we'd discovered.

Once we got back to the centre of the city and met up with the others, I began to wonder whether Harry's motivations in documenting the gate had actually been more involved than I'd suspected, for although he presented the evidence of our find quite persuasively, he seemed reluctant to mention the connection back to Africa.

Not that there was any real contest with what the other groups had found, purely in terms of size and the use of stone for construction it seemed our gate was more likely to be the main gate, but still he seemed to hesitate.

Finally though, perhaps after seeing the questioning looks from myself and Peter, he also told the others about the reference back to Africa.

It was like a small shockwave running through the group, even Androus seemed taken aback.

Very little was said in response, everyone clearly having questions but knowing nobody would be able to answer them.

Talking about the night with Nelion did however seem to put Luke understandably out of sorts, and he just walked off to his horse to wait for the rest of us.

The revelation also seemed to affect Marlow, who strangely just thanked Harry before he also moved off.

Following the initial shock there was no mistaking the anticipation in the air as we moved through the city on our way to the gate.

It was a difficult task clearing the rest of the road of its millennia of hard baked earth to reveal the entire pattern of stone blocks. But Harry and Peter had been thorough in the equipment they'd purchased in Jerusalem, and in no time, we had a winch in place and were ready to start lifting the stones themselves.

It was a slow job and everyone was anxious not to allow anything to drop once we'd started to raise them up, but gradually we managed to remove the central stone and then those surrounding it.

Beneath, there seemed to be distinct layers of clay and then sand, below which was a sheet of hammered copper, and then another layer of stone into which were set nine perfectly preserved and exquisitely carved tablets of lapis lazuli, covered in cuneiform script.

Androus and Harry examined these shimmering blue stones in situ for well over half an hour before even attempting to lift them, which Harry did with the greatest reverence, before passing them one at a time to Androus.

For his part, Androus was visibly shaking as the tablets were each passed to him, before he wrapped them in a cloth and placed them in a canvass bag.

It was scorching hot by now with no escape from the sun, which made us all tired, but both Harry and Androus insisted we again take the trouble to sketch and document the site, before reconstructing the road with all its layers. Even burying it with all the compacted earth covering that we'd worked so hard to remove, in order to preserve the site until it was time for us to tell the world of our discovery.

POINTS OF LIGHT

WE MADE OUR WAY SLOWLY back to the camp in almost complete silence, Androus carrying the tablets like a child cradled in his arms the whole way.

Once back though, it was a different matter, and we all crowded around as he took out the tablets one at a time, and placed them side by side across the low mound of earth we'd earlier used as a map table.

Even to my ignorant eye they were exquisite creations, the intermingling shades of blue, highlighted here and there with flecks of shining gold. Each tablet perfectly shaped and carved with flowing unbroken lines of script.

As for the text, before we even knew what it said we could still marvel at the precision and elegance of it, carved deep into the stone, each figure perfectly chiselled, but on a scale that could compare to any modern printed page.

Androus and Harry were in a world of their own, apparently oblivious to our crowding, questioning and chattering, but eventually, after reclaiming the tablets from the greedy hands surrounding them, and spending several minutes examining the start of each, Androus attempted to describe what the text said.

'These tablets are written using the same language as the scroll, with those same unusual word forms and script, but there seem to be some differences...

'There are at least three distinct sections, here a version of the story we know...

'Sha nagba imuru... The one who saw all... who knew all and who still walks amongst men, I will tell about... He has seen the great mysteries, and knows the hidden, and tasted the fruit of the earth before the great flood.

'Ah yes,' continued Androus, completely absorbed. 'Here, here this looks like it could be more detail describing Gilgamesh's journey or route to the African temple from this very place.

'This seems to continue for three full tablets, and then there is some kind of break. The fourth tablet then starts with what looks like a description of Ziusudra and the ordeals Gilgamesh had to endure, presumably before being granted the breath eternal.

That takes up a further three tablets, at which point there is another break and... This seems to be Ziusudra speaking of his first great temple and the story of how he travelled from there to Africa.

'I need to study this section in more detail, but it does look like there are place names and descriptions in the text.'

'A chronicle of the journey?' broke in Harry, enthusiastically. 'Descriptions of the places and route taken to get here.'

'Yes... yes possibly.' responded Androus, clearly only half-hearing Harry's question.

It was going to take some time for Androus to get

to grips with the translation, so after another few minutes of unsuccessful questioning we reluctantly decided to leave him to it.

The first stage, as we all knew after seeing Androus working on the translation of the scroll, was to accurately transcribe the endless lines of lettering from the tablets to paper. This would allow the text to be more conveniently studied and broken down into individual words, phrases and sentence-like sections.

Being familiar with the text and the technique would enable Harry to help with the first part of the work, and remove a laborious step in the process. But the segmentation of the words and subsequent translation was still the most skilled and difficult task, and that was something Androus would have to do by himself.

At best it would probably be several days, if not a few weeks effort, which we couldn't really expect even Androus to complete from a camp site.

It was too late in the day to be thinking about packing up and starting the journey back to Jerusalem, so with the intention of making an early start in the morning we busied ourselves as best we could preparing, packing and making arrangements.

It was a slightly surreal time, I don't think I'd quite come around to thinking about what we would do next, once we'd successfully located the map we were looking for.

In truth I don't think I'd quite gotten to the stage of thinking we'd actually find anything, yet here we were with the tablets literally 'in the bag'.

There was still a good hour of daylight left by the time we'd finished our preparations, and the evening air was beginning to cool down again to a more comfortable level, so I decided to try and find someone interested in an evening stroll.

There was no point even asking Harry or Androus, and it seemed that several of the others had had enough exertion for one day. But Jean with just a hint of that theatrical exuberance, which seemed to occasionally possess him, readily agreed.

We decided to set off in the opposite direction to the gate, toward the great Ziggurat that lay outside the city on its western edge, on the off chance there might be a better perspective of the city from that side.

We'd been walking for a few minutes, and I was just about to try and draw out Jean's thoughts on how long it might take Harry and Androus to come up with a first draft of the translation, when Jean pre-empted me with a comment of his own.

'It has been an interesting day, has it not, George?'

There was something about his tone, that made me look at him, and I could immediately see something was amusing him.

But Jean being Jean, I knew he wouldn't answer a straight question, especially when he thought it more entertaining to make his audience guess.

So, with a good-humoured sigh, I played along in the hope that his revelation wouldn't be too far off.

'Such a fascinating city, is it not,' he continued to torment me, his smile almost consuming his entire face. 'And so nice to be able to spend some time with one's friends.'

I couldn't imagine where he was going with this, but just as I was beginning to think I'd have to concede, it occurred to me that he'd paired up with Luke in the morning.

'You asked Luke about the young lady we saw him with in the park, didn't you?'

His exasperation couldn't have been more perfect, he veritably exploded with disappointment at being thwarted.

'How could you possibly have guessed so easily?' he blustered, before continuing to give me the details.

'But yes, as it happens, George, you are correct. After failing to get him alone while we were in Jerusalem, I had been attempting to pin him down on the journey, but with all the changes in our transportation, he managed to elude my grasp.

'But we Gascons do not give up easily in our hunting, especially when we know our quarry will not stray far. When we entered the city to begin our search, I saw my opportunity.

'What I had not considered was how I was going to broach the subject once the moment presented itself. But I was determined to get him this time, so I eventually decided to pursue a 'conversational' approach, as though I were not so very interested.

'By the way Luke, says I, while pretending to be interested in some half-collapsed doorway, I did not know you had friends in Jerusalem. Almost as though the thought had only just occurred to me.

'Quite naturally he walks into my not so clever trap and claims to not understand my meaning.

'In the park at the bottom of the Armenian quarter, I was walking with George on the morning that Androushan awoke us all so early, I'm sure it was you we saw walking and talking with a young lady.

'Well, that stopped him, I do not think poor Luke could have been more shocked, had I taken my revolver out and fired a shot over his head.'

'Yes, but what did he say, Jean, why did he greet her so formally?' I couldn't help but ask.

'Now, that is the interesting thing. After a moment or two of desperately trying to escape me by pretending not to recall the occasion, he eventually claimed not to have known the young lady at all, she had simply approached him after getting slightly lost, to ask for directions.

'By chance, she happened to be a fellow countrywoman of his, so he had offered to guide her as best he could, which according to Luke must have been the point at which we saw him.'

We both had to admire Luke's quick thinking, while

at the same time being disappointed not to find out who the young lady really was.

We walked and talked for a while longer, before turning around to make our way back to the camp. But just as we did so, Jean stopped suddenly and stooped to examine the ground.

'Hoof marks! It must be at least a dozen riders going into the city,' he said, moving back and forth to try and get a better look at the prints in the fading light. 'But I cannot tell how recently they were made.'

We quickly examined the tracks to either side of where our paths had intersected, to see if we could get a better idea of how old the marks were and how many riders there were, but the ground was far too dry and hard. So much so, that if we hadn't crossed their path at a slightly sandier point, I don't think we'd have even noticed them.

We quickened our pace on the way back, both to warn the others, but also to make sure we didn't get caught in the open in the now deepening gloom.

It didn't take long to explain the situation, and although we were probably too large a group to be in any real danger from local bandits, we decided it would be wise to take a few extra precautions just on the off chance. This meant keeping the fire low, and surreptitiously making our camp a little more defensible.

We were all rather tired out by the heat and exertion of the day, and I was struggling to stay alert by the time the attack finally came, in the small hours of the night. But in addition to our two obvious lookouts, we'd also taken the precaution of deploying two extra people covertly inside the darkened tents to keep watch out of the rear, with one person sleeping and the other on watch. Harry had just relieved me in our tent, and I was just beginning to doze when suddenly he called my name and then started shooting through the hole we'd made at the back of the tent.

I was stunned for a moment, caught half way between sleep and wakefulness, and then I was grabbing my rifle and following Harry out of the front of the tent.

It seemed like there were hundreds of them at first, galloping at full speed straight through the centre of our camp.

Whooping and screaming as they came and firing rifles at anything and everything, before disappearing out of the firelight and back into the darkness.

I came to my senses though, as a bullet hit the ground a few inches in front of where I was kneeling, spraying my legs and chest with grit. But the attacker had already fallen from his horse with a bullet from Harry in his chest.

It was then I realised our assailants weren't quite as numerous as I'd first thought, and that my friends were very effectively picking them off.

I'd known Harry, Jean and Luke had all served in the army, but what I hadn't realised was the degree to which the years of hunting had refined their skills and efficiency with their rifles.

Our attackers had just begun to understand their mistake as half a dozen of them lay dead or dying in the firelight, and probably twice that number had fallen amongst the shadows outside our camp, when I noticed three riders streaming through the camp and converging on Marlow and Jean.

Marlow had just managed to put a bullet in the back of one rider who'd tried to decapitate him with a great curved sword.

But, in dodging round the edge of the tent to get his shot off, he'd turned away from the centre of the camp and so couldn't see the sudden approach of the other three. He turned back at a shout from Jean, but hadn't had time to reload his rifle.

I could see Jean get a shot off, but it must've gone wild, because his man just kept coming, I quickly tried to put him down myself, but rushed it, and only managed to clip his shoulder.

Fortunately, it caused him to drop the rifle he'd levelled at Jean's head.

Unfortunately, not being able to shoot didn't seem to bother the man too much and instead he just rode at Jean and delivered a savage kick to his head as he went past, knocking poor Jean spinning back onto his tent.

At the same time, I saw Marlow heave his empty rifle at the two horses bearing down on him, and grab for his revolver, before being obscured from my view. The rifle must have connected well, for the next instant both horses were rearing up onto their back legs. Not that it seemed to disconcert either of the riders, who I swear were still trying to aim their rifles one handed at Marlow past their rearing steeds.

What did disconcert them considerably though, was the head of the first rider's horse exploding backwards in a shower of blood and bone into its owners face and chest.

I could see both men nearly lose their seats with shock. Marlow was completely obscured behind them, but it was clear he'd fired his revolver, which I knew was a large calibre Webley, at point blank range, destroying the animal's head.

There was no mistaking the effect, as the poor beast's hind legs simply collapsed, and an agonising moment later it fell backward trapping its rider.

At the plight of its companion the second animal tried to rear again, while simultaneously twisting to the side to try and get away from both Marlow and the collapsing horse beside it. But that only served to open the line for Marlow's second shot square in the chest of the second rider, who was flung back onto the animal's haunches before it bolted into the night.

Checking to see there were no other attackers coming his way, Marlow quickly moved around the dead horse, to dispatch its former rider, who even with a leg still trapped beneath his dead mount was shouting and trying to free his rifle for another shot.

And then, as suddenly as it had started, the mayhem and noise ceased. Marlow regained his position in front of his tent, collecting and reloading his rifle, before checking on the unconscious Jean.

Peter and Luke moved to take up their lookout positions re-stacking the saddles and other equipment they'd piled around them for extra protection.

Androus, after spending a moment trying to free his jammed rifle, drew his revolver and filled his other hand with a big curved sword from one of the attackers who'd fallen nearby.

We sat amongst the carnage that had become our camp, alert and ready for them to return. For hours we waited, before the sky gradually started to lighten and we were able to safely give up our defensive positions.

It was amazing no-one from our camp had been seriously injured, though one of the guides we'd employed had also been ridden down like Jean and knocked out.

Having said that it seemed some of us had been quite lucky, including Androus who'd been saved by his rifle which had caught a bullet right in the mechanism, missing his hand and face by inches.

As the light improved though it became clear our assailants had not been so lucky, and we counted a further nine dead men outside our camp in addition to the eight which we already knew about within.

It was a tragic scene made all the worse by the dead horse that accompanied them. But I only needed to remind myself that if we hadn't stumbled across their tracks as they entered the city then the story could have been very different.

We did our best to bury the men, but as we were preparing the holes, I noticed Marlow and Jean talking and moving over to re-examine each of the bodies before they were interred.

On seeing my approach, they turned and asked for my opinion.

It seemed that while searching the bodies, both Jean and Marlow had noticed something odd. All the men seemed to be carrying a similar amount of silver coin.

'The three men I've examined,' said Jean. 'All have slightly different amounts of money with them, but amongst the other coins, they all have six identical silver coins, not European, could be Turkish.'

Marlow had found the same on the two men he'd examined. We decided to ask Androus if he could shed any light on the matter, but just as we were about to go and find him, we saw him coming out of his tent looking completely aghast and ashen faced.

FRAGMENTS

DURING THE RAID A BULLET had found its mark in the bag containing the stone tablets we'd unearthed only hours before.

Fortunately, it hadn't destroyed them entirely, but at least two of the tablets had been severely damaged, and from what the distraught Androus could tell, the two worst damaged were those describing the route to the lost temple.

It was a massive blow to our moral, both because the damage had likely robbed us of the very information we sought, and the fact that a priceless and beautiful piece of antiquity had been destroyed while in our keeping.

On top of all that, we still had to deal with the dead from the previous night before we could pack up and get out of there.

Amongst all the bad news about the tablets, we almost forgot about the oddly consistent coinage we'd found upon the bandits, but eventually we managed to distract Androus long enough to confirm our suspicions.

'I could not suggest why these men have been paid so much,' Androus commented, distractedly. 'But it is clear to me they have recently been hired or paid for their banditry, and quite handsomely at that. They have all been paid in Turkish Lira, a coin which contains a large proportion of silver, and is therefore acceptable almost anywhere in this region, making it ideal for those who are intent upon doing no good, but have the ability to quickly move on.'

None of us could believe it might be us, these men had been paid to attack. There were few people even knew where we would be, let alone who might have an objection or grudge about what we were intending to do once we got here. As such, we could only conclude it must've just been ill luck that had placed us in the bandits' path after they were flushed with success from some other exploit or criminal activity.

With the bodies buried we packed up the camp and set off back to Jerusalem.

Strangely the return journey proved much easier than the way out, and three days after leaving Uruk, we were checking back into our hotel in a sunset tinged Jerusalem, just as the mournful sound of the Muslim call to prayer were echoing around the city.

The first job for Androus, before any of the translation work could begin, was to try and piece the shattered tablets back together.

He began by laying out the damaged pieces in one of his library's laboratories, which after much pestering he finally agreed to let us see.

Two small calibre bullets had hit the bag of tablets square on the end, seriously damaging the last two tablets and less seriously damaging a further two.

Of the nine pristine tablets we'd removed from beneath the city gate, that left five that were still perfect, two more that could still be read, and the last two which Androus advised us, we should only hope to recover fragmentary sections of text from.

Three days later we were summoned back to the laboratory to view the finished reconstruction work, which had resulted in seven pristine looking tablets and the last two having been reconstructed into a series of lumps held in their correct positions between two sheets of a lightweight and flexible glass like material, which they used in the library to hold tattered documents together.

The end results were far better than I think any of us had imagined would be possible, and now that the reconstruction was complete Androus could once again return to work on the translation.

In the meantime, Harry did his best to help with the transcribing and to give us regular updates on Androus' progress.

At Androus' suggestion, he began by completing his work on the scroll. As it had already been transcribed and had after all led us to Uruk and the tablets, it would also give Harry time to work on the transcription.

Using this approach Androus was able to give us an outline of the scroll's contents after just a week, and we were summoned to the library one Friday afternoon, to hear of ten individuals who were listed on the scroll as having succeeded in claiming the 'breath eternal'.

Like Gilgamesh, these individuals had apparently found their way to the African temple by often quite challenging routes, some of which included landmarks and locations that Androus could identify, others he'd had more difficulty with.

'The problem, as I hope you will all appreciate,' he began, slipping unconsciously into his professorial manner. 'Is that through time so many things can change about a place. Not only its name, but also its prominence in the locality, its major industries, culture and even geography.

'Now, with such things in mind I have translated the words and phrases which lie within the scroll, and placed them before you as best I am able. But I fear the map which you seek is still far from clear.'

With that warning, Androus began to detail what he'd translated within the scroll, along with all its likely inaccuracies and ambiguities, and as he spoke, I began to appreciate just how different the distant past must have been.

He illustrated the point further by working again through the account of Gilgamesh, the earliest entry on the scroll, and his circuitous journey from the city gate in Uruk, to his arrival at Ziusudra's temple. Which we attempted to plot upon our maps as Androus recounted the details contained on the scroll.

So many of the details just made no sense, or sounded like they could be describing anywhere, until it came to the places that we'd actually visited in Africa, then the details suddenly seemed obvious.

The Luangwa River and Muchinga Escarpment in Zambia, that we'd travelled down while the river was swelled from the rains and full of floating detritus, was one location we all recognised instantly, because we'd been there at the same time in the season.

But many of the other locations described, we still found immensely difficult, and that was with us already knowing where the journey started and ended.

After the account of Gilgamesh, Androus outlined each of the other accounts. It was an amazing and somehow humbling moment, to hear those accounts, each preceded with a list of the individuals great deeds or titles, and then to realise these once remarkable people had now been so completely forgotten.

There was one account from antique Anatolia, or modern-day northern Turkey. Another from the shores of the Black sea, at least a couple from different islands in the Mediterranean, mainland Greece, Egypt, Sub-Saharan Africa, and one that seemed from much further to the East, beyond the ancient city of Samarkand on the old Silk route, possibly from China or India.

But most remarkably there was the account of a woman. One Agina, amazingly both a warrior and a chieftain, who it seemed had travelled the length of the Mediterranean, possibly from the fiercely independent and mountainous Basque area of northern Spain.

She was, in all probability, from one of the great Celt-Iberian tribes, but like all the other accounts, the description of her exact home was just too dependent on details now changed and lost to history.

One interesting thing, which slightly surprised me, was the repeated reference to the tablets describing the achievements of these adventurers.

Like Gilgamesh, each successful seeker was described as carrying a set of the tablets back to their homelands.

In some cases, this was done despite the fact they came from cultures who had yet to develop any kind of advanced writing system, let alone possess an understanding of cuneiform!

More interesting still were the details of what these individuals did with the tablets once they reached their homelands, for they all seemed to be buried or hidden, but in such diverse locations. Beneath city gates, within sacred groves, behind revered waterfalls, under temples, upon mountaintops or in burial grounds.

The more I thought about it, the more I began to think the scroll and the tablets must've been intended to be found and used together. The scroll led to the tablets, the tablets led to the scroll.

Within the scholarly comfort of Androus' office the conversation was beginning to move toward what we should do next. How we might track these places down, and where we would be best to start, and so on.

But the more we talked, the more the thought that we were following a deliberate trail laid down for us, kept going through my head.

I was sure I must've misunderstood something

along the way, but couldn't for the life of me see what it was. So as much to dispel it from my mind as to make a serious suggestion, I voiced my thoughts to the rest of the group.

'Sorry to change the subject,' I began, somewhat hesitantly. 'But, well, this thought has occurred to me, and I can't help but think I must've gotten something slightly wrong. Why was it these people did this?

'I mean, they travel for months, if not years in some cases to find this place, enduring all manner of hardships along the way.

'Then, when they achieve their goal and decide to return to their own homes, they first carve their story carefully into a set of semi-precious stones, just so they can then bury them, or in some other way hide them away when they get home?

'Am I right in thinking, none of these accounts describes the tablets being used to help others find the African temple, and achieve the same "Breath Eternal" as the seekers.

'In fact, if Gilgamesh's account is any indication, then he returns with the tools to fake his own death, before he goes on to take up his new true life.

'Now, to my mind,' I continued, waiting for someone to interrupt or stop me. 'I can't help but wonder.

'If these remarkable individuals didn't take these tablets back to their homelands to help their own people, then why did they take them back at all?'

I could see everyone thinking about what I'd said, and I was sure Harry or Androus, or someone else, was going to say I'd missed something, but they all just sat there.

Finally, it was Harry who tried to respond.

'Well, George, that's a good question,' he began, still obviously thinking. 'We know that in the case of Gilgamesh, he returned to Uruk and placed the tablets on display which described his journey, but we now know they were different to the tablets we found beneath the city gate, because they told a different story.

'There doesn't seem to be any religious element to it, in fact if anything the references to the sacred and divine which we would normally expect to see are suspicious in their complete absence.'

'I ask the question,' I interjected, cutting Harry off mid thought. 'Because it seems to me that the entries on the scroll are pointing us toward the ten sets of tablets, buried across the ancient world.

'But from what Androus was able to tell us about the tablets while we were in Uruk. The information on them points back to the African temple and either Ziusudra himself or the scroll.

'I mean, have I missed something, or are these adventurers not taking these tablets back to their homes to provide a trail back to the African temple, and from there, onto this other temple.'

'You're suggesting,' responded Marlow. 'That this was always intended to be a map rather than just a historic record. Not something for their contemporaries, family, friends or countrymen to follow. This was a map laid down for future generations to find and follow?'

'And you are also perhaps conjecturing,' Jean continued, waving his half-full coffee cup dangerously. 'That these people intended this trail to be intelligible perhaps even to us so many years later…

'To conceive of such a plan would be… incredible!'

'That would change things dramatically,' replied Harry, clearly still weighing the consequences. 'If these directions were created with a view to standing the test of time. Then it might be possible for us to follow them, provided we travelled as these adventurers travelled, and saw the landscape in the way they would have seen it.

'But we could only do that if we first identified the right starting point, a landmark or place we could be sure was the same as that mentioned in the scroll.'

I was keen to try and find out more about the

Iberian woman, who'd travelled all that way from Spain to the unknown interior of Africa in her quest. But it seemed the accounts from northern Turkey, the Black Sea, Greek mainland and possibly one of the Mediterranean islands were likely to be the easier to trace.

We just needed that starting point, from which we could attempt to back track our adventurers' routes.

This was something we could all help with, so we divided into pairs to research the four accounts we'd thought likely to be the easiest.

Androus would help out as much as possible to get us all started, but would then turn his attention back to the tablets we'd found in Uruk.

Harry and Marlow would start with the account from Anatolia, as it was geographically closest and probably our best bet. Jean and me would take the account from the Greek mainland, while Luke and Peter would focus on the account we thought was going to be from Crete or one of the other big Mediterranean islands.

Then if one of us finished or got stuck, we'd move on to the account from the Black Sea.

It was a daunting task, but Androus was able to recommend colleagues for us to talk to within the library, and provide all the reference material we could want, as well as a bit of help here and there from some local undergraduate volunteers who helped out at the library.

It was stimulating work, and a week later we had the first breakthrough.

Harry and Marlow figured out a reference in the account from that area of northern Turkey once known as Anatolia. It referred to what they thought might be the ancient city of Byblos, modern day Gubayl, just a day's drive up the coast into the Lebanese Republic.

From there they managed to trace a likely route through the mountains and cedar forests of northern Lebanon and across the broad plains of Syria into Turkey, and back into the mountains.

Here the description within the scroll focused on features that became more difficult to identify accurately on the maps.

'It's a guess, I have to admit,' confessed Harry, as he presented the details to us in one of the map rooms of the library. 'There are a number of features along the way we just haven't been able to place. Including another city that should be somewhere in northern Syria if we've interpreted right, but of which we can find no trace.

'In any event, if we're right, we should be able to tell fairly quickly once we get going. Either the terrain and distances will seem right or they won't. At least until we get to the border with northern Turkey that is. Here the mountain passes are so difficult to tell apart on a map, we'd really need to see the route first hand.

'Having said that,' Harry continued, more cautiously. 'There is a route through the mountains, and a destination that seems to make sense. If we're not talking about somewhere that's been completely lost to the modern world… then we could be talking about Caesarea and Mount Erciyes.'

We ran through the details of this account from the scroll again.

The account was related by one Arathes of Kanesh, or as Harry and Marlow thought, Caesarea. He was a prince and great hunter who presided over what must've been one the early trade routes to Europe from Asia through ancient Assyria. But after being bitten by a snake and nearly dying on one of his hunting trips, he had a vision that caused him to set out to find the home of the gods.

After years of travelling, and losing all he had, he'd become what must've been a gaunt and ragged figure, subsisting by trading what he could hunt for food and shelter. Eventually, almost dead from exhaustion he'd found his way to the temple in Africa, where he studied and regained his health before taking the tests and winning the prize.

Upon returning to his home, he took the tablets with him and placed them in a sacred grove on the side of the great mountain overlooking his home. Here, unable to live amongst his own people after his many years of travelling, he chose to once again live by his hunting as a hermit, before moving on to take up his true life.

DEPARTURES

THE CLUES POINTING AT CAESAREA and Mount Erciyes looked promising, and after throwing the options around between us for a while, we decided to try and follow the route Harry and Marlow had identified overland from Byblos.

After the problems we'd had on our last excursion we decided to travel by car the whole way. This would allow us to retrace the route contained in the scroll precisely. Hopefully confirming the landmarks and features described in the scroll as we went, while at the same time giving us a better understanding of the distances, and difficulties presented by the different types of terrain. It also promised to be a more comfortable journey, with less dependence on the vagaries of the local transport systems.

In actuality, while there may have been less packing and unpacking of equipment travelling by car, with all the stopping to examine landmarks and views along the way it still took us four days to cross the plains of northern Syria and reach the border with Turkey.

On the up side, with every mile we travelled, the evidence for Harry and Marlow's interpretation was building, with many of the subtle nuances mentioned in the scroll being credibly and often obviously located along the route.

The rivers, mountains, woods and plains also seemed to be roughly in the right place, or certainly close enough to have been so all those years before.

We still had no luck finding the elusive 'City of the White Rock', but there were noticeable limestone outcroppings across the entire Syrian plain, which could potentially have supplied just such a distinctive building material.

But it was once we got into the mountains of ancient Anatolia in north-western Turkey, that the description in the scroll really came into its own.

Here the terrain had apparently changed less over the years, and we were easily able to identify the route described in the scroll as leading to Mount Erciyes and ancient Caesarea.

The only problem was, the city appeared to be in the wrong place. While the mountain was an unmistakable feature clearly described in the scroll, the modern-day city of Kayseri, which supposedly stood upon the site of ancient Caesarea, was just too close.

As we'd travelled, we'd developed a good idea of how far it would have been possible for a person to walk or ride over the different types of terrain, and Kayseri was only a day's walk at best from the mountain, across a gently undulating and easily traversed plain.

Yet according to the scroll it should have been almost two days travel. There was nothing else for it, the city couldn't have moved, and if another had once stood nearby there was no sign of it now.

In any event it was the mountain we were interested in, and after establishing ourselves at a hotel in the city centre, we proceeded to try and find some local information to help narrow the search.

Unfortunately, while there were any number of people who professed to know the mountain well, after a while it became clear the city residents were a little too far away to visit the mountain regularly.

It was only as we got closer to the mountain itself, travelling through the small towns and villages which surrounded it that Androus managed to find an old man who used to regularly go hunting on its slopes.

He told of an old path, part way up the mountainside where some of the stones had been carved or inscribed with markings since before his grandfather was a boy.

It was exactly this kind of information we'd been looking for. The old man was too old to act as a guide himself, but his intimate knowledge of the slopes and the details he provided about them was almost as good.

The weather was still very mild, though winter couldn't be far off, so after retrieving our equipment we drove out the way the old man had directed until we could take the cars no further, and then began making our way up the lower slopes of Erciyes on foot.

Even now in late summer the mountain was high enough for its peak to still have a snowy cap and white patches visible on the upper slopes. We all knew it wouldn't be long before those patches started to enlarge and extend again, until they reached right down to the plains.

Just a few more weeks and we might've had to wait until next spring before we could even attempt this search.

Strangely though, seeing where the snow and ice extended to, even in summer, helped us to narrow the area of our search.

There was no way anyone, including our adventurous Arathes, could live for several years amongst the permanent snow and ice on the upper slopes of this mountain. So that narrowed the area down to within a day or a day and half's climb from the plain.

We'd brought enough food and equipment with us to spend a few nights on the mountain, provided the weather didn't get too bad. Carrying it all would make the climb a bit more arduous, but we'd only have to do it once, and then we could focus on the search without having to worry about getting back.

If anything, as we climbed it was a little too warm to begin with, but after a couple of hours the temperature seemed to drop to a more bearable level.

It was a lovely day, and I could easily have been tempted to pitch camp in one of the small meadows along the way and enjoy the views. But every now and again we'd come across some carved or worn stone indicating we might be on some kind of trail, so we kept pushing on.

I was expecting Androus to struggle a bit with the exertion, but not only did he manage to make the climb, he also managed to maintain a lively discussion with Harry about the various small features we encountered along the way.

'Ah yes,' I could hear Harry enthuse. 'More carved steps if I am not mistaken, Chuk.'

'Yes, yes, Harrison, and they are still carved into the resident stone, rather than being built from carved blocks.' Androus enthused back. 'But impossible to date. These could have been carved anywhere from a few hundred to a thousand or more years ago.'

We'd been climbing for about six hours and the temperature was still dropping with the altitude, so we decided to pitch our camp when we came across a good spot, so it would still be comfortably warm, and to use that as a base from which to do further exploration.

We were quite high up now, and the view out over the Kayseri plain and the lower mountains and valleys beyond was quite spectacular in the crisp and clear Anatolian air.

The campsite we settled on, was in a lightly wooded area, that bordered onto a sloping mountain meadow, with a small stream running through it.

The lower reaches of the snow-line were probably another day's climb further, so we couldn't go that much further before we'd be getting beyond the area that could reasonably be described as permanently inhabitable.

The old man in the village had directed us well, and after a sound night's sleep, it seemed we'd no sooner started our search the following day when we found what must have been the stones he had told us about.

Peter and Luke had gone a little further up the mountain, and moved across toward the west, and a rocky outcropping that ran like a spine up the side of the mountain into the snow-line.

As they moved along toward the base of this feature, they'd found a shaped stone lying in the grass at an angle, suggesting it may have fallen from above and planted itself in the soft ground.

Further along, they'd come across some more stones that may have been part of the same block, including a couple that had what looked like the same symbol we'd found in Uruk carved deeply into their surface.

It was enough of a lead for us to abandon our other search areas and concentrate our efforts. Peter and Luke would move further up the mountain to see if they could locate the site from which this rock might have fallen. Marlow and I would move further down the slope to see if anything might have fallen further, while Harry, Androus and Jean would make a more detailed examination of the area surrounding the rocks that had already been found.

It was a laborious task, and after a couple of hours of scrutinising and examining every odd shaped rock and boulder amongst a field of rocks and boulders, I couldn't help but smile to myself at the apparent hopelessness of our task.

Marlow must have seen the expression on my face.

'It's like looking for a needle in a haystack, is it not, George?' he joked.

I couldn't help but smile in return at his ability to read my mind. 'I was thinking more like a needle "on" a haystack,' I suggested.

'And is that perhaps what you still think about this entire venture, as well?' he asked with a slightly more earnest tone to his voice.

I stopped and looked up the slight slope we were on, towards him. It was strange, but as we looked at one another I was reminded of that first time we'd met, on the veranda of the hunting lodge in Africa.

On that occasion we'd been bathed in the flame like shades of an African sunset, whereas now we were surrounded by the crisp alpine light of the Anatolian afternoon.

There remained within him that stillness that I'd noticed in Africa, and which seemed to be growing since our experience at the Singing Stones, but somehow here, looking out over huge distances toward the far-off horizon it seemed more natural, and I felt comfortable returning his gaze and talking.

'Yes, or more precisely, that's how I think I should feel,' I replied, simply. 'But I think this particular needle wants to be found, and is perhaps even drawing us toward it.

'Whether we like it or not, whether we're ready or not, and whether we understand what it will mean once we have it.

'Somehow,' I continued, feeling a sudden urge to see how he'd react. 'Somehow, I know we will find it, Rob. I'm just not sure we'll all still be friends when we do.'

He seemed to think about this for a moment before responding. 'Perhaps, but I hope you're wrong about that last part, George.'

We continued our search for a few more hours, talking of other things, The growing unrest in Europe, especially Spain and Germany, as well as the turmoil within the Soviet Union and East Asia. Before eventually we were summoned back up the mountain by a call from the others.

We arrived to find everyone a bit further up the mountainside toward where Peter and Luke had gone to search.

There was a small meadow up there with some

stunted and ancient looking oak trees around a chilly looking pool. Hidden toward the back of the meadow, behind a dense thicket of young trees, Peter had found a carved rock face beneath a natural overhang. And nearby, the remains of a stone slab similar to the one we'd excavated in Uruk, in which the nine lapis tablets had been housed.

'We found another section of this stone block further down the slope,' Harry explained, to bring me and Marlow up to speed. 'It seems the tablets that were brought back by Arathes, were placed in this block in a similar configuration to what we saw in Uruk, but then, rather than burying it, it was located vertically in this alcove beneath the overhang. Another, larger block, was then placed in front of this one and carved with the same nine-point clock symbol we saw before.

'Sadly,' continued Harry. 'The tablets seem long gone. They must've been removed deliberately, and then the site destroyed afterward, with the ruined stone cast down the mountainside.'

'You refer to the fact that these substantial stones were deliberately thrown down the slope?' Jean asked.

'Yes,' Harry replied. 'While part of the housing stone was found here, next to the alcove, the cover stone would have required a considerable amount of either time or effort to move across this clearing.

'I don't think it likely this happened naturally, either by the ice and snow which covers these slopes in winter, or as a consequence of some rock fall, subsidence or tremor. It's just too far to the edge.'

'It seems our journey has been wasted then,' chipped in Luke, with a tone of resignation in his voice. 'The tablets have been taken, probably hundreds of years ago. Either that or they too were precipitated down this slope to their destruction.'

'No,' interjected Marlow thoughtfully, looking around the group. 'This journey has told us a great deal.

'Some of these tablets may have been found or

destroyed by others who came before us. But to see such consistency in the way they were concealed and preserved, that tells us there will be others out there still hidden away and protected, just waiting to be found.'

'Has this journey not also given us a better understanding,' contributed Jean. 'Of what we can and cannot expect to deduce from the descriptions and directions contained within the stories and the accounts of these ancient and heroic individuals?'

For a moment I thought I saw a cloud pass across Luke's eyes, some dark thought, or resentment at the response he'd received, but a moment later it was gone and his natural good humour seemed to return to him.

Despite what we'd said to Luke, it was still a considerable disappointment to find this ancient site, but not to find the tablets that were once hidden here.

However, the afternoon was getting on, and with it a suggestion of cooler air had started to creep down the mountainside toward us, motivating us to get moving.

Perhaps it was only the first hint of winter coming to the region and making a tentative grasp at the high ground, but it spurred us on.

There was the usual documentation of the scene to go through, but with sketches and drawings complete, we made our retreat down to the camp in the rich evening light, before heading back down the mountain the following day.

We'd been fortunate with the weather on this occasion, but as we headed back to Jerusalem, even though we were travelling toward warmer climes, it was obvious the seasons were now changing everywhere.

A few days later and we were back in Jerusalem and re-installed in the hotel which I was almost beginning to think of as home.

Returning to the relaxed atmosphere of the old town in Jerusalem made it easy to fall into a pleasant daily routine of researching, exploring the city, and lively discussion with the rest of the group, but as the weeks turned into months without another breakthrough on the scroll, that pleasant routine began to feel more like a rut.

Winter arrived, and to my wonderment snow fell in Jerusalem, instantly transforming the old city and surrounding countryside into an even more exotic and magical environment.

A welcome break in the routine came when Androus finally finished his translation of the Gilgamesh tablets. But while the library restorers had done all they could with the shattered tablets, the damage in the end had been too great and Androus was left with just an uncertain collection of letters and odd words from which he could decipher very little.

We still had the undamaged tablets, which while interesting, only turned out to contain a more detailed version of the account we'd already obtained from the scroll.

The disappointment was made all the worse by the fragmentary hints and suggestions retrieved from the restored tablets.

Having said that, we all knew how much work Androus had put in, to translate this more detailed version of the Gilgamesh story from the tablets. So, once complete, we all dutifully made our way through the snow blanketed streets to the library and the fire-warmed map room to work our way through it.

I can't pretend I was persuaded of the value of spending so much time on this second account of the Gilgamesh journey, especially when we'd already retrieved the tablets it led to.

But as soon as we started to work our way through it, it became clear why Androus and Harry had been so insistent we do it.

Just the odd additional comment here and there seemed to provide us with that little bit of extra information necessary to actually pinpoint the route and direction.

Comments as insignificant as where his shadow fell upon the ground while he was walking, or sight of a lake or river in the distance seemed to make the route suddenly obvious.

And then we found it, the key to the other accounts on the scroll and of all things it took the shape of... Butterflies.

Gilgamesh in his quest to find immortality, had travelled around the Levant, through modern day Syria, Lebanon and Turkey, as well as down into the Sinai Peninsula and Egypt before finally making his way deeper into Africa and ultimately to Ziusudra's temple.

But despite knowing the start and the end points of this journey, and even being able to conjecture upon some of the more significant settlements and locations along the way, the detail in the scroll just wasn't enough to be sure of the exact route.

Now, with the tablet translation it suddenly became clear, and a section of the journey fell into place.

Where we had previously thought an excursion to Cyprus had been followed by a return to the mountains of Lebanon, it now seemed he may have left the island and continued on to somewhere else, either on the mainland or even another island.

The geography still sounded very much like that of Lebanon, with mountains, lakes, springs and an abundance of deer, pine and cedar trees.

But Gilgamesh had visited this place, because it was rumoured that the sacred pools and grottoes were often inhabited by gods and spirits who hid their presence by summoning great clouds of butterflies and other insects.

'That could be Rhodes', interjected Peter, looking slightly shocked. 'I travelled there with my family when I was a boy, so my father could visit the medieval city. But while we were there we travelled into the high mountains to a remarkably beautiful area of springs and streams, that every year attracted an unimaginable number of butterflies.'

None of us had heard of this before, but this unknown land of Telina was mentioned in several of the other accounts on the scroll.

'Rhodes would fit the other accounts well,' suggested Harry, thoughtfully. 'In the account of Faron, whom we think may have originated in Crete, there is mention of Telina as one of the places visited. The same with the account of Alcathos of Ephyri.'

The cold and snow beyond the windows was forgotten now, as we bent our attention to the other two accounts on the scroll that mentioned this place. It was engrossing work, and when next I looked up from our task the inky darkness of the winter night had transformed the windows into a lightless reflection of the room.

But more importantly in that short time we'd confirmed that all three of the accounts that mentioned Telina could credibly be referring to Rhodes.

It took us a week to trace the two routes mentioned in the scroll. Faron it seemed had indeed hailed from the southern shores of Crete, while Alcathous appeared to have come from an area just outside ancient Corinth.

Better still, while we were tracing these two routes to Crete and Corinth, we also managed to identify the locations of several other sites mentioned in other sections of the scroll, thus opening up further accounts for study that would previously have been immensely difficult for us.

It was like a switch had been thrown, and the rut we'd had so much trouble escaping, was now forgotten, and we could be on our way again.

But our suddenly rejuvenated enthusiasm was just as quickly cooled by the winter weather, which was now firmly against us.

The snow, which made Jerusalem so picturesque, would not only make it more difficult for us to get out of Jerusalem, but also make it doubly difficult to find the sites we were looking for when we got onto the ground in Crete or mainland Greece, where the thinnest covering of snow or frost would completely obscure those subtle clues and markings we'd be so dependent on to find what we sought.

The waiting was frustrating, but for the sake of a few more weeks, we would not only have a much easier journey, we'd also be able to conduct our search in the ideal early Spring conditions, when the snow and ice had gone, but before much of the native vegetation started to grow again.

The enforced wait also gave us a good opportunity to work on some of the other accounts, and possibly add a third or fourth location to our journey. Not that we'd need to bother with these if we found what we were looking for in either of the first two locations, we just knew from our last trip, there were no guarantees.

We spent the next few maddening weeks, half preparing for our journey, half researching the other accounts, and all the while watching the weather.

We had more information to go on than ever with our search, but some of the accounts still seemed to evade our understanding.

Certainly, the Indo-Chinese adventurer was beyond our immediate abilities, as it seemed was the account of an indigenous African hunter and priest, whose tale, while crammed full of descriptive detail seemed to include not a single place name.

In contrast the account of the explorer from the Black Sea area, abounded with the names of places and geographical features, all of which were wholly unknown to us.

But that still left us with some promising options. I was still keen to try and find the home of the Iberian woman who was also both warrior and chieftain.

The place names and directions leading to her home were still vague, especially toward the western end of the Mediterranean, before the route crossed any of the locations we'd now identified, but it was enough to confirm part of the route and ascertain she was indeed likely to be Iberian.

This wasn't enough for us to try retracing the route on the ground, but it might just be sufficient to make it worthwhile contacting someone who knew the area.

Androus and Jean had a few possible contacts to try, who might in their turn know of some knowledgeable locals they could recommend. It would doubtless take a while, but we sent off the letters and hoped.

In the meantime, the snow and cold were persisting, much to my mixed delight and frustration, and the apparent indifference of the local inhabitants. But as the waiting continued, I noticed it seemed to be getting to Jean, who was uncharacteristically sullen and irritable.

Thinking a bit of exercise would do us both good I decided to seek him out and suggest a long walk around the city, possibly stopping off along the way for some warming coffee or chocolate.

I caught up with him in his room, just as he was donning his boots and coat to go out,

'Splendid,' I said, with slightly exaggerated good humour. 'I was just coming to see if you'd like to venture out for a stroll, and here you are putting your coat and boots on in readiness.'

'Unfortunately, my friend,' he replied. 'I have just a simple errand to run, which I do not think would interest you.'

I'd have taken the hint normally and left him to his own devices, but something in his manner made me hesitate, and on a whim, I decided to push the boundaries of good manners a little and impose myself upon him.

'Nonsense, I shall walk out with you while you perform your errand, and try to persuade you to stretch your legs a little further as we go.'

I didn't ask where we were going as we exited the hotel and courtyard, and walked out onto the streets. The snow had started again, a light gusty fall this time, made up of tiny ephemeral flakes that seemed barely heavy enough to fall to earth. We walked first toward the centre of the city, and then as we entered the Muslim quarter, northward toward the Via Dolorosa.

I didn't want to dissemble, or keep up the act with Jean, which I knew he'd soon see through if he hadn't already, so once we got into the swirling snow, I just outlined my concerns.

'I'm getting a little worried about you, Jean,' I said, looking fixedly ahead. 'You seem to be struggling with something, the waiting perhaps, I don't know. But whatever it is I'd like to help if I can.'

The rhythm of his steps beside me faltered briefly as I spoke, but then regained their regularity.

'Thank you, George,' he responded, after a brief hesitation. 'But while I am indeed straining beneath a burden, it is unfortunately not something I am yet able to share.'

I couldn't think what it was that might be troubling Jean so, but I knew he'd been as open and honest with me as he was able. So, after assuring him, that when he was able to share his burden, I would be more than willing to help hear it, I changed the subject.

We walked in silence for a few minutes, before reaching one of the big Suq markets, where Jean momentarily disappeared to perform his errand, and then we walked back.

The snow was getting a little heavier now, the ephemeral flakes previously so reluctant to fall groundward, now seemed to have plucked up their courage, and had started their descent in earnest.

My walk was now out of the question, but on the way back to the hotel, we decided to take a slightly more circuitous route by way of a compromise for us both.

Many of the stall holders and shops were preparing for the worst and starting to close early, and it seemed anyone with a choice had already made their way home, leaving the streets strangely quiet and serene, with even our footsteps being muffled by the lying snow.

We were halfway back to the hotel and discussing how we would best approach our forthcoming journey to Crete and the Greek mainland, when Jean stopped suddenly, and motioned me back to the intersection of a narrow alley we'd just crossed.

I couldn't imagine what he was playing at to begin with, but after tentatively looking around the corner he drew back and motioned for me to do the same. It was Luke, and he was with the young woman again, the one we'd seen him with in the park.

'Is it not our own Luke and the young lady we saw him with once before?' Jean asked quietly, as he joined me in looking around the corner.

They were stood outside an ancient looking stone building, attempting to shelter from the snow while they spoke. Luke again seemed almost deferential to the young woman, who for her part seemed to accept his respect as though it was perfectly natural.

They were talking quite heatedly though, almost arguing, and eventually the young woman seemed to accept his point, and turning, opened the door into the old building before ushering Luke inside and following him.

It was a perplexing scene.

Firstly, because he claimed not to have known the young lady when Jean had confronted him at Uruk, and now again because of that almost servile respect he seemed to offer her, and which she so readily accepted.

This was all just beginning to go through my head, when Jean suddenly moved past me into the alley, and toward the building Luke and the young woman had entered. I followed, half-expecting Luke to step out and accuse us at any moment.

'Perhaps there is a name or address beside the door,' Jean was saying, as I followed him. But there was nothing to indicate who might live in the house, so as quickly as we'd come, we turned and made our way back to the main street.

I could tell Jean was still thinking about it, but we'd

gone barely a hundred feet, before he disappeared again up a slightly larger side street.

The cold and damp from the snow was starting to seep through my clothes now, and I wasn't really in the mood for random exploration, but he went only about forty feet, before stopping in the shelter of a large doorway.

'What do you think, George,' he said looking out across the street, to an old stone church opposite.

'It's very nice, Jean, but I don't think now is really the time for us to be studying the city's architecture.'

'Perhaps not,' he replied, with that entertained light in his eyes, which always indicated when he was playing with someone. 'But the stone is the same, is it not, and the age also, and it is the same distance from the road down which we were walking.'

It took me a second or two to figure out what he was talking about.

'You think this church is in some way connected to the building we've just seen Luke enter? Perhaps even the same building, and we were just looking at its rear entrance?'

'Did you notice?' Jean continued, mercilessly. 'The building into which Luke entered, in addition to having no number or name, also had no windows or even a keyhole in its door.'

'But why would Luke be entering the back door of a church in central Jerusalem with that young woman?' I asked.

'That I cannot say, my friend,' Jean responded. 'But it will be interesting trying to find out, will it not?'

Once we'd got back to the hotel and had a chance to dry off and think about things, there were of course any number of possible reasons for Luke's actions, that it would be pointless for us to speculate upon.

Just as importantly though, it was clear now, for whatever the reason, this was not a matter Luke wanted to discuss, which meant it was not something we could in fairness ask him about. Whatever it was, we would for now just have to leave the matter alone.

INTO THE SUNSET

AS QUICKLY AND UNEXPECTEDLY as the snow had come, it went, and Spring seemed to rush into its place.

Most of us were eager to be underway, though Luke, for perhaps very understandable reasons seemed happy to dally a little longer.

'For the weather to improve,' being the rather transparent reason he actually gave.

But the time had come for us to leave, and as we weren't sure how long our journey might be, that meant it was also time to say goodbye to Jerusalem, with all the treasures and distractions it held.

Androus made a case for us to leave the tablets and the scroll behind in safekeeping at his library, being such valuable and irreplaceable artefacts. But as we couldn't predict how or whether we might need them again we decided to take them along with us. Though only after having them even more thoroughly catalogued and photographed, and obtaining an almost indestructible, waterproof and fire proof, vacuum-sealed lock box for them to travel in.

Then suddenly, the city walls were receding behind us and we were retracing the route by which we'd arrived all those months previously. There was still a pronounced chill in the air as we drove back toward the port of Jaffa, where we boarded a small passenger ship to Rhodes.

In other circumstances I would've been quite happy to tarry a while on that earthly island paradise, for even in the early spring its beauty was unmistakable. But for us it was merely a starting point, and our attention as a consequence was focused squarely upon how we would move on from Rhodes to retrace the route of another of those ancient seekers.

As chance would have it, we were able to charter a small yacht, which had also come from Jaffa, to sail us along the route described in the scroll, to Crete, and the home of our next explorer, Faron.

From the scroll we knew he was a sea captain and trader, as well as a husband and father. As a trader he travelled extensively, often spending weeks if not months away from home, crossing the Mediterranean, and occasionally even travelling beyond in his search for new commodities or luxuries to be bought or sold.

It was on one such voyage that he first hears the rumours of a man who has lived for many lifetimes, but remained untouched by age or frailty.

After hearing these rumours Faron begins voyaging even further afield in the hope of finding out more, but in doing so he also damages his business, and undermines the trust of his crew. Until finally, after endangering their lives by trying to sail through a storm, they take his ship and abandon him.

Still he tries to continue his search, until one night, half-starved and exhausted, he is visited by a dream, in the form of a man, who speaks none of the many languages known to Faron, but somehow guides him to the temple through the wilderness.

Like the other seekers, Faron stays within the temple for some time, before making his way back to his own people, with the tablets.

However, upon his return, he finds his wife is now married to another man, his son is grown to adulthood, and like Arathes he can no longer bear to live amongst his own people.

At which point, he also leaves behind the comforts of civilisation, to live beside a waterfall high up in a nearby gorge, emerging only rarely to exchange the rare herbs and other plants he is able to collect for some meagre necessities.

I had no idea just how many islands there were in the Mediterranean until we started our journey from Rhodes to Crete. But as we sailed across the still dark and wintry waters, it seemed as though we were never out of sight of one island or another.

Some just tiny outcroppings, barely big enough to sustain a few scrubby plants, others larger and clearly inhabited, or at least possessed of enough land to graze a few goats or sheep.

We'd decided to try and enlist the help of our boat captain in understanding some of the details mentioned by Faron, in the hope that features thought worthy of mention by one experienced seaman, would somehow make sense to another.

It was apparently a more difficult concept to convey than we might have thought, either that or Harry's command of modern-day Greek was not as good as he thought it was.

Still, we got there in the end, even after inexpertly deflecting the odd question as to the identity of our historic captain, and why he would not have called the islands by the same name that everyone else did.

But our modern-day captain, Stephanos, finally got the gist of what we wanted and before long he was pointing out details in the descriptions that made sense to him. Either because it would avoid this sandbank, or that shoal of rocks, or just because it made the most of the prevailing winds or currents. Each detail offered additional confirmation that we'd interpreted the directions correctly.

It took us the best part of two days to reach the north-eastern tip of Crete, navigating past the incredibly picturesque Dodecanese islands of Karpathos and Kaisos with their prominent whitewashed houses and Byzantine churches. The very sight of which seemed to draw forth a little more of the precious Mediterranean sunlight.

The day had begun to warm up a little by late afternoon, and now as we drew closer to the mainland, the sun made one last valiant effort to call forth the shimmering blue from the sea around us, before sinking exhausted into the distant horizon.

Stephanos' boat wasn't big enough to accommodate us overnight, but upon a recommendation from him, we found a quiet cove just south of the island's eastern point, with a small, out of season hotel, whose owner was only too happy to put us up for the night.

Even in the comfortable surroundings of the hotel, which we had entirely to ourselves, it was still a restless night for most of us.

To be on the island and possibly so close to finding another set of tablets was just a torture of anticipation. The directions had been good so far though, and I couldn't help but think a gorge would be an easier thing to search than an entire mountain. But there was just no knowing, until we got there.

The following morning, we left the hotel bright and early, heading back to the boat to continue our journey.

None of us were particularly familiar with this part of the island, though both Harry and Androus had of course ventured to Crete before, to visit the legendary excavations of Knossos in the north.

Our hope therefore was that the directions on the scroll would continue to provide enough detail once we left the sea and moved back on to the land.

Out of habit we politely interrogated the hotel owner before leaving, on the off chance he might have heard of some local legend or myth which might guide us.

Fortunately, archaeological exploration was in no way unusual on Crete, so we could be almost entirely honest about our motivations and reasons for questioning him.

I couldn't help but think it was a long shot personally, as we were right at the opposite end of the island. But our host turned out to be an absolute font of information. Not only about our destination, which he thought likely to be in one of the many gorges, possibly including the well-known Samaria gorge located in the Chania area in the south-west of the island.

In terms of the directions we had for navigating the coast, he also recognised and knew several of the features described well, if by slightly different names.

Surprised by the discovery of this new-found knowledge, we went back to the boat, and in no time were picking out the features described in the directions.

This line of rocks, that cave, reef, promontory, all framed in the background by the ever-present Cretan lowlands, and the more distant spine of mountains that ran along the entire length of the island.

Faron it seemed had been a master mariner who had left a description of his route which people who knew the coast in that area could still to this day follow with ease, so it took little more than an hour for us to arrive at the wide-open bay, that was the last stage of our journey by boat.

From here we would see if his directions away from the water were as good.

Stephanos agreed to wait for us for a week, before taking his leave and heading back to Jaffa. This should be more than enough time for us to find the whereabouts of Faron's sanctuary and the tablets it contained.

We'd had to bring a bit more equipment with us this time, on account of the colder and wetter weather, and we'd been hoping to find some pack animals before we set off, to help carry the additional burden, but it seemed the village where we'd landed, which was towered over by a set of sheer cliffs that encroached almost to the sea, had loaned out several of their animals to another party just a few weeks earlier.

A party that had then for reasons known only to themselves, left those animals at a village on the other side of the island, from where they had yet to be reclaimed.

This left us humping the rest of the weight on our

own backs, and trusting much of our heavier and more valuable items, including the scroll and tablets, to the barely secure strong room in the village's post office. A situation that none of us was very happy with.

We'd squandered our early start by trying to find some animals, and then a storage room, so it was well-past lunchtime on another distinctly overcast and grey day, before we finally set off through the crack-like opening in the sheer cliffs behind the village.

The crack opened out into a steep sided gorge, that Harry had identified as the most likely match to that mentioned in the scroll.

It was a tiring climb, with lots of loose rock and shale underfoot, that often sent us sliding back a step for every two we took forward.

Added to this, there was very little in the way of an established path, which meant we ended up crossing and re-crossing the broad stream that ran down through the gorge as we tried to find a way up.

Thankfully the ground levelled off after a while and the going became a little easier.

There were a few cryptic details on this bit of the route in the scroll, including that we were looking for one of the side gorges or hanging valleys that fed into the main gorge, and that Faron had placed the tablets near to a waterfall there.

These directions sounded helpful enough, until Peter showed us a map of the area, which revealed the entire topographic layout in this part of the island.

There were hundreds, if not thousands of gorges, valleys and ravines, any number of which would probably be a good match for the description we had.

On the plus side we were never more than a few yards walk from an abundant supply of fresh water, which would have been a very unwelcome additional weight to carry.

Once over the initial hump at the start of the main

gorge, it seemed only a few hours before the light started to wane, and we were forced to think about a camp for the night.

The nights were still drawing in quickly, and bringing the cold and onshore wind with them, but we'd no sooner decided to focus our efforts on finding a good site, than we came across a side gorge that matched the description on the scroll, high up on the right-hand wall of the main gorge.

There was a small trickle of a stream, flowing down from it, hardly enough to suggest there could be a waterfall above, like the one we sought, but we had to check it out.

After a quick conference amongst ourselves, we decided that rather than back-track the following day, or risk not finding a decent camp for the evening, we'd split our forces.

Harry, Peter and Jean would go up to investigate the side-gorge, while the rest of us scouted further up the main gorge for a camp site.

This meant they could also drop their packs, to save climbing with them, and just reclaim them on their way back.

As for finding a decent campsite. There were plenty of options to pick from, but the valley walls near to the side gorge were very steep, which meant the entire base of the main gorge was littered with rocks and debris that had fallen from above.

A few hundred meters further on though, and the gorge not only widened out, but the angle of the walls also mellowed into a more gentle slope, allowing a small woodland to survive at the bottom.

There was also a natural hollow in the ground encircled by a dry stone wall, with a shepherd's stone hut at one end.

The hut was far too small to accommodate more than a couple of us, but the encircling wall was high enough to give us some protection from the wind, and any falling rocks that found their way through the trees.

We collected some wood from the little woodland, which contained some dead-standing trunks amongst them, then built a good-sized fire with the dry wood.

The last of the daylight was fading as Harry, Peter and Jean walked up to the camp.

Apparently, the side valley had held little of interest, but had afforded a good view further up the main gorge, revealing several other side valleys for us to explore the following day.

Later, when we turned in for the night, I realised how accustomed I'd become to the comforts of hotel living during our time in Jerusalem.

I still got some sleep, but the hard ground woke me up several times in the night, until just before dawn I gave up altogether, and shivered about the camp until I could get the fire going again and some water on to boil for a cup of tea.

Whether the firelight helped to rouse them, I wasn't sure, but the others all stirred and got up a few minutes later, giving us an early start to the day.

There was still nothing of use in the directions from the scroll, so we just had to make our way methodically up the main gorge, splitting off in twos or threes to check out the side valleys as we came across them.

It was laborious work, with a lot of climbing and then time-consuming searching, made none the easier by the occasional rain shower and the fact that some of the little hanging valleys extended a long way from the main gorge.

By midday, we'd checked out another two valleys, and were waiting for Luke and Marlow to catch us up from their search of a third.

The floor of the main gorge was beginning to get a little steeper now, but at the same time, its sides were sloping at a shallower angle, making the side valleys increasingly accessible.

The afternoon's searching was much the same as the morning; steady progress, but nothing to indicate whether we were getting any closer.

We'd come across another good campsite in the late afternoon, and after we each returned from our last searches for the day, we made our way back down the gorge a little to the site we'd chosen, and started to make our camp.

There was still a good hour of light left by the time we'd finished setting everything up, and started to prepare the evenings meal, but it had been a long day and we were all in need of rest.

While still cool and a little damp, the wind had dropped and the sun had emerged, so while Peter and Luke laboured over the food, the rest of us were all able to enjoy the last warming rays of ruddy sunlight before it sank behind the valley wall.

'That is a very welcome sight, is it not?' commented Jean, as he leaned back against a convenient boulder, and looked up at the sun glittering through the tree branches and leaves on the opposite side of the gorge.

'Almost as though the leaves perform the pirouette in order to catch every last ray of the evening light.'

We could always rely upon Jean for the unexpected poetic insights, and I couldn't help but smile at the thought, as I looked over toward him.

But as I glanced at Jean, I also couldn't help but smile at the rather rueful frown on Harry's face, as he sat next to him looking up at the gilt-edged trees and shrubs of Jean's inspiration.

'You know, Jean,' Harry said with an almost exaggerated hesitation, as he stood up. 'There are times when I wonder what we'd do without you.'

This brought Jean's attention back to earth, but he clearly suspected there was a trap in Harry's complimentary words.

'As always you are too kind, mon ami,' he replied

with a patient smile and raised eyebrow.

'Not at all, Jean,' said Harry, walking over toward the sunset, and then turning to face us all with the setting sun and gilded trees behind him. 'Does this not remind you of the story of the cave and shadows, so eloquently described by Plato himself?

'As the sun sets behind the valley wall, we all sit and admire the golden light as it falls upon the trees and bushes closest toward us, without of course considering where the source of that light might come from.'

'The trees are concealing a small valley,' responded Jean, with sudden realisation in his voice. 'If there were a valley wall behind those wonderful golden edged leaves, then they would be in shade and not illuminated anywhere near so prettily. It is only because the sunlight is free to shine through them, that we see them thus.'

As with so many things, as soon as it was pointed out, it was obvious.

The top of the valley walls were of course quite irregular, and what looked like a slight dip, with perhaps a few trees growing on a protruding ledge in front of it, was now revealed to be another small gorge, with its entrance quite naturally overgrown and hidden.

It was a bit of a scramble to get up there, and take a tentative look, before the evening light would become too weak for us to safely descend.

But tired as we all were, the proximity and mystery of this hidden valley was just too much for us. We had to climb up and take a quick look at what lay beyond, before almost immediately turning around to head back down.

Like several of the other hanging valleys, it extended back at least a quarter of a mile, so we didn't have time to investigate that night, but first thing the following day, after a quick breakfast and packing up the camp, we decided to take a look around as a whole party before embarking on the search proper.

It was a nice enough spot, much like the other side

gorges we'd already investigated, and with all of us looking it took no time at all to rule it out as yet another dead end.

More importantly though, we'd learned a valuable lesson, and at least knew now that we needed to be much more careful in our searching.

As the morning wore on, we once again split into our groups in order to search the various small valleys and crevices we came across.

Unfortunately, half way through the morning, we got to the point where the main gorge split into two equally sized channels going off in different directions.

There was no way we'd be able to pursue both of these routes simultaneously without leaving one group or the other short of equipment.

There was nothing really to choose between them, but there was a small comment in the scroll which seemed to indicate the valley we wanted was on the eastern side of the main gorge, either that or we should follow the eastern most path, when it presented itself.

Androus could shed no further light on the question no matter how he tried to re-interpret the scroll, but with nothing else to go on, it was as good a choice as any, so we went to the east.

The sunlight seemed to be becoming a bit more reliable again, and as the day wore on, the temperature rose to quite a pleasant level for walking and climbing, which we all appreciated after having endured the cool and damp of the previous night.

By mid-afternoon, we'd moved quite a way further up into the mountains, and had split up again to examine a couple of small ravines.

Harry, Luke and Peter splitting off into one group, Androus and Marlow a second, leaving Jean and myself as a third group to continue further up the main channel.

We'd fallen into the habit of dropping our packs in the main valley rather than trying to climb with them, just carrying a little water and some basic tools to do the actual searching.

This helped to cut down on any unnecessary exertion, and served as a convenient marker for the rest of the group, so we all knew where one another were. But sometimes it was also just impracticable to do otherwise, and now with just the two of us left in the main valley, we came across just such a time.

Periodically, as the makeup of stone along the main valley altered, the entire character of the gorge would change.

The softer the stone, the broader the valley became, and the more gently sloping and weathered the sides. Where the stone became harder, the width of the gorge would constrict and the walls would become more vertical.

Well, the stone was evidently a little harder at this point, and as we approached a narrow point in the gorge, we both saw the tell-tale signs of a small stream running down the valley floor toward the main stream from a small copse of mature trees up against the valley wall, hiding the stream's source.

Above the treetops, we could see the water falling down the rock face, bouncing and splashing from one shelf of rock to another.

'I believe it is your turn to lead, is it not, George?' commented Jean as we made our way over to the copse of trees.

'It is, Jean, it is,' I responded, eyeing the formidable looking climb ahead of me. 'Though of course I'd be more than happy to allow you to take my place, as the more experienced climber.'

'Thank you, mon ami, that is most kind,' he replied, with a good-humoured smile on his face. 'But I could hardly deprive you of such a valuable learning experience.'

It was a lovely spot, once we got to the base of the rock. With the small cascade of water shimmering and falling into a perfect little pool, which overflowed into the stream and thence down into the valley.

I was a little preoccupied in trying to decide how to approach the climb, to really pick up on the details, until Jean brought my attention back to our surroundings.

'That is a little odd, is it not?' he observed, walking over toward where a group of birds were squabbling over a small patch of ground. 'It appears that someone else has recently stopped here, and not done a very good job of clearing up their campsite when they left.'

I don't think we'd have noticed, had it not been for the birds, which had been fighting over some scraps of food carelessly disposed of.

But once we'd moved closer it was clear a good-sized party of people had spent some time here.

Most of the camp had been cleaned up of course, at least superficially, the fire being properly buried, and the animal dung disposed of. Which should have been enough for the site to go unnoticed by anyone not looking for it.

But when you were right on top of it, it didn't take a seasoned tracker to spot the footprints and other traces left in the soft sandy soil.

'It looks like a bit too much activity for one of the local shepherds,' I ventured. 'Perhaps it was that group the villagers mentioned, the ones who failed to return their pack animals. Perhaps they camped here.'

'Yes, but why here my friend?' Jean responded, squinting up at the rock face overhead. 'Does not the risk of falling rocks make this a little too inconvenient for most people?'

We decided to leave it there, as there was little more to be done, even if other people had stayed here. Turning our attention back to the rock face and the climb that lay ahead of us.

Once we got going, the climb itself was a little easier than it looked, and while still strenuous in places, with the two of us, to help one another out, it was more a question of picking the right route, than needing any real expertise.

I was a little disappointed once we got to the top,

the valley only seemed to go on for a few hundred meters, before gradually petering out.

Having said that though, there was another very attractive waterfall at the far end of the valley, with another pool and bubbling stream. Just as impressively to the left, the valley wall and surrounding hillside fell away almost entirely revealing the most amazing views across the surrounding hills, and down to the impossibly attractive sea beyond.

It was a spectacular vista, that would have been well worthy of one of Jean's sketches, but we were here for a purpose, and with the climb out of the way, the question of why someone would be making their camp in this particular location started to nag at my mind again.

It didn't take us long to find the reason.

We followed the stream as it meandered across the small valley, and up to the second waterfall. For a few minutes it looked like another dead end, but we were nothing if not thorough. So after ruling out one side of the waterfall, we automatically moved across to check the other, and immediately saw the entrance into a cave behind the sheet of water.

I almost forgot to breathe for a second, as I realised this might suddenly be the place we were looking for.

A moment later my impatience got the better of my shock and I was plunging through the chilly water into the cave beyond, closely followed by Jean.

It was gloomy inside, so it took a moment for my eyes to adjust, as we hadn't thought to bring a torch with us, but there was just enough light coming through the curtain of water to illuminate the shallow cave behind the waterfall.

Unfortunately there was also enough light for us to see that we hadn't arrived here first.

My heart, which had been aflutter with anticipation, now sank at the sight before us.

Whoever it was that had beaten us to the tablets, had taken considerably less care in excavating them from their setting than we had in Uruk. The cover-stone with the deeply incised clock symbol, had obviously just been smashed in from above, and now lay in a dozen fragments against the cave wall, beneath where it had lain for centuries.

Above the broken fragments of stone I could see that the bedrock had once again been carved and shaped to provide perfectly shaped cavities for the tablets, now nine empty spaces open to the air.

There was another copper sheet green with age, which had been discarded along with the cover-stone, and several small piles of sand, which must have again acted as packing.

With a sunken heart I continued to look around for any sign of the missing tablets, my eyes gradually adjusting to the gloom until I could look around comfortably.

I couldn't believe we'd failed again, the bitter taste of bile rising to the back of my throat, which I had to wash away with some of the ice-cold water from the waterfall.

Thoughts of how much time and energy we'd wasted again, and for nothing, filling my mind.

I looked at Jean, expecting to see the same disconsolate feelings written upon the features of his face, but was surprised to see an expression of deep concentration and even an edge of stern resolution.

'We must be quick, George!' he said, turning to me steely eyed. 'We must get back to the bottom of the rock face, before any of the others get there, and cover the tracks that were left.'

'Wait, no, Jean,' I said, almost spluttering, 'All is lost here, the tablets are gone, what is there to gain from anything other than abandoning our search and heading back to the boat.'

I saw it then, a dark edge of sorrow and disappointment in his face, that I almost missed in my confusion, and which for a second, I thought was directed at me.

'We are betrayed, George,' he said, quietly. 'It is no

coincidence that others have come here, mere days before us, and removed that which we seek. One of us is a traitor, and for reasons known only to himself, does not want us to achieve our goal.'

I simply couldn't believe what he had just said to me, it was like a thunderclap in my brain, completely paralysing me.

I simply looked at him, too shocked to even speak, as I grappled with the idea of what he was saying. It was unthinkable that he could be right about one of our friends.

If the implications of what he was saying affected Jean in any way, then somehow, he'd already managed to move beyond the shock and back into action.

'The only power we have,' he explains, patiently. 'The only thing we can do, is to use this betrayal against them. To make them think we do not realise what has happened.

'Do you understand, George? The traitor must not know they are discovered.'

Though I was still too stunned to think, I indicated I understood what he was saying, and followed him back to the rock face and the main valley.

Somehow, we managed to climb back down the way we'd come to the copse of trees and the valley floor, and then Jean was telling me what to do, and I was just doing what he said.

We scattered the food that had been attracting the birds, and then smoothed out the tracks, removing any other sign we could find, before making our way out of the clearing and back down to where we'd left our packs.

We'd been fortunate that the others had taken a while in their searches, so I had a few minutes to pull myself together, before they turned up.

Realising I was struggling, Jean had kept me busy, sorting out our camp for the evening.

But as the others came into sight a little way down the valley, he took me aside again to make sure I was coping, and wasn't going to give the game away by acting unnaturally.

'George, I know this is difficult,' he began. 'But you have to try and treat everyone exactly as you would have done beforehand, or they may begin to suspect.'

'Who do you think it is, Jean, just tell me that,' I replied. 'Because I can only imagine it is one person.'

'Alright,' he said. 'But then we must put the matter behind us until we have had a chance to speak to those who we know cannot be the traitor.

'As far as I am able to see at the moment, it can only be either Luke or Androus, and I do not think it is Androus.

'It would be madness for it to be Robert or Harrison, as it is down to them that we have undertaken this enterprise. Peter and yourself likewise. I believe if either of you were uncomfortable with what we are attempting to do, then you would simply have told us as much and then gone your own way.

'Equally, Androus has done much work for us, if he truly wished to thwart us and claim these treasures for himself, then he would only need to fabricate the translation upon which we are all so dependent.

'In contrast, we know Luke has concerns about what we are trying to do. It may be that he is honestly just trying to protect us, but for whatever reason he is the person I suspect.'

It hadn't even occurred to me that Jean might have considered me along with everyone else as a possible suspect, but moving past that additional shock, I had to agree with his assessment of the situation, and told him so.

By this time the others had come quite a bit closer, so we left off our camp-making to go and join them.

I felt like a traitor myself putting on a fake smile to greet my friends, and then despondently telling them the news, all the time watching Luke whenever the opportunity provided itself, to see if there was some sign that he was in fact the traitor.

After a while our camp routine took over, and if I seemed a little quieter than usual, then I'm sure everyone put it down to tiredness or our second failed attempt at locating the tablets.

Jean, in contrast was his usual gregarious self, smiling and joking with everyone, even Luke.

Complimenting Harry our cook for the night, and valiantly attempting to stay positive about what we had learned, even though we'd once again failed to find what we were looking for.

ENTRAPMENT

WITH TWO OF US ALREADY 'in the know' about the traitor, it was a relatively easy task to split off our suspect in order to discuss the situation with the others.

Marlow went for his usual evening walk to watch the sunset, conveniently accompanied by Harry with his pipe, at which Jean effortlessly pounced on the opportunity, by distracting the others with the offer of a game of cards.

Taking my cue I declined the game, instead deciding to join Marlow and Harry on their walk.

Neither of them were happy at the news I delivered, but Harry was almost affronted at the idea that Androus could be a suspect, only calming down when I explained that neither myself nor Jean thought it a serious possibility, which left us with Luke.

We walked for a bit longer than usual that night, in order to give both Harry and Marlow time to adjust, time I was only too aware I had not had myself.

I wasn't sure what I was expecting from either of them, they had after all been friends with Luke for far longer than I, but if I was expecting anything, it wasn't compassion.

We'd stopped a little way further up the valley, where its sloping sides lowered enough to be easily climbed, so affording a better view of the setting sun. As we reached our viewpoint, it was Marlow who spoke.

'We shouldn't have allowed him to join us again,' he said, unconsciously rubbing the scar on his right forearm, where he'd been gashed by the lion. 'It was unfair of me to even consider that this journey would be one he could bear to make.'

'No, Rob, that's not being fair on yourself, or on the rest of us,' cut in Harry. 'Luke is, or was, a good friend. It was only fair we gave him the chance to come along.

'Just as,' Harry continued. 'If we're going to be fair to Luke now, then it's my feeling we must also try to understand why he's done this.

'There's no viciousness in this act, no selfishness, revenge or pettiness. When we started all this, beneath that great overhanging rock with the Shaman, none of us really knew what we were doing. And afterward, as I think about it now, maybe it was just a bit too easy for us to not understand how badly that experience might have affected both him and Silvio.'

We talked for a while longer, moving through the sorrow and disappointment until they felt able to face the group without raising suspicions, and then we headed back.

We'd decided to bring Androus and Peter into the fold as soon as possible, and after discreetly letting Jean know the plan, it became simplicity itself to pick an opportunity when they would both have the chance to absorb the information and compose themselves.

Our small world seemed to take on a strange new perspective for me in those first few hours after discovering our betrayal.

As the last vestiges of twilight faded, and a cobalt dark sky filled the gap between the steep gorge walls, I went from feeling almost like a traitor myself, for concealing my true emotions, and putting on a pretence to my friends, to now feeling like one of a pack of circling wolves.

All knowing the truth, and all watching our unsuspecting quarry, while Luke became the helpless lamb in our midst, seemingly oblivious to the change in our natures and the eyes that now followed him.

As we rose the following morning, it was our routine that once again helped me to put the situation out of my mind.

We all climbed up to take a look around the ravaged site and complete the usual sketches and description of the cave, the tablet enclosure and its surroundings, which didn't take long, and then after quickly packing we were off down the valley to the sea and our boat. It was much easier going on the way back, without the many diversions we'd taken on the way up, and though we arrived late in the day, we managed to get back before the light completely failed.

There were no hotels in the village, so we were obliged to split up and lodge in some of the larger houses for the night, which provided another ideal opportunity to make our plans.

We were still intending to go and search for the next set of tablets in Ephyri, just outside the ancient city of Corinth, but now there was a new game to be played. How would we use Luke for our own advantage, whilst at the same time, appearing to pursue our regular course.

Marlow and Harry were lodging with him for the evening so we couldn't consult them, but Jean as ever, was ahead of the game.

'My friends,' he began earnestly. 'The reality that we must face, is that by delaying our departure from Jerusalem, we have given Luke and his accomplices all the time they might want to beat us to our goal here in Crete, as well as to our next destination in Corinth.'

I think we'd all had time enough on our walk down the gorge, to realise that this was a possibility, but it was still demoralising to hear it voiced.

'As such we must now use our time well,' Jean continued. 'We must still make the show of travelling to Corinth to seek out nearby Ephyri. But while we do this, I suggest we must also be researching and preparing for where we will go afterward.

'All the while making the pretence of thinking of nothing beyond our current target.

'Once we have figured out where we go after Ephyri, then I fear Androushan we must ask you to engage in a little manipulation of the facts, in order to deceive both Luke and his accomplices.'

'Yes, I understand you, Jean,' was Androus' simple reply.

'Forgive me my friend, but this may be more complex than you realise,' pressed Jean, apologetically. 'However you alter or change the information that we give to Luke, it must not only deceive him and his accomplices, but also be convincing, as an 'honest' mistake, when Luke finally discovers the truth.'

'I have already provided a translation of much of the material we have to work upon,' replied Androus doubtfully. 'Any kind of significant change or alteration, will look very suspicious.'

'And if we do change something, how can we possibly make it seem like a mistake,' interjected Peter. 'Without Luke picking up on it as soon as we deviate from the route.'

'You are both quite correct,' responded Jean. 'That is why, I suggest we make an 'honest mistake' in our interpretation of the evidence, perhaps blaming the poor copying and transcription by Harrison, while he was assisting with the copying of the scroll.

'In this way,' Jean explained, with that entertained gleam returning to his eyes again. 'We can give Luke's accomplices time to commence their journey, to get ahead of us, which they will surely wish to do. And then at the point where the two routes diverge, we can 'suddenly discover' our mistake, and head off in the corrected direction.'

'Of course!' I said, suddenly realising where Jean was going with his plan. 'If we just change one of the distances or directions, then as long as Luke doesn't get a chance to contact his accomplices, they will already be committed to their route, travelling with all haste in order to get there before us, and unable to double back to the real destination in time.'

'Exactly, George,' Jean replied. 'Such a mistake should give us enough time to find the next set of tablets. Or, in the event our search should go badly again, Luke will still be none the wiser.'

It had been a tiring day, and time was now definitely getting on, so after clearing up a few of the minor points, and talking through the plan for the following day, it was time to rest.

The following day arrived clear and bright, with enough of a breeze to make for a good days sailing, so with the minimum of fuss and delay, we collected our things and prepared to leave the island.

As we were leaving the house we'd lodged in, I stopped off with Jean to thank our host and say goodbye.

Knowing that the gentleman of the house had good English and had been one of those whose pack animals had been left on the other side of the island, I asked if he yet knew when they would be returned to him.

'Yes,' was the rueful reply. 'My son will travel with two other men from the village, to meet those who have our animals in a week's time.'

Luke wasn't nearby, so I thought it safe to question the man further in the hope we might find out a little more about this group that we suspected of being Luke's accomplices.

'Can you tell us who these people were,' I asked, openly. 'In case we should come across them in our travels?'

'Please do not trouble yourself on my account,' our host graciously replied. 'The matter is done with, and should another lady wish to use my animals it shall be on the condition that I accompany them personally.'

'It was a lady who hired your animals?' Jean interjected, with a tone of mild shock in his voice.

'Yes, M'sieur,' was our hosts simple reply. 'A very beautiful and important lady, travelling with two of her female friends and several of their servants.

She was very sure she did not need help to look after the animals, and now see what has happened.'

I was a little bit taken aback to hear that the group we'd suspected of being Luke's accomplices were being led by three young women, so naturally assumed them to be a group of well-to-do young gentlewomen, perhaps touring the Mediterranean for a holiday.

But then our host mentioned how they must have been very important, judging by the level of respect they demanded from their servants. Perhaps even royal princesses he mused, in which case they couldn't be expected to understand the ways of livestock and ordinary folk.

It was such an incidental detail, but it instantly reminded me of the young woman we'd observed Luke with in the park in Jerusalem, and then again entering the side or back entrance of the church. The young lady that both Jean and myself had assumed to be nothing more than a gentle romantic interest.

I don't know why it should have affected me so, but for some reason the idea that she could somehow be involved with Luke's betrayal sent a chill into my spine.

I thought I saw a flicker of recognition in Jean's face too, but his natural composure was, as always, too good for me to be sure.

A minute or two later and we'd said goodbye to our host, and were heading over to the boat where the others had finished loading and were waiting for us.

'Is there any chance it could be a different woman,' I asked him, bluntly, as we walked.

'No, George, there is not,' was his simple reply. 'Now compose yourself and do not attempt to breathe a word of this to anyone else, or even me, until we get off this boat, and we know Luke is not around.'

The granite hardness of Jean's tone was such a contrast with his amiable expression that it would have seemed quite inhuman to anyone else happening to observe him, but to me it was simply my cue to drop the subject and do as he instructed.

Like a dream within a dream we set sail from Crete and travelled north toward that narrow bridge of land that joined the mainland of Greece with its southern-half known as the Peloponnese, and our next two destinations the legendary cities of Athens and Corinth.

As we started the voyage I was constantly scanning the boat and my friends for any untoward sign that might tip off Luke. But after a few hours, as golden sunlight broke through the clouds and the shimmering aquamarine of the passing ocean was revealed, I started to relax into the routine and rhythm of the boat.

I hadn't had the opportunity to update my journal for a few days, it being one of the things I'd left behind on our trip up the gorge, but in my slightly dazed state, now seemed like a good time. So after retrieving it from my things, I went forward to find a comfortable spot in the sun to do a bit of writing.

I'd written no more than a few lines when the thought suddenly occurred to me that I must be careful.

Everyone was aware that I kept a journal, and I never made much of an attempt to secure it, both because it had never contained anything I wouldn't have been happy to say to my friends, but also because I had trusted them all implicitly.

Now, of course, the situation had changed. I could no longer trust Luke, and clearly couldn't just suddenly start hiding or locking my journal away. Which meant I had no option but to exclude any mention of our suspicions or true plans, and instead view the exercise as a form of propaganda.

The situation got to me for a moment, and I briefly considered just throwing the entire thing overboard. But, as I thought about it, and the rashness of the moment passed, I managed to collect my thoughts enough to realise that my journal writing was just as much a part of our routine, which needed preserving for Luke, as anything else we did. So I not only had to resist the temptation to throw anything overboard, but also had to keep up appearances, both outwardly and in the things I wrote about, to ensure Luke didn't find anything to make him suspicious.

With the potential propaganda value of my journal firmly fixed in my mind, I settled down again to write and document the past few days. It was all factually correct, with the odd contrived musing upon our 'lack of luck' from time to time, and the occasional space here and there, just big enough for me to squeeze in a few details at a later date, when the same constraints might not apply.

Although we could have headed straight for Corinth via the great canal connecting the Aegean and the Ionian, we'd decided to make a detour to nearby Athens, under the pretence, that the more comprehensive research resources available at the university, would help us identify where to start looking in Corinth.

We would only be able to drag our feet for so long before making Luke suspicious, but a few days for Androus to work on where we should aim for after Corinth could make all the difference.

Androus also had a few connections in Athens, which enabled us to get access to the university archives and map rooms.

These appeared to be just as comprehensive as those available in his own library, and with most of the students having only recently returned from their winter break, we all but had the place to ourselves.

We knew that Ephyri was one of the ancient names for Corinth or the area around and about, but as with all the other accounts on the scroll, that of Alcathos of Ephyri ended with him removing himself from the local population centre and living as a hermit, in this case a cave by the sea.

Aside from that, the scroll gave very little additional detail. We knew for example that he was able to subsist largely on what he could catch from the sea or hunt from the land, and that he was incredibly strong, and would occasionally earn bread and other necessities by labouring and using his strength for those living around and about.

There were also a couple of references to the sun and views of the great white escarpment behind the ancient city of Corinth. All of which we'd hoped was going to narrow the search area.

It wasn't much, and before we'd discovered Luke's betrayal, we'd hoped that a day or two in Athens would be enough to refine our target areas on a map, before we started our search on the ground.

Now, of course, we wanted to string out our stay in Athens for all it was worth, in order to locate where we would go after Corinth.

We'd been in Athens for a couple of days, spending almost every minute at the university poring over maps of the coast and surrounding area around Corinth, and we'd pretty much identified all the areas that we thought would be worth searching.

Harry and Androus were supposedly going through the details from the scroll again, but in actuality, were devoting their time to the other entries, and deciding which one we should pursue once we failed to find the set of tablets hidden in Corinth.

While we were taking a break, I accompanied Luke, who'd decided he wanted to take a stroll. I thought I'd broach the subject with him, just to see if he was getting impatient or suspicious of the delay.

'You know,' I started, speculatively. 'I'm not sure how much more there is we can do here, the research has helped, but I think we must have taken it pretty much as far as it can go.'

'I think quite the opposite,' responded Luke, without a heartbeat's hesitation. 'Now is the time when we need to be as thorough as possible, especially as we do not know where we might go afterwards should this expedition also prove fruitless.'

'Well, I suppose,' I heard myself say, trying not to sound too surprised. 'But I'm sure once we get on the ground it will be easier to follow the directions, just as it has in the past.'

'Perhaps, George,' he responded, not quite indifferently. 'But could we not have so easily gone astray in the past also?'

It occurred to me as he was speaking, that it was almost as though Luke was trying to delay us, and with that thought my mind immediately started working through the possible motives.

Perhaps his accomplices had failed to take advantage of their head start, either that or they were playing an even more clever game, than we'd thought.

I had to get back and let the others know, so that we could decide what to do next, but I couldn't risk alerting Luke.

We were passing a notice board with posters and leaflets pinned all over it, and in an attempt to buy some time while I thought, I steered us over to have a look.

It was the usual hotchpotch of posters and leaflets all plastered and pinned over the top of one another competing for space.

Books for sale, rooms to let, part time jobs and a couple of advertisements for different events, including a music recital that very evening, by the resident orchestra performing 'An evening of Russian music'.

I can't say I fancied the prospect much, but making

a brave face of it, I pointed it out to Luke and suggested it might make a nice change. The recital wasn't due to start for another several hours, but we had yet to dine, so it didn't leave us long.

Twice Luke tried to get rid of me on the way back to the others, by pretending he needed to stop for a while or go back the way we'd come. I presumed it was to contact his accomplices. so I amiably stuck to him so he couldn't get any time to himself, and eventually we made it back to the others, with me accidentally banging a door or two along the way to alert them of our arrival.

I had a comical few minutes of enthusiastically explaining about the recital, before Harry and Jean finally cottoned on that I was probably just covering and needed to speak to them. But they got there eventually, and after a few more minutes, I ended up walking out with the two of them to supposedly find out a bit more about the programme and where we could buy tickets.

Fortunately Luke seemed to have had enough of my company for a while and decided not to join us, so I was able to quickly outline the conversation I'd had with him and my suspicion that he still wanted to delay us.

'Is it possible the next location still evades them,' mused Jean.

'With a ten-day head start! I'd have said it was unlikely,' responded Harry, filling his pipe as he spoke. 'But we don't know much about who these people are, so perhaps not.'

'If we've wasted days here in Athens, while we still stood a chance of beating them to the tablets in Corinth…' I started, before being interrupted by Harry.

'No, George,' he said kindly. 'There is little point speculating or second guessing ourselves, we must decide what to do now in the situation in which we find ourselves.

'We could be in Corinth by lunchtime tomorrow if we got an early start,' he continued, between puffs to light his pipe. 'And if nothing else we might get a better look at our adversaries, gauge their strength and resources.

'Who knows, while they think we're still in the dark they might even get overconfident and allow us to get close to them,' he mused.

'That is a risky game, my friend,' answered Jean, shaking his head. 'If we were to seem too interested in what they were doing, or even too watchful of Luke, we might give away our only advantage.'

I could tell Jean was thinking about it though, and probably just voicing his concerns as part of the process.

'But then,' he continued, a few seconds later. 'We might still get to the tablets before them, or...' and he hesitated here. 'Be able to take the tablets off them before they got away.'

That idea caused me to take a breath, beating them to the tablets in the first place, and hanging on to them was one thing. Targeting other civilised people, and women at that, who'd, albeit underhandedly, beaten us to our goal, that was entirely another, and I could tell Harry was none too comfortable with the idea either.

'Now, steady on Jean,' he replied. 'I know you're probably just thinking through our options, but if you're thinking about theft, or worse still, using force against these people?'

'I am merely, as you say, thinking through the options,' was Jean's slightly melodramatic reply. 'Opportunities may present themselves, and if they should... I simply suggest it may be useful to have agreed our response.'

I had the distinct impression that he was playing with us now, seeing how far he could push the idea before we caught on. But moving past Jean's occasionally exasperating sense of humour, the idea of packing up and moving to Corinth had clearly started to appeal to him.

There was no way we could know what we might find when we got there, but if we went soon, then we might well stand a chance of finding the tablets first, and ultimately after discussing our options for another few minutes, that was too much of an opportunity to miss.

There was still our pretence to maintain for Luke's sake, and we decided to use the recital to trap him for a few hours, so he wouldn't be able to give his accomplices too much notice of our plans.

It was a bit sticky letting the others know what we were planning without letting on to Luke, but somehow we muddled through, and managed to raise the subject of leaving Athens without it seeming too contrived.

Luke, as predicted, was all for spending a few more days where we were, even suggesting we do a bit of research into where we might go after Corinth, should we again fail to find the tablets, which I couldn't help but be quietly amused at.

Getting him to come along to the recital afterward was a bit more difficult. He clearly wanted to get away to contact his accomplices, but with a combined effort, and much coaxing we finally managed to get him to agree.

It was a pleasant evening in the end, with some surprisingly beautiful music composed by Rachmaninov and Borodin, only moderately diminished by our never-ending game of tag with Luke, who we successfully managed to distract or accompany for the entire night.

The following day we managed to make an early start, but we still had to keep an eye on Luke, and try to contrive the situation so he didn't get the opportunity to send a message to his friends.

With the benefit of travelling by sea, once more on Stephanos' boat, it was a straight-forward journey to Corinth, and involved us simply hugging the east-coast as we travelled south, until we reached the great canal that cuts Greece in half, and joined the Aegean to the Ionian Sea, via the Gulf of Corinth.

I'd never travelled much as a youth, and Greece, like Jerusalem, was an entirely new experience for me, but even those amongst our group who knew Greece well, were still amazed at the scale of the Corinthian Canal.

That great channel carved through the ancient bedrock that divided the north of Greece from the south.

It was an amazing feet of engineering expertise, with the sheer stone wall rising almost vertically above us, the countless layers of stratified stone laid bare for all to see, a geologist's dream.

Harry was of course his usual font of wisdom, telling us of previous attempts that had been made in antiquity to accomplish the same goal of connecting the east and west of Greece, via both roads and canals, so in what seemed like no time, we were through the canal and into the Gulf of Corinth.

It had been a bright, if overcast, day when we'd set out, and as we sailed south to the mouth of the canal, I'd begun to think the warm Mediterranean sun was going to burn the cloud off and give us a dazzling day. But as we emerged from the canal into the more westerly gulf, the temperature seemed to drop a little and the clouds become darker.

Minutes later as we cleared the collection of boats waiting to go through the canal from the western side, the first few drops of rain started to fall.

We hadn't had time to make a hotel reservation before leaving Athens, but we had been given a recommendation from one of Androus' university acquaintances, to try the newly built Grand Hotel overlooking the gulf. So it was to there that we made our way as soon as we got onto shore.

The rain was starting to fall more heavily as we stepped through the front doors, and into the enormous foyer.

As its name suggested, it was indeed a very grand and fine hotel, built in the Deco fashion, with clean, elegant, modern lines, and the bright welcome of polished marble and an airy electrically lit crystal chandelier.

At the same time it was obviously a popular location, even at this quiet time in the season, and for a minute I doubted they'd be able to accommodate us. But a moment later we had rooms and were following our respective belongings up the stairs, escorted by a small army of uniformed porters.

I couldn't help but compare the bright opulence of the Corinthian Grand with the altogether more humble old hotel I'd grown so fond of in Jerusalem.

Here was luxury, a bedroom with a wide curving panoramic window taking in the huge expanse of sea front, a sumptuous bed, sofas, chairs, dresser, all exquisite, even a radio and reading lamps.

In contrast Jerusalem had been almost austere, with its plain furniture and small square window looking out onto the surrounding rooftops.

Then I remembered the difficulty I'd had acclimatising even to that simplicity, after living for so long in the wild. How I would've coped going from Africa to this luxury, I could only speculate and smile.

By the time I'd finished unpacking, the rain was coming down quite heavily and looking like it was staying for the rest of the day. So after a quick conflab with the others, we reluctantly decided to postpone starting our search until the next day, and to just rest up and relax for the remainder of the afternoon.

With little else to do, I decided to try and find a quiet spot in the hotel lounge to watch the rain and maybe do a little reading or writing.

It didn't take me long to find a comfortable window seat, overlooking the sea and the front entrance to the hotel, and for the staff to furnish me with a pot of tea, sadly without the option of the added mint, but with ample milk, and a fine china cup and saucer.

It was a very comfortable spot, and I settled easily into a relaxing daydream for a while, before Jean came over and joined me to read one of the papers.

The day was just beginning to fade, with the dusky light darkening the pale marble of the hotel lounge walls.

I was staring aimlessly out along the sea front, when the setting sun suddenly appeared from behind a distant bank of cloud.

As it did so a flash of light caught my attention, and I noticed the approach of two cars out of the sunset, their rain covered bodywork catching and reflecting the dying sunlight like they were covered in a thousand shimmering jewels.

Moments later, as the cars stopped outside the hotel, and the sun disappeared again behind the cloud, I knew it must be Luke's accomplices.

They were dressed rather boyishly in outdoor attire, strong boots, trousers and jackets, and were attended by half a dozen servants. But as unconventional as their clothing was, it was the air of confidence and command that really singled them out.

Realising who they were must have sent a shock through my frame, for Jean immediately turned to see what I was looking at.

It was an extraordinary thing to suddenly be so close to our so recently discovered adversaries, especially without them being aware of our presence. The shock made all the greater with the realisation that they were staying in the same hotel.

They didn't dally in the pouring rain, but at the same time, they didn't seem to pay the same heed to it that most young women would've done. Walking briskly, but without rushing into the hotel.

As I turned from the window to watch them enter the foyer, I looked at Jean, whose expression held a strangely rueful quality.

'It appears, we will have ample opportunity to study our opponents after all,' he commented, before being distracted by something over my shoulder.

Marlow had descended the main staircase while we

were looking out of the window, and had then been directed by the reception to the lounge where we were sat.

There was no way to warn him, and as he turned to make his way over to us, he came almost face to face with Luke's accomplices. They all stopped, almost bumping into one another, and for an agonising second I thought the game was up.

But then Marlow simply smiled and courteously stepped aside to allow them to approach the reception desk.

The three young women were almost as equally at their ease, only one of them seemed to react as they encountered Marlow. But a second later they had passed, and seemed unconcernedly to be retrieving their room keys.

As Marlow turned away from them and walked over to join us, I noticed he had that faraway look in his eyes again. Yet as he drew closer, I could see he was also smiling.

'Well, gentlemen. It appears our situation has suddenly become much more interesting,' was his simple and rather entertained greeting to us.

'I was just saying the very same thing to George here.' Jean replied. 'We had wanted to know more about Luke's conspirators, and now it seems we will have a great many opportunities.'

'It will be interesting to see how Luke responds,' I interjected. 'When he realises we are all beneath the same roof.'

'Yes, but we must warn Harrison, Peter and Androushan,' replied Jean. 'To ensure the surprises are only those in our favour.'

It was a good point, and as I needed to get changed for dinner, I offered to stop off to see them on the way and pass on the warning.

SIREN SONG

NERVES WERE DEFINITELY IN EVIDENCE amongst my friends as I stopped off to inform them about the arrival of our adversaries.

But for as much as they were nervous about the proximity of Luke's accomplices, they were also curious to find out who these people were. So much so, that a task which should have taken me moments, very nearly made me late for dinner.

When I finally got back to my room, I was ready for a lie down, but something made me think I should take a little more trouble dressing for dinner, so I resisted.

It was probably because of the opulence of our surroundings, but there was also something that made me think it would be worth putting on more of a show for our newly encountered fellow guests.

In any event, I took a little more time getting ready, and before I went back downstairs to meet up with my friends, I felt the fellow in the mirror looked rather the dapper sort, even if I did say so myself.

I discovered the others sat in one of the hotel bars having an aperitif. I was pleased to see I was neither the last to come down for dinner, nor the only one who felt the merit of making a little extra effort for the evening.

Jean and Luke were the others who hadn't come down yet for dinner. While the conversation flowed and ebbed its way around the current news and gossip of the day, Peter leaned over to tell me Luke had decided not to join us for dinner, as he was feeling a little tired.

Nothing else was said on the subject, but I could see in Peter's eyes, he was thinking exactly the same as myself.

Jean appeared a few minutes later, and while we were waiting for our table to be prepared in the dining room, the conversation turned toward the subject of the three young ladies who seemed to be assisting Luke.

'Well, there's no way for us to know how things might go,' Harry observed. 'But it strikes me, we should probably try and get our story straight, just to be on the safe side.'

'A very good point,' interjected Jean, thoughtfully. 'For while these young women know a great deal about us, they may yet hope to learn more, or perhaps create a confusion between us.'

'And we should accomplish all this without also seeming too practised?' asked Androus, with more than a hint of doubt in his voice.

'Yes, my friend,' responded Harry, with an amused air. 'But I know you're far better at this kind of subterfuge than you seem to be letting on. Need I tell our friends here about our trip to Cairo in… '26 was it?'

That caused more than one or two smiles and quizzical looks from around the table, but Androus quickly dispelled any chance of the tale coming out, by graciously conceding the point and bringing the subject back to the present.

Over the next few minutes we agreed the broad outline of what we would tell Luke's accomplices, should we somehow enter into conversation with any of them, including what we were doing, how we'd met, and where we were going. All based around half-truths and the completely fabricated idea of a new archaeological theory that Androus and Harry were supposedly researching.

It definitely wasn't water-tight, but it was all we could manage by the time our table was ready, so it would have to do.

The dining room was possibly the finest room in the whole hotel, with tall, fluted columns lining the walls, and the most exquisite chandeliers and lighting, above immaculately laid tables and a mirror polished stone floor.

We were one of the larger groups in the room, which seemed already full of contented diners, but it hadn't taken too long to get the table, so we must have arrived at just the right moment.

I was again struck by the opulence and comfort of this hotel by comparison with our former 'home' in Jerusalem, and wondered if in time this place might as easily come to feel the same.

We'd ordered our wine, and had been talking and discussing the exquisite menu for half an hour or so when they arrived.

I was just finalising my thoughts about the appetiser, when Jean nudged my arm and indicated I should look down the room.

Somehow it hadn't occurred to me they might look any different to when I'd seen them arrive at the hotel earlier on in the afternoon, but as I gazed down the room and saw them being led to their table by the maître d', I was simply awe struck. Individually I would quite happily have described each as a vision of beauty, but together… As they made their way across the dining room, their combined elegance and beauty gave them almost an air of the divine, condescending to walk amongst we poor mortals for but a few hours.

Several times I had to stop myself from staring, so great was the transformation from earlier on, and looking around the table as they passed, I could tell their appearance had much the same effect upon my companions.

I glanced at Jean beside me, who noticing my look, turned toward me with a very quizzical smile upon his face.

'It seems,' he said musingly, after taking a sip of his wine, 'We may have found the worthy opponents we so fervently wished for all those months ago, back in Africa.'

I was just considering saying something in return when the maître d' appeared between us, and addressed the table.

'Gentlemen, please forgive my intrusion, but the group of young ladies, ask if they might join you for dinner this evening.'

It felt like an electric shock had been passed through my body, so surprised was I. But as I reeled in momentary confusion, it was Marlow who responded with perfect equanimity.

'Not at all, please tell them we would be delighted to make their acquaintance.'

So it was, almost in a daze I saw them join us, chairs and table settings were brought, introductions were offered, and within moments we were sat at the same table as our adversaries.

Confidence and vivacity radiated from them, as they even chose to sit equally spaced between us around the table.

Slowly my shock receded and I felt able to think again. Marlow had done our introductions, and was now saying something about us having travelled for a while and only just arrived in Corinth. Then it was their turn and Selene, who appeared to be the leader of their little group responded in her clear, unaccented English.

They were all apparently Italian, though I might never have guessed from their speech or manner, and were supposedly just travelling for the pleasure of it, indulging their passing interest in mythology and history, by exploring the less well-known areas around each of the places they visited.

I was sat beside Thea, who it seemed was the youngest of the group at just twenty-one. I was fairly sure it was she whom I'd seen start slightly, when they'd unexpectedly come face-to-face with Marlow earlier on in the day. And, as my wits returned, I realised rather un-chivalrously that as such, Thea might be a weak point we could use to find out more about these friends of Luke's.

Amongst the various introductions and chit-chat we somehow managed to order food, but just before we dispensed with the menus, I was able to make a slightly closer study of our new dinner guests.

Selene was certainly the most self-possessed of the group, and while perhaps not as conventionally beautiful as Thea, she was taller and more athletic in appearance. An impression enhanced by the black silk evening gown she was wearing, very low cut at the back and with a simple halter neck that showed off the toned alabaster skin of her long neck and shoulders.

More striking though were her eyes, pale green and framed by her dark hair they had an almost haunting quality of stillness, a stillness I could see almost perfectly mirrored in Marlow's eyes, where he was sat just a couple of seats over from her.

Next there was Miriam, almost as tall as Selene, but where Selene was a moonlit night, Miriam was the sun warmed afternoon. Golden complexioned with dark hazel eyes and shadow-filled wavy auburn hair.

She had the lazy grace and broad knowing smile of a Cheshire cat, and was wrapped in a gown of flowing emerald satin and chiffon.

She seemed to enthral Androus and Jean, who were sat on either side of her, almost immediately.

Finally, and sat between myself and Marlow, was the slighter younger but strikingly beautiful Thea. Shorter than the other two, she was the cool dawn to Selene's moonlit night and Miriam's sun warmed afternoon. With pale blonde hair and large blue eyes, she wore an exquisitely embroidered gown of ivory taffeta.

There was an element of innocence about Thea that I found quite disarming, especially when she smiled.

In fact I think it was only the fact that she was far more interested in Marlow that saved me from becoming completely besotted.

Our food arrived, but we continued to talk while we ate, often about such random subjects, the news and gossip of the day, travel, literature, music. But in and amongst that intoxicating mix of eloquence and charming conversation, my wits occasionally alerted me to the more probing, less innocuous questions.

What our plans were, interests, where else we'd visited, how often we wrote to family or friends.

It was so subtly done, I honestly don't think any of us would've noticed had we not already been on our guard, and even then, I still wasn't sure we weren't giving more away than we intended.

Our conversations fractured and split a hundred different ways during the course of the evening, so I wasn't always able to follow what was being said, but even so, I occasionally caught the sound of our own return fire.

It was equally subtle and unobtrusive, more side arms than artillery, but even so, from time to time, I think our questions might've come close to exposing some of the gaps in their own cover story.

But a miss as they say is as good as a mile, and before too long I realised we were outmatched and lucky to be holding our line together.

Somehow, we managed to make it through the meal without tripping over our rehearsed story too many times, but our interlocutors were only too happy to retire back to the bar with us, where even the sparse cover offered by the meal would no longer be present.

I was beginning to feel despondent about the prospect of us being cornered in some way or another, and was sorely tempted to quit the field, and leave the ongoing campaign to my friends.

But then, as the rain once more hammered against the windows, I started to think about some of the other adversities we'd come through together.

The brigand attack outside Uruk, the torrential downpour in Kenya, the overland trip to Zimbabwe, not to mention the various trials and tests along the way.

For some reason the foolishness of my own thoughts suddenly struck me. I was honestly afraid of what I might inadvertently say to three charming and beautiful young women. When a few months ago I'd been on foot in the African bush, having to wait and hope that some of the most dangerous animals on the planet would just pass by. And suddenly I couldn't help but smile.

'You seem amused, Mr Whitaker,' was Selene's, sudden and rather unexpected comment to me. 'Is it a private thought, or perhaps something you might consider sharing were I to offer you an English penny in exchange?'

I'd suddenly become the centre of attention, but whereas a few minutes before I would've been terrified, now I let my amusement fill me, and as I did so, allowed myself a little Jean-style mischief into the deal.

'Ah, Ms Autieri, you have indeed caught me out,' was my slightly melodramatic response. 'And now of course I shall have to share my thoughts or you will think me very rude.

'I was just thinking,' I continued, with another dramatic pause. 'That here I am, near to one of the most charming ancient sites in the world. The very location, I believe you were saying during dinner, where the daughter of the Titan Oceanus stepped forth from the sea and founded the ancient city upon which Corinth was later built...

'Of course, I've travelled here to stumble around with my dusty academic friends, expecting to find only rocks and with luck a few traces of antiquity. Yet our path crosses that of three beautiful young ladies, possessed of such sophistication and elegance as to suggest their direct descent from the very goddess who stepped ashore here, and I suddenly realised... l had no idea archaeology could be so rewarding.'

It was a truly grotesque piece of flattery, worthy of Jean himself, but it was accepted with much good humour, even drawing a delightful smile from the irrepressibly tranquil Selene.

It also reduced the conversation to mere light-headed conviviality, with much mock indignation from Harry and Androus at being described as dusty, and many equally barbed enquiries from both my friends and Luke's accomplices as to what I was drinking, and how much of it I'd already had.

In no time the evening seemed to have passed, and it was time to retire.

Thea was the first to excuse herself, closely followed by Miriam and Selene. But it was as they were leaving, saying good night to each of us, that I noticed Marlow and Selene finally coming eye to eye.

I'd actually had a few drinks by that point, but as their two gazes finally met long enough to linger upon one another, I could almost feel time slowing.

I wasn't aware of either of them speaking, but for a moment their eyes just seemed to lock upon one another. I don't think anything could have withstood that combined gaze, even the legendary Gorgon would have had to look away, but finally Marlow kissed the hand Selene had proffered to him, and received her smile again in return.

A few minutes later, after we'd finished our drinks we also decided to retire for the evening, and it was as we were making our way upstairs, and I was walking alongside Jean, that I saw him smiling.

'You are quite the dark horse, mon ami,' he said, chuckling quietly. 'One moment I think you are almost drowning in the conversation, the next you effortlessly gather all the attention to yourself, and deliver the most elegant coup de grâce to the inquisition. It was all I could do not to applaud you.'

With that we'd reached the landing and it was time to bid one another good night. I didn't explain to Jean just how close he'd come to the truth, or for that matter how close I'd come to being overwhelmed, for that night I was happy to just enjoy the moment.

DREAMS AND VISIONS

I SLEPT DEEP AND WELL THAT NIGHT, roused only once by a tumultuous storm of thunder and lightning that seemed stuck over the bay in front of the hotel, but after watching the crimson tinged light-show from my bedroom window for a few minutes, I returned to bed and once again fell into a deep and dreamless sleep.

It was a glorious morning when I next awoke, with clear blue skies as far as the eye could see, and the calm untroubled waters of the bay showing no sign of the previous day and night's wet weather.

I'd also got away scot-free from the previous evening's over indulgence, clear headed, bright-eyed and feeling thoroughly refreshed.

Which was just as well, considering the day ahead was likely be an interesting one, if Luke and his accomplices had anything to do with it.

But it was too nice a morning to worry about such things before they happened, so putting them out of my head I got ready for the day ahead.

I was washed and dressed in no time, eager to get out and about in the fresh air, so was pleased to discover everyone else had risen early was well, and headed down to breakfast.

They'd probably gone down without rousing me because they expected I'd be a little the worse for wear, which just added to my pleasure when I strolled into the dining room full of beans and with a hearty appetite.

There was much good-humoured banter round the table as I settled down to some hot coffee and poached eggs.

All censored for Luke's ears of course, and all to the benefit of my previously non-existent roguish reputation. And then with an ease and simplicity, that proved my suspicions completely unfounded, we were setting off once more on our search.

After figuring out that the location we sought was likely to be close to the sea, we'd decided to start our search using Stephanos' boat. From there we could travel quickly and comfortably up and down the coast, using the dinghy to land or get a closer look at the cliffs and shallows.

With no sign of Selene and her companions we simply strolled down to the boat and after setting sail in our own time, headed a couple of miles down the coast to the first point we'd identified on the maps.

The Gulf of Corinth was like a giant horse-shoe as far as we were concerned, with the opening between the heels representing the far western end of the gulf, and the toe of the shoe representing the east where the canal, modern day city, and ruins of the ancient city were located.

One of the main pieces of evidence we had from the account of Alcathos, was his description of the great white escarpment that lay directly behind the ancient city. It was an impressive curved cliff face of pale limestone visible from miles away to the north-west and west.

It wasn't visible to the north, because a substantial headland jutted straight into the gulf just above the canal, hiding the pale cliff face from view for half of the northern shoreline.

All of this, when combined with some of the other references in the scroll, conveniently narrowed our search area to the southern coast of the gulf, a little bit of the headland, and a couple of areas on the slightly more distant northern shore.

As soon as we got under sail, I could feel my eagerness and enthusiasm returning, something I don't think I'd really experienced since we'd found out about the betrayal. But I was still on my guard, and when the situation permitted, I took the opportunity to observe Luke for any tell-tale signs of nerves or furtive behaviour.

Now, as we made our way along the coast, he seemed relaxed and at ease, his normal-self even. But of course that probably meant we were doing what Luke and his accomplices wanted and therefore he felt he could relax.

It was a pleasant, if fruitless day. We made extensive searches of several areas of coastline, either using the dinghy, walking the craggy shoreline or scanning it with binoculars from the boat. All the while, making various positional checks from the boat to confirm lines of sight and directions of light throughout the day.

We also scanned the shallows where we could, in case of changing water levels, or other evidence that might have been lost through the constant earthquake activity in the region. Even doing a little diving, which to our credit, resulted in quite a few interesting odds and ends, all far too modern to be of any real value, but it included a few bits of pottery, some engineering parts and a pair of spectacles.

Of course our own diving and swimming was nothing by comparison with that of the local children, as was amply demonstrated by one group of young boys and girls who we encountered hurling themselves off a small cliff into the azure water below.

The situation becoming more concerning for us, and more entertaining for them, when one the boys didn't immediately appear back at the surface. But just as we were getting ready to go in after him, he appeared again smiling and laughing atop the cliff face, having swum underwater and unobserved by us through a natural arch of stone, and then surreptitiously clambering up some back route to his comrades above.

It was a neat trick, which they demonstrated to us again with huge smiles on their faces by swimming back and forth under the arch like a playful school of fish.

It was a long day, but we'd got a lot done, and while

tired and in need of a hearty meal, it seemed like a good start, with some honest progress, even if only to rule out a few places.

The day was getting on a bit by the time we got back, and when we finally made it down for dinner after getting cleaned up, the sociable aspect of dining was definitely running a distant second to the need for something to eat.

The hotel restaurant was busy again, so rather than wait for a table we decided to eat out at a nearby restaurant recommended by the concierge.

Of course, it turned out to be a French restaurant, run by another one of Jean's irrepressible countrymen, which inevitably lead to all manner of deliberation, exaggeration and enthusiasm from Jean, and it being very nearly midnight by the time we took our leave to make our way back to the hotel and much needed beds.

As a consequence we had neither sight or sound of Selene and her companions, and had inadvertently probably also prevented Luke from being able to contact them too.

Not that I had any illusions about things staying that way, but I couldn't help but wonder what they would be thinking.

The following morning was again warm and bright with barely a cloud in the sky. I was the first one up, so took my turn to rouse the others on my way downstairs.

Luke was already moving around and answered his door straight away. While Jean, slightly the worse for the previous evening's enthusiasm was a little more sluggish than usual.

When I'd given them all a call and received an answer of one form or another, I headed on down to the dining room for breakfast.

The swimming and diving of the previous day had given me more than a few aches in my muscles, but it was nothing serious, and by the time I got to the ground floor, I could already feel my limbs loosening up.

The swimming had also given me a ravenous appetite, so I was already giving my breakfast some serious consideration by the time I crossed the hotel reception on my way to the dining room.

Just then, I noticed through one of the windows at the front of the hotel, the arrival of the two large motorcars which I'd seen Selene and her companions arrive at the hotel in a couple of days before.

But with no sign of the three young women, I concluded they must just be arriving to pick them up.

I didn't have much time, and fleetingly considered skulking away to some quiet corner to simply watch their departure. But then, it occurred to me, if they were about to leave, they could hardly corner me for very long, and even if they did my friends would also soon arrive.

So, after surreptitiously spotting them in the dining room, I picked up a daily newspaper, as though anticipating being by myself, then feigned to notice them as I strolled across the room, before detouring to go and say hello.

They'd finished their breakfast, and were sat with coffee, clearly waiting for their cars to arrive. They were in their outdoor attire again, though now after having seen them in their evening gowns, they appeared distinctly less boyish, and much more reminiscent of the elegant and adventurous Amelia Earhart.

'Why good morning to you, Mr Whitaker,' was Miriam's sunny greeting. 'How nice to see you again, we missed you yesterday.'

'Ah yes, Ms Sabbadini,' I responded, with what I hoped was a relaxed smile. 'I'm afraid my friends rather exacted their revenge upon me yesterday for daring to call them dusty, and we arrived back a little too late to dine at the hotel.'

'Such cruelty,' Selene interjected, with a smile. 'I hope you at least found something worthwhile for all your efforts.'

'Alas no,' I responded. 'Though as I predicted, we

did seem to discover a great many rocks. And yourselves? Did you have a pleasant day exploring?'

I was expecting to see one or other of their drivers coming across the room at any moment, and was keeping a weather eye out for him when I spotted Luke enter the dining room and look around.

On an impulse I decided to try and cause a bit of trouble, so waved to attract his attention and bring him over to 'meet' his accomplices.

'Ah, how fortunate,' I said affably, and being careful not to let anything else show in my eyes. 'Here is the friend we mentioned the other night, a fellow countryman of yours, who was feeling a little run down and not up to joining us for dinner, when we met you.

'Here he is. Luke, come and meet the three young ladies we told you about yesterday morning, the ones who were kind enough to join us for dinner, while you were feeling under the weather.

'Ms Galanis, Ms Sabbadini, Ms Autieri, may I introduce another one of my good friends Mr Luke Cassanelli, not only one of your countrymen, but also from Rome and an intrepid hunter of dusty rocks like myself.'

We exchanged pleasantries for a few minutes during which I watched them all like a good-natured hawk, especially Thea and Luke who I suspected were the two weakest links. But there was very little that gave them away.

Luke was a little stiff both physically and conversationally, while Thea looked a little nervous for a moment or two, but Selene and Miriam were completely at their ease, picking up and juggling the conversation until the others had a chance to recover.

A moment later and the maître d appeared to inform the ladies their cars had arrived. This was closely followed by Harry, which put the shoe on the other foot for a few heartbeats, as I waved to bring him over, hoping that he wouldn't show too much surprise or interest at seeing Luke and his accomplices together.

But my concern proved unfounded as unflappable Harry walked over without batting an eyelid and moved straight into extolling his pleasure at seeing Selene, Miriam and Thea again, especially in the company of Luke, after he'd missed the opportunity to meet them the other night.

A few more moments idle chat and our elegant adversaries took their leave, crossing paths with Peter on their way out, before finally making it to their cars.

I was itching to get rid of Luke so I could talk to Harry and Peter about the effect of bringing them together, but there really wasn't that much to tell, so I decided not to try and engineer the situation.

Jean was a bit slower at coming down than everyone else, which delayed us by a short while, but he didn't want much to eat, so it wasn't all that long before we could once more take to the open water and continue our searching.

We finished off our search of the southern shoreline before moving on to examine the headland right at the toe of the horseshoe, and then on the following day the more distant northern shore.

We even ran into Selene and her group on one occasion, as we were searching the headland, but all was politeness, and we simply waved from the boat and went on our way, as did they.

After another two days of searching, we were beginning to run out of ideas, when the weather turned again, and we were once more confined to the land.

There wasn't a great deal we could do cooped up in the hotel, so I took the opportunity to do a bit of reading and some writing. Eventually getting a bit bored of my room, I thought I'd pop down and see the concierge, to ask if he could recommend anything in the way of wet weather entertainment.

Unfortunately, just as I got there, he was busy dealing with another guest looking for somewhere interesting to go for lunch, so I indicated I would wait, and while he dealt with the issue at hand, I gazed about looking for something to distract me until he was finished.

On a whim, I moved over to look at a tropical fish tank stood in a corner of the foyer, beside a few comfortable chairs.

I'd never been a fan of such things back in England, they'd always seemed remarkably dark, unattractive things, full of dull, bored looking fish. But this one, by comparison, was a corker.

Not only because it was so large and well kept, but also because of the variety and number of brightly-coloured, energetic fish within. There was even a small forest of underwater plants and an artificial reef for the inhabitants to play in and amongst.

But it was as I watched the fish swimming around the reef that they really caught my attention. One of the rocks was obviously hollow underneath, and I could see some of the smaller fish swimming underneath it, leaving the bigger fish to go around the outside.

I don't know why, but the hidden route beneath the rock seemed such a curious thing to think of putting into a fish tank, that I bent down to try and see into the gap beneath it.

As I did so, I was surprised to find the dark underside of the rock, was actually quite well-lit with reflected light from a window on the far side of the tank, and there was even a small silvery air pocket, at which the fish would occasionally gulp as they passed.

It was like an electric charge had been passed through my body, and I stood up rather too suddenly, my head reeling as I tried to grasp the idea that had suddenly leapt into my brain.

I don't know how long I just stood staring at those fish, until eventually I became aware of someone talking to me, and pulled myself together.

It was the concierge, politely asking what it was he could help me with.

I apologised, saying something about it being a

fascinating fish tank, and eventually managed to recall the question I'd originally come down to ask him about.

There wasn't much in the nearby city worth venturing out into the rain for, but he did suggest a small art gallery and studio, that wasn't too far away, and which one of the other guests had recently visited and then recommended.

I thanked him, doubtless still seeming terribly distracted, and then went to find the others, to run my sudden inspiration past them.

I found Peter on the stairs on my way back up. As it happened, he was looking for someone to play cards with, and I'd caught him before he'd found anyone else.

We managed to find a quiet spot, and I ran the idea past him that the place we were looking for could be a cave with an entrance below sea level, like the famous Blue Grotto at Capri.

He knew a bit more about geology than I, and thought it a distinct possibility, especially with the type of rock found around and about the gulf. But of course had no idea how we might find such a place, especially if the entrance was wholly submerged, and not partly visible as it was in Capri.

This would explain why Selene and her companions wouldn't have found the place, even with the considerable head start they'd had on us.

But of course now, the difficulty would be in figuring out how we could search for such a thing without letting Luke know, and hence without turning the search into a simple race.

We needed to discuss this with some of the others, but again, without making Luke suspicious. Between the two of us we quickly hatched a plan.

Peter and I would split up, and then I would find Luke and ask him if he'd like to accompany me to the art gallery I'd just found out about from the concierge. If Luke said yes, then Peter would say he wasn't interested, and while we were out he would discuss the idea with anyone else who hadn't wanted to go. If Luke said no, then we'd simply leave him to it, and find a café or bar along the way.

I was fairly sure Jean would be interested in going, and now as I went off to find Luke, I wished we'd arranged some kind of signal, so we could let one another know when we had something to talk about that we didn't want Luke around for. Maybe I'd suggest it if Luke decided to stay behind.

I finally caught up with Luke in one of the bars having a coffee with Selene and Thea. Now they'd officially met of course they could meet openly without attracting any undue attention.

They saw me coming from a mile off, so there was no chance of catching them unawares, but we'd seen quite a bit of one another over the previous couple of days, what with dinner in the evenings and the like. And we'd also run into one another around and about the hotel when we were all rained off, so it was unlikely anyone was going to slip up now anyway.

I put the proposal to them all, though didn't perhaps sell it as well as I might, made all the less convincing by a heavy downpour just at that moment too, and Selene's very astute question about whether I was sure the place would even be open in such weather.

They wavered for a minute or two, I suspected more out of politeness than any real interest, and then declined.

That gave me a free hand, and after searching out the others, including Peter, we decided to split into two camps so as not to arouse too much attention. Myself, Jean and Marlow would head out to the gallery, while Peter, Androus and Harry would find somewhere to discuss things at the hotel.

TIME AND TIDE

THE GALLERY WAS NOT ONLY OPEN, but turned out to be a wonderful place to shelter from the rain. We'd been dropped off by one of the hotel cars, and upon discovering it open, sent the car back with instructions to return for us later in the afternoon.

Away from the rain and inside it was a positive treasure-trove of local art. Watercolours, sketches, a few oils and some locally crafted items, driftwood scrimshaw, decorative pottery and the odd sculpted piece.

Better still the gallery owner was also a working artist who, while originally from Spain, had walked and studied the local area intensively, and was only too willing to show us around and talk about the various pieces he had for sale, and artists that created them.

Unfortunately, whilst the gallery was thoroughly charming in every way, we had business to attend to and the gallery unsurprisingly had nowhere that could accommodate us.

However, having spent an hour or so looking at his exhibits, we imposed upon the owner to recommend somewhere we could get a bite of lunch, before we went on to examine the rest of his stock later in the afternoon.

We found the place he recommended without any difficulty, a small but friendly little bistro, serving some of the delicious local delicacies along with strong black coffee for Jean.

I was also delighted to discover the mint tea I'd become so accustomed to in Jerusalem, but here served in ornate little glasses.

We settled into a quiet corner and then got down to business.

'Of course!' was Marlow's immediate response, when I suggested the idea of a submersed cave.

'With the more moderate climate of this area the shelter provided by the cave would be of less importance than the inaccessibility created by the water. He may even have lived outside and kept the presence of the cave entirely secret.'

'Alternatively,' responded Jean. 'It may just be that the level of the water has risen slightly, or the shore subsided, and what was once open to the air is now no longer.

'In any event,' he continued. 'The coast is an obvious place to find a cave. Did we not see the young children jumping off the rocks and swimming through some hidden passage, in order to amuse themselves at our concern.'

'If we think it's plausible that there is a cave with an underwater entrance,' I asked. 'Then surely the question we should focus on, is how do we go about searching for it, without Luke realising what we're doing?'

It was a tricky question, but as we discussed it, with the benefit of having now examined most of the coast, we began to put together some ideas of where we should take another look.

For a start we could ask Androus to re-examine the scroll, just in case the wording might convey some additional meaning when considered alongside the idea of an underwater cave.

At the same time we could re-examine those sites we'd originally short-listed, but we could do it when the light would give us the best chance of seeing the submerged rock, or the pale sand of the sea floor.

We probably wouldn't be able to see the cave itself, but it might be enough to limit the number of dives we might have to do to check it out, and that would reduce the chance of Luke guessing what we were really up to.

With a working plan, we finished our lunch, and stopping off at the gallery, finished our tour with the purchase of a few small items.

I even thought Marlow was going to be tempted for a minute when he seemed to get lost in a wonderful sunset seascape showing the gulf from the headland. But like every other sunset, he seemed content to view it only once and then wait for the next.

It often amazed me just how much he enjoyed that same evening ritual. Always the sunset and never its rise, forever bathing only in the fading light.

The weather was just as filthy and horrible when the car turned up to collect us, as when it had left, and after our excursion I found I was only too happy to be returning to the bright light of our hotel with all its many comforts.

I hadn't bought much from the gallery, as I didn't really have much of an eye for such things. But I had found a wonderful pocket-sized photograph that I thought would make a nice memento, and which showed the modern city, and in particular our hotel in the lowering light and long shadows of a late Mediterranean afternoon.

But it was Jean who predictably found the greatest treasures, which he duly brought back to enjoy and show off before sending them on to his home in Paris.

It was an easy matter to catch up with Peter, Androus and Harry once we got back, and to compare notes on how to progress our search.

They'd already thought of re-examining the translation but had been a bit stumped about how to take the search any further. But after hearing our idea, Harry did suggest a rather splendid fabrication we could use to explain our new approach.

Namely that we were starting the search over again, but this time we were going to try and re-enact the conditions mentioned in the scroll, particularly the time of day and the light.

Once we got going it was only a few hours work to draw up a map showing the direction of light at the different times of day. All the same, by the time we'd finished adjusting the information to account for the different times of year, and for each of the locations, the sheer amount of information had become quite overwhelming, and needed a better grasp of geometry than mine to properly understand.

Of course while we could map the direction and rough angle of light at the different times of day, it was all but impossible to match that detail to the surrounding hills and mountains. The height of which could probably add twenty minutes or half an hour on to the dawn in places, and meant we could still have quite a bit of work to do when we got out there.

We staged a mock decision-making meeting later on in the day for Luke's benefit, in a corner of one of the hotel bars.

Initially talking in slightly demoralised tones about our lack of success, and then seemingly coming up with the cover story suggested by Harry.

We'd agreed to be a bit cagey about the prospect at first, with some of us pretending not to be convinced by the merits of such an approach, only to be talked around later on.

Most interestingly, the cover story we were using to explain our search seemed to be something that Luke didn't want us to do, because he again started to become obstructive and agitated at the prospect.

And then of course it hit me, this must be the approach that Selene and her companions were actually using, which was why we kept missing them in the mornings, and why they were occasionally so late in returning. They were already checking different locations at the different times of day mentioned in the scroll, to see how the evidence matched.

It might have only been the cover story we were using to prevent them from guessing the real focus of our search, but it clearly indicated that Selene and her friends were as determined as we were, and not about to easily give up.

And then another idea fell into place for me.

For the entire time we'd been in Corinth, Selene and her companions had been focusing their efforts on the headland to the north of the city. We'd seen them there several times and had even come close enough to wave on one occasion.

Now the thought occurred to me. Suppose their search was more advanced than ours, and by some means they'd narrowed the search area down to the headland.

It was time for me to try out one of the new signals I'd suggested to the others, when any of us wanted to talk about something without Luke.

We hadn't discussed using it when we wanted everyone to play along, but I was hoping they'd get the message and do exactly that.

We'd agreed four signals, to fit the different kinds of situation we might find ourselves in. From pretending to have a stone in a shoe, or to have lost or dropped a hotel key, to the one I was just about to use, which was to pretend my watch had stopped at the very specific time of quarter to three. There was no flicker of recognition from anyone, as I went through the motions, which is as it should have been.

But then while supposedly correcting my watch, I dropped the point I wanted to make into the conversation.

'Perhaps we should compromise,' I said, almost innocently. 'Rather than just starting the entire search again, which Luke is quite right would be a bit demoralising. Why don't we pick one particular area to try out the new approach just to see how it goes? We could start with the headland, that was one of our likely sites to begin with, and you never know we might run into Selene, Miriam and Thea again while we're over there.

They seem to have spent quite a bit of time there,

and who knows, they might even be able to point us toward something of use.'

It was amazing to see the change come over Luke as I suggested this. He'd clearly been winding up to agreeing with me, and then suddenly found himself wrong-footed.

He noticeably stiffened at the sudden prospect, and stumbled over his words for a bit, even slipping back into Italian for a moment, which was something I'd never seen him do before. Then, pulling himself together and finding his feet again he launched into a dozen reasons why the headland would be the worst place to start, including the brazenly impudent suggestion that we might rouse the unwanted curiosity of Selene and her friends!

But my friends seemed to have picked up on my signal, as well as perhaps the implications of Luke's response, and without any further coaxing threw their support behind the idea.

I met up with Jean and Marlow shortly afterward when we could get a few minutes away from the others, and explained my thinking, which they'd largely already figured out.

But it was Jean who particularly liked the irony of the situation, and the possibility that it might be our adversaries themselves who led us to our goal.

'You were quite right, mon ami, this is surely the plan that Ms Autieri and her friends have been working to all along,' he said, thoughtfully. 'And if they could be so far ahead of us in this respect, why not also in terms of the location?'

'Absolutely,' added Marlow. 'But if Selene and her friends are convinced that the headland is the location, then they will pay particular attention to us while we search there, and it won't take long for them to figure out we're really looking below the water.'

He was right of course, we might be able to hide the real focus of our search from Luke, if we were to start somewhere else. But picking the same area that Selene,

Miriam and Thea were searching meant we were bound to be more closely scrutinised.

It was definitely a gamble, but we had no guarantees with anything, so we would start with our new search as soon as the weather permitted.

After another whole day of wet and desultory conditions the weather finally changed, and we arose early on the Friday morning, an hour before dawn, to discover the day promised to be cool, but with clear skies and only a gentle onshore breeze.

We needed to be at the headland as soon after sunrise as possible, if we were to make the most of the light that would let us see down to the seabed, while at the same time giving credence to our cover story.

All of which meant a rather gruelling start to the day, but after a false start the previous morning, it felt good to be up and out, even at such an unreasonable hour.

We'd warned Stephanos that we would want to make an early start, as soon as we got a dry day, and true to form he had the boat ready and waiting when we got there, so that in no time we were off and moving over the dark water toward our destination.

I'd again thought we might run into Selene and her friends at some point, but yet again they surprised me by just letting us get on with things without any attempt at hindrance or delay.

It took less than half an hour for us to get to the headland once we cleared the other boats moored in the marina. Then it was just a short wait before the first spears of light appeared over the horizon to hit the rocky shore of the headland behind us.

We had to adjust things to account for the different arc of sun at this time of year, but even taking that into account, I was still surprised by the angle at which the light appeared. You can never quite get a true impression of how things will work out when looking at a map, even a detailed one. But I'd judged the headland to be much more east-west than it was, and therefor presumed it would catch much more light first thing than it actually did.

It was still a glorious sight and no mistake, but I think it was clear to all of us that we'd over estimated the number of places we should include in our search area.

We moved up and down the few miles of coast on the southern edge of the headland, checking and re-checking the places that had both a view of the great cliff face behind Corinth, and which were also illuminated by the first rays of the rising sun.

As the sun grew higher and moved more westerly it bathed more of the coast in its warmth and light, but for that first half hour of the day the sun's rays fell only directly on the handful of places we'd seen picked out at first light.

It was an interesting discovery that caused us to once more question Androus about the translation of the scroll, and specifically the details concerning the description of dawn. But he was adamant that the description he'd translated was emphatically that of first-dawn, or literally the time before 'the ball of the sun had fully emerged from behind the distant mountains.'

With no further dispute possible, and only a handful of locations to search, it was just a question of deciding where to start.

We'd sailed right up to the tip of the headland, which also happened to be one of the most promising looking sites, with a small bottlenecked cove comprised of a tiny golden beach surrounded on all sides by craggy rocks and steep cliff faces.

It was as good a place to start as any, so after getting the dinghy out and dropping Harry and Jean onto the beach, Marlow, Peter and I rowed back out to examine the surrounding cliffs and rocks, while Luke and Androus stayed aboard Stephanos' boat to examine the shore through binoculars.

In truth the light would have been at too shallow an angle if we'd tried to start our dinghy search any earlier, as the sun needed to be that bit higher before it penetrated the water rather than just reflecting off the surface.

There was still a good deal of squinting and peering at the water, even when the sun got into the right place.

We'd been searching for only about half an hour and had just come alongside the mouth of the little cove near to where the boat was anchored, when Marlow spotted it.

We'd already been past this spot once when we'd rowed out of the cove, but the light mustn't have been quite right.

Now as Marlow told us where to look, it seemed quite clear.

'We're a bit too close to the boat for me to point,' he began, 'but you can see the pale sand of the seabed extend right into the cliff, in fact it looks like there might even be two caves rather than one.'

'Luke appears to be interested in what we're doing,' commented Peter, who was on the oars. 'It might be worth waving your arms around a bit as though you're talking about a bit of the cliff-top.'

We followed his advice without looking around, but continued to discuss what to do next.

'It seems a bit early to be getting into the water,' I ventured. 'We could come back later if this still seems a likely spot.'

'No, this is about as likely as it gets,' said Marlow looking thoughtfully at the shimmering area of pale blue sea-bed. 'This is where I'd choose if I wanted to remove myself from everyone society.

'It's remote, and has little to attract anyone, but with that sheltered beach to keep a boat on, you could be back over to Corinth in under an hour, perhaps less with a sail.'

'Yes, I'm with Rob on this one,' said Peter. 'That looks like a cave, and this looks like the perfect location, we might as well get in there.'

Enough had been said. We moved the little boat as

close into the cliff as we could, which wasn't that hard as the water was quite calm on this side of the headland, got our masks on and then it was just over the side.

Marlow went first, slipping into the cool water over the back of the boat, but I followed him a few seconds later.

The water was a little bit cooler than it had been a few days earlier, on account of the overcast weather, but it was still warm enough for us to not have to worry about a chill, as long as we kept moving.

I deliberately didn't look round to see if Luke was still paying attention, and then after taking a couple of deep breaths Marlow was gone. I felt the adrenaline kick in then, and a second later I was following him through the sapphire water.

There was no point discussing what we were going to do, and even less once I saw what lay beneath the water.

From the surface it was fairly clear that the sandy sea bed extended into the cliff face. But the second I got below the water I could see clearly, as the coruscating light of the morning sun penetrated the water it illuminated the shadowy depths of a large cave within the cliff.

The top of the cave mouth was only just below the surface, maybe four or five feet, and Marlow had already swum down far enough to see further in.

As I swam down to join him, I could see he'd hesitated for the briefest of moments before he was off, into the cave.

A moment later I could see why he'd hesitated. It was a wondrous sight, the light filtered through the cave mouth filled the interior of the cave with a pale light. But this wasn't the only shaft of light, there were others that must've been coming from other openings further along the cliff.

Each shaft of light waving and shifting slightly as the waves outside rose and fell, refracting the light a dozen different ways, and giving the sea bed inside the cave an almost theatrical stage illumination.

Not only that, but the entire effect was mirrored in the pale silvery underside of the water inside the cave, which also indicated there was air.

I could have gazed on that spectacle for an age, but Marlow was getting ahead of me, so with no further hesitation, I swam after him.

It was only a short distance, but it was far enough for me to be concerned about swimming back if the air was no good. So, as Marlow made for the surface, I held back momentarily, in case he suddenly came back down or started to show signs of distress.

But instead, I saw him rise slowly to the surface of that silvery mirror, extend a hand before him, which disappeared through, followed by his head and shoulders. His arm came back down and as he started to tread-water I could tell he was looking around at the inside of the cave.

Following, I emerged beside him into the cave, and was again stunned by the beauty of our surroundings, though this time it was the beauty above the water.

It was a biggish space that swelled and grew as it went further back into the hillside. In addition to the limpid light reflecting from the pale sand of the sea bottom, up through the water around us, which gave the interior a wonderfully tranquil, almost magical appearance, there was a single shaft of light coming straight through a narrow fissure in the rock face.

Together, there was more than enough light to see around the entire cavern, which I was still overwhelmed by the wonder of, when Marlow pulled my attention back to our purpose.

'George,' he said, simply. 'Do you see it, over on the far wall?'

I turned around in the water to look where he indicated, and could clearly see the familiar shape of the ancient clock symbol carved out of the wall above a ledge at the back of the cave.

'I do indeed,' I said, feeling my heart begin to race.

We swam over quickly, aware that our friends would be getting concerned about us if we didn't go back soon, but just needing to take a quick look first.

The ledge was just above water level, and as we climbed out onto it, I could immediately see that it had been shaped to make it more regular and probably more useful, including what may have once been a tunnel leading to the surface.

But I could also see that the site was badly damaged, and there was a great deal of broken stone, including pieces of lapis lazuli strewn all over the ledge.

I saw Marlow bend down and pick up a small piece of the blue stone, and understood exactly the expression on his face as he turned it over in his hand and saw the remains of those deeply incised symbols.

I swam back out of the cave, taking Marlow's mask with me so that someone else could use it to swim in, feeling my enthusiasm and eagerness once more waning, but desperately trying to hang on to the hope that somewhere in the wreckage there might be something we could salvage.

We'd clearly been a bit too long in the cave, and when I surfaced back beside the boat, I found Peter getting ready to go into the water himself, and everyone on Stephanos' boat gathered on the near side rail looking expectantly towards the cliff.

I explained the situation briefly to Peter as he helped me back into the dinghy, and then rowed us back over to the main boat.

Peter hadn't told them anything, so as he rowed, we quickly put an excuse together for why we'd both gone into the water, where we'd just happened upon the cave, just to make sure we were consistent with our cover story.

As we got back on the main boat, I was immediately assailed with questions about what was going on, to which I was finally allowed to answer.

'It's the most extraordinary stroke of luck,' I began.

'We thought there was something unusual about the sea bed, it seemed to be piled up against the cliff face below the water, and we thought maybe the sand had built up to cover something, so we went down to have a look.

'But it wasn't a build up at all, it was the entrance into a large cave. There are carved walls and pieces of lapis. This is it, this is the cave of Alcathous that we've been looking for.'

I really didn't want to get into any more detail until we'd had a chance to pick up Harry and Jean from the shore, but Luke just kept pressing me.

It was clear he didn't know what to think yet. Horror that we'd found the cave before Selene and the others, or relief that it seemed as though the tablets had been destroyed. His emotions were so clearly written upon his face, that for the first time since we'd discovered his betrayal, I found it hard to even look at him.

Fortunately, Androus was there with his much more pragmatic approach and questions that made me concentrate on the work to be done.

I went back into the dinghy with Peter to retrieve Harry and Jean from the cove, which also gave me the opportunity to vent my anger about Luke, and meant I could brief them all properly on the way back, not only about the cave but also about Luke.

Androus didn't really fancy trying to make the dive, as he was not only a poor swimmer, but also seemed to be getting a bit of a cough, but Luke was unfortunately more than happy to have a go.

Neither Harry or Jean were particularly keen on the prospect of an underwater swim, as neither were particularly strong swimmers, but with the aid of a couple of ropes we managed to get them inside.

Marlow had done what he could while we were outside, and had already collected together quite a few of the larger fragments of lapis, but he'd been thwarted by some of the large pieces of stone that still made up much of the rubble.

Once Harry had got his breath back and was able to assess the situation, he took control and brought order to our search, starting with a more thorough search of the area and of course the documentation.

Getting the paper in and out in a dry state proved an unexpected challenge, until Stephanos remembered he'd got a water-tight aluminium map case we could use.

After we finally got the basics out of the way, Harry tried to piece together a theory of what we were looking at, and what might have happened.

'There's a whole load of damage here that's for sure,' he began, as he re-examined the debris pile and the wall at the back. 'But this, this looks like natural damage to me. Maybe subsidence, or an earthquake or both.

'And it looks old too, there's evidence of lichen growing over some of the broken edges, and much of this dust and dirt is not only settled, it's compacted as well.

'All of which can only really happen over a considerable period of time.'

'Precisely what I was thinking,' chipped in Peter. 'Some kind of ground movement caused the tunnel and part of that back wall to fall first, dislodging the cover stone and the tablets from their carved housing. Then, judging by the presence of this large rock on top of these two which look like they've fallen from the ceiling and the wall, I'd say at least this section of wall fell next, which undermined the ceiling above and caused that to fall later.'

'So if there's anything left of them, then the tablets could be underneath all of this?' I asked.

'It's possible,' answered Harry. 'Some may have escaped over the edge into the water, so we should probably check there first. Then we remove the rest of this stone one piece at a time.'

It hadn't occurred to me to look in the water, so while the others were figuring out how to tackle the larger blocks of stone, I went back in with Peter, and we started to search the sandy sea floor.

The sand was very fine, and in no time visibility was down to nothing, but between us we managed to find a large piece of one tablet, and another, almost entirely intact barring a chip out of one corner. But their time in the water had come at a cost, and while they were still intact, they were worn quite badly in places, leaving only about fifty percent of the writing still easily legible.

Similar results were achieved on the ledge. As the debris and stones were cleared away, the remains of the tablets were gradually recovered, but only one tablet came out entirely intact, miraculously preserved from the falling rocks.

The rest, were either entirely destroyed or reduced to an intricate jigsaw puzzle of fragments that might take years to put together again.

But at least we'd got something, and there was always the chance that the one undamaged tablet held something significant, or might give us a pointer to one of the other locations where another set of tablets was hidden.

Much as he tried to conceal it, Luke was definitely not happy that we'd come away with so much, and after a while simply fell silent, doing what was asked of him, but nothing more.

It was an exhausting day, made all the worse by the need for so much swimming back and forth, in order to carry what we'd recovered out of the cave.

If we'd thought about things before we started, we'd have brought some more appropriate equipment, instead of having to make do with the things we managed to cobble together from our belongings, or the items aboard Stephanos' boat.

At one point, we even found ourselves bringing the remains of two tablets out in knotted handkerchiefs.

The cave was particularly hard on Jean and Harry, who just weren't up to the swimming, but they stuck it out until there was nothing else they could help with, and then they swam out and stayed on the boat, collating what was brought out.

I was completely done-in by the time I swam out of the cave for the last time, with the map case holding the drawings and observations of the site. And it was really just a toss-up as to whether I had something to eat first, or got some sleep.

We'd been here since before dawn, and barring a couple of short breaks for something to eat, had worked through the entire day, to excavate the site and retrieve everything of interest, only finishing our work as the sun started to go down over the western end of the gulf.

We didn't talk much on the way back, we were all so tired, barring Androus who was immediately immersed in the study of what we'd retrieved.

Trusty Stephanos managed to rustle up a hot drink for each of us before we set off, which we had with a packet of biscuits that someone had thought to bring.

I think Marlow was as tired as the rest of us, but as the boat turned southward and we started back to Corinth he once more went through his timeless evening ritual.

Hauling himself to his feet, and taking his tea with him, he carefully stepped over and around everyone, to the back of the boat where he could watch the sun as it sank beneath the distant horizon.

The rest of the evening became a bit of a blur, as the momentary boost from the tea and biscuits wore off, and all my muscles started to cool down and stiffen up.

I remember getting back and bathing, and then Jean almost forcing Peter and myself to join him for a meal in his suite, before he'd allow us to go off to our beds.

Before I turned in, I also remember becoming aware of a change in the atmosphere.

There was a small outpouring of energy and activity from Androus, a weary underhandedness from Luke, as he, no-doubt, forced himself to go and tell Selene about our day. But there was also a hint of stress coming from Jean, who seemed anxious about something.

I wasn't sure if it meant anything, but just as we were saying goodnight, Marlow happened to pass by.

He was himself ready to turn in, but it was as we all said goodnight and left to go to our respective rooms, that I noticed a hint of concern and worry in Jean's eyes as he watched Marlow leave.

It wasn't the time or place to try and pursue it further, but even as I drifted off to sleep, I could sense the concern I'd seen on Jeans face taking root in my own mind.

SMOKE AND FIRE

OVER THE NEXT DAY OR SO, as Harry and Androus started work on the transcription and preservation of the tablets we'd pulled out of the underwater cave, the waiting became an agony.

If we'd got lucky with what we'd retrieved, then our search could be over, and we could start making plans for the next phase of our journey, to find the first great temple of Ziusudra, and the place where these extraordinary individuals went after abandoning their mortal lives.

Alternatively, if we weren't so lucky, then the fragments we'd retrieved might hold nothing more than the detail of Alcathous' life, or his discovery of the African temple.

If that were the case, then I didn't want to think about what we'd do next, perhaps move back to Jerusalem, or Athens, maybe even stay where we were.

There was nothing else for it but to try and keep busy, and try not to pester Androus too much while he worked.

Thankfully the weather stayed fine, so I was able to

get out of the hotel and do some walking and sight-seeing. I even tried to start the habit of going for a swim in the mornings, having discovered I rather enjoyed the exercise and feel of the water while we were exploring the underwater cave.

We still didn't see much of Selene and her friends, who seemed to be keeping up the appearance of their routine, but I was sure they weren't going to just accept defeat.

It wasn't until just before lunch on the third day that we found out what form their action would take.

I'd returned from my morning swim invigorated, and after wolfing down a hearty breakfast I was talking to Peter about the prospect of heading out of town, maybe for a stroll around the ancient acropolis, when we were interrupted by one of the hotel staff with a message from the manager.

Apparently, there was a matter that required our attention downstairs in his office.

It immediately raised my suspicions, and looking at Peter as the messenger left us, I could see he was thinking the same thing.

We arrived at the manager's office just as Luke and Jean got there, and after exchanging a quizzical look or two we entered the room.

Inside we found Marlow and the others sat on the opposite side of a large desk from the hotel manager and two other Greek men in plain suits.

It was a delicate situation, but the hotel manager was the very soul of tact, and after introducing the two men with him as police officers, one Inspector Laskari and his assistant, he proceeded to try and 'clear up the obvious mistake and confusion that must have occurred,' by asking the inspector to explain exactly why he had come.

The inspector was a man of average height and build, but with a polite bookish manner, and excellent English, who reminded me of Androus, but without the added flair and exuberance of our Armenian friend.

'Gentlemen,' he began, in a good-humoured tone. 'As Mr Alexandrakis has suggested, I'm sure this matter can be settled quickly and easily, if you will be kind enough to answer a few simple questions for me.

'As you may know, our government here in Greece has experienced some difficulties over the past year, as a result of a clouded decision at our last national election, and the unwillingness of one of our less experienced political parties to help find a compromise.

'Unfortunately, this situation has made the great historic treasures of our troubled country seem all the more tempting to admirers and collectors, who wish to remove items from our soil.

'Now, the customs service where I am engaged, has recently received information indicating that your group may have come into the possession of a small number of artefacts, perhaps unaware that our law forbids the unlicensed excavation and removal of such items.

'As such, I have come here today to ask you to hand over any artefacts you may have unknowingly removed and to desist from any further excavations of this kind.'

I could feel a knot forming in my stomach as the inspector talked to us. And I could only imagine the inevitability of us having to hand over the tablets to this bureaucrat, so he could bury them on a shelf in an anonymous cupboard, ignored and inaccessible for who knows how long.

Even with Androus and Harry's impressive academic credentials it could be years before we'd get permission to see them again.

But I'd failed to consider that Androus and Harry might not be quite so easy to put off.

'Inspector Laskari,' Harry began. 'I have to confess my surprise at what you've just told us. For, as I'm sure you know, both myself and Dr Chukjadarian here have worked in the field as archaeologists for our respective institutions

221

for a great many years. Including quite substantial amounts of time and work on the Greek mainland, islands and throughout the Peloponnese, and I have never encountered this legal restriction of which you speak.

'Have you, Dr Chukjadarian?' Harry enquired, innocently of Androus.

'I have not, Dr Sutherland,' responded Androus. 'But perhaps it is a very recent addition to the legislative body, something which I would have imagined my colleagues at the University of Athens would have mentioned when we stopped off there on the way here.'

It was like watching the inspector swallow something that tasted bad, as Harry and then Androus so unsubtly showed off their credentials before him.

He must have come unprepared, thinking perhaps he was just dealing with tourists. But to his credit, he collected himself quickly, and bristling slightly at being caught out, he immediately straightened his posture and adopted an altogether more formal tone.

'Yes, well, some allowances are made for the work of recognised institutions, especially in the pursuit of academic excellence, but even then, the treasures of Greece must still be safeguarded, and the due revenue from their export collected.

'Is it your assertion that you are here as part of an authorised and official dig, conducted on behalf of a recognised institution?'

I knew neither Harry nor Androus would be prepared to claim the work we were doing was for either of their institutions, and again I could feel my heart sinking.

But Harry and Androus continued to argue from our side, forcing the inspector to do more thinking on his feet.

Still it was clear he wasn't going to let the matter go, and eventually we had to agree to him taking the tablets back to Athens for the Customs Service to have them appraised by an expert from the university.

Worse still, he knew about the scroll and other tablets we had with us, and insisted they also be taken for appraisal.

This, despite the hotel manager's own testimony that the items in question had been put under secure lock and key on the day of our arrival and not been touched since.

For a moment I had visions of us having to make a run for it, back to the boat before he would have time to call for reinforcements. But Androus also knew how to apply the pressure.

'As you wish, inspector,' he said, with a very business-like formality. 'If you are insistent upon this ludicrous course of action, then you will of course be prepared to give me a full financial guarantee for the value of the artefacts you wish to remove, authorised by a signatory of your Prefecture.'

'Yes, yes, Dr Chukjadarian, that will not be a problem, I'm happy to give you a receipt myself, and take full responsibility for the artefacts while they're in my care.'

'Forgive me, inspector,' responded Androus with perfect equanimity. 'I don't think you quite realise the nature of the artefacts we're talking about. Not only are these artefacts made in part of semi-precious materials, they are also to the best of my knowledge totally unique in the world. And certainly when they were examined by myself and my colleagues in Jerusalem, before bringing them to Greece, we estimated their value, conservatively... to be in the region of thirty to fifty thousand dollars.'

My heart skipped a beat at this pronouncement from Androus, surely he couldn't be serious. The inspector would be lucky to earn the equivalent of a hundred dollars a year. So, as shocking as it was to me, it must have been unimaginably so for him.

His face noticeably blanched at the idea, and his assistant, who must have been a fairly new recruit, looked like his legs were going to buckle beneath him.

The hotel manager looked a little unstable too, though that was probably at the thought of his own liability in agreeing to safeguard the artefacts for us in the hotel strong room.

'I… I see,' said the inspector clearing his throat and looking distractedly at the table before him. 'You are correct, I had not realised the value of the items in your possession.

'But this is all the more reason for them to be appraised by an expert trusted by my service.'

'Perhaps, if we were to accompany you to Athens,' suggested Androus?' You have a car at your disposal?

'Good, then might I suggest myself and another member of my party travel with you to Athens, to properly safeguard our valuable property.

'The artefacts can be appraised by your expert in our presence, and then when everyone is satisfied that these items are in no way part of your country's historic estate, we can travel back in the same fashion.

'If your expert is available, we could be there and back in under three days.'

Somehow, even though he was completely unprepared, Androus had managed to take control of the situation, and the inspector was only able to agree to his terms.

The arrangements were quickly made, with Peter volunteering to go along as well. Apparently, he'd studied the law for a couple of years, before moving on to engineering. He conceded he was no expert, but was confident he'd be able to help out if need be.

It was going to be a long drive to Athens, and probably a lot less comfortable than Stephanos' boat. But nobody wanted to try and open up the negotiations again, so we agreed to leave things as they were, and they set off less than an hour later in the police car.

Androus and Peter guarding the box containing everything we'd found.

It could've been worse, but we'd still been out-manoeuvred by Selene and her friends, and now we faced an even longer wait before we'd find out whether our latest find was going to be of any value.

The entire thing seemed to put Marlow into a particularly dark mood, and as soon as Androus and Peter had left in the inspector's car, he quickly excused himself and left without another word.

I could tell Jean and Harry were concerned about the situation, but there was nothing to be said, especially in front of Luke, who now seemed intent upon lingering, no matter what.

This being the case, I decided to continue with my planned diversion for the day anyway, and get out for a walk around the old acropolis.

So, after skulking around for a while longer, I arranged for a car to drop me off, and left them all to it.

It would have been nice if Harry had come along to the Acropolis and once more acted as guide and educator, as I had no doubt he'd have been able to enrich my visit with his knowledge and understanding of the place. But it was not to be, and instead I had to settle for the nice views, elegant ruins and my own imagination.

It was a wonderful place, well worthy of a visit, and I thoroughly enjoyed exploring the ruins and escarpment top, before making my way back across the bottom of the great white cliff-face.

The exertion and fresh air had completely taken my mind off everything back at the hotel. In fact, it was only as I made my way back to rendezvous with the car that I once more started to think about what we were going to do.

I'd arranged for the car to come and pick me up fairly late in the afternoon, so I wouldn't have to kill too much time before dinner. So, after getting back to the hotel, retrieving my key from the desk and checking for messages, I'd just got to the top of the stairs along from my room, when I saw Luke hurrying down the corridor with an expression full of anxiety and consternation.

He was almost upon me before he even realised I was there, so preoccupied was he with whatever was troubling him.

Flinching as he saw me, and stopping directly beside me on the staircase, he almost seemed frenzied as he spoke.

'I cannot, will not, go through that again,' he said, almost reaching for me as he spoke, eyes roving wildly around and barely settling upon me. 'To even contemplate such a thing is a… is a… Stop him George, plead with him, he cannot know what he is doing.'

I tried to get him to explain, but he just moved past me, unwilling to stop, almost not recognising who I was again.

As I watched him go down the stairs, concern now rising in my own mind as to what could have provoked such a reaction, and then moving past my own room, I made for Jean's. If anyone could tell me what was going on it would be him.

He was waiting patiently inside, sat in a comfortable armchair looking out of the window at the sea and surrounding hills of the bay, just as the light was beginning to fade.

He smiled a welcome as I entered, immediately guessing what I was about to say.

'You have just seen Luke, have you not?' He asked politely, and then continued as I confirmed I had.

'He is… not happy about a decision that Robert has made,' he explained. 'You remember, my friend, when we were back in Jerusalem just after Christmas. The snow and ice had covered the place and we were waiting for the weather to break before we could head off to Crete?

'You caught me in a rather poor mood, just as I was preparing to go out to run an errand to the Al-Dabbagha suq, yes? Well what I could not tell you at the time, is that the errand was one I had agreed to run for Robert.

'Although, perhaps it would be more accurate to

say, an errand which I had asked him to allow me to perform for him. To procure a selection of… substances, with the aid of which he could recreate, or at least better remember the dream visions he had in Africa.'

'You mean some variety of narcotics?' I asked, rather warily.

'I once had a little knowledge of these things,' Jean conceded with a reluctant nod. 'As a result of some time I spent in the orient as a young man.

'Enough knowledge for me to be able to speak with several of the fakirs and dervishes plying their trades within the suq, and to be taken seriously.

'Anyway, before the visit we made together, they had agreed to provide me with the components of a powerful potion used only in a rare mystic rite. It was this powder that I collected when you insisted upon accompanying me, and which I have subsequently been holding for Robert.

'For some time now I have tried to dissuade or discourage him from its use, to counter his increasing willingness to take the risks involved.'

I was shocked to hear what Jean was telling me, it must have been three months since the day he was talking about, which was a disconcerting amount of time for him to have kept such a secret, let alone to have discussed and argued with Marlow about it.

But it was the idea of the drugs that sounded particularly risky to me, especially while there were still other channels of research we could follow.

These were after all still powerful narcotics even if they didn't have the desired effect, what would happen if they simply didn't work, would it mean trying a string of potentially damaging concoctions one after another.

All of which I was open about and told Jean as much in no uncertain terms.

'Yes, yes, you are quite correct, mon ami,' he responded, patiently. 'But if I had not done this for him, I am certain he would have found a way to pursue it himself. And at least this way I have been able to moderate, and yes, delay him from following this path.'

'You mean he's wanted to try this before now,' I asked, slightly surprised that I'd had no suspicion.

'I have attempted to be discreet, partly because of the reaction I thought it might cause in Luke, but also because I hoped it might somehow be avoidable. But Robert is acutely aware of the visions fading within his mind, and it has taken every scrap of my persuasion to get him to delay this long.

'Now, of course, I have failed, and he is determined to make his experiment this evening.'

The others it seemed were already preparing, and Jean had just been waiting for me to return to tell me of the plans.

I don't know why it had popped into my mind, but that very afternoon, while I'd been walking back along the base of the escarpment, I'd found a small overhanging area of the cliff face, with a shallow depression in the ground below.

It was an idyllic little spot, that would be perfect for a summer nights camping, the overhang sheltering those below from falling rocks, as well as reflecting back the heat from a fire.

It must have been the thought of a fire beneath the overhang, that made me think of Africa, and our encounter with Nelion beneath that much greater rock face covered in shadow-dancing figures.

I felt the hair rise on the back of my neck, as I explained about the place I'd found to Jean. At the same time telling myself, it was just coincidence I'd been thinking of that particular experience only a few hours earlier.

The others thought the place I'd found would be ideal, so with nothing more to say, we got on with our preparations. It was probably going to take us an hour to get there, more if we had to try and find our way in the dark, so we had to do things quickly.

After the last storm the weather had been warming up, and didn't look like it was going to deteriorate for the next few days, but we still needed to sort out bedding, food and a few other bits.

Jean had already assembled a small medical kit with purgatives, stimulants and charcoal, and then of course there were a few other precautions to take and make, and we were ready.

The afternoon was turning to twilight by this point, so there wasn't time to do much thinking about whether we were doing the right thing, and from the sound of it there was no point bringing the subject up with Marlow again. If Jean had finally failed to dissuade him then there was little the rest of us could hope to achieve.

Luke, as expected, was absent, so had we been in the mood for further conversation about our plans it would have been an ideal time, but somehow no-one seemed to feel much like chatting.

The car dropped us off, where it had picked me up only a couple of hours earlier, and a few minutes later we were retracing my route across the bottom of the cliff face. The light noticeably fading as we walked, but the last vestiges of sunset providing just enough light for us to find the spot I'd suggested.

The routine of making camp came back quickly, and with the familiarity came the conversation, and the reminiscences, and in no time we had a small fire going, along with a supply of wood for the rest of the night.

We'd sorted everything out for the evening, and were just standing around having a light bite of supper, when Harry suddenly started slightly, and turned as though to listen.

'Did you hear it,' he said, suddenly pale in the firelight.

'What is it, my friend?' asked Jean concerned.

But it was Marlow who responded. He was stood

on the opposite side of the small fire from me, and as he answered I could see he was looking past us all toward the far horizon. 'The drums,' was all he said.

And then I heard them.

Soft and distant, fading in and out, just as they had in Africa, as though borne on fickle winds that changed and danced with the starlight, one moment bringing the sound to us, the next casting it in another direction.

But I'd heard it, I was sure of that, and it was enough for that 'other' state of mind to start insinuating its way into my brain, sending a shiver down my spine despite the warm evening, blurring the boundaries just a little between dream and wakefulness.

The others had all heard it too, and in that state of half-dream, I heard Marlow tell Jean it was time, at which, Jean moved without argument, retrieved a small sandalwood box from his pack. Inside which were two linen bags, which he removed before pocketing the box.

The drums were becoming a little clearer now, more urgent in their call, almost as though they would draw us closer to them. Slowly, their tempo increased with that strange undulating African rhythm, compelling my heartbeat to follow.

While I was watching Jean, Marlow produced a bowl he'd bought at the gallery, and held it out for Jean to put the contents of the bags into.

I had a strange moment of thinking it odd that Marlow should have bothered to bring that ornate little bowl with him, and then suddenly I realised he must have been thinking of using it for this purpose all along. But then Jean was pouring hot water onto the powders and dried herbs he'd sprinkled into the bowl.

I watched as the steam and vapours rose from the hot liquid and encircled Marlow's face, a swirling, billowing motion, that again matched the rhythm of the drums as they soared and climbed toward their climax.

Then, as Jean stepped back, I saw Marlow, eyes

closed, raise the bowl to his mouth and drink deep of its contents.

Until this moment I'd had no intention of actually taking part in this 'experiment', but with the evocative sound of Africa once more in my ears, and that strange sense of otherness gliding over my mind, I was no longer certain.

I saw the bowl pass to Harry, who seemed so sure, acting without hesitation, almost impatient to drink and then pass the thing on to me. As I took the bowl in my hands I became aware of Jean watching me.

Holding it before me, I pulled my gaze away from the swirling liquid to look him in the eye. I think I was searching for some kind of disapproval or rebuke, perhaps even some guidance as to what I should do, but as always, there was no judgement in those eyes.

Almost as though they were aware of my hesitation, the distant heartbeat of drums swelled once more on the night air, twisting and twirling around my mind, as they had back in Africa, and bringing my attention back to the bowl of liquid I held in my hands.

As though dreaming, I saw my hands raise the bowl to my lips, and once again I drank of the bitter liquid within.

As I passed the bowl on to Jean, I could see that he too was feeling the pull of the drums now, but was fighting the impulse to drink.

But the drums and drug had me now, and my attention drifted from Jean to the fire, which burned so brightly in the night air.

At some point I sat down on the ground beside the fire, to watch it more comfortably, and then, before I knew it, I was lying down to watch the flickering shadows on the rock face above us.

Finally, as my eyelids began to droop, I vaguely remembered there was something I should have done.

If only I could concentrate for a minute, but the drums kept distracting me and I couldn't quite seem to remember what it was I'd had in mind.

It was irritating and I thought to mention it to the others, but even as I looked for them, they had already gone, and my Father was approaching from the other side of the fire.

He was older this time, more like how I'd remembered him when I was a young child. He simply came walking out of the darkness on the other side of the fire, a warm smile upon his face.

No longer tired, I stood up and walked around the fire to join him, half expecting we'd suddenly find ourselves racing across the surface of the cliff again, chasing after some fleet footed game.

But instead he simply welcomed me with a handshake, and then indicating the inky darkness beyond our circle of firelight, we walked off into the night.

We talked of many things, the journey I was on, my journal keeping, home, and my friends. But we both knew it was all just a polite preamble, and eventually I saw the fire coming into view that Marlow had spoken of in his dream.

I felt the warmth from the flames on my face from quite a distance away, and could only imagine how hot it must be for the circle of strange figures I saw gathered around it.

As I looked upon them now, I realised it was these strange and shimmering individuals that had asked questions of me in my first dream, but that I hadn't recognised them at the time.

I stopped a short distance behind the circle they were standing in, unsure that I wanted to move any closer to them, or whether I even wanted to stay, but not knowing what else to do. Eventually it was my father who spoke, and helped me to decide.

'You've come a long way, my son,' he said, simply. 'But this is no place for doubts and uncertainties. The flames of time that burn so brightly here, can consume a person not ready to look upon their brilliance or feel their heat. We cannot stay here for long.'

I knew what he was saying was the truth, it was almost as though the heat from the fire was felt not upon my skin, but upon my doubts, and even so far removed it was becoming more than I could take.

But just as I was about to leave, I saw Marlow approach out of the darkness a little further around the fire.

He was walking and talking with a tall Maasai man wearing a lion skin across his back, who for a moment reminded me of the Shaman Nelion, or rather as I imagined he would have looked when he was young.

The brightness of the fire seemed to grow a little as they approached, forcing me to take a few steps further back into the darkness. But even as I stepped away, I could see the circle of figures around the fire break and make way for Marlow and his companion, and then, with scarcely a heartbeats hesitation in his step, I saw Marlow walk toward the fire.

How that blistering inferno arose to meet his presence, the explosion of heat and pain became unbearable, as the flame suddenly brightened and grew in its intensity.

I was forced to withdraw further, even as the figures that had been standing so comfortably around the fire threw themselves away from the now scorching heat.

Only Marlow's companion, and one or two of the others remained, forcing themselves to stand against the searing heat, which almost physically forced them back by its incendiary power.

I couldn't stand to even look at that white-hot furnace, but before I fled into the cooling darkness, I saw Marlow as he stepped into the centre of that impossible flame, arms extending outward as though in welcome, letting the fire wash over him, feeling and embracing its purifying touch.

It was an agony to stand there for even that

moment, before I allowed my father to pull me away into the night.

I couldn't imagine the force of will it must have taken to step into that blaze of light and heat, let alone to stay there. I only hoped it was worth it to Marlow when he awoke.

We moved out amongst the stars again for a while, my father stopping off to show me Harry, as he walked and talked with someone I presumed to be his old professor.

I wasn't sure, because the man seemed too young to be the person of whom Harry had referred. But they seemed to be engaged in some intense conversation, and to be walking once again around the site of the Singing Stones, looking at the wall paintings and smoke marks, and who knew what else.

There was no sign of Jean, so after seeing Harry, we simply walked and talked some more, until eventually we'd made it back to the camp, where I once more said good bye to my father, before laying down to rest.

ENDINGS AND BEGINNINGS

I AWOKE EARLY THE NEXT MORNING clear-headed, but slightly tired as though I hadn't quite had as much rest as I could've done with. The sun was already up, but our camp was still firmly in the shade, so it was a bit on the cool side. Fortunately Jean had been up and around for a bit, and had rekindled the fire to warm the rest of us, before disappearing off somewhere.

He returned a few minutes later with a couple of canteens full of water and some more wood for the fire. He immediately greeted me upon seeing that I was awake, and promised hot coffee within half an hour now that he'd got some water.

While the water was heating, I took the opportunity to go and wash and freshen up beside the nearby spring, and when I returned I discovered the coffee ready and Harry already awake, but clearly feeling the effects of the previous night, much like myself.

'Well your potions definitely do the job, Jean,' he stated, with a good-humoured smile. 'But I don't think you've got the recipe down to quite such an art as old Nelion.'

'Practice, my friend, that is all I need,' Jean retorted with mock seriousness. 'Once I have experimented upon you another ten or twenty times I should have something comparable!'

'Well I'm happy to say my friends,' responded Harry, with a strange glint in his eye. 'That particular pleasure will not be necessary.'

I didn't quite understand what he was driving at for a moment. But Jean was as ever ahead of me. 'Do you mean to say, your dream has revealed something to you?' he asked warily.

But before Harry could answer we were all distracted by Marlow suddenly starting in his sleep, and coming awake.

He'd been sleeping perfectly quietly while we were talking. Though it was unusual for him to sleep in for longer than the rest of us, but Jean had checked on him at least once, and come away without any concern.

But now as he sat up, he was wild-eyed, and almost delirious.

He seemed to look around not seeing us for a moment, and then as he spotted the fire he stopped and gazed fixedly at it.

We'd all gone over to see that he was alright, but he wasn't aware of us, and seemed to be talking nonsense, with just the odd word being audible for us to understand.

I couldn't tell what he was rambling on about, and

he wasn't responding to us, but then suddenly his face set into a mask of steely determination, and for the first time in my life I saw rage enter those unnervingly calm eyes. For a moment then I was afraid of him.

Yet it was what he was saying that really transfixed us.

'Selene' he said, over and over again. 'Selene hold on. Keep pressure on the wound and just try to stay awake... I'll get help.'

And then as suddenly as he'd woken, he again fell unconscious, and we had to place him back on his sleeping mat.

None of us were quite sure what to make of it or what to do. Jean checked Marlow's pulse, to discover it beating quickly, and his eyes could still be seen to be moving frantically beneath his closed lids, but for the moment he was still.

'Is it the drug?' asked Harry, bluntly. 'Did he drink too much, and he's unable to awake properly?'

'No,' responded Jean, quietly. 'It cannot be the drugs.'

'But I thought you were concerned about their potency,' asked Harry, slightly confused.

'Yes, yes I am indeed concerned about both their strength and their effect,' answered Jean, rather too frankly. 'But that is why they are still in my pack, and last night I gave you all nothing more than a mild sleeping draught.'

'What... but how?' Harry stammered, in confusion.

But now was not the time for such questions, and after trying to form his question for another moment, he abandoned it to turn his attention back to what we could do for Marlow instead.

'What are you thinking, Jean?' he said, getting back to the matter at hand. 'Is there anything we can do to help him?'

'I do not know,' Jean replied still thinking, 'I have never known Robert to experience or suffer from such a condition before, though it is far from uncommon. I have heard that such dispositions can often be relieved by reassuring the subject about whatever it is that troubles them.'

'He was talking about Selene,' I said. 'Something about getting her some help. Though why he should be concerned about such things, I cannot imagine.'

'I think I can imagine,' Harry responded rather thoughtfully. 'He wasn't just talking about bringing help for her, he said something about her being injured, perhaps even dying.

'Now I cannot imagine what that circumstance might be,' he continued. 'Neither can I say what vision or dream Rob might have been having, but I do know, no matter what our differences with these women, he'd still go out of his way to help if they were in danger.'

'Then we must reassure him that she is safe, and perhaps this will help him to awake,' suggested Jean.

It took only a few moments of Jean's calm voice assuring Marlow that Selene was well and safe before his pulse started to slow and he seemed to relax before falling back into a more normal sleep.

We were still too concerned to try and wake him, feeling it better to let him come around, or at least out of that state of deep sleep, in his own time.

As we watched and waited we began to talk again about the previous evening. I knew Harry had some news he wanted to share, but I was also curious as to what had happened to Jean.

'It was without doubt a strange evening,' Jean began, after I put the question to him. 'When those drums began again, it was almost as though I were transported back to Africa. I saw each of you drink the sleeping draught I had prepared, but even knowing what it was, I still felt myself wanting to join you and drink also.

'But I struggled against it. Telling myself over and over that it was all just foolishness, until eventually I gained enough control to dash the bowl into the fire.

'As I think of it now, I cannot imagine why it should have been such a trial. But by the time I came back to myself, and was able to look toward your care, you had all been unconscious for some while.

'I do not recall looking at the time, or even having much sensation of it passing. I busied myself making you all more comfortable by moving you back to your sleeping mats, all the while aware of the drums continuing to sound, ever more distant and faint, but still pulling at my mind, until eventually I too fell into unconsciousness.

'I still dreamt much as I had done back in Africa, of things and people now passed, but without the force and persuasion of before.

'I do not know why, but I awoke several times in the night, long enough to check upon each of you before once more falling back to sleep. The rest you know.'

'How is it possible that we could hear those drums again,' asked Harry. 'Let alone feel such a strong compulsion upon hearing their sound?'

But none of us had any answers for him on that point, so we moved on again, and I asked him about what he'd meant earlier, when he'd said we wouldn't need to try this experiment again.

'I know where there is a full set of intact and pristine tablets,' he said, quite simply. 'And I don't mean, I know where they are roughly, or even that I'm just fairly sure they are there. I mean I can put my finger on them exactly, because we've already been there.'

I was simply too shocked to speak, his entire manner and tone was so confident and matter of fact, as to be almost comical, I simply couldn't believe he was saying what he was saying.

Eventually, Jean managed to collect his wits and beg for an explanation.

'Well, you may well want to kick me when you hear,' Harry said, half-amused and half-apologetic. 'You remember when all this started, we travelled to the Singing Stones, and drank that potion, just like we re-enacted last night?

'Well, I was a bit giddy with the entire experience afterward, which might explain things a little. But do you remember, I said that in my dream I'd seen a strange, almost clock-like symbol carved deep into the stone of that overhang, but it wasn't there the following day.

'At the time I simply didn't realise the significance, not until we found that same symbol carved into the threshold stone at Uruk. Well... don't you see? I dreamed that symbol was carved into the rock face of that great overhang, but when I looked for it the following day, all I could find was a hunting picture painted onto the surface of the stone.'

'Of course,' exclaimed Jean. 'It would be the simplest thing in the world to fill in the carved stone symbol with mud or clay, and then to paint over the entire thing, especially with the thick paint used by the Maasai for their wall painting. It would perfectly disguise the mud on the stone.'

'Precisely,' echoed Harry. 'Well, after I drank the potion last night, I again met my old professor. But this time I was prepared.

'I explained about the symbol, and the tablets we'd found or been beaten to, and asked him whether there were any other sets that were still complete, that we might yet be able to find.

'Well, he showed me that night in Africa again, all beneath the stars and fire-lit overhang, as we drank the potion and then fell asleep.

'It was strange to see it again, and even stranger to see my own sleeping form and that clearly visible symbol where it was carved into the stone. The remains of the previous lot of mud plaster clearly visible on the ground beneath it. I even saw the mud being reapplied afterward and the hunting scene being painted back over the top again.'

'So that must be the set of tablets taken by the African seeker,' I said, thinking out loud. 'And the Maasai obviously know about the symbol, so how can you be sure the tablets are still there?' I asked, expecting Harry to have just not considered this.

Harry was looking altogether more serious now, and although he didn't look flustered or put out by my question, I could tell there was something he wasn't sure how to tell us.

Jean must have picked up on Harry's changed expression too, and tried to reassure him.

'Come now, my friend,' he said, encouragingly. 'There is little point in your hesitation, what after all can you have to add that could be more amazing than what you have already told us?'

I saw a wistful amusement enter Harry's expression then as he began to answer.

'I know the tablets are still there,' he said simply. 'Because I know the person who brought them to that spot and placed them in the cliff, is also still there, guarding them, and waiting for someone to claim them.'

It was a good job I was already sat down, I felt as though the ground had gone from under my feet. I just looked at Harry unable to believe what he'd just said. Jean stood up and then sat down again, and then somehow managed to find his voice.

'Nelion?' he asked.

Harry nodded, before going on to explain.

'My guide, my old professor, had shown me the carved symbol and how it was disguised, but then I had exactly the same thought as you, George. What if they'd already been removed, especially as others had already realised the symbol was significant in some way and taken the trouble to disguise it, all of which I put to old Professor Zimmerman.

'Do you not recognise what it is you see, Harrison?'

he asked me, his smile indicating I'd missed something. 'Perhaps seeing him when he first brought the tablets here all those ages ago will help you.'

With that he showed me the same scene again, the overhang once more with the fire below it, perhaps even more enormous than it is today, and perfectly clean of both paintings and smoke stains.

'And then I finally recognised him, the young Nelion. Unmistakably the same person, that same scar across his shoulder, though more vivid now, as though still not fully healed. But here he was, with the lithe strength and power of the practised hunter, his eyes almost afire with the life that pulsed within him.

'I don't know how it's possible that he still remains in that place, how he has managed to continue to live amongst humanity and his own people, when so many of the others have found it so difficult. But I know he has guarded those tablets for all this time, and that we'll find them there, in that exact spot.'

'It is incredible to even think about such a thing,' commented Jean. 'On the scroll, the African account is listed as one of the earliest, from more than three thousand years ago.

'I cannot even conceive what it would be like to live for such a time, let alone what changes such a life span would have upon the mind. What could possibly be of interest or importance to a person after such a length of time?'

In many ways it truly was an inconceivable prospect, in no way within reach of our understanding. But we had other issues to attend to that demanded our more immediate attention.

Firstly there was Marlow, who as we were talking seemed to have come out of that deep state of sleep, and into a more relaxed form instead.

We still weren't quite sure what would be the best course of action, but we had to do something, so eventually we decided to try and rouse him.

He was clearly still very tired, which made rousing him a little more difficult, but with much gentle coaxing he came round, and amazingly, while slightly surprised to find us all gathered about him, seemed to have no ill effects.

We still had a short while before the car was due to come for us, so we took things easy while he woke up properly, explaining as he breakfasted about what Harry had discovered, as well as the strange bout of sleep-walking he seemed to have suffered.

It would have been a lot for anyone to take in, but being tired as well can't have helped. Somehow though he managed to absorb what we had said, albeit with the same questions and thoughts repeated again.

Jean tried to press him about his dream and what he'd said whilst still asleep, and the reference he seemed to make to Selene, but Marlow was reluctant to try and explain, until he'd had time to properly rest and digest it all.

After checking his pulse and that his eyes were focusing properly, it was time to head back to the hotel and hopefully catch up with the others.

The car was waiting for us when we reached the pick-up point, and in it we found Androus and Peter, waiting for us, and freshly returned from Athens.

They were a little jaded from their journey, and it was obvious the news wasn't good as soon as we saw them. It was all we could do to bundle all the equipment and everyone into the car before they told us we had to leave Greece, and we had to do it today.

We all had news to tell, but Androus was insistent about needing to go first.

'We have miscalculated the situation my friends,' he began, taking out one of those colourful handkerchiefs to mop his brow. 'We have only just managed to return from Athens with the artefacts in our possession, and I was only able to achieve this by lying to one of my friends and colleagues from the university, who in turn has used his influence on my behalf.'

This sounded serious indeed, and we all fell silent as he continued.

'As you know, we left for Athens knowing that the law and precedent was on our side, and suspecting that this was nothing more than a manoeuvre to slow us down and maybe to tie us up in the local bureaucracy.

But as soon as we got to Athens I knew we'd made a mistake. The customs officer, Laskari, had evidently had time to make a few calls, and when we reached the University there was a very senior official waiting there for us with his legal representative and several other people.

'Well, I immediately became concerned that this was far more than a delaying tactic. But I knew all their legal representation and high powered argument would still be useless unless they could find some kind of link to Greece in the artefacts, which meant they'd be dependent upon an expert from the university, and I thought I knew who that would be.

'Now, while I hadn't predicted the level of support the inspector might have, I had given my friend at the university a call before we'd set off, to explain the situation, and ask for his help in sorting it all out. I'd guessed right, and when my self-same friend entered the room as their expert witness, I knew there was still hope.

'Well, we still had to go through the motions. They looked at every angle they possibly could to try and confiscate the artefacts. But when it came down to the appraisal, there was simply nothing to indicate anything had any link to Greece. The language, the materials, the craftsmanship and of course the provenance that I was able to provide, all pointed to these items coming from the near east.

'My friend was more than a little interested in the artefacts, but he put it to those people very simply, that unless there was some evidence to suggest these things had been found on Greek soil, then there was nothing to suggest

Greece had any title or interest in them.

'That's when I had to lie, and I told them that we'd brought all these things with us, and were just trying to verify some of the references made within the various writings, with a view to possibly locating new sites worthy of investigation.

'I'm not proud of having to do this, but it is what I learned after that meeting, when we had finally been able to reclaim the artefacts and had started to head back to the car.

We'd checked into a small hotel near to the university, and as we headed back there yesterday evening, with our possessions intact, I found my university friend waiting for us with a look of grave concern on his face.

'Androushan,' he said to me. 'You must leave this place, and Greece as quickly as you are able. I do not know what it is you are involved in, but a lot of very powerful people are interested in stopping you, and confiscating those unique and beautiful items you carry with you. Before joining you today in that meeting, I avoided going back to my own office, because I could see that an official was waiting there for me. I now know he was from the Phanar and had travelled from Mount Athos to see me.

'My university friend wouldn't talk any more, fearing that he had already put his job at risk by coming to warn me. But I believe what he was saying, which means that whoever Luke's friends are, it is not just those three attractive young ladies we've been sharing a hotel with, they have far too much influence and support to be working by themselves.'

This could've been a body blow to us, and we all realised how narrowly we must have side-stepped it. But that didn't mean we were out of danger, and our best bet, as Androus said, would be to get away from here, and at least make ourselves more difficult to find.

'It's time to confront Luke,' Marlow said, with sadness in his voice. 'We cannot hide from these people, whoever they are, if he is with us.

'It may be his continued presence within our group, is what has convinced his associates they do not need to rush to deal with us, but I am sure when they realise we've been playing them for so long, they will redouble their efforts.'

'We could just leave without him,' Jean suggested, not very convincingly. 'Simply steal away upon some pretext.'

'We could,' conceded Marlow. 'But he was once a friend, and I would like to continue to treat him as such if we possibly can.'

There was a general agreement at this, and as we continued our journey back to the hotel, we brought Androus and Peter up to speed with our own news, which made for yet more shocked expressions.

Then we laid our plans, so we could do the proper thing by Luke, without giving him the opportunity to stand in our way.

It was a relatively simple plan to execute, especially with the help of the hotel manager, who still felt he had to apologise for the inconvenience we'd been put to, so was willing to go out of his way to help us sort everything out.

It was made all the easier by Luke's absence, doubtless he'd taken the opportunity to contact Selene and her friends to make their next round of plans, and of course we'd had Stephanos on standby for a couple of days since Androus had been forced to go to Athens.

Now we were left with the difficult part, how to confront Luke. There was no easy way to go about it. So, after we'd discreetly packed and sent all our things to the boat, we again imposed upon the manager to allow us the private use of one of the bars for an hour or so, at the same time leaving a message for Luke to join us there.

We weren't all going to confront him, just Marlow, Jean and myself. The others would leave on the boat and navigate back through the great canal while the direction of traffic was in our favour from west to east. We'd then arranged for a hotel car to drive us overland to a point where we could rendezvous.

We hadn't been waiting for long in the bar, when Luke finally found us. He knew that something was up, when he saw us waiting there, but he was still prepared to try and bluff things out.

'Has it not gone well in Athens?' he asked, probably knowing more about what had transpired than we did ourselves.

'No, it's not Athens, or the artefacts, they're all safe and beyond the reach of the Greek authorities,' began Marlow. weariness showing in his every word. 'It's time for us to leave Corinth, and to end the charade that we've been playing.'

Luke was still looking confused and was obviously going to try and continue his act, but Marlow cut him off politely with a gesture before continuing.

'We know that you betrayed us, Luke. That you've been working with Selene and her friends, and a much larger organisation to prevent us from achieving our goals. We know you tried to delay us in Jerusalem and again in Athens.

'We know your friends beat us to the tablets on Crete, and that they tried to beat us to the tablets here in Corinth.

'We also know that they tried to steal these artefacts away from us by using the police, and we know that if you continued to stay with us, then you would continue to help them.'

It was amazing to see the transformation coming over Luke as Marlow said all this to him, he looked incredulous at first, then indignant and angry, before finally becoming resigned, and with it more relaxed than I think I'd seen him for months.

'Yes, it's true,' he finally said, with such a stark simplicity as to be almost shocking. 'All of what you say is right, and I am glad that the pretence is finally over…

'It is a strange thing, In the heat of the moment,

convinced you were all on the path to self-destruction and certain damnation, I betrayed you with hardly a moment's regret. But the constant lying and deceit once I made that decision, the shame of treating my friends in such a manner, even for their own good, was almost unbearable.

'As for hiring the bandits to attack us outside Uruk. If I had imagined they could fall to such measures… I would never willingly risk your lives, when it is to save you that I strive.'

We talked for a few minutes more about various things.

For our part, we explained how we discovered the betrayal.

For Luke, it was more of a confession. He wouldn't give us any more information about who Selene and her other friends were working for, other than to tell us that 'they' would not be known to us.

But he did tell us it had been him who'd tried to destroy the first set of tablets, not one of the bandits. He'd fired blindly into the bag with his revolver, thinking it would be enough to reduce the contents to dust.

I think it was this last confession of wonton destruction that finally pushed Harry over the edge and forced him into asking him why he'd done it.

'I simply don't understand Luke,' Harry stated, with bitter disappointment in his voice. 'We've known one another for years, and I know you used to appreciate the beauty and art of the ancient world, even when it was just fragments.

'Yet in that bag we had some of the most beautiful, complete, unexpected treasures from a time so long ago, and still you turned a gun on them. How could you do that Luke?'

I could see Luke was hesitating, as though he didn't really want to try and explain it to us, but eventually he responded.

'I don't expect you to understand, Harry, or any of

247

you,' he began.

'It was the dream to begin with, the horror of that night is not something I would ever wish to try and remember, let alone to try and re-create, though I think perhaps Silvio had it even worse than I.

'You were so pre-occupied with trying to figure out what it could all mean, that you forgot to even stop and ask, what it was I had seen.

'After I swallowed that poison passed around by the Shaman, I saw you all, at least as you started your dreams. But I also saw the malevolent flame in that old man's eye as we all slipped into his world, a world of deceit and lies conjured by spirits and apparitions. Visions of the past, of other places and people, all designed to pull you in.

'My 'guide' was an old friend, a girl from Rome whom I could have loved, but who'd decided to be a missionary in India instead.

'I didn't even know she was dead until she came walking out of the darkness to meet me. She knew I'd loved her, so didn't want to talk to me about how she'd died, but when I insisted she took me there, powerless to help, able only to stand and watch as she was mutilated and abused beyond the help of friends or family.

'It took me over a week to confirm the details when I got back to Rome, after leaving you. And it was me that had to visit her family to tell them what had happened to their daughter, while sparing them the details that would have destroyed them.

'That is the reality of what you are all trying to do. These spirits that you are all thinking of as benevolent are offering you a knowledge and understanding that mankind should not possess…'

I could see he was still hesitating about telling us something.

'Even if, by some ungodly means, these tablets you seek were hidden by people able to extend their lives. You already know it will mean no longer being able to live amongst the rest of humanity.

'Living instead on the fringes of society, away from those who cannot or will not understand what you have become, and all of you, just like those mentioned in the tablets, will end up existing apart from society until you too finally find a way to die.'

A lot of what Luke was saying echoed and resonated with my own initial thoughts, and to hear about the terrible experience he'd had after drinking the potion at the Singing Stones, well, that helped to explain even more. But even while he was telling us all of this, I think he realised he'd made a mistake.

It was a polite exchange, heavy with regrets, but without recriminations. We talked about things for a short while longer before saying our final goodbyes, and leaving the hotel to get into our waiting car.

Luke came out to join us, never asking what we planned to do next, and as we drove away to rendezvous with the boat on the other side of the canal, I looked back only once to see him walking down toward the sea front and away from the hotel.

He could've rushed off to tell Selene and her party what had transpired, and perhaps try to catch us before we could get to the boat, or out of Greek waters.

But instead, it seemed he'd chosen to give us some time to make good our exit.

COMPLETING THE CIRCLE

IT WAS A SAD MOMENT leaving Luke behind, even knowing how he'd betrayed us. But we'd taken the risk of confronting him, with full knowledge that we might then have a race to get away from Greece and Greek waters, before the authorities could catch up with us.

We'd done it anyway, both because it was the right thing to do, but also because, despite everything, we still felt some bond of friendship toward him.

After leaving the hotel we sped through the Greek roads, expecting to see signs of pursuit by the police, or to be stopped by a roadblock at any moment. But neither happened, and in no time the hotel car had dropped us off and we'd rendezvoused with the boat on the other side of the island away from Corinth, before heading out into the open water.

With every mile we sailed the odds of us being caught shrank, until finally after skirting past the western edge of Crete, toward north Africa, we began to relax.

Stopping overnight in Alexandria, it was then only a short hop by boat along the north African coast and down through Suez into the Red Sea, and the east coast of Africa.

As soon as we entered Suez I began to smell Africa again, and that rich aroma of fertility and decay so redolent of the land beyond the coast.

But it wasn't until we came out into the Indian Ocean and started to head south toward Mombassa, that the heady scent of East Africa, brought out to sea by the warm offshore breeze, really got its claws into me.

I hadn't realised how much I'd missed it, but as I stood on the deck of Stephanos' boat watching the land come closer, I almost started to crave the feel of that rich red soil beneath my feet again.

And then we had arrived, and I was stepping ashore, just as I had done nearly three years previously.

A few minutes later and we'd unloaded our things and it was time for Stephanos to leave us, sailing away into the fading light.

Stephanos had brought us as far as he could. He wasn't particularly comfortable taking his boat out of the Mediterranean and the waters he knew, only agreeing to do it as one final kindness before leaving us.

But as we lost our guide to the waters of the Mediterranean, we regained one we'd lost when we left Africa, for even as we alighted at the port in Mombassa I found Mkize waiting for me.

He'd dreamed of the drums on the same night we'd heard them, so had come down to the port to meet us somehow sensing we would return.

It was a peculiar thing to be retracing my steps again after so much had happened in the meantime, but it felt good to be back, and good to know exactly where we were going this time.

No research, no maps, no attempting to match antique descriptions to landmarks. This was a route we all knew by heart, and we followed those hearts first to Nairobi, then on to the hunting lodge where we'd all first met.

And just as we'd picked up Mkize in Mombassa, Nbutu was also waiting for us at the lodge. Much to the exasperation of the otherwise affable hotel manager, who welcomed us back warmly, but couldn't understand how this inscrutable Maasai could know of our return, before even he himself had known we were coming.

In some ways our return to Africa and to Kenya had been a bit too quick.

We were suddenly here, back in the heat and humidity but without the time to become accustomed to it. It was particularly tough on Androus who didn't have the more recent experience of the climate, nor the long days in the saddle that the rest of us did.

Consequently, by the time we reached the lodge he was clearly beginning to suffer from the exertion.

The rest of us had lost most of our African conditioning ,having spent over eight months in the far more moderate Mediterranean climate, but after even just a couple of days I was beginning to get used to it again.

Still, by the time we reached the lodge, it was clear to us all that we'd have to stop for a day or two to give Androus time to acclimatise.

We all knew this environment, as well as what to expect from the journey ahead. So it was vital for Androus, and the rest of us, to be up to it.

On the plus side, the spring rains had already been and gone, so the Serengeti was now filled with that verdant lushness that twice a year turned it into a paradise on earth. Another few weeks and the colour would start to slowly bleach and fade beneath the unrelenting sun. But for now, the bush was an Eden of plenty for all, and had an almost relaxed feel, which we knew to make the most of while it lasted.

On the journey back through Mombasa and Nairobi we'd had a lot of planning and preparation to do, so hadn't really stopped to digest the situation we now found ourselves in. But having got to the lodge, with all the equipment and supply arrangements made, we now had the time to start thinking about things more seriously.

As usual it was Jean who started us off. We'd had a pleasant evening at the lodge, with a good meal inside us, and comfortable beds to go to. And as we'd now decided to have a least a couple of days here, I'd decided to get up early the following day in order to go out for a ride before the heat became too much.

Nobody had really seemed interested when I'd asked, but when I came down the following morning, Jean was already up and dressed to join me.

It was a nice surprise, but I thought nothing more of it until we got out into the cool morning air and started our ride. The Serengeti is a glorious place even at the worst of times, with its low rolling hills and vast plains, but just after dawn when the bush is green and full of life from the rains, it becomes almost magically beautiful.

We'd ridden out to a small area of rocky high ground that would afford good views of the surrounding country, and had been chatting amiably and drinking in the enchanting view for several minutes, when Jean suddenly changed the subject.

'I must apologise, mon ami, I do not wish to spoil such a pleasant morning,' he began. 'But I have been thinking again, about Selene and her companions, and I am having difficulty resolving some of the things we now know.'

I knew better than to doubt Jean when he chose to raise something, but I had to ask him why he wanted to talk to me about it, rather than getting everyone together to talk it through.

'Well it is very easy to jump to conclusions, is it not?' he continued. 'Especially when so little is known for certain. But I particularly wanted to discuss my thinking with you, because you were also a witness to much of what we know.

'Now, our encounter with the officials in Greece could not have been predicted by any of us,' he began thoughtfully. 'There was no way we could have guessed Selene and her friends might have such influence. But... the fact that these young women have this kind of power made me reconsider some of the other things we know.'

I was with him so far, but wasn't quite sure where he was going. 'Are you talking about one of the times we saw Luke with Selene in Jerusalem?' I asked uncertainly.

'Precisely! Perhaps not the first encounter in the park. But you recall the second when we stumbled across them in the alley?' he asked.

I indicated I did.

'You remember then that it appeared as though Luke had gone there to meet her for some reason, but she seemed reluctant to allow him into the building?'

'Yes, yes,' I answered, still not quite understanding where he was going with all this. 'It was at the back of some old church, which you subsequently insisted we stop and admire the front of, even in the falling snow!'

He smiled at my description, but seemed hesitant to go on, as though I hadn't quite answered in the way he would have liked. But after another moment he continued.

'Well the question has been going through my mind,

why would he go to meet her at a church, or more specifically at the private entrance to a church? Could it be that Selene and her companions are in some way linked to that church, and if so, in some way be acting in that organisation's interests?'

I couldn't help but smile at this last point. 'Well,' I replied, diplomatically. 'It may be possible... But isn't it more likely she was just meeting Miriam or Thea there and didn't want to intrude upon them?'

'Yes, I have considered this,' he responded. 'And if it were the only link to the church then I would probably think your interpretation plausible.

'But then there is the presence of the Phanar in Athens, when Androushan and Peter had been forced to go there and defend our possession of the tablets and scroll. His colleague at the university was under no illusions about the dangers for us all if we stayed in Greece.'

I remembered Androus mentioning this Phanar organisation before, but I hadn't understood the relevance at the time, so asked Jean to explain.

'The Phanar, mon ami? It is almost as ancient as those very artefacts to which we devote so much of our time. Perhaps you have heard of it by one of its other names; the Church of Constantinople perhaps, or the Eastern Orthodox Church? Just as you will have heard the Church of Rome referred to as the Vatican. Well it is the same with the Orthodox Church, based in the Phanari district of Constantinople they are sometimes referred to as the Phanar.'

'And this Church of Constantinople is in some way related to the church we saw Luke entering in Jerusalem?' I asked trying to put the pieces of Jean's thoughts together in my own mind.

'Ah, if it were only so simple,' Jean replied, as we turned our horses to continue our journey along a track. 'But unfortunately, the church into which we saw Selene and Luke disappear was related to a Jesuit order of the

Vatican.

'Now you may know from your history that the two great traditions of Christianity had a violent separation in the Middle Ages?' he continued. 'Well, they may not be as mutually antagonistic as they once were... but the possibility of someone having influence within both would be... unlikely at best!

'But if it is not a link through the church, then what could it be,' he continued, thinking out loud. 'Perhaps I am missing something, or perhaps the organisation these young women are working for was just fortunate, and in going to Greece we happened to enter a country where their influence is at its greatest.'

Seeing Jean so evidently struggling to put the various points he'd mentioned together. I began to wonder whether I might have listened a little more patiently or tried to be more constructive in my criticisms. We had the time to kill after all and it couldn't do any harm if I tried to go along with his thinking for a bit, and not to dismiss his ideas quite so quickly.

'Alright!' I conceded. 'Just to be thorough, and to make sure we're not underestimating anyone.

'We know that Selene and her friends are working for someone else, but according to Luke someone whom we would not have heard of. We also know Selene, Miriam and Thea are all from Italy and have the means to travel with a large retinue of servants. And, that they have quite a bit of pull within the Greek government, but not so much that they can afford to just ignore the law, like they did at Uruk.

'And now, it seems they may also have influence within the Greek Orthodox Church, as well as access to one of the Catholic churches in Jerusalem...'

'If only we knew how Luke came into this situation,' Jean continued to speculate. 'Then we might have a clue to the organisation or individual for whom these young women are working.'

'I don't think it matters, Jean,' I said, feeling a shiver

run down my spine, as I suddenly realised a mistake we'd made. 'Before long they'll know where we are, and they'll come in force to stop us.'

I'd stopped my horse and was turning it around now as I spoke.

'What is it, George, how can you suddenly know such a thing?' he said, also turning his animal around.

'Stephanos,' I said, simply. 'Whoever it is Selene is working for, they'd have to be fools not to look in Jerusalem for us after we disappeared. And if they look in Jerusalem then they'll look at the coast to try and find the boat, where by now they'll find Stephanos, who will probably tell them where he took us, because we never thought to tell him it was a secret.'

We weren't far from the lodge. But by the time we got back, and got everyone together I was already beginning to think we might be too late to set off that day.

'My friends,' I began my explanation. 'I believe we may have made a very unfortunate mistake, which means we cannot stay here a moment longer than we have to, and that we may not be able to come back to this place once we leave.'

There was an understandable surprise and concern at this. But with Jean's help I explained about our early morning conversation, and the sudden realisation that Selene, and the organisation she worked for, would even now be travelling toward us, and may even be upon us before the day was out.

'You're both convinced of this?' was Marlow's simple question.

There was an energy and determination about him as he asked us this, which seemed to grow in intensity when we indicated that we were indeed both sure of what we were saying.

'Then we must leave within the hour,' was his equally straight forward suggestion. 'And you can explain your reasons in more detail once we stop and have time.'

He looked at each of us as he said this, that becalming gaze of his travelling from face to face, to invite further discussion, but there was none. And then we were all off in our respective directions preparing and packing with all possible haste.

THE HUNT

THERE WAS A LOT TO GET DONE within an hour, especially if we weren't sure we'd be coming back this way. But somehow we managed it without everything descending into chaos, even taking a few minutes to convince the hotel manager to misdirect anyone who might happen to turn up looking for us, before we set off.

We wouldn't be difficult to find, even once we'd left the lodge, not until we got a few miles away at least.

But, if anyone from the outside knew Africa, and how to hide in the bush then it was us. We were still like children by comparison to the natives, who had an almost intuitive communion with the land. But we knew enough, that with a few hours head start, we could become very difficult to find.

We were following the same route we'd taken the first time, and I knew that if Luke was still with Selene and her friends, then he'd have a pretty good idea of which way we'd gone. So it all depended on how far behind us they might be.

As we travelled with Nbutu again leading us onward, I tried to do the sums.

We'd left Mombasa six days ago, wasting at least two days while we made arrangements and sorted out supplies and equipment. But in that time Stephanos would be back in the Mediterranean, where I was sure he'd have been found almost straight away. Even if it took them a day to find him and get the information out of him, then they might only be three days behind us.

But how would they travel here? If they went by boat and train as we had, then they couldn't do any better than we had, and would therefore be at least five days behind us.

But if they got a plane, that would completely change things. They could be in Mombasa the same day they found Stephanos, and it wouldn't take them long to figure out where we might be headed from there, perhaps even flying straight to Nairobi if their plane could do it. In which case they could even have arrived on the same day we left.

The heat of the day had started to build now, and even in the shade it was already hot, but at the thought of them being so close behind us I felt a chill creep into my spine, and a cold sweat form upon my brow.

It had taken us three days to travel to the lodge from Nairobi, not a slow pace, but it could be done quicker, especially in a car. The roads and tracks weren't good, but at this time of year, and with a bit of luck, you could do it in a day. Which meant they could've been upon us already if everything had gone their way.

I wasn't feeling the heat anymore, I was so convinced they had to be close upon our heels, and the more I thought about it, the more I realised that in some ways we'd played straight into their hands.

We had all the artefacts they wanted with us, and we were far enough away from civilisation and the law for them to be taken by force, without fear of recrimination. Luke had mentioned that either Selene or her employer had been responsible for the brigand attack just outside Uruk. That kind of thing wouldn't be as easy to arrange in East Africa, but it could be done, especially if they brought their own people in for the job.

We'd been travelling for about an hour and a half before being obliged to stop for a few minutes by a herd of elephant.

There weren't many of them, but they looked like one of the small packs of young bulls that one occasionally sees tearing up the place. They weren't intent on mischief this time, but equally they didn't seem in any great hurry to move on, so we just had to stop where we were and wait for them to wander off out of our way.

I took the opportunity to have a quiet word with Mkize while we were stopped, to let him know I was concerned about being followed, and therefore to keep an eye out for any sign that might indicate others coming this way. But he did better than that and also informed Nbutu, who nodded his understanding also, and indicated he would go and look while we waited for the elephant to move on.

I tried to watch him as he moved effortlessly over to some higher ground, with that long efficient stride of the Maasai, but in no time he'd blended into the bush and disappeared.

A few minutes later, as the elephant finally decided to move on, we rode forward again, as best we could until Nbutu came back to guide. We were all keeping an eye out for his reappearance, but he still managed to pop-up practically beside us before we'd realised. I'd no idea where he'd come from, but without a moment's hesitation he was directing us off to the side toward a more open area of land a short way off.

Nbutu made no attempt to tell us what was going on, but it was clear he was leading us as quickly as he could. I couldn't see where he was taking us until suddenly a few hundred yards further on we crested the edge of a small wadi, into which Nbutu now led us and then stopped, indicating we should all dismount, and then get our horses to kneel down.

I'd seen the Maasai do some amazing things with their cattle, which they had an almost mystic control over, but I couldn't have been more surprised when, after seeing us struggle for a few minutes, this tall Maasai stepped forward and with no effort at all made each of our horses kneel down in turn.

We'd gone along with all this so far, guessing and trusting that there was an explanation. Now as we waited, crouched in this hollow in the middle of the bush, we listened via Mkize as Nbutu explained that we were pursued by a motor vehicle.

I'd been dreading this news, it could only be Selene and her friends, and here we were still out in the open on horseback. They must have gone for the quicker option of a car to get to the lodge, and then had no choice but to try and catch us before the ground got too rough for them to follow.

We heard them a long time before we saw them, the petrol engine of the small truck they were using sounding so completely alien in the bush. It was a good ten minutes before they finally came into sight. It looked like something they'd hired from a local farmer or business delivery service, as it was by far a poor relation to the two shining saloons they'd had at their disposal in Corinth. But it was clearly a more rugged vehicle, with what looked like Selene and Luke in the cab with a driver, while the servants we'd seen them with in Corinth, rode open topped on the flatbed of the truck with Miriam and Thea. They were all alert, perpetually scanning the horizon with binoculars as the truck jolted along.

We were as good as trapped now. They came out into the clear open area where we were hidden, and then stopped, too far away for us to hear what was being said. But it was clear from the way the people in the back were searching with their binoculars that they were taking the opportunity provided by the more open terrain to do a more comprehensive scan of the area.

We couldn't move. The wadi was too shallow for us to even think about trying to get the horses back on their feet, but if Selene and her friends decided to drive further into the open, then they'd have to come our way, and there was no way they could miss us.

To the west, the direction in which we wanted to travel, the ground dropped slightly to form a large verdant basin, before rising again, and becoming a little more rugged, as the terrain climbed into the hills beyond. This basin could easily take us several hours to travel through, and there was no way we could pass through unseen as long as they were behind us.

After taking a long time to satisfy themselves that we weren't in sight, they eventually started to move off to the west, and not toward us. I was just beginning to relax when suddenly the truck drew to a halt, and a moment later both Thea and Miriam were firing large calibre rifles from the back of the truck over the cab at a target I hadn't seen.

It took me a second to take in the scene, and then to comprehend what I saw.

As the truck had started to move off they'd crossed the path of a young Rhino, which unusually, had attempted to charge their vehicle.

Now a Rhino is a formidable creature at the best of times, but they're so short sighted that on horseback one can just stop and wait for them to go on their way, just as it was with a great many of the larger game animals, when one wasn't deliberately hunting them.

Unfortunately for this animal, it must have strayed close to their vehicle while the engine was quiet, and had then become alarmed at the noise, when the truck started up again, causing it to attack.

But it was the speed and accuracy of those two young women on the back of the truck that was the truly shocking thing. The servants in the back of the vehicle barely managed to get a shot off in the time it took Thea and Miriam to down the animal.

Now that was an impressive feat, period. Even a large calibre round won't stop a Rhino unless you hit it in the right place. But for two young women to show that kind of proficiency, and with such powerful and difficult to manage weapons, why that was practically unheard of.

It had all caused a bit of a stir, with our own horses becoming restless for a moment before they were calmed again by Nbutu. Over at the body of the Rhino, our pursuers stopped again to examine the unfortunate creature, before unceremoniously moving on.

I could tell my friends had spotted the efficiency with which they'd wielded their weapons too, and as their vehicle moved away into the distance, I could see from the expressions on their faces they were thinking over what we'd seen.

We had no option now but to wait, and it was another twenty minutes before Nbutu checked the coast was clear. Only then could we carefully raise our animals and head off in the same direction.

The horses might have gotten a bit nervous if we'd taken them too close to the dead Rhino, so we took them around, and left them with Nbutu, Mkize and the other guides, before walking back to take a look at the animal.

'Four clean head shots,' remarked Marlow, after examining the body. 'One more straight into the horn, another into the neck.'

Another couple of smaller calibre rounds had hit the animal in the leg and grazed its side.

'I'd wager the head shots were from Thea and Miriam, and these others were from one of the servants grabbing the wrong weapon,' Marlow speculated.

It was a very business-like kill. Far too business-like for anyone who hadn't spent the last few years hunting.

We had to continue on our journey for now, and try to make sure we didn't run into them again, but I could tell we were all now wondering who these people could be, and where on earth they might have developed the kind of skill they'd just exhibited.

Regardless, we got back to the horses and set off again at a good pace. Nbutu had watched our adversaries as they'd travelled into the bush ahead, and had noticed that while they scanned the terrain before them and to the sides with great alertness and care, they seemed to be paying little or no attention to what lay behind them. Their tracks were certainly easy enough to follow, and the din from their engine seemed to be driving most of the animals away before they got anywhere near. So, by following them as close as we dared, we were able to not only avoid them, but also much of the more dangerous game that might have otherwise slowed us down.

It was tough going mind, and I was beginning to get concerned for Androus, as we were obliged to travel a little more recklessly than we would normally, just to try and stay up with them, all of which was taking its toll on the already tired Armenian.

They did gradually get ahead of us, even though we clearly heard them stop and presumably search the area ahead on several occasions. But by then they'd led us across most of the lower plain, and we were getting close to the point where the terrain would become impassable for their vehicle.

This was the tricky stage, and Nbutu started to lead us away from the vehicle track and through areas that afforded us more cover, just in case they suddenly decided to double back and retrace their steps.

We could hear the engine, but it was difficult to tell where exactly it was coming from, and now we had the added problem of having to avoid the animals that were being made nervous by the sound of the truck.

We slowly managed to move forward, but then, just as we were starting to think we were making progress, Nbutu stopped us dead, and pointed out a rocky outcropping atop a Kopje three-quarters of a mile or so up ahead, from where he'd seen a flash.

We were moving through a small stand of acacia trees at the time, but had been just about to move across an open area toward some tall grass, when Nbutu had raised the alert. Jean had his binoculars handy, and a moment later was scanning the outcropping for the source of the flash.

'Ah, but they are too clever,' he half mused to himself, before describing what he could see. 'There are two, no three of them. I cannot tell for sure but it looks like Thea and Miriam and one of their servants, all using their binoculars to scan the land around them.'

'And the others,' asked Marlow. 'With the truck, are they anywhere to be seen?'

We could hear the distant sound of the truck engine, which indicated it was being driven rather than parked, but it was too far away to be able to tell clearly where the sound was coming from.

'I cannot see it,' responded Jean after a moment of looking, 'No wait, that could be it. Half a mile away from the outcropping to the north, something disturbs a flock of small birds, it could be the truck.

'Yes, that's it. There's quite a bit of cover over there, but it looks like it's beginning to circle round, back toward us and the direction in which they came.

'They must suspect we are hiding when we hear the sound of the truck drawing near, so they're using it as a decoy while the others watch from the rocks.'

It was a good idea, which could have easily caught us out if we hadn't had Nbutu leading the way.

Hence, it became a game of cat and mouse. They knew we hadn't had time to get past them yet, but we now knew where they were and how they were looking for us.

If we could get past them and into the rougher terrain of the hills beyond they wouldn't be able to follow.

Whereas, if they could find us while we were in the open, they'd be able to cut us off and close in without difficulty.

It made our journey much longer, having to stick to the cover of the trees, or banks and hollows in the ground, while at the same time trying to maintain an idea of where the truck was.

Though now we knew it didn't have as many people

keeping look-out in it we didn't have to worry about giving it quite such a wide berth as we had earlier.

It was slow going, but we'd managed to get most of the way round the hillock where the main watchers were based, while the truck had gone off way over to the other side of the plain.

Unfortunately, we'd also attracted the attention of a group of hyena, that had shadowed our movements as we skirted round the outcropping.

They didn't normally bother with people, especially once they'd had a couple of warning shots put amongst them, but we just couldn't risk making that much noise, so they'd started to get a bit curious.

Slowly they began to get their nerve up after still not being sent off, drawing closer and fanning out around the rear of our line. We had to do something about it before they started to spook the animals, or worse to nip and bite at our heels.

We knew the rifle shots were going to give our position away, so we tried to get to a location where we'd have some cover, and then if the gunshots echoed, it might still take our pursuers a while to home in on where we were... or had been.

Hyena are an evil-looking bunch, especially when they spread, ready to start their nip and run type of hunting, trying to encourage their target to wheel this way and that, using up energy while the Hyena use very little, eventually getting confused and tired.

But we knew exactly what was coming, having seen it dozens of times before. While Androus stayed mounted the rest of us slid off our horses, and slowly moved to the back of the line, and then let the horses move off a bit. Hyena might be powerful beasts, but they're also one of the smartest animals in the bush, and they won't attack when they know you've seen them, they'll just sit and wait for a while to see what you're doing.

It really wasn't very sporting when we finally

opened fire. A dozen of them just sat there watching us, but we wanted to try and keep our shots down to a minimum to give our pursuers less to go on. So, at a signal from Peter we all took aim and then fired once at a different animal each.

It was a complete overkill just to deter them, but we didn't want to have to repeat ourselves in ten minutes time.

Sure enough they scattered at that, leaving their dead or dying companions where they were, but we didn't have time to stop and look. Now we had to try and put as much distance as possible between us and this spot. The chase was on.

We moved quickly but carefully for twenty minutes or so, sticking to the cover and checking the outcropping every now and again to see if the watchers were still in place.

We could hear the truck getting closer, but we guessed they would stop off to pick the others up on the way before it could come for us, at which point we'd have a few minutes to try and put some real distance between us and the place they thought we'd be.

We heard the lull in the engine noise from the truck, and when we checked the rocky Kopje where the watchers had been it was now clear.

I wasn't sure quite how far we'd have to go before the truck wouldn't be able to follow us, but it would be close. If we could just stay out of their way for a bit longer we might be in the clear.

We were moving as quickly as we could, but unlike our pursuers we still had to watch out for any game that might cross our path, if we didn't want to go signalling our location with rifle shots every few minutes.

We were relying upon Nbutu to find a route for us around all the obstacles and delays while still giving us some cover.

He seemed to have an idea of what to do and started to lead us a bit further toward the south-west, where we crossed first a steep-sided dry river bed, then through a patch of more dense trees, before turning more westerly back toward the hills.

We could hear the engine getting closer again now, quarter of a mile at the most, when suddenly it roared and went silent.

The ground was beginning to rise a little more steeply into the low hills, where we hoped to gain refuge, but it wasn't so steep or rough that they'd have to abandon their vehicle. So why had they stopped? We couldn't risk stopping to find out, so we continued going, expecting the engine to roar back into life again at any moment.

But after another ten minutes or so, with still no sound of the truck pursuing us, it seemed that something must have happened.

We all knew Selene and her companions were here to catch us, and probably weren't going to be too fussed about what they might have to do to stop us.

But at the same time, an accident in the bush was no way to die, which meant we should at least try and make sure they weren't in need of help.

Still, we didn't want to compromise our own goals in the event of it being a trap, so decided that Marlow and Peter should go with Nbutu to try and find out what had happened, while the rest of us continued on our journey, just to make sure it wasn't another clever trick.

Nbutu was as impassive as ever as we explained to him what we wanted to do, before dutifully leading Marlow and Peter off toward where we'd last heard the truck.

We continued to move further up into the hills, balancing the direction we needed to head, against the need to stay out of sight from below. With every step it seemed the terrain became more rugged making it less and less likely that the truck would be able to follow us.

But it had also been an exhausting day, with few stops or opportunities for rest since we'd set out, and now, as the threat from our pursuers seemed to recede, I could feel myself getting tired.

The afternoon was beginning to get on a bit by this time, and even though we could've gone on a little further, when we stumbled upon a good campsite, with the remains of a thorn fence still intact around it, we decided to stop and make camp.

It didn't take us long to get the camp set up, though without any fresh meat for a meal we didn't have to worry about cooking, instead just relying on the cold provisions we'd brought with us from the lodge.

Androus was attempting to put a brave face on things, but it was clear he was done in. His normally jovial and expansive humour had all but disappeared now, replaced by a slightly ashen tinge to his features and a deathly tiredness in his eyes.

I suggested he get some sleep as soon as the camp was set up, on the pretence that we might need him to take a turn keeping watch later on, but it was really just to give him the excuse to get his head down.

We'd done our best to hide the fire with a couple of make-shift blanket screens, but I was hoping it was a precaution we wouldn't need.

Two hours later, Marlow, Peter and Nbutu walked out of the growing gloom to join us, and while you'd never have guessed it from Nbutu, the smiles and friendly chatter between Marlow and Peter were a clear indication that something had gone our way.

'I tell you,' said Peter, smiling warmly and gratefully accepting a cup of hot coffee, 'Nbutu is a genius, he anticipated Selene and her friends perfectly. When we found them, they were all fine, but they'd driven their truck over the edge of that dried up riverbed we crossed. It was a little bit deeper at the point where they'd hit it, which would probably have made it more difficult to get out of than in. But they also managed to pick a spot where there were a number of large rocks, one of which seemed to have completely destroyed their front right wheel.

'They were having a terrible time trying to move the truck onto level ground, so they could change it, I can tell you.

'Better yet, the spare they had was almost useless, it had evidently been punctured at some point in the past and never been fixed, so it was looking like they were going to have to stop every few miles on their way back to re-inflate the thing! Anyway we stayed to watch them, just to make sure they were able to get moving again, without them even suspecting we were within earshot.'

'Earshot, mon ami?' Jean suddenly enquired. 'Did you by any chance hear them talking about anything of interest?'

'Well, there were a few unusual things, now that you come to mention it,' Peter replied, enigmatically, stringing Jean along in exactly the same way that Jean liked to do with the rest of us.

'For example?' Jean played along.

'Well, it did strike me as odd the way they talked when they thought nobody else was around,' Peter replied, thoughtfully. 'They spoke in Italian mostly, and my command of that language is perhaps not as good as it should be... but at one point I could swear one of the servants referred to one of his mistresses as Sister.'

'Yes, you understood it correctly,' indicated Marlow, looking more serious now. 'Miriam obviously has the hotter temper of the three, and after rebuking one of the servants over some small thing, he responded with a request for forgiveness, and used the name Soura... which she seemed none too happy about, and rebuked him further.'

'You are sure it could not have been Sorrella?' asked Jean carefully.

'No my friend, he definitely referred to her as a holy sister, not as a relation,' was Marlow's simple reply.

I hadn't quite followed the significance of these two words, until Marlow explained it in these terms, and even once he made the issue clear it still took me a moment or two to think through the implications of what it all meant.

'The more we learn about these people, the less I understand,' mused Jean, as we all made ourselves more comfortable around the fire. 'If these young women hold some kind of religious office, then that might explain the strange deference Luke paid to Selene when we saw them together in Jerusalem.

'But then they have wealth, political influence, and they use firearms as though born to it.'

It was an entertaining conundrum for us to throw around while we ate and relaxed, coming up with some truly silly ideas.

But really it was just a relief to know that we could no longer be pursued, and hence that we could relax for a while.

It might turn out to be a bit tricky on the way back, if they were still around. But once we'd got what we came for, we could make our way in any one of a dozen different directions, or even just find a village and sit it out for a week or three. We just had to get to the Singing Stones and retrieve the tablets before anyone could beat us to it.

ANOTHER COUNTRY

IT WAS GOOD TO BE BACK UNDER the stars in Kenya, away from the towns and villages and with the earth once more beneath my head. I slept a deep and dreamless sleep for the first time since we'd left Corinth.

Waking early the next morning to find Androus already up and about, and looking very much like his old self.

It was cool and ever so slightly misty, which gave the verdant bush an even more enchanted feel.

'I thought you were going to wake me to take a watch,' Androus asked smiling, clearly understanding the motivation for my deception.

I apologised to him for my dishonesty, then filled him in on the conversation he'd missed while asleep, including the news that our pursuers had turned back, and the strange enigma of Miriam being referred to as a holy sister.

'I would have to agree with Jean and the rest of you,' he declared. 'That just doesn't seem to make any sense. Although if Selene, Miriam and Thea are linked to the Jesuits through the chapel in Jerusalem, then anything is possible.'

'Why is that?' I couldn't help but ask. 'Have you heard something about that chapel?'

'No, no it's not the chapel itself, or even the modern order, it is more that the Jesuits, of all the different orders of the church, have had a rather... chequered history.' He began, before going on to tell me about the various historic intrigues in which the order had once been reputedly involved.

'I forget the details,' he continued, pouring and handing me a coffee as he tried to explain more about the order's history. 'But the order was unusual to begin with, in that it was founded by a Spanish nobleman, who before becoming a priest, had been quite a successful soldier and diplomat. According to some, this is the foundation upon which the later society was developed.

'To begin with though, the Society of Jesus, or Soldiers of Christ as they are sometimes known, developed as a response to the growing popularity of Protestantism, which it successfully opposed in a number of countries, especially Poland, Prussia and Russia.

'But as the order started to gain support in India, Japan and China, it also became more secretive, and supposedly began exerting its influence against governments and monarchs in Europe.

'At the time, it was rumoured to employ not only the advancements in learning and science that had been discovered in the west, but also some of the mystical abilities that were practised in the orient, to achieve their goals.

'Eventually, as a consequence of their political manoeuvring they came unstuck and the order as a whole was suppressed by the pope. Aside that is, from in…'

I could see something had just struck him, as he suddenly froze and didn't move for several moments.

Whatever it was, he was thinking hard about it. So, tempted though I was to give him a nudge and get him to continue, I held myself in check until he was ready.

'That could be the link,' he eventually said, as his eyes once again focused on me. 'They must be one of the few connections…

'I'm sorry, my friend,' he said, finally remembering my presence. 'But, you see, when the order was suppressed in the 18th century, it was suppressed by a papal decree. A decree which was ignored in Eastern Europe and Russia, because they had recently become aligned with the Eastern Orthodox Church and not the Church of Rome.

So, whilst the Jesuits today are very much part of the Catholic Church, there will be some elements of the order, that still have strong ties to the Orthodox Church which once sheltered them.

'Ah, but I know too little of such things,' he continued, exasperated at his own lack of knowledge.

'I know as a religious order they were thought to be incredibly wealthy before they were suppressed. And, were commonly considered to have infiltrated all walks of society, from the government and legal systems, to the universities and military, but they were always a strictly male order.

'That was over two hundred years ago, and the modern order has nothing but the highest reputation for its learnedness and missionary work. So where these three young women could fit in, is a very great puzzle.'

I could be of no help to him in his musings, so just did my best to listen and ask the odd, hopefully intelligent, question until someone else woke up.

It was an interesting start to the day for all of us, no sooner did someone open their eyes than they were questioned upon their knowledge of the church and European history.

But even Harry and Jean, who probably had the greatest knowledge and interest in such things, still couldn't shed any further light on Androus' speculation.

Fascinating as all of this was though, we just didn't have the time to stand around talking, and even though we'd been able to relax for the evening we weren't in the clear yet, not by a long chalk, so we once again pushed on, as soon as we were able.

As we moved further and further into the foothills to the west of the lodge, the terrain continued to get rougher. The rocky outcroppings, or kopjes became more and more frequent, until the ground was as much rock as it was soil, and the trees and shrubs took on a more shrunken and shrivelled appearance as the soil on which they subsisted became ever thinner and less fertile.

As we climbed the temperature also started to reduce, which made the travelling more comfortable, allowing us to appreciate the beauty of our surroundings a little more.

Nbutu lead us unerringly on, past a Maasai village that I didn't recall seeing the first time, and beyond until the terrain started to get too rough for the horses.

It was a tiring day, with as much time spent leading the horses as riding them. Though with the stress of the previous day now replaced by the nervous anticipation of what lay ahead, it seemed nowhere near as psychologically tiring.

When we could no longer move forward with the horses we found a sheltered spot to make our camp, packing and re-packing the equipment and supplies we'd need the following day, before settling down for the night.

We hadn't had to worry about attracting attention as we travelled, so had managed to bag some small game for a decent evening meal, and with that inside us we once again had the time to think about and discuss our situation.

The conversation and speculation continued around whether Selene and her friends could actually be working for some offshoot of the Jesuit order. But as we still didn't know any more we quickly exhausted the subject, and instead started to consider what our pursuers might do once they got back to the lodge with their damaged truck.

'They couldn't hope to catch us on horseback, could they?' asked Peter, looking around the fire to the rest of us. 'I mean, by the time they got back and arranged for horses and a guide, they'd have to be at least two days behind us, surely.'

'If they got to the lodge just after we'd left,' replied Harry, thinking out loud. 'And then set off as soon as they could without making any other arrangements. Then they might be that far behind us by the time they got horses and equipment sorted. But…'

'But if you were to place yourself in their shoes, Harrison?' Jean enquired, knowingly.

'Then I'd have considered a great many eventualities well before I got to the lodge, and upon finding us recently departed would've asked for horses and equipment to be arranged before I set off again in the truck.' Harry replied. 'I might even have asked for them to be sent out to meet up with the truck to save the group having to come all the way back.'

I hadn't even considered they might have such forethought. But as soon as Harry voiced the idea I knew I should have.

'So they're perhaps half a day to a day behind us?' I asked.

'I would estimate perhaps a little more,' replied Jean, thoughtfully. 'Do not forget, we were ourselves fairly well prepared before we chose to begin our journey. Our guides were already at the lodge, much of our equipment was packed. We just had to prepare our personal things and some provisions.

'In contrast, Selene and her friends will have had much preparation to do. To call in a guide from one of the surrounding villages would alone have taken three or four hours at the least, perhaps more.'

'And of course, they may not find a Maasai guide who would be prepared to lead them to a site like the Singing Stones,' added Marlow. 'It is after all a sacred place to them, at which women may not be welcome.'

It was all a good reminder about why we still couldn't afford to relax. We had the advantage, and to keep it, we just had to continue making good time, find the artefacts we sought, and then disappear via another route before they could catch up to us.

Granted, our horses and all the heavier equipment that we'd be leaving at our current camp, would be lost if the camp were discovered. But provided the men looking after the camp didn't do anything foolish to give away their position, the odds were against anyone stumbling upon their location.

The big question for me was whether Selene and her friends would try to follow us, or whether they'd just try to catch us when we next surfaced. I put it to the others on the off chance they had some insight into this as well, but there was little anyone could add.

'In my own opinion,' said Jean. 'There are not enough of them to divide their forces and still hope to over-power us. So they cannot guard the lodge or the route back to Nairobi, and pursue us.

'At the same time they must realise their chance of catching us, if they choose to follow, is small. Equally, because we could so easily bypass the lodge, or take another route out of Kenya, the odds of catching us by sitting in wait are also small.'

I could see where Jean was going, there was no right answer or way of knowing what Selene and her friends might do, but then he surprised me.

'Having said all that,' he continued. 'These young women, I do not know, but I think they are people of action. Intelligent, thoughtful, energetic and forceful, I do not think they are the kind to sit and wait. So if I were to guess, I think they will follow us and try their very best to catch us, either on route, or while we excavate.'

We continued to talk into the night, the anticipation of what might lie ahead the following day keeping us awake until late.

The following morning saw us rise with the dawn, ready for the day ahead. We knew it was going to be a long day, especially as we had to carry the scroll and strongbox of artefacts and notes with us, in addition to the shovels, picks, trowels and brushes we'd brought to excavate Nelion's tablets. But we were starting early in the day, and the air seemed cooler and a bit less dry, which made the going easier.

We set a good pace as we went, climbing higher into the mountains, making our way along the stream beds and gullies like we had the first time, ever steeper, and rougher under foot, leaving more and more of the tree cover behind us.

We'd have stopped and rested more if we hadn't been pressured to keep our advantage. But we were also eager to get there, especially Androus, who was keen to see another intact set of tablets in situ.

So we slogged our way upward, pushing our legs and lungs as far as they could go, and always looking for those tell-tale signs that might indicate we'd come this way before.

When we did finally start to recognise where we were, we were almost on top of the place, and no sooner had we started to point things out to one another, than we were climbing the ravine wall to reveal that towering overhang that dominated this place so sacred to the Maasai.

I was completely over-awed once again, and had to really force myself not to just stop and stare at that great wave of stone, that looked as though it were about to crash down upon us.

We'd arrived with a good couple of hours' of daylight left, which subdued and flattened the figures and pictures painted across that rocky surface, while at the same time somehow enlarging and highlighting the sheer size and extremity of the overhang itself. I'd just managed to tear my gaze away, when everyone again stopped suddenly, and seemed to be looking up at the top of the overhang.

I don't know if I'd just missed them the first time, but there, atop the very tip of the rock face, I could clearly see the three shaman that we'd met the last time we'd come here. They were too far away to see in detail, but their silhouettes against the pale sky were unmistakable.

Nobody said anything, we all just stopped and stared for a moment, before the three figures one by one turned and walked away from the edge and out of our sight.

It was almost impossible to imagine one of those figures had somehow survived down through the ages, millennia after arriving here with a set of tablets from the temple in Rhodesia.

As the last of the figures moved out of sight, the spell was broken, and we were once again free to move over to the rock face where Harry had dreamed he saw the symbol carved into the wall.

It appeared exactly as we'd left it, with dozens of exquisite paintings covering the entire rock face, from high to low.

As we stood beneath that colossal weight of stone, we each looked at one another in hesitation, and then Harry, after dropping his pack, removed a small metal hammer from it, walked over to one of the paintings on the wall and struck it squarely in the centre until it cracked and fell away.

Despite the fact that he was destroying a piece of

art in the process, he moved without a trace of hesitation as he cleared the plaster, until he finally turned back to us and revealed the clock symbol he'd told us would be there, carved deep into the rocky surface.

There could be no more doubt as we stared at that deeply incised symbol, but for a moment we all just stood there looking at it, a thousand different thoughts no doubt going through each of our minds, before we again got to work.

Exposing the cover-stone, into which the symbol was carved, was actually a much easier job than any of us had anticipated.

An entire section of the wall turned out to be nothing more than a sham, and rather than being a solid stone wall carelessly covered in patches of mud plaster. It was actually several large pieces of stone plastered into the face around the symbol, to make it look like the solid bedrock of the cliff.

As soon as we removed the mud, much of the stone also came away, until we were again looking at the perfectly flat, carved cover-stone that lay beneath.

Jean was asked to sketch the arrangement and layout, which he did with lightning speed to Androus' satisfaction. And then it was time to remove the cover stone.

It was perfectly vertical, just like the arrangement we suspected had been used on Mount Erceyes and in the Cave of Alcathos on the headland to the north of Corinth.

It was heavy, but between us we managed to safely move it to one side, exposing a sheet of copper, then sand, and then the nine pristine lapis lazuli tablets, inset perfectly into nine carved recesses in the cliff wall.

It was a poignant moment for us all, and for several seconds I held my breath, so transfixed was I by the sight. And then Androus and Harry, very carefully removed each of the tablets, wrapped them one at a time in a piece of cloth before placing them together in a leather bag, and then putting the bag into the strongbox we'd brought with us.

The day was beginning to fade now, but there was enough light left for Jean and Harry to finish up their documentation of the site, and for the rest of us to return things, as much as possible, to the way we'd found them, minus the tablets.

As soon as we'd finished, Nbutu lead us away from the site to a campsite that was surrounded by a crude stone wall.

It wasn't a huge distance away from the great overhanging cliff face, but it was far enough for us to be able to make camp without any risk that we might be discovered by Selene and her friends, should they somehow manage to find their way here in the night.

The enclosure was located in a bit of a hollow amongst a few scrawny looking trees and surrounded by a high stone wall, which would hide our fire light.

It was a good place to stop for the night, but if anything, getting to it had taken us a bit out of our way, meaning we'd have a slightly longer walk the following day, going down the mountain to get back to our horses.

Of course, it didn't take long once we'd made camp, for Androus and Harry to get the tablets out for a closer inspection. And it was almost like being transported back to that day outside the ruins of ancient Uruk, as we all gathered around to see that first set of tablets that we'd excavated from beneath the city gate.

The tablets we had before us now, seemed an almost exact copy. The shimmering shades of aqua and ultra-marine stone, flecked here and there with glints of gold, all inset with perfectly incised cuneiform lettering, row after tiny row, first on one side then the other, a marvel of craftsmanship and beauty.

We all knew much more about the process and the amount of work it would take for Androus to properly translate the huge amount of text the tablets contained. But we still couldn't resist asking him to do his best and tell us whatever he could of the message they contained.

'Well, I shall attempt to read it for you my friends,' he began, slipping into his polite professorial manner. 'But you all know that I am far from able to just read them to you as I would the newspaper.'

After asking first for a few minutes to study the text, he began. He was sat next to the fire, in a cross-legged position that allowed him to lean forward in order to catch as much firelight on the tablets as possible, while the rest of us sat on our sleeping mats, filling our pipes or just relaxing,

'The writing again seems to be divided into the same three sections we saw on the tablets from Uruk. Starting with the journey this particular seeker made to reach the African temple of Ziusudra, then the trials endured once there, and finally a section written by Ziusudra, describing the location of his first temple.

'As for the seeker, the first section here, lists his name as Nulayan, or Nula-an. Just as it is written on the scroll.

'How similar to Nelion it now seems with the benefit of hindsight,' he mused aloud, looking up briefly from the text before going on.

'Again there is a list of titles and achievements, I cannot make much of these, but there seems to be a reference to hunting and the slaying of a lion. There is more here, but I would need to study it further.

'Moving on to the story of the journey to the African temple… There seems to be another reference here to the killing of the lion, and a wound received in the process.'

'That could be the scar across Nelion's shoulder?' chipped in Peter.

'Yes possibly,' replied Androus. 'Though I cannot make out the phrase being used to describe the wound location or type. Then there is a reference to visions or dreams, which could be reminiscent of visions received in some of the other scroll accounts.'

There wasn't much more that Androus could really translate about the journey to the temple, so loaded was the text with unfamiliar names and descriptions. So he skipped on to the next section, which it appeared was similar in some ways to the account we had on the remaining tablets from Uruk about the tests and trials that were endured before Nulayan succeeded in achieving his goal.

But it was the last section that we were all eager to hear more about. This was the section written by Ziusudra, directing us to his first temple. The same section that had been destroyed by Luke, when he'd fired his revolver into the bag containing the Gilgamesh tablets, during the brigand raid just outside Uruk.

'This section will take a lot more work,' commented Androus, as he tried to find something he could translate for us. 'Again the temple is described as beyond or away from the African temple, but then it becomes more complex… I think this may be a reference to the rising sun as a direction of travel, which would indicate the east somewhere, and further on there seems to be some mention of water again, and interestingly there is a familiar phrase here, about the source of the waters.

'Now as some of you may recall,' he explained, looking up from the tablets again. 'That phrase is commonly used in the description of the Noah or Utnapishtim character who we know from the scroll and the Uruk tablets as Ziusudra. In the later Biblical story of Noah this earlier description is interpreted more figuratively and 'the source of the rivers' becomes a mountain top, where of course many rivers were thought to begin.'

He looked down again to examine the tablets further, and we could all see he was checking them thoroughly for anything further he might be able to translate for us. But eventually, with an apology, he looked up again and confessed himself defeated until he had time to study the text in detail.

'I am sorry my friends, but I really need to sit down

and study this much more carefully. This writing is so detailed and precise in its description, that picking out odd words would be as likely to deceive as it would to inform.'

If we hadn't all known the difficulty of the task in advance, then it might well have been disappointing not to hear more about the contents of the tablets. But we all understood the process by now, and the amount of work required to give even a basic rendering of the text. So after offering our thanks for his attempt, we relaxed and allowed the conversation to take us where it would, until we were all ready to rest again.

INTO THE FLAMES

THE NIGHT PASSED QUIETLY, and the following morning saw us up with the dawn, and heading back to where we hoped to retrieve our horses.

We had to move with caution again, on this leg of our journey, as it was now that we'd be most likely to run into Selene and her friends. But we were heading down hill and as usual had the eagle-eyed Nbutu leading the way.

I was hoping we might just pass them on route, without either party coming within sight of one another. But, about two hours after we set off, Nbutu stopped us and pointed out a movement further down and along the slope, and sure enough, when we checked through binoculars it was them.

They were a good way off, and probably wouldn't come anywhere near us, unless we did something to attract their attention. But they were also only half a day behind us, at the most. In fact by the time they got to the Singing Stones, realised we'd already left with the tablets, and turned back, we'd probably have less than four hours head start on them.

Of course we had to ensure they didn't spot us first, and the easiest way to do that was for us to sit still and wait for them to pass, which we did, before once more setting off to reclaim our horses.

Because we'd seen Selene and her friends on the way up we didn't have to worry too much about checking the site before going in to get our horses and equipment.

With four hours head start, we decided to risk heading back to the lodge. It would be tight, but it was just enough time to allow us to re-provision and set off again, provided we didn't run into any delays along the way.

We might even be able to disable their truck as well if it hadn't already been sent back. It was risky, and we were all far too aware of the delays that could slow us down and hand the advantage back to Selene.

But if we could get a reasonably good run through the bush then this could be the deciding point. Even if Selene and her friends decided to push things, and take a few risks, they just couldn't make up that much time, not unless we were delayed, at which point we could just bypass the lodge and stay off the main roads anyway.

The artefacts would only be safe if we could make it to one of the big administrative centres where we could be sure of a strong police presence. From the lodge, Nairobi as the capital was the safest option, with a good train line that would allow us to easily make it back to Mombassa and thence Jerusalem.

If we couldn't make it to Nairobi, then Nakura to the north, would be the next easiest place. Though much smaller, it would still be safe enough.

We were not without other options, if we had to we could always head south into German controlled Tanzania where we could try and make it to Arusha or Moshi. Both had good train lines, but it was a longer journey, and without a German national amongst us the authorities would naturally be less inclined to help, should we get into a fix.

I could feel the tension and excitement growing again now. It was a race, but this was our home ground so to speak, and we were starting with a good lead.

We made good time heading back down the mountain, and managed to get back to the horses with a good two hours of light left. The men we'd left behind had kept as low a profile as they could while we'd been away, and as we approached the camp now, we could see it was almost invisible to anyone who didn't know it was there.

We didn't want to waste the time we'd made on the way down, but in such rough terrain we equally didn't want to risk the horses by trying to move them after dark. So after talking to Nbutu, through Mkize and discovering there were no obvious places we could reach in the light we had left, we eventually decided to stay the night and head off again in the morning.

We were all aware of the fact we'd probably be giving away some of our lead by not pushing on for another hour or two. But we also knew that this was how mistakes were made, and it would only take an injured horse for us to lose the lead we had altogether.

It was another quiet and uneventful night, with nobody really being in the mood for conversation, each of us instead preferring the company of our own thoughts.

Marlow once again resumed the sunset ritual he'd had to forgo for the past few days, while I took the opportunity to update my journal.

I hadn't gone back yet and filled in the spaces I'd left while we were travelling with Luke. So after finishing a fresh entry to describe my view of events over the last couple of days, I went back and started to correct some of the deliberately inaccurate entries.

It was absorbing work, and I hadn't realised just how much time I'd spent on it, until I looked up after finally finishing, to discover that almost everyone else was asleep, bar the couple of men who were keeping watch.

I walked over to offer them both some coffee, and

to stretch my back a bit before I turned in.

Writing often seemed to invigorate my senses, almost as though the act of committing my thoughts and observations to paper, somehow gave me a greater appetite to experience more.

Now, after hours of what should've been tiring work, I found my perception enlivened and hungry for the sights and sounds of the night.

Away from the fire, as my eyes adjusted, I could see the sky was clear and could feel the temperature was dropping, with a bright almost full-moon bathing the grove of trees we camped in with a silvery light.

It put me in mind of Selene, as we'd seen her with her friends in the dining room of the hotel in Corinth, the very incarnation of the night in human form. It was a momentary indulgence which I enjoyed, before reminding myself of the ruthless intelligence, power and determination that also dwelled beneath that beautiful visage.

As much as I'd enjoyed my late night, it was definitely more of an effort to rouse myself the following morning, when Peter woke me just before dawn. But I pulled myself together, and joined the others packing up the camp ready for the sunrise.

We'd kept the camp to a minimum, and had packed up the food and a few other bits after we'd finished with them the previous night, so were ready to go quite quickly, and well before the first glimmerings of dawn.

There was no point in guessing or speculating how far behind Selene and her group might be, the only thing that mattered was how quickly we could make the journey back to the lodge.

The ground was tough going to begin with, but we'd had over a week in the saddle again by now, so as soon as the terrain became less rugged, we were able to mount up and really get going.

We still had to be careful with the horses, and to avoid some of the dangerous animals, though at least we could use our guns now without worrying about giving our position away. But even with the odd stop to look for our pursuers, we still managed to make good progress, and effectively reduced the distance we'd have to cover the following day by a good three hours.

But what we made up for in distance travelled, we sacrificed in our choice of camp site, and were forced to eventually make camp amongst some low rocks on a small outcropping.

It was risky not having somewhere more enclosed, so, with Nbutu's help, we did our best to pull a thorn fence together to keep the big cats out, and build up a couple of good sized fires to provide more light. But despite our efforts, it was far from perfect, and we were all woken more than once during the night, when our watchers were forced to fire warning shots to deter the more curious of the nocturnal predators.

We got through the night, and were again ready to set off before first light, albeit a bit more tired than we had been the morning before.

It was delightfully cool and misty during that pre-dawn time, and we made good progress over the firm dew-covered ground. But the mist also prevented us from spotting Selene's group.

An hour later, as the sun finally broached the horizon, the mist started to burn off, though it would probably be mid-morning before it was completely gone.

Now as we travelled, we could occasionally pick out the tracks that the truck had left as it had pursued and then preceded us on the way out, as well as the site where the rhino had been shot, now picked perfectly clean, bones skin and all.

We even managed to avoid the group of rowdy young elephant this time, though they were definitely still in the area.

By mid-afternoon we were probably only ten miles or so from the lodge and had made good time all the way. I was sure we must've beaten Selene and her friends back here, though we'd seen no sight of them after the mist had cleared.

But even so Jean was still urging us to be careful, we could after-all, still turn aside and avoid the lodge if we needed to.

It was beginning to look like our caution was unmerited though. We were taking a slightly circuitous route to the lodge, following a thicker line of trees and brushwood that offered us more cover, when we heard the unmistakable sound of the truck's engine ahead of us, as someone started it up and then began to drive. It was too far away to see, but there was no mistaking it had started at the lodge and was coming our way.

There were no hollows to hide in this time, so we just had to do our best with the cover we had, making the horses kneel, and hoping the trees and brush would do the rest.

We didn't have to wait long for it to appear, it was being driven at speed, following the more open ground we'd fortunately decided to avoid. All we could do was get our guns ready and hope we wouldn't need them. But as the truck approached, although we could see it was manned as before, it was also clear the occupants weren't really looking for us, let alone searching.

We were a good three hundred yards away from the path they were following. But I could clearly make out the three young women again, one in the cab, and two in the back with their usual abundance of servants.

I couldn't tell if it was still Selene in the front or not, but I could see that Luke wasn't with them this time, either in the front or back.

I was just about to comment on the fact that they didn't appear to be searching for us, when Jean suddenly spoke.

'It is not them,' he said quite simply, but sounding a little surprised, as he studied the vehicle through his binoculars.

'It is three young women again, and their servants, but it is clearly not Mademoiselles Thea, Miriam and Selene.' He said handing his binoculars to me.

'You're right, Jean,' I heard Harry say, as I quickly found them myself.

'Those three young women have all got blonde hair unless I'm mistaken,' Harry continued, before handing his own binoculars on.

I could see them now, and with the binoculars it was as clear as day. They were certainly of a similar age and appearance to our pursuers, as were their servants, but it took only a moments scrutiny to realise this was an entirely different group of people.

After waiting a moment or two for the truck to move out of sight, we raised our horses, and led them off to try and find some thicker cover where we could discuss things.

We heard another engine and then another as we cautiously moved around the north side of the lodge, trying to find somewhere we could temporarily hide. But we'd travelled almost right the way around to the far side of the lodge, before we finally found a good spot amongst a thick copse of trees behind a small hillock.

It was Harry who started us off. 'If that wasn't Selene and her friends, then who was it?' he asked looking around at the rest of us.

'Reinforcements?' suggested Marlow, not looking convinced.

'It cannot be a coincidence,' responded Jean gravely. 'Three young women, with half a dozen identical servants, all carrying rifles and travelling about in the bush like they were born to it, they must surely be working together.

'But then,' he continued, more thoughtfully now. 'If there is a second group like the first, then why not a third or fourth, or more?'

I could feel my mind reeling with the implications. Implications that we didn't have time to think about, but that we couldn't just ignore.

'We need more information,' stated Marlow. 'If these people are working with Selene and the rest of her group, then we need to act. That first truck that passed us could meet up with Selene at any time, and then even if there are no others, we could be facing both groups searching for us within an hour or two.

We need to take a closer look at the lodge, and if there's nobody suspicious around, maybe even have a few words with the manager.'

We were all agreed, and quickly decided amongst us that Marlow and Peter should scout out the lodge, whilst the rest of us tried to keep a low profile.

Mkize and Nbutu went with Marlow and Peter, to try and get them closer. Which left the rest of us to sit and stew for a while until they returned.

They were gone for nearly an hour in the end, though it seemed like an age longer. As soon as they came back into sight we could all see from their faces it wasn't good news.

'Well, Robert,' was Jean's uncharacteristically impatient enquiry. 'What did you see?'

'It isn't good news, I'm afraid,' he replied. 'Selene's friends are considerably more numerous than we'd anticipated.

'There are four cars and two other trucks parked around and about the lodge and its outbuildings, which doesn't include the one we saw go past us, or any that may be parked out of sight from where we were hidden.

'As for the occupants,' he continued. 'They could almost be sisters to Selene, Thea and Miriam, some older or younger perhaps, but all with the same manner.

'We saw at least ten, maybe fifteen, with a similar number of male servants. We couldn't see them very well, but from what we could make out they're well-armed and equipped for the outdoors.

'There was also one older woman, white haired, but fit and strong looking, like the rest, from whom they all seem to be taking orders, though what she was organising them to do, we couldn't discover.'

'Perhaps thirty people! Are you sure it is so many,' asked Jean.

'At the very least,' responded Peter. 'We didn't see them all at the same time, they were that busy. But we watched them going about their work for long enough to be sure there are at least that many.

'I don't know what they've got planned,' Marlow added. 'But they've got all the equipment and supplies they could want. That includes horses, and by the look of it guides, weapons, camping gear, food, they seem to have brought everything with them.'

There was a moment's silence, as we tried to absorb what Marlow and Peter had said, and then Marlow continued.

'We've clearly underestimated the resources these people have at their disposal, and for all we know this could just be the tip of the iceberg.

'But with the equipment and people they've got, bearing in mind there are at least another eighteen that we know of in the bush, that will soon be on their way back, they could easily track us down before we got anywhere near Nairobi.

'Even if they just sit on the hilltops with binoculars, like Selene and her group did before, it wouldn't take them long to corner us.'

'Well if we cannot disappear into the bush,' asked Jean. 'Then what do you think we can do, Robert. Have you another option?'

'I'm not ruling anything out yet, and I certainly don't think we should just surrender to them,' was Marlow's response. 'There is one option, which it might be worth looking at, it's risky, but could work.

'We've clearly made it back here before they were expecting us,' he explained, cautiously. 'So they're preparing and setting up a perimeter without realising we're already inside it.

'They've got more than enough people and vehicles to do it, but it looks like they're either expecting to catch us on the way in, or they're getting ready to head out into the bush to hunt us down.

'Either way they don't seem to be paying that much attention to their flank.

'Now, that will probably change as soon as they make contact with Selene and realise we could have already bypassed the lodge, but right now it gives us a window of opportunity.

'A window in which we might be able to sneak around behind them and take one of their cars without them noticing.'

'Now, it's a full day's drive to Nairobi, but with a car we could travel through the night, and if we get an hour's head start, they might not have another vehicle quick enough to catch us.'

'That could land us in a whole pile of trouble with the police, Rob,' threw in Harry. 'If we were to be caught, they might even be able to make the case that we'd stolen the artefacts along with the car!'

'You are quite right, Harrison,' Jean interjected. 'But the worst thing we might expect from the authorities here is a delay, is it not?'

'Quite so,' added Androus, with a suddenly mischievous glint in his eye. 'And let us not forget that the majority of these artefacts have been recorded in our possession by our friends in the Greek police!'

It was far from perfect. But we knew we didn't have much time to decide what to do, so after a few minutes of planning, we prepared as much of our equipment and possessions as could quickly be loaded into a car. We also settled our account with Mkize, Nbutu and the other guides, and then carefully started to make our way around toward the cars.

We wouldn't be able to take the horses very far, so decided to just leave them where they were, with a couple of the men, who had agreed to return them for us the following morning.

Then carefully, we started to make our way forward through the bush, toward the cars, Mkize and Nbutu going ahead to scout the way for us.

The afternoon was beginning to get on a bit now, and it wouldn't be long before that chorus of insect voices would once more begin its song of sunset celebration. For the moment though, there was still more than enough light for us to be seen.

We carefully made our way through the all too sparse trees and scrub, back to the vantage point that Peter and Marlow had found, which was still a good sixty yards from the rear porch of the lodge, and maybe twenty to the side of the nearest car.

We all knew the lodge and environs well, but it's amazing how you don't really notice the details when you're living with them every day.

The lodge itself was a large building, with verandas all round, a few scattered out-buildings laid out in no particular order, presumably just built where the land was easiest to clear.

Wilderness veritably crowded in around the place, forming thick bush within a few dozen yards, hiding the lodge and its outbuildings perfectly until you were practically on top of them, leaving just a twisting track through the bush, that could be leading anywhere or nowhere.

It wasn't really a place designed for cars. But over the years the continual use by carts and horses had not only created the track, it had also cleared a turning area at the rear of the lodge, that was now littered with more vehicles than I suspect the place had ever seen before.

There was no real order to the way in which the vehicles had been parked, the drivers had just drawn up where there was space, and inadvertently formed a bit of a pyramid, blocking in the vehicles closest to the lodge.

A couple of trucks and smaller cars at the front, then another car and truck behind, and a couple of larger saloons right at the back, so that the vehicles further back were partially obscured from the view of the lodge by the vehicles in front.

It was the saloon cars at the back that we had our eye on. They were easily big enough to take us all, while at the same time hopefully quicker than the trucks, should we need to try and outrun them.

A couple of servants from the lodge were unloading the car right at the front, but otherwise the activity seemed to be focused on the other side, outside the western veranda.

We waited patiently, and then, when they seemed to have finished, we carefully started to steal over to the rear most of the two saloons. Jean went first, then Androus, and the rest of us one at a time until we were all gathered around it, equipment in hand.

Harry was going to be the driver, and as he slowly slid into position behind the wheel, the rest of us tried to quietly load the car with our bags and possessions.

There weren't many people around, but my heart was in my throat as we made ready. Jean had gone forward to try and disable a couple of the cars in front, and I saw him stuff something into the exhaust pipe of the other saloon, and then move on to the smaller car in front of that one.

We were ready to go, and were slowly and silently rolling the car back a bit to allow it to more easily pull away, when I heard it. The unmistakable sound of the truck that had passed us as we approached the lodge.

There was no need for words, we all knew it must be Selene and her group returning with those others that we'd almost mistaken them for.

Jean had finished with the second car in front of us, and I could see he was just about to head for the truck beside it, when he too heard the approaching engine.

Of everyone I knew, I think it was Jean who surprised me the most. He was always self-possessed and intelligent, but there were times when his complete lack of hesitation said the most about the darker, more troubled times in his past.

Instantly his military training seemed to come to the fore, and like a thought he moved forward, drawing his knife as he went. First to the tires of the truck, then those of the car in front parked straight in front of the lodge, before he turned and glided back, weaving between and around the vehicles he'd disabled, to the car we were in. At which point Harry started the engine and began to pull away.

There was nothing sudden of suspicious about the way Harry pulled the car around in a gentle arc toward the track leading to Nairobi. Nothing to attract attention to the hammering hearts and strained senses of its occupants. Though we could all now hear the sound of the truck as it arrived on the other side of the lodge.

It was the perfect diversion to help us get away, but there was no way of knowing if it was going to be good enough. So, as soon as we went round a bend in the road, and out of sight of the lodge, Harry increased our speed to as fast as the uneven track would allow.

Despite not being able to detect any immediate signs of pursuit, we knew we were far from being in the clear. As the afternoon light dimmed, and turned into twilight, Harry was forced, even with the headlamps, to reduce his speed. But even with all his care we were still pushing it, and barely an hour after we'd set off into the gloom the road claimed one of our tyres and nearly sent us crashing off into the undergrowth.

There was a good spare on the back, and in no time

we had the car up and the old wheel off. But we'd apparently used up all our luck getting away from the lodge, because as Peter laboured with the spare wheel, we all turned at a word from Marlow to see several sets of lights in the distance behind us.

They were perhaps thirty minutes behind us, but we knew only too well that our adversaries were prepared to be reckless if it was needed. We were trying not to rush Peter, who was working as quickly as he could, but there was nothing we could do to help, so we just had to watch the lights as they came closer and closer.

'Just another thirty seconds should do it,' he eventually told us, as he worked furiously away. He barely had time to get in the car once the jack was down, before Harry was pulling away again. The jack, damaged wheel and associated equipment just left in the road behind us as we went.

The sun had disappeared behind the distant hills by now, leaving just a crimson edge across the horizon, which left Harry with the all-too-poor car headlamps to light the way ahead. There were moments as we reached relatively good bits of track when the car surged forward, then others when we had to slow almost to nothing as a sudden corner or obstacle loomed.

All the while the car headlights picking out surprised pairs of eyes amongst the surrounding bush, as various animals were momentarily caught in the beams.

Harry was hunching further and further over the wheel in an attempt to see into the gloom, but no matter what he did, the lights behind seemed to just get closer and closer.

Behind us, it looked like the lights of four vehicles were in the chasing party, with others occasionally visible further off in a following group.

We were losing the race, and we knew it.

It was miles before the track would join a proper road, and we might be able to use the speed of the car, but right now that seemed an impossible way off, with the lights behind sure to catch us before we could get there.

On we drove, into the night, constantly checking behind us to see how much closer our pursuers had come.

Eventually we figured out it must be the trucks coming up behind, their greater height and road clearance allowing them to plough along the track far more quickly than we could in the saloon.

And then it happened, though I don't think even Harry knew what animal he'd hit. But whatever it was, it was enough to make us swerve and put one of our front wheels into a deep rut, and then suddenly we were out of control.

Time slowed to a honeyed-crawl, as Harry struggle to bring the vehicle back on to the track, and for one agonising moment, I thought he might just do it. Then there was a bang as we hit something and the car skewed to the side, tipped, and then rolled, crashing over the uneven ground beside the road, doors flying open, and glass showering around us, before the car finally came to a rest.

I clambered out of the ruined vehicle, and instinctively dragged myself away, looking back to see the headlights casting their beams askew into the night sky.

The engine roared for another few seconds, before wheezing to a stop as it haemorrhaged oil and fuel onto the now glass-littered ground.

I was dazed and confused, but as I gathered my senses, it was Jean who was leaning over me checking I was alright.

As my wits returned, I got back to my feet to help the others, at which point I discovered I'd had a relatively lucky escape.

Marlow and Jean were largely unhurt, barring a few scratches. However Androus was clearly in pain as he breathed and couldn't put any weight on one leg, Peter was better off, but seemed to be having trouble moving his left arm. It was Harry though who was causing the most concern. One of the others had pulled him out from behind the wheel, but he was still unconscious, just lying very still beside the car, a nasty gash along his forehead and temple.

I don't remember the trucks arriving, or the throng of people that came out of them, as they surrounded us with guns in their hands. But my attention snapped back with a jolt when I saw Marlow unclip the flap of the holster on his belt.

Suddenly there was tension in the air. I hadn't heard what was said. But I saw that two of the male servants that travelled with these young women, had taken a few steps toward the wreck of our car, and Marlow who was stood in their way, had stopped them in their tracks by putting his hand on his pistol.

While there were several of those strangely self-possessed young women surrounding us, along with their servants, it was clear that one of them was somehow in charge, and she spoke again now, the air of authority flowing from every fibre of her being.

'Mr Marlow, you will stand aside,' she demanded, dispassionately. 'So that we may remove the box of artefacts from your car, or I will order my people to kill you where you stand.'

I could see my friends respond to this. We knew these people could be deadly, but to have the fact so casually disclosed, and to our faces! I had no doubt she was telling us the truth, and palpably felt the shock travel through me.

But even as I registered that shock, and saw it travel through my friends. I saw it break upon Marlow like a wave upon a cliff face.

Not a single atom of his being seemed moved by the force of her words. And it was in that moment I realised a greater truth.

I couldn't see his eyes and the gaze he levelled at the speaker, and for that I was thankful, because now I saw in the line of his body something I'd never noticed before.

The dreadful calm or stillness I'd seen so often in

his gaze, wasn't confined to his eyes.

I understood it now, as he stood there, perhaps more motionless than he'd ever allowed himself to be before. That fathomless well of stillness, up until now so well concealed, possessed every fibre of his body. It was less visible when he moved, the idea of stillness within movement just too alien for our minds to conceive, making us see it as grace or balance.

It was more noticeable possibly in those moments of natural repose or quiet, when he watched the sunset, or stopped to gaze across to the far horizon. But now, confronted by this strange group of armed individuals, when the pretence was stripped away, the stillness possessed and consumed him.

On some level I knew nothing could stir that calm now, not even the guns raised against us, and I remembered that second dream-vision we'd all had, when we'd tried to re-create our experience at the Singing Stones.

How in my dream, I'd seen Marlow step straight into the heart of that raging inferno, a fire that burned with such heat and light I could hardly bare to look upon it. What impurities that crucible must have removed from his soul I cannot imagine, but it was clear to me now that only something purer remained.

I don't think he even bothered to respond. In that moment he seemed to exist outside time, as immobile and immovable as the earth. But it was his antagonist I was becoming more interested in now, and as I watched I think she too caught a glimpse of what I had just understood.

I don't think anyone could've described exactly how that young lady changed. But to me, it seemed the shining and flawless confidence within her began to crack and crumble, as doubt took hold, and then overwhelmed her, to leave only the hollow-eyed façade of command.

The tension in the air gradually evaporated. Nothing was going to happen, and everyone knew it. They'd lost their will, and without it, even with their numbers they were powerless to act.

If our car had been salvageable I think we could've driven away in that moment without them even trying to stop us. But our car was finished, and there was nowhere we could even try and walk to, not with Harry still unconscious.

Our car was leaking fuel and oil all over the place, so once the tension had been dispelled, we moved the injured and a few of our things a little further away. Harry still couldn't be roused, and the gash along his head now seemed compounded by some nasty bruising and swelling.

I couldn't see what we could do. The lodge was probably the closest point, and that was at least several hours walk. As for the track, we couldn't rely on anyone coming this way even in the daylight.

There was a sudden flicker and whoosh of air as the fuel and car suddenly caught alight. It was a desperate scene without doubt, now illuminated in the infernal light from our car as it began to burn.

But the light from the fire did more than destroy some of our things, it also distracted us from the arrival of two more cars, which we didn't notice until they pulled in behind the trucks.

The young woman who had so casually threatened us was the first to move over to the new arrivals, presumably eager to explain the situation.

And then I recognised them, it was Selene, Miriam and Thea, again with Luke in tow, and a slightly older woman, who I presume must have been the figure that Peter and Marlow had observed.

To say that this strange collection of young women were all cut from the same cloth, would in many ways be to do their individual beauty and charm a considerable disservice.

But as these new arrivals stepped forth into the firelight to confront us, it felt more like we were facing an army unit than a group of individuals.

There was an obvious deference to the older woman, as she stepped forward into the light and toward us. She was tall and slender, with shoulder length pale hair perfectly framing the high cheekbones and elegant features of her still beautiful face.

'Mr Robert Marlow, M'sieur Jean de Gris, Dr Androushan Chukjadarian, Mr George Whitaker, Mr Peter McAndrews, and your unfortunate friend Dr Harrison Sutherland,' she said, naming each of us as she looked at us.

'You have led us upon a merry dance, as you English would put it, demanding far more of our attention and time than anyone in quite some while.

'But your journey is now over, gentlemen, and I must insist that you persevere in your little… hobby, no more.'

'Madame, you seem to have us at a disadvantage,' replied Jean, with a soft charm in his voice and steel in his eyes.

'My name, M'sieur de Gris is of no consequence,' she replied with perfect equanimity. 'All that is of importance, is the care of your injured companion and the relinquishment of those artefacts that you have worked so hard to recover.'

She'd assessed the situation perfectly. She knew she neither needed to demand nor threaten, she had us exactly where she wanted us.

I didn't dare look at Marlow as she said this, instead diverting my attention to poor Harry, as he lay on the ground with Peter attempting to do his best for him.

But it was Marlow that spoke next, and with a depth of feeling that surprised me, and caused me to turn back toward him.

'Do you even know what these things represent,' he asked, stepping toward her almost menacingly. 'Do you care that these artefacts could rewrite history as we know it, or that they may contain a knowledge that could transform our world… our very existence or nature as human beings.'

'Do I know what these things represent,' she responded with equal force. 'How arrogant you are! I think perhaps I have a better understanding than you do yourself, Mr Marlow.

'Mine after all, is not the interest of an idle sportsman like yourself, grown bored of his privilege and leisure. Mine is a life of devotion. A life, Mr Marlow, not a season or whim.

'So yes, I do understand what these artefacts represent. For you they represent the life of your friend and your ability to get him to a hospital before it is too late. For me they represent chaos and turmoil, knowledge that it is not our lot to possess.'

'We are all acutely aware of the hold you have over us, madam, or would you prefer, Mother?' chipped in Jean. 'We are also acutely aware of the ruthlessness that your… Order, has displayed in opposing us, so you need not remind us again. As for forbidden knowledge, you will I trust forgive me if I prefer not to live under the delusion of such primitive notions.'

I couldn't tell whether Jean had been genuinely irritated by something this woman had said, or whether he was just trying to provoke her for reasons of his own, but whatever the motivation, it had an effect, as I saw her posture stiffen in response to his words, and the elegant lines of her face harden into something altogether less attractive.

'So you have learned something of our Order, it appears you are more perceptive, than we have been careful,' she said, looking pointedly at Selene, Thea and Miriam. 'No matter, such information has availed you little.

'As for the "primitive notion", that some knowledge is and should remain beyond the grasp of mankind. I do not expect you to understand such things, let alone to comprehend that there could even be a spiritual consequence to your actions. For myself, and the Order which I serve, I am content to safeguard such knowledge, and to let others with greater wisdom than myself decide its fate.'

'Is it really so easy for you to abdicate your responsibility?' asked Marlow, with sadness in his voice. 'You are right, I do not fully comprehend what such knowledge may mean, either for the wider world or myself. But, if I cannot see with a perfect clarity, then I can at least catch glimpses of what may be, both the good and the bad, the choices that may need to be made, and the decisions that may follow.

'And yes, I may not have the faith or devotion that you lay claim to, but I do know that at the heart of mankind, and perhaps at the root of your own faith, freedom of choice is paramount.

'Take these things if you must?' he said, gesturing to the box containing the tablets, scroll and all of Androus's work. 'And hide it away in some dark place, for your masters to ignore or eventually make judgement upon.

'But know this, despite your best efforts and prohibitions, I think you will live long enough to see the world grow and decide these things for itself.'

With that he turned his back on her and walked over to where Harry was lying, still unconscious and unmoving.

I thought she might be about to say something else, but after a moment's hesitation, she indicated to Selene and Thea to retrieve the box, and then instructed some of the men who attended upon her, to bring forward one of the smaller cars for us to use.

I joined Marlow and the others over beside Harry, who wasn't looking well. Peter could only speculate upon why he wasn't waking up, but he suspected he must have a severe concussion.

Neither Selene nor Thea said a word as they came over to retrieve the box, but for a moment I thought I saw a genuine look of concern on Selene's face.

I don't think any of us wanted to watch as they took the box away, but our eyes followed it nonetheless as they took it over to the pale-haired woman, who opened it and examined the contents, before turning back to us with a satisfied smile on her face.

'A considerable amount of work. I complement you on your industry,' she said, before turning and addressing herself to Selene.

'Burn the scroll and the notebooks and take the tablets back with us.'

It hit me like a hammer blow between the eyes. I couldn't tell whether she was just doing this to torment us, or for some other reason known only to herself. But the idea of such wilful destruction stunned me.

I saw Marlow and Jean start to move toward her, only to be stopped as thirty guns suddenly raised and pointed toward them.

'There is no need to destroy anything,' Marlow said, through gritted teeth. 'You've won your prize, why not just take it and hide it away.'

'Unfortunately, you've proven to be just that little bit too resourceful, Mr Marlow,' she said, still smiling pleasantly. 'With a car and your experience in this land, who knows what contacts and connections you might be able to exploit?

'Better to teach you your lesson now, I think. The scroll will be destroyed.

'Should you in any way attempt to interfere with us again, before we leave this country, I will personally empty my revolver into the contents of that box to reduce these tablets to dust. Do I make myself abundantly clear?'

As much as I hated to admit it, her reasoning was beyond question, and if anything I'd have been more surprised if Jean or Marlow hadn't already been thinking along exactly those lines.

It was agonising to watch as Selene and Thea carried the box over to the burning wreck that had been our car, and started to throw Androus' notebooks into the fire. I was waiting, hoping that they would somehow choose to spare the scroll, but eventually I saw Selene draw it too out of the box, and for a moment hesitate, before with a small tremor in those pale hands remove the scroll from its case.

'Ms Autieri… Selene, please do not do this,' implored Jean.

'M'sieur de Gris,' broke in the pale-haired woman, 'I have warned you about the cost of any further interference.

'Now do as you were told, my child,' she said addressing Selene.

'Yes, Mother Agostine,' she replied.

We then all watched as Selene, holding the scroll, stepped a little closer to the flames and then threw it still furled deep into the fire.

Marlow tried to take another step, but was held back by Jean who'd taken a firm grasp of his arm.

We all watched as the papyrus caught light and began to burn brightly. For a moment or two I thought we might have been able to retrieve some portion of it, if our captors had left quickly enough. But Mother Agostine was not to be so easily fooled, and we were forced to stand and watch until the entirety of the papyrus had turned to ash.

When all was irretrievably lost they prepared to leave us, turning all their vehicles around with the exception of the car they'd given us to transport Harry. As they climbed into their respective vehicles, the pale-haired Mother Agostine addressed us one final time.

'You have achieved far more than most of those with whom we have become involved,' she began, almost complimenting us. 'But you should not make the mistake of thinking this is an end of our… oversight, or that we will tolerate your continued pursuit of these goals. We are everywhere gentlemen, and will be watching you from this day forward.

'So take this warning in the spirit in which it is intended, abandon this quest of yours, seek no more of these tablets or scrolls, because next time we will be neither so tolerant, nor so lenient in our response.'

And with that final threat she stepped into her waiting car and drove away, back toward the lodge, leaving us alone again in the night.

We had a long way to go if we were going to get Harry some decent medical help, so we quickly set about preparing the car to carry him as comfortably as possible. Unexpectedly they'd left a small medical kit on the back seat, with some drugs that might help. But as soon as he was in and we were ready to go, I noticed Marlow wasn't getting in the car with us.

'I'll catch you up, I need some time,' was all he'd say.

I could see in his eyes there would be no arguing with him, so after making sure he had a rifle and ammunition, we set off without him.

I watched him briefly, as our car moved away. He watched us for a moment only before walking back over to the burning car, to stand and watch his own personal sunset.

ASHES

I T WAS THE END OF EVERYTHING. We managed to get Harry to the hospital in Nairobi, where he was given the medical attention he needed, not only for what turned out to be a fractured skull, but also his broken ribs, collar bone, and assorted other minor injuries, but also for the ensuing complications that had arisen due to the delay in getting him there.

It was much the same for the rest of us, the doctors insisting upon checking us out thoroughly, as well as treating our respective injuries. And all despite the insistence that we had to get back for our friend who'd stayed behind.

Eventually though we managed to get them to contact the police, who immediately sent a car out to collect Marlow, only to find him gone, and a message left in his place.

'My dear friends,' it read.

'I am most sincerely sorry to abandon you at such a time, but I need to walk for a while more in this land of broad horizons, before I can decide what to do next.

Yours in earnest

Rob'

I think the police were almost as concerned as I was myself when I read this note. The idea of Marlow heading off into the bush to do something foolish sprang immediately to mind.

Jean was convinced otherwise though, and managed to persuade the police that it was not worth organising a search party, or posting a bulletin for him.

All of which left us at a bit of a dead end. We'd lost a good portion of our possessions and other personal effects, had several rather nasty injuries between us, and in many respects had lost the main reason that had kept us together.

Harry was going to take a while to recuperate, but once he regained consciousness with no indications of any lasting brain trauma, the doctors were confident it would only take a matter of time before he'd be back on his feet.

With such a positive prognosis, the bonds holding us together started to loosen.

Androus and Peter were the first who decided to head back to their respective homes in Jerusalem and Edinburgh.

They waited just over a week, until Harry was well on his way to being discharged, and then arranged to be on their way.

It was a strangely emotional and yet numb moment

when they were finally ready to leave, but came back to the hospital to say goodbye to Harry, Jean and myself.

He was being kept in the hospital more as a precaution by this point, nursing his sore ribs, and keeping his arm immobilised, but his head injury was now all but forgotten.

'A year and a day my friends,' he said, with confidence. 'Let us not part without first agreeing when we will meet again.'

'Very good!' chimed in Jean. 'And let it be in Paris a year and day from today. I shall arrange all, and at the very least we can drink some fine wine and speculate upon what might have been.'

It was a nice idea, and we all readily agreed to the appointment, even though we were perhaps not feeling positive about things yet.

Harry was discharged from hospital a few days later, so we each arranged to travel back to our homes, Jean back to Paris, me to Shropshire, and Harry via boat back to New England.

I was hoping we might have heard something more from Marlow before the last three of us separated, but it was not to be, and before too long I found myself back in England again, and the house in which I'd grown up.

It didn't seem as dark or as dreary as it had done when I'd left, though the soil wasn't red enough, and the horizon seemed far too close.

For a while I almost enjoyed being back, looking out over that rolling landscape, often from the tiny window in my father's old room.

But it was only almost. I had a bit too much of Africa and Jerusalem and Corinth in my blood now.

A year and a day would pass quickly, though perhaps not quickly enough for my liking.

The story continues in
'The Embers of Time'

If you enjoyed reading this book, please consider visiting my website and signing up for my newsletter, so I can tell you about the other books I'm writing and publishing.

www.knytewrytng.com

All comments and feedback gratefully received.
Peter Knyte

And finally:

     In the next few pages you'll find a sample from the next book in the Flames of Time trilogy – The Embers of Time.

Here's the back page blurb, followed by the sample.

'In the heart of the Eternal City secrets have a price.
  A price to keep, and a price to finally reveal. . . '

The ancient artefacts containing directions to an impossibly old temple have been recovered by Marlow and his friends, only to be stolen at gunpoint by a shadowy organisation determined to preserve the status quo.

But has the mysterious Order, which seems to have its roots intertwined with those of the Vatican, misjudged the people they stole the artefacts from.

Will Mother Agostine's warning to the group, to leave this particular secret alone, backfire and turn the hunters into the hunted? Or will the price of keeping this one secret end up costing the strange religious order the secret of its own existence!

THE
EMBERS
of
TIME

BOOK
TWO

PETER
KNYTE

"IN THE HEART OF THE ETERNAL CITY SECRETS HAVE A PRICE,
A PRICE TO KEEP, AND A PRICE TO FINALLY REVEAL."

THE EMBERS OF TIME

THE CHASED

I WAS THIRSTY, THE AIR WAS DRY, and the sound of the drums was all around me, racing against the thundering in my chest as I strained to keep my legs moving. The hunters were close behind me, and I could smell the copper tang of blood as I raced to get away from them.

Panic clawed at the edges of my mind as I crashed blindly through the bush. Unable to see where I was going, hoping my pursuers would lose my trail in the tangle of long grass and thorn bushes. But I was getting weaker, the pain in my side from the spear wound sapping my strength and dragging me down.

I stumbled, unable to get my legs back beneath me, and nearly went down, but somehow managed to stagger a little further, as much sideways as forward, and then it was all over. I crashed to the ground, legs flailing, unable to get back up, my lungs burning and heart breaking with the effort.

The hunters were close, I could hear the sound as they too crashed through the bush, closing in on me, with more spears in hand....

My skin was covered in sweat. The bedclothes plastered around me as I awoke in the small room that had once been my father's bedroom, at the house in Shropshire.

For a moment I thought I still heard the sound of the drums, fading into the distance, only to realise it was the pounding of my own heart.

I had been back for almost a year, the remains of

the summer flying past, succeeded by the warm regret of autumn and the cold grey of winter.

This place had never been my home, and the life I lived here had never been my own, it was just assumed by me and everyone else that I'd find my place here, a routine, within its gentle ebb and flow.

But that was before I went to Africa.

Before the dark red soil had mixed with my blood, and before the dreams had come drifting through the ether on the soft rhythm of distant drums to find me.

The time had almost come when I had agreed to meet once more with those friends I'd left behind in Africa, when we'd all agreed to come back together again and decide what, if anything, our fate was to be.

I didn't think it would be a hard decision for most of us. More than once, Harry, Jean or Marlow had expressed their doubts about ever being able to return to their old lives with friends and relatives. Even though these were people they loved, admired and missed, they somehow knew they could never go back to living amongst them, not without giving up some essential part of their own being.

I honestly don't think I'd really understood them at the time, my own home life holding so little by way of family or friends. But now I knew what they'd been talking about, and what Marlow had meant after he faced and killed that lion with just a sword in his hand.

Life back at my father's house would have been quiet and comfortable, and in time might even have become pleasant, but that rich red soil and those impossibly wide horizons had changed me, and the very idea of 'just' a pleasant life now left a bitter taste in my mouth.

There was still a little time before we had promised to meet up again at Jean's house in Paris, certainly time enough to put my affairs in order; to sell or let the house, to move the few private things that I could not bear to part with, and of course to once more pack my things.

The things I would need for a prolonged, if not

permanent, life away from England.

My solicitor was to take care of the house and its belongings, including the furniture and contents, with a signed authority to manage it as he would any other form of long term investment. The exceptions were my father's journals, and now also my own, which had been boxed up and stored away securely.

I had no way of knowing whether that mysterious organisation, which employed those dangerous young women, was still waiting and watching for any indication we were resuming our search, but discretion would cost only a little extra time. So, while I was preparing for my journey to France and then on to who knew where, I also went to the trouble of doing a few things around the house and garden to throw any potential watchers off the scent.

I began by planting some new fruit trees and laying some much-needed hedging. I also arranged for some decorating to be done inside the house, all the while ordering in my equipment and supplies through my local post office.

In order to further disguise my preparations I also made open enquiries about travelling to America through a local travel agent, even timing my train journey to London to coincide with a similar train leaving for Liverpool.

Whether my little subterfuge would be of any interest to anyone I had no way of knowing, and even if it did work for me, it would only take one of the others to be less cautious, and what little advantage it might deliver would be lost.

Jean, of course, could do little to hide our arrival at his home, but he would, I was sure, manage to disguise his own travel preparations.

The end of April finally arrived, which was when we had agreed to re-unite, and I walked out of my house for what was likely to be the last time, and into a waiting taxi cab.

As the car slowly pulled away and I looked back at

the place where I grew up, I found my mind concerned only with what might lie ahead, rather than what I was leaving behind.

The idea of once more meeting up with my friends, after the unfortunate way in which we had been forced to part company, preyed upon my mind.

Time and again, I found my thoughts returning to the question of whether our friendship would be the same, or whether our time apart had caused it to wane.

The journey down to London and then on to Paris was a simple one, and while I tried to be vigilant for any sign of those dangerous young women who worked for the mysterious Order, I knew if they had even half the ability of Selene, Miriam or Thea, I would have very little chance of spotting them.

I had only ever visited Paris once before while I was a child, travelling with my father many years previously. Unfortunately, my few memories of the trip consisted almost entirely of the fine French pastries and sweets which at that time had completely absorbed my attention, and which had, for a short while, convinced me that being a French pastry chef was surely the most glamorous and attractive of all occupations.

It was a pleasantly warm spring afternoon by the time I alighted from the train in the cavernous Gare du Nord train station, and then made my way to the exit with my bags.

I was a little peckish after the journey, and was considering stopping off for some lunch as I walked out of the station onto the bustling Rue de Dunkerque, when I spied an elegant little patisserie positively glowing in the warm afternoon sunshine.

My childhood fascination with exactly the type of pastries that would be contained within this bright jewel of a shop immediately brought a smile to my face. A smile which very nearly turned into laughter, when I considered how easily my second visit to this great city could result in very similar memories to the first.

But I did laugh a moment later, when I saw Peter McAndrews come strolling out of the self-same patisserie, with a very handsome-looking box of the bakery's produce.

'Peter!' I called out, before I even realised what I was doing.

'George!' he yelled back.

All semblance of our low profile entrance into Paris ruined in a moment.

'I just couldn't help myself,' he said, after crossing the street and holding up his trophy. 'I was waiting here to grab a cab over to Jean's place, and the next thing I knew I'd crossed the street and ordered half the shop.'

I confessed I had very nearly done exactly the same myself, and then as we fell into a light-hearted conversation about our shared childhood memories of Paris's great pastries, I knew my doubts about our old camaraderie had been pure foolishness.

We shared a cab over to Jean's house on the Ilse St-Louis, our bags and cases crammed in around us, with all the while the delicate white box of pastries placed prominently on top.

I think Peter was a little relieved to have run into me before getting to Jean's house, and to have dispensed with any potential awkwardness.

'So, George,' he began, looking a little more serious as we drew closer to the river and Jean's house. 'Do you think everyone else will still be the same? Jean, Harry, Androus, Rob?'

'I do,' I said, meaning it. 'If anything I think Harry and Rob will be even more eager to continue the search than they were before. Jean will be his usual pragmatic self, so will probably have spent some time considering all manner of eventualities that the rest of us haven't even guessed at, and Androus, I think he may just have stopped seething about the destruction of the scroll and the theft of his notes, but will otherwise be adamant that the truth must be revealed.'

'I see,' Peter replied, looking rather serious. 'So you don't think Jean will be upset?'

He had me for a moment, and could have strung me along for much longer, but Peter, unlike Jean, had at least a trace of civility when it came to his jokes.

'He won't be upset that I've brought cakes to his home?' Peter continued, before slipping effortlessly into an almost perfect imitation of our Gascon friend.

'You are perhaps concerned I will not feed you, mon amie. Never has Gascon hospitality been so cruelly misjudged…'

I could not help but laugh at the impersonation, despite having been taken in so easily, because I could imagine Jean getting into exactly that kind of melodramatic huff about it… before going on to thoroughly enjoy the very pastries that had so terribly insulted his household.

It took about half an hour in the cab from the train station to Jean's house, and we had started to discuss what we had each been up to for the past year when we arrived.

Jean lived in one of the tall old town houses made of pale stone that can be seen almost everywhere in the city.

It sat, rather grandly, overlooking the gently flowing waters of the Seine, and beyond that, to the increasingly infamous Rive Gauche, which seemed over the last few years to have become a positive Mecca for artists, poets, writers and philosophers from all over the world.

Jean must have seen our car arrive, because no sooner had we paid the driver than he was on the pavement at the bottom of the steps shaking our hands and leading us up to his front door. It was unimaginable to think of him ever changing, and as we greeted one another with warm embraces I realised, that with the exception of being a little less tanned and in his city clothes, my friend appeared exactly the same as he had when we parted all those months ago.

At the sight of Peter's box of cakes though, we both learned we had completely misjudged him.

'Ah, you have succumbed to the siren call of Madame Villandry's pastries, I see,' he commented, with a broad smile. 'A wise choice, my friends, and perhaps also just what the doctor ordered.'

Intrigued by this odd comment, we shuffled and stumbled our baggage and trappings into his house, with the assistance of a couple of Jean's staff, and were then ushered through into a spacious lounge, where we could sit and talk properly over coffee and sandwiches, provided by his housekeeper.

We did not have long to wait to discover the cryptic meaning of Jean's comments about the pastries.

Apparently both Androus and Harry had arrived the day before, and had popped out a couple of hours earlier, before Peter and I arrived, to stroll around one of the local museums.

I could barely believe it when they returned and Harry walked in through the door. He was practically a shadow of his former self, having lost a lot of weight in the last year.

We greeted one another as the old friends we were, and then settled down with fresh coffee and the cakes Peter had brought, to hear what had happened to Harry.

'It was the broken collar bone that started it all,' he explained, tucking into the sandwiches and then pastries with a will.

'I convalesced in Nairobi for a few days after Peter and Androus returned to their homes, as I'm sure you remember, but after I was discharged from the hospital a week or so later, I decided to travel back to the United States and catch up with a few folks, while my ribs and collar bone finished healing.

'Well, I decided to travel through the Mediterranean on the way to Le Havre or Portsmouth. Wherever I could get the next birth across the pond, but I stopped off along the way in Cairo, then Tunisia and Morocco just to break the journey up a little.

To begin with, when I started to feel lethargic, I presumed I'd just eaten something that didn't agree with me. I was after all trailing around some of the less frequented sites of antiquity along the way, and visiting some of the quieter restaurants and hotels in the process.

'We've all suffered with an upset stomach from time to time after eating something we probably shouldn't, and for the first few days I thought it was just a dose of the usual, so thought nothing more of it. I took it easy, made sure I stayed well hydrated and didn't stray too far from the hotel.

'But despite resting up, after another couple of days, it seemed to suddenly get worse, and by the time I got onto my Atlantic crossing, I'd developed a mild fever followed by chills, even though the weather was quite warm.

'Anyway, after another day of feeling terrible, I thought I'd best take myself off to see the ship's doctor.

'He was clearly an experienced old hand, and after taking one look at me, he starts asking if I've spent any time in Africa, or near to swampy ground or places with a lot of standing water.

'Well, half the old troglodytic Roman sites I'd visited in Tunisia were swimming in stagnant water, which still hadn't dried up after the winter, at which point I remember what a pest the midges and mosquitoes had been, after which, the penny finally drops.'

'Ah, le Paludisme,' Jean commented, shaking his head slightly. 'It was the malaria, mon ami?'

'Precisely,' replied Harry. 'But because I didn't twig to it straight away I'd given it the chance to get well-established before I even went to see the doctor.

'He prescribed the strongest medication he had available, but the next thing I know, I'm waking up several weeks later with my family and friends around the bed, looking at me as though my time on this mortal coil is up.

'The doctors told me afterward, that the pain killers I'd been taking for my collar bone had probably masked the real start of the fever, and given the parasite time to affect my brain, which despite treatment aboard ship, had swelled up, resulting in me slipping in and out of consciousness for a couple of months.

'By all accounts they were seriously concerned about me for a while there, with me at one point even falling into a coma. So, if I hadn't gone to see the ship's doctor when I did, who knows what might've happened.

'Well, needless to say, after a couple of months of lying around on my back I was as weak as a kitten, and could barely sit up in bed for the first week, let alone walk. On the plus side my collar bone had healed nicely, it just took a few weeks before my arm was strong enough to hold a glass of water without shaking.

'It's been a slow and steady journey since then, but I'm getting my strength back now, though it's probably going to take a little while before my old clothes fit me properly again,' he said, patting his rather hollow-looking stomach.

We talked amiably for a while longer, as the rather slender Harry quietly polished off a handful of sandwiches followed by eclairs, tarts, then macaroons and dacquoise, much to our mutual wide-eyed enjoyment.

None of us had asked about Marlow yet, but as the last of the afternoon light started to fade with still no sign of him, I finally felt I could wait no longer.

'I don't suppose any of you have heard anything from Rob in the last twelve months?' I asked simply.

'I exchanged a couple of letters with him while he was in northern Spain, a few months back,' Harry confirmed. 'Enquiring about my health, and informing me he'd continued to travel.'

'I myself had heard nothing until a week ago, when I received a telegram from the very tip of Sicily,' Jean added. 'Telling me he would be here, but would probably not arrive until a little later in the day, and asking me to prepare a few things.'

'Did he mention what he was doing in Sicily?' asked Androus, rather quizzically.

'Only that he was on some tiny little island which was positively covered in Carthaginian archaeological ruins, and he was learning a bit more about archaeology, by helping with the continuing excavations.'

'Ah yes, this sounds familiar, but I cannot recall its name,' Androus replied. 'Harrison, can you remember it? '

'I recall it was just across the water from Marsala, and that the entire island had been bought by an Englishman so he could excavate it,' Harry replied, 'But I can't recall the details.'

'I believe it is Motya that you're thinking of,' chipped in Marlow from the doorway, obviously having just arrived.

'Ah, Robert, welcome,' replied Jean, springing to his feet to usher his friend into the room. 'You found my secret key without any problem?'

'I did, my friend,' responded Marlow holding up the key in question, much to everyone else's curiosity.

'I'll explain the details of my stealthy visit a little later,' he promised, handing the key to Jean, and then sitting down in one of the spare chairs.

'It is very good to see you all again, though I see that some of us have a tale of their own to tell,' he joked, looking at the new, slimmed-down Harry.

We talked a little more about the archaeology he had been helping with on his Sicilian island, and quickly recapped Harry's brush with malaria, before Jean herded us through to his dining room, and a delicious meal he had arranged, which by his own admittance was comprised mostly of traditional Gascon fayre.

As it had a hundred times before, the conversation rambled its way around the table, splitting and dividing any number of times. Jean regaled us with his countless forays into the latest artistic, philosophical and cultural thinking that he had been liberally submersing himself in on the other side of the river.

Peter then countered with news of the more practical developments in his home city of Edinburgh, the Athens of the north, with its almost simultaneous clearances of the city centre slums and the opening of both a new city museum, and the even more highly anticipated public swimming baths.

I had little to contribute beyond my planting of a few trees, but I was content to simply sit and listen to my friends, once more united, and engaged in the gentle exchange of raillery and nonsense.

I didn't have a particularly good vantage point from which to observe Marlow, but I managed to steal a few glances along the room all the same, and discovered him doing much the same as me, quietly sitting and enjoying the company of his friends.

Our meal was, in true French style, a long and unrushed affair with one course after another of rustic but delicious food, accompanied by equally fine wines, before the obligatory coffee and cognac to finish. Even the half-starved Harry apparently was satisfied by the end of it.

As pleasant as the conversation and the meal had been though, we all knew there was something we needed to discuss, and it was Jean our host who finally broached the subject, as he slowly toured the room refilling everyone's coffee.

'I feel I must once again offer my thanks to you all for coming to my home, and allowing me to enjoy a last wonderful meal here for what may be some time,' he said, smiling faintly as he looked around the room at each of us.

We all knew, of course, to what he was referring, and one by one offered a silent toast to our host in return.

'It has been a year, my friends,' he continued, thoughtfully. 'And as I look around this room I believe I see hearts and minds unchanged from when we parted. But perhaps it would be wise for us to be sure and discuss the topic a little first. Shall I open the windows so that we can listen once more for the sound of those distant drums?'

'For my part, Jean, there is no need,' replied the ever enthusiastic Harry. 'Even while I was convalescing back in the States there were quiet times when I swear I could still hear that soft rhythm on the night air.'

'I dreamed of them on the very night before I left England to travel here,' I admitted, quietly. 'And have done so on countless other occasions during the year.'

'Even I have occasionally half heard or half remembered the cadence of some incredibly distant tribal drumming,' confirmed Androus.

'And you, Jean?' asked Marlow, quietly. 'You who have often been the voice of reason, reminding us to be sceptical.'

'Ah Robert, it is true I am gifted not only with a great and passionate heart, but also with a precise and logical mind,' he replied, with a playful twinkle in his dark eyes. 'But it is also true that I am first and foremost a philosopher, and as such over the past year, I have continued to ask myself the question, of whether my mind has been sufficiently open to the strange and unusual things we experienced on our adventure together.'

'And let me guess,' broke in Harry, with an equally impish glint in his eye. 'Your mind is still undecided, but it can now see both sides?'

'Really, Harrison, for a man of such academic achievement your understanding of philosophy is still far too simple. But as chance would have it on this occasion my thinking has been greatly improved by a number of discussions I have had during our little sabbatical, and I must concede, that however inexplicable some of the things we experienced were, there is without doubt, both truth and value in this search, and as such I cannot in good conscience allow you to continue alone.'

'Thank you, my friend,' replied Marlow. 'Your

support means a great deal to me.'

'Well, if we're all agreed that we should continue,' Harry summarised. 'Surely the next question we must try to fathom is where we begin? We have, after all, lost the vast majority of our information and research.'

'We could head back to the temple we found near to Great Zimbabwe to recover all the information captured on the walls,' Peter offered.

'I would certainly like to visit this site that you have described to me,' replied Androus, with unrestrained enthusiasm.

'I have already travelled back there, just to confirm it remains undisturbed,' responded Marlow. 'And I could find no indication it had been tampered with in any way.'

'Robert, that is a very dangerous part of the world for you to have travelled to alone,' commented Jean, clearly concerned.

'You're right, my friend,' conceded Marlow. 'But I was in a dangerous frame of mind at the time, and as dangerous as it might have been for me, I think you will agree it would have been an impossible location for our adversaries to have followed me.'

'All the same, mon ami…'

'I mention this,' Marlow continued, looking at Jean steadily for several moments, 'So that you are each able to weigh my next suggestion in the full knowledge that there is a genuine alternative.

'However, in contrast to the temple, which I suspect may contain a copy of what was written on the scroll carved upon its walls, the location I have in mind is one we're already aware of, and where a full set of the ancient lapis tablets are located, along with countless other artefacts that may be of relevance to our search.'

'Robert, I think perhaps you are mistaken,' began Androus, slipping into his professorial manner. 'My memory may not be perfect, but I assure you we have already sought and found all the sites we were able to identify from the scroll.'

'I do not think Robert is talking of the locations listed on the scroll, Androus,' replied Jean with an unreadable expression on his face.

'Forgive me,' responded Androus. 'But if the place you are thinking of was not listed on the scroll then how could you possibly know that there is a full set of tablets located there?'

'I know they're there, Androus, because it's where the people who took them from us take all their recovered treasures,' Marlow said simply, before standing up and walking over to retrieve the brandy decanter and glasses from the side table in the corner of the room.

'Let me be clear,' he said, putting the decanter and glasses down in the middle of the table and pouring a glass for each of us. 'I know that the tablets we found in Africa were taken back to the Vatican City in Rome. I know which archive they were interred in, and I'm suggesting we should break into the vaults where they're stored and take them back, along with anything else we find on site that may help us in our search or may make up for the destruction of the scroll.'

I watched stunned as Marlow then slowly poured a glass of the brandy for himself before sitting back down at the end of the table to wait for our questions.

To find out what happens next in the Flames of Time trilogy - read:

'The Embers of Time'

Available from all good retailers.

Or for more information visit:
www.knytewrytng.com

www.ingramcontent.com/pod-product-compliance
Lightning Source LLC
Chambersburg PA
CBHW031149120726

47905CB00006B/1871